# THE MERLIN CONSPIRACY

Diana Wynne Jones' first children's book was published in 1973. Her magical, humorous stories have enthralled children and adults ever since, and she has inspired many of today's children's and fantasy authors. Among Diana's best loved books for older children are the Chrestomanci series and the Howl books. Her novel *Howl's Moving Castle* was made into an award-winning film. She was described by Neil Gaiman as "the best children's writer of the last 40 years".

### Titles by Diana Wynne Jones

#### Chrestomanci Series
Charmed Life
The Magicians of Caprona
Witch Week
The Lives of Christopher Chant
Mixed Magics
Conrad's Fate
The Pinhoe Egg

#### Howl Series
Howl's Moving Castle
Castle in the Air
House of Many Ways
Archer's Goon
Black Maria
Dogsbody
Eight Days of Luke
Enchanted Glass
The Homeward Bounders
The Merlin Conspiracy
Deep Secret
The Ogre Downstairs
Power of Three
A Tale of Time City
Wilkin's Tooth
The Game

#### For older readers
Fire and Hemlock
Hexwood
The Time of the Ghost

#### For younger readers
Wild Robert
Earwig and the Witch
Vile Visitors

# THE
# MERLIN
# CONSPIRACY

HarperCollins *Children's Books*

*To Rowan Dalglish*

First published in hardback and paperback in Great Britain by
Collins in 2003. This edition first published in paperback in
Great Britain by HarperCollins Children's Books in 2013.
HarperCollins Children's Books is a division of
HarperCollinsPublishers Ltd, 77-85 Fulham Palace Road,
Hammersmith, London, W6 8JB.

The HarperCollins website address is:
www.harpercollins.co.uk

Text copyright © Diana Wynne Jones 2003

The author and illustrator assert the moral right to
be identified as the author and illustrator of this work.

ISBN 978-0-00-750776-4

Printed and bound in England by
Clays Ltd, St Ives plc

**MIX**
Paper from
responsible sources
**FSC** www.fsc.org **FSC™ C007454**

# Contents

# PART ONE
## RODDY

# CHAPTER ONE

※

*I* have been with the Court all my life, travelling with the King's Progress.

I didn't know how to go on. I sat and stared at this sentence, until Grundo said, "If you can't do it, I will."

If you didn't know Grundo, you'd think this was a generous offer, but it was a threat really. Grundo is dyslexic. Unless he thinks hard, he writes inside out and backwards. He was threatening me with half a page of crooked writing with words like "inside" turning up as "sindie" and "story" as "otsyr".

Anything but that! I thought. So I decided to start with Grundo – and me. I am Arianrhod Hyde, only I prefer people to call me Roddy, and I've looked after Grundo for years now, ever since Grundo was a small, pale, freckled boy in rompers, sitting completely silently in the back of the children's bus. He was so miserable that he had wet himself. I was only about five myself at the time, but I somehow realised that he was too miserable even to cry. I got up and staggered through the bumping, rushing bus to the clothes lockers. I found some clean rompers and persuaded Grundo to get into them.

This wasn't easy, because Grundo has always been very proud. While I was working at it, Grundo's sister Alicia turned round from where she was sitting with the big ones. "What are you bothering with Cesspit for?" she said, tipping up her long, freckled nose. "There's no point. He's useless." She was eight at the time, but she still looks just the same: straight fair hair, thick body, and an air of being *the* person, the one everyone else has to look up to. "And he's ugly," she said. "He's got a long nose."

"So have you got a long nose," I said, "Lady Sneeze." I always called her "Lady Sneeze" when I wanted to annoy her. If you say "Alicia" quickly it sounds just like a well-behaved sneeze – just like Alicia, in fact. I wanted to annoy her for calling Grundo Cesspit. She only said it because Sybil, her mother, called Grundo that. It was typical of the way they both treated him. Grundo's father left Sybil before Grundo was born. Ever since I could remember, Sybil and Alicia had been thick as thieves together. Poor Grundo was nowhere.

It got worse when Grundo started lessons with us and turned out to be dyslexic. Sybil went around sighing,

"He's so *stupid*!" And Alicia chanted at him, "Stupid, stupid, stupid!" Alicia, of course, did everything well, whether it was maths, magic or horse-riding. She got chosen as a Court page when she was ten.

Our teachers knew Grundo was not stupid, but his inside out way of going on baffled them. They sighed too and called Grundo "Our young eccentric" and I was the one who taught Grundo to read and write. I think that was when I started calling him Grundo. I can't quite remember why, except that it suited him better than his real name, which is Ambrose of all things! Before long, the entire Court called him Grundo. And while I was teaching him, I discovered that he had an unexpected amount of inside out magical talent.

"This book is boring," he complained in his deep, solemn voice. "Why should I care if Jack and Jill go shopping? Or if Rover chases the ball?" While I was explaining to him that *all* reading books were like this, Grundo somehow turned the book into a comic book, all pictures and no words. It started at the back and finished at the front, and in the pictures the ball chased Rover and Jack and Jill were bought by the groceries. Only Grundo would think of two people being bought by a huge chunk of cheese.

He refused to turn the book back. He said it was more fun that way, and I couldn't turn it back into a reading book whatever I tried. It's probably still where I hid it, down inside the cover of the old teaching bus seat.

Grundo is obstinate as well as proud.

You might say I adopted Grundo as my brother. We were both on our own. I am an only child and all the other Court wizards' children were the same age as Alicia or older still. The other children our own age were sons and daughters of Court officials, who had no gift for magic. They were perfectly friendly – don't get me wrong – but they just had a more normal outlook.

There were only about thirty of us young ones who travelled in the King's Progress all the time. The rest only joined us for Christmas or for the other big religious ceremonies. Grundo and I always used to envy them. They didn't have to wear neat clothes and remember Court manners all the time. They knew where they were going to be, instead of travelling through the nights and finding themselves suddenly in a flat field in Norfolk, or a remote Derbyshire valley, or a busy port somewhere next morning. They didn't have to ride in buses in a heatwave. Above all, they could go for walks and explore places. We were never really in one place long enough to do any exploring. The most we got to do was look round the various castles and great houses where the King decided to stay.

We envied the princesses and the younger princes particularly. They were allowed to stay in Windsor most of the year. Court gossip said that the Queen, being foreign, had threatened to go back to Denmark unless she was allowed to stay in one place. Everyone pitied the

Queen rather for not understanding that the King *had* to travel about in order to keep the realm healthy. Some said that the whole magic of the Islands of Blest – or maybe the entire world of Blest – depended on the King constantly moving about and visiting every acre of England.

I asked my Grandfather Hyde about this. He is a Magid and knows about the magics of countries and worlds and so on. And he said that there might be something in this, but he thought people were overstating the case. The magic of Blest *was* very important for all sorts of reasons, he said, but it was the Merlin who was really entrusted with keeping it healthy.

My mother did quite often talk of sending me to live with this grandfather in London. But this would have meant leaving Grundo to the mercies of Sybil and Alicia, so, whenever she suggested it, I told her I was proud to be a member of Court – which was quite true – and that I was getting the best possible education – which was partly quite true – and then I sort of went heavy at her and hoped she'd forget the idea. If she got really anxious and went on about this being no sort of life for a growing girl, I went on about the way Grandad grows dahlias. I really do hate dahlias as a way of life.

Mam had her latest worry session in Northumbria, in the rain. We were all camped in a steep, heathery valley waiting for the Scottish King to pay our King a formal visit. It was so bare that there was not even a house for the King. The canvas of the royal tent was turning a wet, dismal yellow just downhill from us, and we were slithering in shiny, wet sheep droppings while I went on about the way Grandad grows dahlias.

"Besides, it's such a stupid thing for a powerful magician to do!" I said.

"I wish you didn't feel like this about him," Mam said. "You *know* he does a great deal more than simply grow flowers. He's a remarkable man. And he'd be glad to have you as company for your cousin Toby."

"My cousin Toby is a wimp who doesn't mind being ordered to do the weeding," I said. I looked up at Mam through the wet black wriggles of my hair and realised that my dahlia-ploy hadn't worked the way it usually did. Mam continued to look anxious. She is a serious person, my mam, weighed down by her responsible job in the travelling Exchequer, but I can usually get her to laugh. When she laughs, she throws her head back and looks very like me. We both have rather long pink cheeks and a dimple in the same place, though her eyes are black and mine are blue.

I could see the rain was getting her down – having to keep the water out of her computer and having to go to the loo in a little wet flapping tent and all the rest – and I saw it was one of the times when she starts imagining me going down with rheumatic fever or pneumonia and dying of it. I realised I'd have to play my very strongest card or I'd be packed off down to London before lunch.

"Come off it, Mam!" I said. "Grandad's not *your*

14

father. He's Dad's. If you're so anxious for me to be in the bosom of my family, why not send me to *your* father instead?"

She pulled her shiny waterproof cape around her and went back a step. "My father is Welsh," she said. "If you went there, you'd be living in a foreign country. All right. If you feel you really can stand this awful, wandering existence, we'll say no more."

She went away. She always did if anyone talked about her father. I thought he must be terrifying. All I knew about my other grandfather was that Mam had had to run away from home in order to marry Dad, because her father had refused to let her marry anyone. Poor Mam. And I'd used that to send her away. I sighed with mixed relief and guilt. Then I went to find Grundo.

Grundo's lot is always worse when we're stopped anywhere for a while. Unless I think of an excuse to fetch him away, Sybil and Alicia haul him into Sybil's tent and try to correct his faults. When I ducked into the dim, damp space, it was worse than usual. Sybil's manfriend was in there, laughing his nasty, hissing laugh. "Give him to me, dear," I heard him saying. "I'll soon make a man of him." Grundo was looking pale, even for him.

The only person at Court that I dislike more than Alicia is Sybil's manfriend. His name is Sir James Spenser. He is very unpleasant. The astonishing thing is that the whole Court, including Sybil, *knows* he is nasty, but they pretend not to notice because Sir James is useful to the

King. I don't understand about this. But I have noticed the same thing happening with some of the businessmen who are useful to the King. The media are constantly suggesting these men are crooks, but nobody even thinks of arresting them. And it is the same with Sir James, although I have no idea in what way *he* is useful to the King.

He gave me a leer. "Checking that I haven't eaten your sweetheart?" he said. "Why do you bother, Arianrhod? If I had your connections, I wouldn't look twice at young Ambrose."

I looked him in the face, at his big, pocky nose and the eyes too near on either side of it. "I don't understand you," I said in my best Court manner. Polite but stony. I didn't think my connections were particularly aristocratic. My father is only the King's weather wizard and much further down the order than Sybil, who is, after all, Earthmistress to England.

Sir James did his hissing laugh at me. *Hs-ss-szz.* "The aristocracy of magic, my dear child," he said. "Look at your grandparents! I should think at the very least you'd be setting your sweet young adolescent cap at the next Merlin."

Sybil said sharply, "*What?*" and Alicia gave a gasp. When I looked at her, she was speckled pink with indignation. Alicia has even more freckles than Grundo. Sybil's long, jowly face was furious. Her pale blue eyes were popping at me.

I didn't understand what made them so angry. I just thought, Bother! Now I shall have to be very polite – and rather stupid – and pretend I haven't noticed. This was typical of Sir James. He loved making everyone around him angry. "But we've got a perfectly good Merlin!" I said.

"An old man, my dear," Sir James said gleefully. "Old and frail."

"Yes," I said, truly puzzled. "But there's no knowing who'll be the next one, is there?"

He looked at me pityingly. "There are rumours, dear child. Or don't you listen to gossip with your naïve little ears?"

"No," I said. I'd had enough of his game, whatever it was. I turned, very politely, to Sybil. "Please would it be all right if I took Grundo to watch my father work?"

She shrugged her thick shoulders. "If Daniel wants to work in front of a staring child, that's his funeral, I suppose. Yes, take him away. I'm sick of the sight of him. Grundo, be back here to put on Court clothing before lunch or you'll be punished. Off you go."

"There's motherly love for you!" I said to Grundo as we hurried off into the rain.

He grinned. "We don't need to go back. I've got Court clothes on under these. It's warmer."

I wished I'd thought of doing the same. It was so chilly that you wouldn't have believed it was nearly Midsummer. Anyway, I'd got Grundo away. Now I just had to hope that Dad wouldn't mind us watching him. He doesn't always like being disturbed when he's working.

When I cautiously lifted the flap of the weather tent, Dad was just getting ready. He had taken off his waterproof cape and was slipping off his heavy blue robe of office and rolling up his shirtsleeves. He looked all slim and upright like that, more like a soldier preparing for a duel than a wizard about to work on the weather.

"Over in that corner, both of you," he said. "Don't distract me or you'll have the King after us in person. He's given me very exact instructions for today." He turned a grin on us as he said this, to show he didn't at all mind having us there.

Grundo gave him one of his serious, deep looks. "Are we allowed to ask questions, sir?"

"Most probably not," said my father. "That's distracting. But I'll describe what I'm doing as I go along, if you want. After all," he added, with a wistful look at me, "one of you might wish to follow in my footsteps some day."

I love my dad, though I never see very much of him. I think he really does hope that I might turn out to be a weather worker. I'm afraid I am going to be a great disappointment to him. Weather does fascinate me, but so does every other kind of magic too. That was true even then, when I didn't know more than the magic they teach you in Court, and it's more true than ever now.

But I loved watching Dad work. I found I was

smiling lovingly as he stepped over to the weather table. At this stage it was unactivated and was simply a sort of framework made of gold and copper wires resting on stout legs that folded up for when we travelled. The whole thing folded away into a worn wooden box about four feet long which I had known for as long as I could remember. It smelt of ozone and cedarwood. Dad and that box went together somehow.

He stood beside the table with his head bent. It always looked as if he was nerving himself up for something. Actually, he was just working the preliminary magics, but when I was small I always thought that weather-working took great courage and I used to worry about him. But I've never lost the queer amazement you feel when the magic answers Dad's call. Even that day, I gasped quietly as mistiness filled the framework. It was blue, green and white at first, but almost at once it became a perfect small picture of the Islands of Blest. There was England in all its various greens, except for the small brown stains of towns, with its backbone of the Pennines and its southern hills as a sort of hipbone. All the rivers were there as tiny blue-grey threads, and dark green clumps of woodlands – very important each of these, Dad tells me, because you bring the picture into being by thinking of water, wood and hill – but it still defeats me why I could even see the white cliffs in the south. And Scotland was there, too, browner, with travelling ridges of grey and white cloud crossing the brown. The fierce greyness at the top was a bad storm somewhere near John O'Groats. Wales lurked over to one side, showing only as dim greens under blue-grey clouds. But Ireland was entirely clear, living up to the name of Emerald Isle, and covered in big moving ripples of sunlight.

Dad walked round it all, bending over to look at the colours of the seas particularly. Then he stood back to see the patterns of the slanting, scudding clouds. "Hm," he said. He pointed to the north-east of England, where the land was almost invisible under smoky, whitish mist. "Here's the rain that's presently being such a pest. As you see, it's not moving much. The King wants it cleared up and, if possible, a blaze of sunlight when the Scottish King arrives. Now, look at Scotland. There's very little clear sky there. They're having sun and showers every ten minutes or so as those clouds ripple. I can't get any good weather from there, not to make it last. Quite a problem."

He walked slowly in among the green landscapes and the moving clouds, passing through the wires of the framework underneath as if they were not there. That part always gave me a shudder. How *could* a person walk through solid gold wire?

He stopped with his hand over dim, green Wales. "*This* is the real problem. I'm going to have to fetch the weather from Ireland without letting this lot drift in across us. That's really appalling weather there in Wales at the moment. I shall have to try to get it to move away north and out to sea. Let's see how the bigger currents are going."

Up to his waist in moving, misty map, he gestured. The whole picture humped up a little and moved away sideways, first to show a curve of heaving grey ocean, ribbed like a tabby cat with strips of whitish cloud, and then, giddily, going the other way to show green-brown views of the Low Countries and the French kingdoms and more stripes of cloud there.

"Hm," my father said again. "Not as bad as I feared. Everything is setting northwards, but only very slowly. I shall have to speed things up."

He set to work, rather as a baker might roll dough along a board, pushing and kneading at clumps of cloud, steering ocean wisps with the flat of his hands, and shoving mightily at the weathers over Ireland and Wales. The dimness over Wales broke apart a little to show more green, but it didn't move away. My father surveyed it with one hand to his chin.

"Sorry, everyone," he said. "The only way with this is a well placed wind."

We watched him moving around, sometimes up to his shoulders in land and cloud, creating winds. Most of them he made by blowing more or less softly, or even just opening his mouth and breathing, and they were never quite where you thought they ought to be. "It's a little like sailing a boat," he explained, seeing Grundo frowning. "The wind has to come sideways on to the canvas to make a boat move, and it's the same here, except that weather always comes in swirls, so I have to

21

be careful to set up a lighter breeze going the opposite way. There." He set everything moving with a sharp breath that was almost a whistle and stood back out of the table to time it.

After a few minutes of looking from his big, complicated watch to the movements on the table, he walked away and picked up his robe. Weather-working is harder than it looks. Dad's face was streaming with sweat and he was panting slightly as he fetched his portable far-speaker out of a pocket in the robe. He thought a moment, to remember that day's codes, and punched in the one for the Waymaster Royal's office.

"Daniel Hyde here," he told the official who answered. "The rain will stop at twelve-oh-two, but I can't promise any sunlight until one o'clock... Yes... Almost exactly, but it couldn't be done without a wind, I'm afraid. Warn His Majesty that there may be half a gale blowing between eleven-thirty and midday. It'll drop to a light wind around half past... Yes, we should have fine weather for some days after this."

He put the speaker away and smiled at us while he put on his robe. "Fancy a visit to the Petty Viands bus?" he asked. "I could do with a cup of something hot and maybe a sticky cake or two."

## CHAPTER TWO

*

*I*t was just as Dad predicted. We turned out for the Meeting of Kings in wet, howling wind that flapped velvet skirts and wrapped robes around legs. Those with headdresses held them in their hands until the last possible moment and then got very uncomfortable because, like the rest of us, they were trying to eat prettybread or pasties in one hand as we all went to our places. Sybil looked more dishevelled than anyone. Her yellow hair was streaming from her head and her hat was streaming green ribbons in her hand while she rushed about wailing cantrips and shouting at bad-luck carriers to get away behind the buses. She was barefoot, being an earth wizard, and she had kilted her velvet skirts up to her knees because of the wet in the grass. She had extremely thick legs.

"Looks just like a sack of sweetcorn balanced on two logs," Dad said unkindly as he passed me on the way to the King's tent. He disliked Sybil as much as I did. He used to say that it didn't surprise him that Sybil's husband had run away. And then he usually added, "They wanted the poor fellow to be the next Merlin, too. If it had been me, I'd have run away long before. Sybil *and* the worst job in the kingdom! Imagine!"

Unfortunately, Dad's remark threw Mam into one of her rare fits of laughter and she breathed in a crumb of pastry. I was still thumping her back for her when word came round that the Scots were on their way. I had to run to my place beside Grundo. We were lined up with all the other children who weren't pages in a row in front of the Royal Guards.

By this time, most of the tents were down except for the Royal Pavilion, and all the buses, vans, lorries and limousines were drawn up on three sides of an enormous square with the north-facing side left empty. The air was loud with the clapping of the household flags hoisted over them. The Royal Guards were drawn up inside that – poor fellows, they had been polishing kit and whitening belts since dawn, but they looked magnificent, a living line of scarlet and white. We of the Court were inside that again, like a bed of flowers in our Court clothes, shivering in the wind. Grundo said he envied the Household servants.

They were allowed to stay in the buses and keep warm, *and* they had a much better view. They must have been able to see the Scottish Court advancing long before we could.

It was all timed perfectly. Hard-worked officials had been talking to one another on far-speakers all morning to make sure it was. The Scots appeared first. They seemed to come over the horizon and get larger and brighter as they came. They had pipers walking on both sides, solemnly stepping and skirling. I love the sound of bagpipes. It is the most exciting noise I know. I was quite sorry when our band started up and trumpets drowned the pipes out.

This was the signal for our King to come out of his tent and walk towards the Scots. When we stop in towns long enough for me to get talking to people, they always say enviously, "I suppose you see the King every day!" No. Actually, I don't. He is nearly always away in the front of the Progress and I often don't set eyes on him for weeks. When I do see him, it is usually like this, at a distance, as a tall figure in dark clothes, and the main way I recognise him is by his neat brown beard – and a sort of shiver of majesty he brings with him.

On this occasion he had Prince Edmund, the Prince Heir, with him too, also in sober, dark clothes. The Prince is eighteen now and he was travelling with his father that year to learn his duties. With them came the Merlin on one side and the Archbishop of York on the other, both old and stately in stiffly flapping robes, and after that a mixture of bishops and high officials and the wizards who are priests and priestesses of older powers. I'm supposed to know the order of them, but I keep forgetting. All I really know is that Sybil walked behind the Archbishop – with her skirts let down and her hat on by then – and my father was near the back, not being a priest.

I was looking at the Scots mostly anyway. Their King was quite young and he wasn't the one I'd seen before. They have dozens of people who have claims to the throne of Scotland. Every so often, the clans back a new claimant, or three, and have a war and the King gets changed. This one, though he was new, didn't look as if he'd get changed easily. He had a strong, eager look, and he walked as if he owned the earth, not just Scotland. He was wearing plaids, which made him stand out from the crowd of courtiers with him. They were very dressy. I have never seen so many styles and colours and French fashions. Their King looked like a hawk among parrots.

He left them behind and strode to embrace our King. For a brief minute, it was the friendliest possible Meeting. Prince Edmund was beckoned forward and introduced, and then a young woman in glorious rose pink silk who may have been the Scottish Queen – anyway the Scottish King grinned at her as if he knew her very well – and then it was the turn of the Archbishop and the Merlin to step forward and bless everyone. This was when the awful thing happened.

The Merlin spread his arms to call down benign magics. Dad says you don't really need to spread your arms or do anything else physical to work magic. This is why he found Sybil so irritating, because she always acted about so, doing magic. But he says the Merlin had to show people what he was doing. So the poor old man held his arms up wide. His face, which was always rather pale, turned a strange colour. Even from where I was, I could see that the Merlin's lips were sort of lilac-coloured where they showed through his white beard. He took his arms in hurriedly and hugged at himself. Then he slowly folded up and flopped down on the wet grass.

Everybody simply stared for an instant. And this was the instant that Dad's fine weather arrived at last. The sun blazed out. It was suddenly damply, suffocatingly warm.

Dad got to the Merlin first. Dad had been spread out to the side when the two groups met and it only took him two strides to get there and kneel down. He swore to me afterwards that the Merlin was alive at that point, even though he had clearly had a bad heart attack. But Dad had to give way to Prince Edmund, who got there next. Prince Edmund put his hand out towards the Merlin's chest and then snatched it back, looking aghast. He turned to the King and started to say something. Then he stopped, because Sybil swooped in almost at once and pulled the poor old man over on to his back. By that time he was definitely dead. I got a glimpse of his staring face among everybody's legs and, as Grundo said, you couldn't mistake it.

"Dead!" Sybil screamed. "My mentor and my master!" She put her head back so that her hat fell off and screamed again, towards the Scottish King. "*Dead!*"

She didn't say any more. She just stood up with wet black patches on her velvet gown where she had knelt in the grass and stared at the Scottish King with her hands clasped to her chest.

Our King said icily to the Scottish King, "I believe Your Majesty was trained as a wizard?"

The Scottish King looked at him. After a moment he said, "I think this is the end of any friendship between us. I bid you good afternoon."

He swung round in a swirl of tartan and walked away with all his people. He didn't have to walk far. Vehicles came roaring over the brow of the hill almost at once, most of them military transports, and the royal party was scooped up into some of them, leaving the rest sitting in a threatening row on the Scottish border.

"We'll move back a few miles," our King said.

The rest of that week was a hot, moist chaos. Grundo and I, along with most of the children, were bundled here and there and sent about with messages because the royal pages were run off their feet, and it took us several days to find out what was happening.

It seemed that the media people had been filming the whole Meeting from their bus and they broadcast it as they filmed it. The Merlin's death caused an outcry all over the country. The King had to go to the bus and assure people in another broadcast that it was an unfortunate accident, and that no one was accusing the Scottish King of anything. It didn't help the situation that he said this in a grim way that made everyone think the opposite. At the same time, the whole Progress packed up double quick and moved south to the borders of Northumberland. The media bus was actually on the road while the King was grimly broadcasting. The rest of the buses had to keep drawing up on to the verges to make way for the army units rushing to take up defensive positions along the Scottish border, so all we knew of things were tilted views of hedges while green lorries thundered by in the road.

It turned out that the Scottish King broadcast too. He talked about an insult to Scotland and he sent army units to the border as well.

"But he must know it was simply an accident," my mam said worriedly, when I did manage to see her and ask what was going on.

This was when we were finally camped around a village where the King could stay in a manor house that was big enough for the wizards to perform an autopsy on the Merlin. There, Grundo and I were sent hurrying with messages to other wizards, to the army HQ bus, the media tent, to the Waymaster's Office and the Chamberlain's, and after a day or so, to the village hall where the judicial enquiry was being held. So much was going on. There was a nationwide hunt for a new Merlin, with most of the wizards involved, while the rest were busy with the enquiry. It seemed that the post mortem had shown that there *were* traces of a spell hanging round the Merlin, but no one could tell what kind. It could even have been one of the Merlin's own spells.

Dad was called into the enquiry. For a whole day, it looked as if he might be accused of murder. My heart seemed to be filling my ears and drumming in my chest that entire time. Mam went around white as a sheet whispering, "Oh, they can't blame him, they *can't!*" The trouble was, as she pointed out to me, everybody else who was close to the Merlin when he died was either royal or very important, so poor Dad got the full blast of the suspicion.

I can't tell you how frantic everything was that day.

Then everything calmed down.

As far as I could tell, it was Grandad's doing. He turned up that evening, shortly after Dad had come out of the village hall looking as if he had spent several sleepless weeks on a bare mountain. Grandad brought the new Merlin with him and they went straight to the King together. We didn't see Grandad until quite late that night, when they all came out on to the village green: Grandad, the King, the Merlin, the judges, Prince Edmund, and a whole string of the wizards who had been tearing about and fussing over finding the new Merlin. The new Merlin was a skinny young man with a little pointed chin and a big Adam's apple, who looked a bit stunned about his sudden jump to fame. Or maybe he was in a trance. Prince Edmund kept looking at him in an astonished, wondering way.

Meanwhile, the Waymaster's Office had acted with its usual efficiency and cordoned off a big space on the green, while the Royal Guard jumped to it and built a bonfire in the centre of it. We were standing watching, waiting, wondering what was going to happen, when Grandad came up to us. Mam flung herself on him, more or less crying.

"Oh, Maxwell! It's been so awful! *Can* you help?"

"Steady," Grandad said. "All's well. Dan's in the clear now. Had to tackle it from the top, you see, on account of the family relationship." He slapped Dad on the shoulder and gave me one of his quick, bony hugs. "Roddy. Hallo, Grundo," he said. "I think I've got the whole mess sorted. Have to wait and see, of course, but I think they'll end up deciding it was nobody's fault. Lord! Poor old Merlin Landor must have been in his eighties at least! Bound to drop dead at some point. Just chose a bad moment to do it. No need for national hysteria about that."

You know that marvellous moment when your mind goes quiet with relief. Everything was suddenly tranquil and acute with me. I could smell the trampled grass and motor fuel that I had not noticed before this, and the sweet, dusty scent of hay from beyond the village. I could hear the crackle of the bonfire as it caught and the twittering of birds in the trees around the green. The small, yellow flames climbing among the brushwood seemed unbelievably clear and meaningful, all of a sudden, and my mind went so peaceful and limpid that I found myself thinking that, yes, Grandad *could* be right. But Sir James had *known* the old Merlin was going to die. I looked round for Sir James, but he was not there. When I thought, I realised I had not seen him for some days, though Sybil was there, in among the other wizards.

As soon as the bonfire was blazing properly, the senior wizard stepped forward and announced that we were here to present the new Merlin to Court and country. Everyone cheered and the young Merlin looked more dazed than ever. Then one of the judges said that the question of the late Merlin's death was now to be settled. He bowed to the King and stepped back.

The King said to the Merlin, "Are you prepared to prophesy for us?"

"I – I think so," the Merlin said. He had rather a weak, high voice.

"Then," said the King, "tell us who, or what, caused the death of the last Merlin."

The young man clasped his hands together with his arms pointing straight down, rather as if he were pulling on a rope, and he began to sway, round and round. The bonfire seemed to imitate him. It broke into long pennants of orange flame that roared and crackled and sent a great spiral of smoke and burning blobs high into the evening sky. The extra light caught and glistened on tears pouring down the Merlin's small, pointed face. He started to give out big gulping sobs.

"Oh, Lord! He's a weeper!" Grandad said disgustedly. "I wish I'd known. I'd have stayed away."

"A lot of the Merlins have cried when they prophesied," Dad pointed out.

"I know. But I don't have to like it, do I?" Grandad retorted.

The Merlin started to speak then, in high gasps, but what with the roaring and snapping from the bonfire and the way he was sobbing, it was hard to hear what he was saying. I *think* it was, "Blame is – where blame lies – blame rests – where dragon flies."

"And what's *that* supposed to mean?" my grandfather muttered irritably. "Is he accusing *Wales* now or *what*?"

While Grandad was mumbling, the King said in a polite, puzzled way, "And – er – then have you any words that might guide us for the future?"

This brought on a new bout of weeping from the Merlin. He bent this way and that, choking and sobbing, still with his hands clasped in that odd way. The bonfire gusted and swirled and golden sparks rained upwards. Eventually, the Merlin began gasping out words again and I found these even harder to catch. They sounded like, "Power flows – when Merlin goes – world sways – in dark ways – a lord is bound – power found – land falls – when alien calls – nothing right – till dragon's flight."

"I suppose this means something to *him*," Grandad grumbled.

Several of the wizards were writing the words down. I believe they all wrote different versions. I can only put down what I thought I heard – and the creepy thing is that the prophecy was quite right, now that I understand what it was about.

After that, it seemed to be finished. The Merlin unclasped his hands, fetched out a handkerchief and dried his eyes on it in a most matter-of-fact way. The King said, "We thank you, Merlin," looking as mystified as the rest of us. The bonfire fell back to burning in a more normal way.

The Household staff came round with glasses of warm spiced wine. I do take my hat off to these people. They have an awful job obeying all the instructions for camping that come from the Waymaster and the Chamberlain, or setting up house if the King decides to stay under a roof somewhere, and then providing meals fit for a King at all times and in all weathers, and they nearly always get it exactly right. That wine was exactly what everyone there needed. The fine weather that Dad had provided was still with us, but it came with a chilly wind and heavy dews at night.

We took our glasses and went to one of the benches at the edge of the green. From there, I could see the Merlin pacing awkwardly about near the bonfire while Prince Edmund talked earnestly to him. The Prince seemed fascinated by the Merlin. I suppose they were the same age, more or less, and this Merlin was likely to be the one the Prince would have to deal with all through his reign when he got to be King. I also noticed Alicia hanging about near them, looking very trim in her page's uniform. She was making sure that the Merlin got twice as much of the wine and the snacks that were going round. Doing her duty. But, well, she was sixteen and quite near the Merlin's age too – not that he seemed to notice her much. He was listening to the Prince mostly.

My parents were asking Grandad how he had managed to find the new Merlin when nobody else could, and he was making modest noises and grunting, "Magid methods. Not difficult. Had my eye on the chap for years." I don't quite understand what it means that Grandad is a Magid, not really. I *think* it means that he operates in other worlds besides ours and it also seems to mean that he has the power to settle things in a way that ordinary kings and wizards can't. He went on to say, "I had to have a serious talk with the King – told him the same as I told the Scottish King. It's vitally important that the Islands of Blest stay peaceful. Blest – and these islands in particular – keeps the balance of the magics in half the multiverse, you see."

"How old is the Merlin?" I interrupted.

"Twenty-five. Older than he looks," Grandad told me. "A powerful magic gift does that to some people. Roddy, do you mind taking Grundo and going off somewhere? We've got things to talk about here that aren't for children."

Grandad is like that. He never likes to talk about the interesting things in front of me. Grundo and I drifted off.

"He's too old for Alicia, the Merlin," I said to Grundo.

He was surprised. "Why should that stop her?" he asked.

# PART TWO
# NICK

# CHAPTER THREE

*

*I* thought it was a dream at first. It was really peculiar. It happened when my dad took me with him to a writers' conference in London. Dad is Ted Mallory and he is a writer. He does horror stories with demons in them, but this conference was for people who write detective stories. This is the strange thing about Dad. He reads detective stories all the time when he isn't writing himself, and he really admires the people who write them, far more than the people who write his kind of thing. He was all excited because his favourite author was going to be speaking at the conference.

I didn't want to go.

"Oh, yes you do," Dad said. "I'm still shuddering at

39

what happened when I left you alone here last Easter."

"It was my *friends* who drank all your whisky," I said.

"With you as a helpless onlooker while they broke the furniture and draped the kitchen in pasta, I know," says Dad. "So here's what I'm going to do, Nick. I'm going to book you in with me, and I'm going to go, and when I go, I'm going to lock up this house with you outside it. If you don't choose to come with me, you can spend the weekend sitting in the street. Or the garden shed. I'll leave that unlocked for you, if you like."

He really meant this. He can be a real swine when he puts his mind to it. I thought about overpowering him and locking *him* in the garden shed. I'm bigger than he is, even though I won't be fifteen until just before Christmas. But then I thought how he isn't really my dad and how we'd both sort of adopted one another after Mum was killed because – usually – we like one another, and where would either of us be if that fell through?

While I was thinking this, Dad said, "Come on. You may even enjoy it. And you'll be able to tell people later that you were present at one of the very rare appearances of Maxwell Hyde. This is only the third time he's spoken in public – and my sense is that he's a very interesting speaker."

Maxwell Hyde is this favourite author of Dad's. I could see I would be spoiling his fun if I didn't let him take me along, so I gave in. He was ever so pleased and gave me one of this Maxwell Hyde's books to read.

I don't like detective stories. They're dead boring. But Maxwell Hyde was worse than boring because his books were set in an alternate world. This is what Dad likes about them. He goes on about the self-consistency and wealth of otherworld detail in Maxwell Hyde's Other-England – as far as I could see, this meant lots of boring description of the way things were different: how the King never stayed in one place and the parliament sat in Winchester and never did anything, and so forth – but what got to me was reading about another world that I couldn't *get* to. By the time I'd read two pages, I was so longing to get to this other world that it was like sheets of flame flaring through me.

There are lots of worlds. I know, because I've been to some. My real parents come from one. But I can't seem to get to any of them on my *own*. I always seem to have to have someone to *take* me. I've tried, and I keep trying, but it just doesn't seem to work for me, even though I want to do it so much that I *dream* I'm doing it. There must be something I'm doing wrong. And I'd decided that I'd spend the whole first week of the summer holidays trying until I'd cracked it. Now here was Dad hauling me away to this conference instead. That was why I didn't want to go. But I'd said I would, so I went.

It was even worse than I'd expected.

It was in a big, gloomy hotel full of soberly-dressed people who all thought they were important – apart from the one or two who thought they were God or

Shakespeare or something, and went around with a crowd of power-dressed hangers-on to keep them from being talked to by ordinary people. There was a lecture every hour. Some of them were by police chiefs and lawyers, and I sat there trying so hard not to yawn that my eyes watered and my ears popped. But there was going to be one on the Sunday by a private detective. That was the only one I thought might be interesting.

None of the people had any time for a teenager like me. They kept giving my jeans disapproving looks and then glancing at my face as if they thought I must have got in there by mistake. But the thing that really got to me was how eager Dad was about it all. He had a big pile of various books he was trying to get signed, just as if he was a humble fan and not a world famous writer himself. It really hurt my feelings when one of the God-or-Shakespeare ones flourished a pen over the book Dad eagerly spread out for her and said, "Who?"

Dad said in a modest voice, "Ted Mallory. I write a bit myself."

Mrs God-Shakespeare scrawled in the book, saying, "Do you write under another name? What have you written?"

"Horror stories mostly," Dad admitted.

And she said, "Oh," and pushed the book back to him as if it was contaminated.

Dad didn't seem to notice. He was enjoying himself. Maxwell Hyde was giving the big talk on the Saturday evening and Dad kept saying he couldn't wait. Then he got really excited because one of the nicer writers – who wore jeans like me – said he knew Maxwell Hyde slightly and he'd introduce Dad to him if we hung around with him.

Dad was blissed out. By that time I was yawning every time Dad's back was turned and forcing my mouth shut when he looked at me. We went hurrying up and down corridors looking for Maxwell Hyde, pushing against crowds of people pushing the other way, and I kept thinking, If *only* I could just wheel round sideways and walk off into a different world! I was in a hotel when I did that the first time, which gave me the idea that hotels were probably a good place to step off from.

So I was daydreaming about that when we did at last catch up with Maxwell Hyde. By then it was just before his lecture, so he was in a hurry and people were streaming past us to get into the big hall, but he stopped quite politely when the nice writer said, "Oh, Maxwell, can you spare a moment for someone who's dying to meet you?"

I didn't really notice him much, except that he was one of those upright, silvery gentlemen, quite old-fashioned, with leather patches on his old tweed jacket. As he swung round to Dad, I could smell whisky. I remember thinking, Hey! He gets as nervous as Dad does before he has to give a talk! And I could tell he had had a drink to give himself some courage.

I was being bumped about by all the other people in the corridor and I had to keep shifting while Dad and Mr Hyde were shaking hands. I was right off at one side of them when Mr Hyde said, "Ted Mallory? Demons, isn't it?"

Just then, one of the people bumping me – I didn't see who, except that it was a man – said quietly, "Off you go then." I stepped sideways again out of his way.

This was when I thought it was a dream.

I was outside, on an airfield of some kind. It must have been early morning, because it was chilly and dark, but getting lighter all the time, and there was pink mist across the stretch of grass I could see. But I couldn't see much, because there were things I thought were helicopters blocking my view one way – tall, dark brown things – and the other way was a crowd of men who all seemed pretty impatient about something. I was sort of squashed between the men and the helicopters. The man nearest me, who was wearing a dirty, pale suede jacket and trousers and smoking a cigarette in long, impatient drags, turned round to throw his cigarette down on the grass and saw me.

"Oh, *there* you are!" he said. "Why didn't you say you'd got here?" He turned back to the rest of them and called out, "It's all right, messieurs! The novice finally got here. We can go."

They all sort of groaned with relief and one of them began talking into a cellphone. "This is Perimeter Security, monsieur," I heard him say, "reporting that our numbers are now complete. You can tell the Prince that it's safe to embark now." And after the phone had done some angry quacking, he said, "Very good, monsieur. I'll pass that on to the culprit," and then he waved at the rest of us.

Everyone began crowding up the ladder into the nearest helicopter-thing. The man who had spoken to me pushed me up ahead of him and swung on to the ladder after me. This must have put his face up against my legs, because he said angrily, "Didn't the academy tell you to wear your leathers for this?"

I thought I knew then. I was sure this was one of my dreams about getting into another world and that it had got mixed up with the sort of dream where you're on a bus with no clothes on, or talking to a girl you fancy with the front of your trousers missing. So I wasn't particularly bothered. I just said, "No, they didn't tell me anything."

He made an irritated noise. "You're supposed to be skyclad for official workings. They should *know* that!" he said. "You didn't *eat* before you came, did you?" He sounded quite scandalised about it.

"No," I said. Dad and I had been going to have supper after we'd listened to Maxwell Hyde. I was quite hungry, now I thought of it.

"Well, that's a relief!" he said, pushing me forward into the inside of the flyer. "You have to be fasting for a major working like this. Yours is the pull-down seat at the back there."

It would be! I thought. There were nice padded seats all round under the windows, but the one at the back was just a kind of slab. Everyone else was settling into the good seats and snapping seat belts around them, so I found the belts that went with the slab and did them up. I'd just got the buckles sussed when I looked up to find the man with the cellphone leaning over me.

"You," he said, "were late. Top brass is not pleased. You kept the Prince waiting for nearly twenty minutes and HRH is not a patient man."

"Sorry," I said. But he went on and on, leaning over me and bawling me out. I didn't need to listen to it much because the engines started then, roaring and clattering, and everything shook. Some of the noise was from the other fliers. I could see them sideways beyond his angry face, rising up into the air one after another, about six of them, and I wondered what made them fly. They didn't have wings or rotors.

Eventually, a warning *ping* sounded. The bawling man gave me a menacing look and went to strap himself in beside his mates. They were all wearing some kind of uniform, sort of like soldiers, and the one who had bawled at me had coloured stripes round his sleeves. I supposed he was the officer. The men nearest me, four of them, were all dressed in dirty pale suede. Skyclad, I thought. Whatever that meant.

Then we were rising up into the air and roaring after the other fliers. I leaned over to the window and looked down, trying to see where this was. I saw the Thames winding underneath among crowds of houses, so I knew we were over London, but in a dreamlike way there was no London Eye, though I spotted the Tower and Tower Bridge, and where I thought St Paul's ought to be there was a huge white church with three square towers and a steeple. After that we went tilting away southwards and I was looking down on misty green fields. Not long after that we were over the sea.

About then, the noise seemed to get less – or maybe I got used to it – and I could hear what the men in suede were saying. Mostly it was just grumbles about having to get up so early and how they were hungry already, along with jokes I didn't understand, but I gathered that the one who had talked to me was Dave and the big one with the foreign accent was Arnold. The other two were Chick and Pierre. None of them took any notice of me.

Dave was still irritated. He said angrily, "I can sympathise with his passion for cricket, but why does he have to play it in *Marseilles*, for the powers' sake?"

Pierre said, slightly shocked, "That's where England are playing. HRH *is* a world-class batsman, you know."

"But," Dave said, "until last night he wasn't going to be in the team."

"He changed his mind. Royal privilege," said Arnold with the foreign accent.

"That's our Geoff for you!" Chick said, laughing.

"I know. That worries me," Dave answered. "What's

he going to be like when he's King?"

"Oh, give him the right advisors and he'll be all right," Chick said soothingly. "His royal dad was just the same when he was Crown Prince, they say."

This is a really mad dream, I thought. Cricket in France!

We droned on for ages. The sun came up and glared in through the left-hand windows. Pretty soon all the soldiers down the other end had their jackets off and were playing some sort of card game, in a slow, bored way. The men in suede didn't seem to be allowed to take their jackets off. They sweated. It got quite niffy down my end. And I'd been assuming that they weren't allowed to smoke in the flier, but that turned out to be wrong. The soldiers all lit up and so did Dave. The air soon became thick with smoke on top of the smell of sweat. It got worse when Arnold lit up a thin, black thing that smelt like a wet bonfire.

"Yik!" said Pierre. "Where did you get hold of *that*?"

"Aztec Empire," Arnold said, peacefully puffing out brown clouds.

I shall wake up from this dream with cancer! I thought. The slab seat was hard. I shifted about and ached. Most of the people fell asleep after an hour or so, but I couldn't. I supposed at the time that it was because I was asleep already. I know that seems silly, but it was all so *strange* and I'd been so used to dreaming, for months now, that I had found my way into another world that I really and truly believed that this was just another of those dreams. I sat and sweated while we droned on, and even that didn't alert me to the fact that this might be *real*. Dreams usually sort of fast-forward long journeys and things like that, but I didn't think of that. I just thought the journey was the dream.

At last, there was another of those warning *pings*. The officer reached into his jacket for his phone and talked to it for a short while. Then he put the jacket on and came towards the men in suede, who were all stretching and yawning and looking bleary.

"Messieurs," he said, "you'll have twenty minutes. The royal flit will circle during that time under the protection of the Prince's personal mages and then put down on the pavilion roof. You're expected to have the stadium secured by then. All right?"

"All right," Arnold agreed. "Thanks, monsieur." Then, when the officer had gone back to the other soldiers, he said, "Bloody *powers*!"

"Going to have to hustle, aren't we?" Chick said. He jerked his head towards me. "What do we do about him? He's not skyclad."

Arnold was the one in charge. He blinked slowly at me as if he'd noticed me for the first time. "Not really a problem," he said. "He'll have to keep out of the circle, that's all. We'll put him on boundary patrol." Then he actually spoke to me. "You, mon gar," he said, "will do exactly as we say at all times, and if you set so much as a toe over the wardings, I'll have your guts for garters. That clear?"

I nodded. I wanted to tell him that I hadn't the faintest idea what we were supposed to be doing, but I didn't quite like to. Anyway the flier – flit or whatever – started making a great deal more noise and going downwards in jerks, hanging in the air and then jerking sickeningly down again. I swallowed and sat back, thinking that it would probably all be obvious what to do, the way it is in dreams, and took a look out of the window. I had just time to see a big oval of green stadium surrounded by banks of seats crowded with people, and blue, blue sea somewhere beyond that, before we came down with a grinding thump and everyone leapt up.

The soldiers went racing and clattering off to take up positions round the roof we'd landed on. They were carrying rifles. It was serious security. We clattered off after them into scalding sunlight and I found myself ducking as the flier roared off into the air again just above my head, covering us in an instant of deep blue shadow. As it did, the others bent over some kind of compass that Dave had fetched out.

"North's up the narrow end opposite," Dave said, "pretty exactly."

"Right," said Arnold. "Then we go the quickest way." And he led us rushing down some stairs at the corner of the roof. We clattered along boards then, somewhere high up along the front of the pavilion, and raced on down much steeper stairs with crowds of well-dressed people on either side. They all turned to stare at us. "Ceux sont les sorciers," I heard someone say, and again, when we got to the smart white gate at the bottom of the stairs and a wrinkled old fellow in a white coat opened it for us, he turned to someone and said knowingly, "Ah. Les sorciers." I reckon it meant, *Those are the mages, you know*.

We rushed out into the enormous stadium, hurrying across acres of green, green grass with blurred banks of faces all round and all staring at us. It really was exactly like my worst dreams. I felt about an inch high as Arnold led us trotting straight towards the opposite end of the oval. I could see he was going to take us right across the square of even greener grass where the wicket was laid out, flat and brownish, right in front of us.

Now, I'm not much for cricket myself, but I did know that you were never, ever supposed to run on the sacred wicket. I wondered whether to say something. I was quite relieved when Pierre panted out, "Er – Arnold – not on the wicket – really."

"What? Oh. Yes," Arnold said, and he took a small curve, so that we went trotting just beside the strip of bare rolled turf.

Pierre turned his eyes up and murmured to Chick, "He's from Schleswig-Holstein. What can you expect?"

"Empire's full of barbarians," Chick panted back in a whisper.

We hastened on to the end of the stadium, where we had to do another detour, around the sightscreen. There was a grille behind it blocking an archway under the seating. Soldiers let us through and we plunged into chilly, concrete gloom beyond, where we really got busy. We were in the space underneath the seats there, which ran right round the stadium like a concrete underpass, including under the pavilion. I know it did, because I was forced to rush all round it three times.

Arnold dumped down the bag he was carrying on the spot Dave said was the exact North and snatched out of it five big sugar-shakers full of water. "Ready blessed," he said, jamming one into my hand. Then they shoved me behind them and stood in a row gabbling some kind of incantation. After that, they were off, shouting at me to come along and stop dossing, pelting down the arched concrete space, madly sprinkling water as they ran and shoving me repeatedly so that I didn't tread inside the wet line, until Dave said, "East." They stopped and gabbled another invocation, and then they charged on, sprinkling again, until Dave said, "South," where they stopped and gabbled too. Then we pelted off once more to gabble at West, then on round to North again. The water just lasted.

I hoped that was it then, but no. We dumped the empty water-shakers and Arnold fetched out five things that looked like lighted candles but were really electric torches. Neat things. They must have had strange batteries, because they flickered and flared just like real candles as we raced around to East once more with our feet booming echoes out of the concrete corridor. This time when Dave said "East", Chick slammed his candle-torch down on the floor and stood gabbling. I nearly got left behind there because I was staring at Chick drawing what looked like a belt-knife and pulling it out as if it were toffee or something so that it was like a sword, which he stood holding point upwards in front of his face. I had to sprint to catch the others up, and I only reached them as Dave was singing out, "South!" They shed Pierre and his candle there and, as we pelted off, Pierre was pulling a knife out into a sword too.

At West, it was Dave's turn to stand pulling a knife into a sword and gabbling. Arnold and I rushed on together to North. Luckily, Arnold was so big he was not much of a runner and I could keep up. I'd no breath left by then. When we got round to Arnold's bag again, he plonked down his candle and remarked, "I hold North because I'm the strongest. It's the most dangerous ward of all." Then, instead of drawing his belt-knife, he took my candle-torch away and passed me a gigantic salt-shaker.

I stared at it.

"All round again with this," Arnold said. "Make sure it's a continuous line and that you keep *outside* the line."

It's one of *those* dreams, I thought. I sighed. I grabbed the salt and set off the other way to make a change.

"No, *no!*" he howled. "Not widdershins, you fool!

*Deosil*! And run. You've got to get round before the Prince lands!"

"Making my third four-minute mile," I said.

"Pretty well," he agreed. "Go!"

So off I went, pouring salt and stumbling over my own feet as I tried to see where I was pouring it, past Chick standing with his sword like a statue, past soldiers I was almost too busy to notice, who were on guard about every fifty feet, and on round to Pierre, also standing like a statue. When I got to him, I could hear the nearby blatting of a flier and cheering in the distance. Pierre shot me an angry, urgent look. Obviously, this Prince had more or less landed by then. I sped on, frantically sprinkling salt, getting better at it now. Even so, it seemed an age before I got round to Dave, and another age before I got back to Arnold again. The cheering overhead was like thunder by then.

"*Just* about made it," Arnold said. He had a sword by now and was standing like the others, looking sort of remote, behind his candle-thing. "Make sure the line of salt joins up behind me, then put the shaker back in the bag and get on guard."

"Er…" I said. "I'm not sure—"

He more or less roared at me. "Didn't they teach you *anything* at the academy? I shall lodge a complaint." Then he seemed to pull himself together and sort of recited at me, the way you might tell a total idiot how to dial 999 in an emergency, "Choose your spot, go into a light trance, enter the otherwhere, pick up your totem beast and go on patrol with it. If you see anything out of the ordinary – *anything at all* – come and tell me. Now go and get on with it!"

"Right," I said. "Thanks." I threw the salt-shaker into the bag and wandered away. Now what? I thought. It was fairly clear to me that what we had been doing in such a hurry was casting a circle of magic protection around this French cricket stadium, but it struck me as pretty boring, mass-produced sort of magic. I couldn't see how it could possibly work, but I supposed it kept them happy, them and this Prince of theirs. The stupid thing was that I had been dying to learn magic. Part of the way I kept trying to walk to other worlds was to do with my wanting, above anything else, to be a proper magician, to *know* magic and be able to work it for myself. Now here was this dream making it seem just boring. And probably useless.

That's dreams for you, I thought, wandering on through the tunnel under the seats. Since I had no idea how to do the stuff Arnold had told me, the only thing I *could* do was to keep out of his sight, and out of Chick's sight too, on round the curve in the East. I trudged past the first soldier on guard and, as soon as the curve of the passage hid him from sight, I simply sat down with my back to the outside wall.

It was a pretty dismal place, full of gritty, gloomy echoes and gritty, gloomy concrete smells. People had used it to pee in too, which didn't help. It felt damp. As

I was soaked with sweat from all that running, I began to feel clammy almost at once. At least it wasn't dark. There were orange striplights in the concrete ceiling and holes in the concrete back wall. The holes were high up and covered with grids, but they did let in slants of bright sun that cut through the gritty air in regular white slices.

Not much to look at except a line of salt, I thought. At least I was better off than Arnold and the rest. I didn't have to keep staring at a sword. And for the first time, I began to wonder how long we'd all have to stay here. For the whole time it took this Prince to play in a Test Match? Those could go on for days. And the frustrating thing about this dream, I thought, as I heard clapping far away over my head, was the way I never set eyes on this Prince all the fuss was about.

# CHAPTER FOUR

✳

*I* think I went to sleep. It made sense to think so. I was quite jet-lagged by then, given I'd set off before supper, arrived at dawn and then flown all the way to the south of France, followed by running round the stadium three times.

But it didn't quite feel like sleep. I felt as if I got up, leaving myself sitting there, and walked off along an inviting, bluish, shady path I'd suddenly noticed. This path led upwards and sort of sideways from the concrete passage, out of the smells and clamminess, into a cool, rustling wood. This was such a relief that I didn't feel tired any more. I stretched and snuffed up the cool green smells – pine trees and a sharp, gummy scent from head high ferns, and bark and leaves and bushes that smelt almost like incense – and I kept on walking, deeper into the wood and uphill.

The incense bushes in front of me started rustling. Then the ferns swayed.

I stopped. I kept very still. I could feel my heart banging. Something was definitely coming. But I was still not prepared for it when it did.

The ferns parted and a smooth black head slid out and stared me in the face with huge yellow eyes. For just one instant I was nose to nose with an enormous black panther.

Then I was up a tree, the tallest tree I could find.

In between was a blur of absolute terror. If I *think* about it, carefully, I think the panther sort of said Oh, *hallo* in wordless panther talk, and I'm fairly sure I screamed. And I do, slightly, remember staring around with tremendous speed to choose the best tree, and then listening to my own breath coming in sort of shrieks while I shot up this tree, and I even remember yelling "Ouch!" when I peeled one of my nails back on the way up.

Then it all stops with me sitting shakily astride a branch watching the panther coming up after me.

"Bugger!" I said. "I forgot panthers could climb trees!"

*Naturally we can*, it said. It settled on the branch opposite mine with one great paw hanging and its tail swinging. *What are we doing up here?* it asked. *Hunting?*

There was no doubt it was talking to me. Well, I thought, this was a dream. So I gave in to it and answered, "No. I'm supposed to be keeping watch in case anything supernatural attacks the Prince."

The panther yawned. It was as if its head split open into a bright pink maw fringed with long, white fangs. *Boring*, it said. *I hoped you might want to go hunting.*

"Let's do that in a bit," I said. I was feeling weak with terror still. "I agree," I said, hoping to persuade it to go away, "keeping watch is really boring. I may have to be here for hours."

*Oh, well*, the panther said. It let down its three other huge paws, put its black chin on the branch and went to sleep.

After a while when I couldn't look away from it in case it went for my throat, and another while when I didn't dare move in case it woke up and went for my throat, I sort of got used to the fact that I was sitting in a tree facing a big, black, sleeping panther, and I began to look about. Carefully and slowly. Arnold had said "pick up your totem beast" and I supposed that this panther might be my totem beast, but I didn't believe this, not really. As far as I knew, totem beasts were a part of a shamanistic magician's mind, which meant they were not really real, and I could see the panther was as real as I was. Anyway, I wasn't going to take a chance on it. I sat and turned my head very slowly.

I was looking out over the tops of trees, but that was

only the ordinary part of wherever I was. Tilted away sideways from the wood was – well, it was a bit like a diagram in lights. The nearest part of the diagram was a low-key misty map of a town and, beyond that, was a sparkling, electric hugeness that seemed to be sea. Nearer to me, at the edge of the lines and blobs that made the town, I could see a striking, turquoise oval. It was like a lighted jewel and it had a blob of whiter light at each end of it and two more blobs in the middle of each side.

"Oh!" I said, out loud without thinking. "Their magic *did* work! Those blobs must be *them* – Arnold and Dave and his mates!"

The panther twitched and made a noise in its throat. I didn't know if it was a growl, or a snore, or its way of agreeing with me, but I shut up at once. I went on staring without speaking. It was fascinating, that lighted diagram. Little bright sparkles moved inside the turquoise oval of the stadium, and one brighter one stood still quite near the middle. I wondered if that was the Prince. But it could have been one of the umpires. After a bit, I noticed moving smudges of light out in the sea that were probably ships, and one or two quicker ones moving in straight lines that I thought were aircraft, because some of them made lines across the town. They were all in the most beautiful colours. None of them struck me as dangerous. But then I wouldn't have known what a threat to the Prince looked like if it came up and hit me.

Anyway, I was stuck in this tree until the panther

decided to leave. So I simply sat and stared, and listened to the rustlings and birdcalls in the wood, and felt as peaceful as anyone could be stuck up a tree a yard away from a lethal black panther.

The panther suddenly woke up.

I flinched, but it wasn't attending to me. *Someone coming*, it remarked, head up and all four paws on the branch again. Then, like a big slide of black oil, it went noiselessly slithering away down the tree.

My forehead got wet with relief. I listened, but I couldn't hear a thing. So, rather cautiously, I let myself down from branch to branch, until I could see the panther crouched along one of the very lowest boughs below me. Below that, I could see bare, pine-needled ground stretching away to bushes. Another animal was walking across the pine needles, another big cat, only this one was a spotted one, with long legs and a small head. This cat was so full of muscles that it seemed almost to walk on tiptoe. Its ugly, spotted tail was lashing. So was the panther's, only more elegantly. The cat looked up, past the panther, and straight at me. Its eyes were wide and green and most uncomfortably knowing. When it got near the tree, it simply sat down and went on staring, jeeringly.

Then a man came out of the bushes after it.

He's a hunter, I thought. This was because of the way he walked, sort of light and tense and leaning forward ready for trouble, and because of the deep tan on his narrow face. But I couldn't help noticing that he was dressed in the same kind of suede that Arnold and his pals were wearing, except that his leathers were so old and greasy and baggy that you could hardly see they were suede. Hunters can dress in leather too, I thought. But I wondered.

He came up beside the ugly spotted cat and put his hand on its head, between its round, tufted ears. Then he looked slowly up through the tree until he saw me. "Nick Mallory?" he said quietly.

I wanted to deny it. I wanted to say my name was really Nichothodes Koryfoides, which is true. But Nick Mallory was what I had chosen to be when Dad and I adopted one another. "Yes," I said. I meant it to sound cautious and adult, but it came out weak and defiant and resentful.

"Then come down here," said the man.

As soon as he said it, I *was* down, standing on the pine needles under the tree, only a couple of feet away from him and his cat. That close, I could tell he was some kind of magic user, and one of the strongest I'd ever come across, too. Magics fair sizzled off him, and he felt full of strange skills and strong craft and deep, deep knowledge. He knew how to bring me down from the tree with just a word. And he'd brought the panther down with me, I realised. The poor beast was busy abasing itself, crawling on its belly among the pine needles, and pressing itself against my leg as if I could help it, absolutely terrified of that spotted cat. The cat was studying it contemptuously.

"I had quite a bit of trouble locating you," the man said to me. "What are you doing here?"

"I'm supposed to watch the boundaries for anything that threatens the Prince," I said. My throat had gone choky with fright. I had to cough before I could say, "You're threatening him, aren't you?"

He shrugged and looked around as if he was getting his bearings. To my surprise, although there were trees all round us, I could still see the lighted turquoise oval of the stadium and the sea shimmering beyond it. It seemed like something on a different wavelength from the wood. But the chief thing I noticed was that the man's profile was like a zigzag of lightning. I'd never seen anything more dangerous – unless it was that spotted cat. I kept as still as I could.

"Oh, the Plantagenate Empire," the man said. "I've no need to threaten *that* Prince. He's going to lose the French part of his empire, and most of his German holdings too, as soon as he comes to the throne, and he'll be dead a couple of years after that. No, it was you I wanted. I've been offered a fee to eliminate you."

My knees went wobbly. I tried to say that I wasn't a threat to anyone. I'd *said* I didn't want to be Emperor. My father was Emperor of the Koryfonic Empire, you see, many worlds away from here. But I just harmlessly wanted to be a Magid and walk into other worlds. I opened my mouth to tell the man this, but my tongue sort of dried to one side of my mouth and only a surprised sort of grunt came out.

"Yes," the man said, staring at me with his dreadful, keen eyes. They were the kind of brown that is almost yellow. "Yes, it surprises me too, now I see you. Perhaps it's because of something you might do later. You strike me as completely useless at the moment, but you must have some fairly strong potential or that panther there wouldn't have befriended you."

Befriended! I thought. *What* befriending? I was so indignant that my tongue came unstuck and I managed to husk out, "I – he's not real. He's my totem animal."

The man looked surprised. "You think she's what? What gave you that idea?"

"They told me to go into a light trance and look for my totem in the otherwhere," I said. "It's the only explanation."

The man gave an impatient sigh. "What nonsense. These Plantagenate mages do irritate me. *All* their magic is this kind of rule-of-thumb half-truth! You shouldn't believe a word they say, unless you can get it confirmed by an independent source. Magic is wide, various and *big*. If you really think that animal is just a mind-product, touch her. Put your hand on her head."

When that man told you to do something, you found yourself doing it. Before I could even be nervous, I found myself bending sideways and putting my hand on the panther, on the broad part of her head between her flattened ears. She didn't like it. She flinched all over, but she let me do it. She was warm and domed there and her black hair wasn't soft like a cat's; it was harsh, with a prickly end to each hair. She was as real as I was. I don't think I'd ever felt such a fool. The man was looking at me with real contempt and on top of it all I hadn't noticed that the panther was a female.

But perhaps, I thought as I straightened up, I'm not very real here after all, because my body *has* to be in a trance back at the stadium. Then I thought, I keep having to do what this man tells me. In a minute, he's going to say *Go on, die.* And I shall do that wherever I am.

I said, "So he – she's not a totem."

"I didn't say that," the man said. "She wouldn't have come to you if she wasn't. I simply meant that she's as much flesh and blood as Slatch is." He reached out and rubbed the head of the spotted cat. His hand was thin and all sinews, the sort of strong, squarish hand I'd always wished I had, full of power. The cat gazed at me from under it sarcastically. *See?* it seemed to say.

I knew it was only seconds before he was going to tell me to die and I started to play for time like anything. "And this wood," I said. "Is this wood real then?"

His thin black eyebrows went up, irritably. "All the paths and places beyond the worlds have substance," he said.

"Even…" I made a careful gesture towards the turquoise oval, making it slow in order not to annoy that spotted cat. "Even if you can see *that* from here? They can't *both* be real."

"Why not?" he more or less snapped. "You have a very limited notion of what's real, don't you? Will it make you any happier to be somewhere you regard as real?"

"I don't kn—" I began to say. Then I choked it off because we were suddenly back in the concrete passage under the seats of the stadium and a little patter of applause was coming from overhead. I was standing in front of this man and his killer cat, exactly as I had been under the tree, but the black panther wasn't there. *She* must be relieved! I thought, and I took a quick look round for my body, which I was sure had to be sitting against the wall in a trance.

It wasn't there. I could see the place where it had been by the scuff marks that my heels had made on the floor. But I was the only one of me there. The time seemed to be much later. The light coming in from the grids slanted the other way and looked more golden. I could feel that the patter of clapping was faint and tired overhead, at the end of a long day.

This is only a dream! I told myself in a panic. Someone can't have made off with my body! *Can* they?

"You were in the wood in your body too," the man told me, as if I was almost too stupid for him to bother with. In here, he seemed even more powerful. He wasn't much taller than me, and a lot skinnier, but he was like a

66

nuclear bomb standing in that passage, ready to go off and destroy everything for miles. His cat was pure semtex. It stared up at me and despised me, and its eyes were deep and glassy in the orange light.

"If you're going to kill me," I said, "you might as well tell me who you are and who hired you. And why. You owe me that."

"I owe you nothing," he said. "I was interested to know why someone thought you worth eliminating, that's all. And I don't think you are. You're too ignorant to be a danger to anyone. I shall tell them that when I refuse the commission. That should make them lose interest in you – but if they send anyone else after you, you'd better come to me. I'll teach you enough to protect yourself. We can settle the fee when you arrive."

He sort of settled his weight a different way. I could tell he was ready to leave. I was all set to burst with relief – but the spotted cat was not pleased at all. Its tail swished grittily against the floor and I just hoped the man could control it. It was a big creature. Its head came almost up to my chest and its muscles were out in lumps on its neck. I knew it was longing to tear my throat out.

Then the man settled his weight towards me again. I was so terrified I felt as if I was melting. His eyes were so yellow and cutting. "One other thing," he said. "What are you doing here in a world that has nothing to do with you, masquerading as a mage?"

"I don't know," I said. "This is a dream really."

One of his eyebrows went up. He had been pretty contemptuous of me all along. Now he *really* despised me. "It is?" he said and shrugged his leather-covered shoulders. "People's capacity to deceive themselves always amazes me. If you want to live past the age of twenty, you'd be well advised to learn to see the truth at all times. I'll tell you that for nothing," he said. Then he did turn and go. He swung round and he walked away as if he couldn't bear the sight of me any longer. The cat rose up on its musclebound tiptoes and walked after him, swinging its tail rudely.

"Wait a moment!" I called after him. "Who *are* you, for heaven's sake?"

I'd expected him just to go on walking away, but he stopped and looked over his shoulder, giving me the benefit of his lightning-strike profile again. "Since you put it like that," he said, "I'm generally known as Romanov. Ask your little mages about me if you like."

Then he turned his head away and went on walking, and the cat after him, round the curve of the corridor and out of sight. In spite of the way he'd made me feel, I nearly laughed. He and that cat – they both *walked* the same way.

I hoped they'd run into the soldier on guard round there, but I knew they wouldn't. The soldier would have come off worst anyway.

# PART THREE
# RODDY

## CHAPTER FIVE

✳

G randad must have done the trick. Though there was a coldness between England and Scotland after this – and there still is – both armies moved back from the border and nobody talked about the Scottish King much or even mentioned the poor old Merlin. Instead, the Court and the media began worrying about the Meeting of Kings that was due to happen on the Welsh border soon. *Will Logres and the Pendragon meet in peace?* That sort of thing. In between, they went back to being angry about Flemish trading practices, just as usual.

Nobody seemed to be suspecting Dad any more. Grandad only stayed with the Court until the King had spared a moment to have a friendly chat with Dad, and then he left, saying he had a book to finish. The new Merlin left too. Part of his duties at the start of his tenure was to visit every place of power in the country, and a few in Wales too, and attune himself to them. I think he was hoping that Grandad would go with him and advise him. He looked wistful when Grandad left. This Merlin was one of those who get what they want by looking wistful, but that never works with Grandad, so he was on his own. He climbed wistfully into the little brown car Grandad had helped him buy and chugged away.

We went back to normal. That is to say, we were rumbling along in buses most of the time, with rumours flying about where we were going next – although nobody *ever* knows that until a few hours before we get to wherever-it-is. The King likes to keep the Court and the country on its toes.

The unusual thing was the exceptionally fine weather. When I asked Dad about it, he said the King had asked him to keep it that way until the Meeting of Kings at the edge of Wales. So at least we were warm.

We spent three unexpected days in Leeds. I think the King wanted to inspect some factories there, but after the usual flustered greeting by the City Council it was blissful. We stayed in *houses*. Mam squeezed some money out of Sybil and took me and Grundo shopping. We got new clothes. There was *time*. We had civilised lessons in the mornings, sitting at tables in a *room*, and we could explore the city in the afternoons. I even enjoyed the riding lessons – which I don't much usually – out on the moorlands in the hot sun, riding past the carefully repaired green places where there had been mines and quarries.

"I'm going to be Mayor of Leeds when I grow up," Grundo announced, as we rode against the sky one morning. "I shall live in a house with a *bathroom*." He meant this so much that his voice went right down deep on the word bathroom. We both hate the bath-tents, even though the arrangements are quite efficient and there is usually hot water from the boiler-lorry and towels from the laundry-bus. But you get out of your canvas bath to stand shivering on wet grass, and there is always wind getting into the tent from somewhere.

We were sad when we had to leave. Off we went, the whole procession of the Court. We spread for miles. The King is often half a day ahead in his official car, with his security and his wizards and advisors beside him. These are followed by all sorts of Court cars, everything from the big square limousine with tinted windows belonging to the Duke of Devonshire to the flashy blue model driven by Sir James - Sir James had turned up again when we were leaving Leeds. The media bus hurries along after the cars, trying to keep up with events, and a whole string of administrative buses follows the media – with Mam in one of them, too busy even to look out of a window – and then the various lorries lumber after the buses. Some lorries are steaming with food or hot water, in case these are needed when we stop, and some are carrying tents and soldiers and things. The buses for the unimportant people follow the lorries. We are always last.

It often takes a whole day to go twenty miles. Parliament is always proposing that fine new roads get built so that the King – and other people – could travel more easily, but the King is not in favour of this so they don't get done. There are only two King's Roads in the entire country, one between London and York and the other between London and Winchester. We spend most of our journeys groaning round corners or grinding along between hedges that clatter on both sides of our bus.

It was like that for the two days after we left Leeds. The roads seemed to get narrower and, on the second day, the countryside beyond the windows became greener and greener, until we were grinding among hills that were an almost incredible dense, emerald colour. By the evening, we were rumbling through small lanes, pushing our way past foamy banks of white cow-parsley. Our bus got stuck crossing a place where a small river ran across the lane and we arrived quite a while after the rest of the Court.

There was a castle there, on a hill. It belonged to Sir James and the King was staying in it. Although it looked quite big, we were told that most of it was rooms of state and there was no space in it for anyone except the King's immediate circle. Everyone else was in a camp in fields just below the gardens. By the time we got there, it looked as if the camp had been there for days. In the office-tents, Mam and her colleagues were hard at work on their laptops, making the most of the daylight, and Dad was in the wizards' tent being briefed about what magic would be needed. And the teachers were looking for us to give that day's lessons.

"We must get a look inside that castle," Grundo said to me as we were marched off to the teaching-bus.

"Let's try after lessons," I said.

But during lessons we discovered that the King had one of his ritual duties that night. Everyone with any magical abilities was required to attend. This meant Grundo and me, as well as Alicia and the old Merlin's grandchildren and six of the other children.

"Bother!" I said. I was really frustrated.

Then at supper someone said that we were going to be here at Castle Belmont for days. The King liked the place, and it was near enough to the Welsh border that he could go to meet the Welsh King in a week's time without needing to move on.

I said that was good news. Grundo said morosely, "Maybe. That's the worst of arriving late. Nobody *tells* you things."

Nobody had told us anything about the ritual duty, except that it began at sunset somewhere called the Inner Garden. After we'd changed into good clothes, we followed everyone else as they went there and hoped someone would tell us what to do when we got to the place. We straggled after the line of robed wizards and people in Court dress, past beds of flowers and a long yew hedge, and then on a path across a lawn towards a tall, crumbly stone wall with frondy creepers trailing along its top.

"I know I'm going to hate this," Grundo said. Rituals don't agree with him. I think this is because his magic is back-to-front. Magical ceremonies often make him dizzy, and once or twice he has disgracefully thrown up in holy places of power.

"Keep swallowing," I warned him as we went in under the old stone gateway.

Inside, it was all new and fresh and different. There was a garden inside the old walls – a garden inside a garden – cupped inside its own small valley and as old and green as the hills. There was ancient stonework everywhere, worn flagstones overhung with flowering bushes or isolated arches beside stately old trees. There were lawns that seemed even greener than the lawns outside. Above all, it was alive with water. Strange, fresh-smelling water that ran in conduits of old stone and gushed from stone pipes into strange, lopsided stone pools, or cascaded in hidden places behind old walls.

"This is *lovely*!" I said.

"I think I agree," Grundo said. He sounded quite surprised.

"Fancy someone like Sir James owning a place like this!" I said.

It was hard to tell how big this Inner Garden was. You hardly noticed all the finely dressed people crowding into it. It seemed to absorb them, so that they vanished away among the watery lawns and got shadowy under the trees. You felt that twice as many people would hardly be noticed in here.

But that was before Sybil took charge and began passing out candles to the pages. "Everyone take a candle – you too, Your Majesty – and everyone who can must conjure flame to them. Pages will light the others for those who can't," she instructed, bustling about barefoot, with her green velvet skirts hitched up. She bustled up to the King and personally called fire to his candle. The Merlin lit Prince Edmund's for him. I was interested to see that the Merlin was back. He looked much less stunned and wistful than he had before. But, as light after light flared up, sending the surrounding garden dark and blue, I found I was not liking this at all. It seemed to me that this place was intended to be dusky and secret, and only to be lit by the sunset light coming softly off the waters. The candles made it all glittery.

Grundo and I looked at one another. We didn't either of us say anything, but we both pretended we were finding it hard to call light. Because we knew Sybil knew we never had any problems with fire, we backed away into some bushes and behind a broken wall and hoped she would forget we were there.

Luckily, she was busy after that, far too busy to notice us. She was always very active doing any working, but I had never known her as active as she was then. She spread her arms wide, she raised her hands high and bent herself backwards, she bent herself forwards and made great beckonings, she made huge galloping leaps, and she raised loud cries to the spirit of the garden to come and vitalise us all. Then she twirled off, with her arms swooping this way and that, to the place where the nearest water came gushing out of a stone animal's head, where she snatched up a silver goblet and held it under the water until it overflowed in all directions. She held it up to the sky; she held it to her lips.

"Ah!" she cried out. "The virtue in this water! The power of it!" With her hair swirling and wrapping itself across her sweating face, she brought the goblet to the King. "Drink, Sire!" she proclaimed. "Soak up the energy, immerse yourself, revel in the bounty of these healing waters! And everyone will do the same after you!"

The King took the goblet and sipped politely. As soon as he had, the Merlin filled another goblet and presented it to Prince Edmund.

"*Drink*, everyone!" Sybil carolled. "*Take* what is so freely given!" She began filling goblets and passing them around as if she was in a frenzy. Everyone caught the frenzy and seized the goblets and downed them as if they were dying of thirst.

This is all wrong! I thought. Some magics do require a frenzy, I know, but I was fairly sure this garden was not one of them. It was a quiet place. You were supposed to – supposed to – I remember searching in my head for what the garden was *really* like, and having a hard job to think, because Sybil's workings had set up such a loud shout of enchantment that it drowned out most other thoughts – you were supposed to *dwell* with the garden, that was it. You were supposed to let the garden come to you, not suck it up in a greedy riot like this. It was a small island of otherwhere and full of strength. But it was *quiet* strength, enclosed in a great bend of the River Severn, which meant that it certainly belonged to the Lady of Severn who also ruled the great crescent of forest to the south. It seemed to me that this garden might even be her most secret place. It ought to have been hushed and holy. Sir James – I could see him in the distance half-lit by candles, tipping up his goblet and smacking his lips – Sir James must be supposed to *guard* the secret place, not open it to frantic magic-making, not even for the King.

I don't know how I knew all this, but I was sure of it. I murmured to Grundo, "I'm not doing any of this drinking."

"She's doctored the waters somehow," he answered unhappily.

Grundo usually knew what his mother had been up to. I believed him. "Why?" I whispered.

"No idea," he said, "but I'm going to have to drink some of it. She'll know if I don't."

"Then let's go and see if there's a place higher up where she hasn't got at it," I said.

We moved off quietly sideways, in the direction the

water was coming from, clutching our unlit candles and trying to keep out of sight. Nobody noticed us. They were all waving candles and passing goblets about, laughing. People were shouting out, "Oh! It's so refreshing! I can feel it doing me good!" almost as if they were all drunk. It was easy to keep in the shadows and follow the waters. The waters flowed down in several stone channels – I had a feeling that each channel was supposed to give you some different goodness – that spread from one of the lopsided pools near the top of the slope.

"How about this?" I asked Grundo beside this pool. It was very calm there and twilit, with just a few birds twittering and a tree nearby breathing out some strong, quiet scent. I could see Grundo's head as a lightness, gloomily shaking.

"She's been here too."

The pond was filling from another animal head in the bank above and there were stone steps up the bank, leading under black, black trees. It became very secret. *This* is where it's all coming from! I thought, and I led the way up the steps into a little flagstoned space under the black trees. It was so dark that we had to stand for a moment to let our eyes adjust. Then we were able to see that there was a well there, with a wooden cover over it, almost beside our feet. The gentlest of trickling sounded from under the cover, and there was a feeling of strength coming from it, such as I had never met before.

"Is *this* all right?" I whispered.

"I'm not sure. I'll have to take the cover off in order to know," Grundo replied.

We knelt down and tried to pull the cover up, but it was so dark we couldn't see how. We stuffed our candles into our pockets and tried again with both hands. As we did, we heard a burst of chatter and laughter from below, which faded quickly off into the distance as everyone left the garden. That gave us the courage to heave much more heartily. We discovered that the wooden lid had hinges at one side, so we put our fingers under the opposite edge and we heaved. The cover came up an inch or so and gave me a gust of the strongest magic I'd ever known, cool and still, and so deep that it seemed to come from the roots of the world.

There were voices, and footsteps, on the steps beyond the trees.

"Stop!" whispered Grundo.

We dropped the lid back down as quietly as we could, then sprang up and bundled one another on tiptoe in among the trees beyond the well. The earth was cloggy there. There were roots and we stumbled, but luckily the trees were bushy as well as very black and we had managed to back ourselves thoroughly inside them by the time Sybil came storming merrily into the flagged space, waving her flaring candle.

"No, no, it went very well!" she was calling out. "Now, as long as we can keep the Scottish King at odds with England, we'll be fine!" There was a rustic wooden seat at the other end of the space and she threw herself down on it with a thump. "Ooh, I'm tired!"

"I wish we could do the same with the Welsh King," Sir James said, ducking down to sit beside her, "but I can't see any way to contrive that. So you've got everyone drinking out of your hand. Will it *work*?"

"Oh, it *has* to," Sybil said. "I ran myself into the ground to make it work. What do *you* think?" she asked the Merlin, who came very slowly in under the trees and held up his candle to look around.

"Very well, as far as it goes," he said in his weak, high voice. "You've got the King and his Court…"

"*And* all the other wizards. Don't forget them," Sybil put in pridefully.

Sir James chuckled. "None of them suspecting a thing!" he said. "They should be dancing to her tune now, shouldn't they?"

"Yes. For a while," the Merlin agreed, still looking around. "Is this where you put the spell on?"

"Well, no. It's a bit strong here," Sybil admitted. "I didn't have time for the working it would take to do it here. I worked from the pool below the steps. That's the first cistern the well flows out to, you see, and it feeds all the other channels from there."

The Merlin went, "Hm." He squatted down like a grasshopper beside the well and put his candle down by one of his gawky, bent legs. "Hm," he went again. "I see." Then he pulled open the lid over the well.

Grundo and I felt the power from where we stood. We found it hard not to sway. The Merlin got up and staggered backwards. Behind him, Sir James said, "Ouch!" and covered his face.

"You see?" said Sybil.

"I do," said Sir James. "Put the lid back, man!"

The Merlin dropped the lid back with a bang. "I hadn't realised," he said. "That's *strong*. If we're going to use it, we'll have to conjure some other Power to help us. Are there any available?"

"Plenty," said Sir James. "Over in Wales particularly." He turned to Sybil. The candlelight made his profile into a fleshy beak with pouty lips. "How about it? Can you do a working now? We ought to have this Power in and consolidate our advantage now we've got it."

Sybil had pouty lips too. They put her chin in shadow as she said, "James, I'm exhausted! I've worked myself to the bone this evening and I can't do any more! Even going barefoot all the time, it'll be three days before I've recouped my powers."

"How long before you can do a strong working?" the Merlin asked, picking his candle up. "My friend James is right. We do need to keep up our momentum."

"If we both help you?" Sir James asked coaxingly.

Sybil hung her head and her hair down and thought, with her big arms planted along her large thighs. "I *need* three days," she said at last, rather sulkily. "Whoever helps me, I'm not going to be able to tackle something as strong as this well before that. It won't take just a minor Power to bespell the thing. We'll have to summon something big."

"But will the effect of the drink last until we do?" Sir James asked, rather tensely.

Sybil looked up at the Merlin. He said, "It struck me as firm enough for the moment. I don't see it wearing off for at least a week, and we'll be able to reinforce it before that."

"Good enough." Sir James sprang up, relieved and jolly. "Let's get this place locked up again then and go and have a proper drink. Who fancies champagne?" He pulled keys out of his pocket and strode away down the steps, jingling them and lighting the trees to a glinting black with his candle.

"Champagne. Lovely!" said Sybil. She heaved to her feet and shoved the Merlin playfully down the steps in front of her. "Off you go, stranger boy!"

Grundo and I realised we were likely to get locked inside the garden. We nearly panicked. The moment Sybil was out of sight we surged out on to the flagstones and then realised that the only way out was down those same stone steps to the lopsided pool. That was almost the worst part of the whole thing. We had to wait for Sir James, Sybil and then the Merlin to get ahead, then follow them, and then try to get ahead of them before they got to the gate in the wall.

We were helped a lot by the queer way the space in the garden seemed to spread, and by all the stone walls and conduits and bushes. We could see Sir James and the other two easily by the light of their flickering candles – and hear them too, most of the time, talking and laughing. Sybil obviously was tired. She went quite slowly and the others waited for her. We were able to scud along behind lavender and tall, toppling flowers, or crouch down and scurry past pieces of old wall – though we couldn't go really fast because it was quite dark by then – and finally we got in front of them and raced out through the gate just before they came merrily along under a rose arch.

I was a nervous wreck by then. It must have been even worse for Grundo, knowing his mother was part of a conspiracy. We went on running beside a dim path and neither of us stopped until we were well out into the lawns in the main garden and could see our camp in the distance, twinkling beyond the fence.

"What do we do *now*?" I panted at Grundo. "Tell my Dad?"

"Don't be stupid!" he said. "He was there drinking with the other wizards. He's not going to listen to you for at least a fortnight."

"The King then," I suggested wildly.

"He was the first one to drink," Grundo said. "You're not tracking." He was right. Everything was all about in my head. I tried to pull myself together, not very successfully, while Grundo stood with his head bent and thought. "Your grandfather," he said after a bit. "He's the one to tell. Do you have his speaker code?"

"Oh. Right," I said. "Mam will have his number. I can ask Dad to lend me his speaker at least, can't I?"

Unfortunately, when we got to the camp we discovered that both Mam and Dad were up at the castle attending on the King. Though I could have asked all sorts of people to lend me a speaker, it was no good unless I knew the code. Grandad's number is not in the directory lists.

"We'll just have to wait till tomorrow," I said miserably.

I spent a lot of that night tossing in my bunk in the girls' bus, wondering how the new Merlin came to join with Sybil and Sir James, and how to explain to Grandad that he had chosen the wrong man for the post. It really worried me that Grandad had chosen this Merlin. Grandad doesn't usually make mistakes. It worried me even more that I didn't know what this conspiracy was up to. It had to be high treason. As far as I knew, bespelling the King was high treason anyway, and it was obvious that they meant to go on and do something worse.

I tossed and turned and tossed and thought, until Alicia suddenly sprang up and shouted, "Roddy, if you don't stop jigging about this moment, I'll turn you into a *statue*, so help me Powers Above!"

"Sorry," I mumbled, and then, even lower, "Sneeze!" If Alicia hadn't been there, I might have tried telling the other girls in the bus, but Alicia would go straight to Sybil. And Alicia had drunk that enchanted water along with the other pages. Heigh ho, I thought. Wait till tomorrow.

So I waited helplessly until it was too late.

# CHAPTER SIX

✳

*I* overslept. I dragged myself up and over to the food-
tent, yawning. I had just got myself some juice and a
cold, waxy-looking fried egg, when Grundo appeared,
looking worried.

"*There* you are!" he said. "There's a message for you
from the Chamberlain."

The Chamberlain had never noticed my existence
before. Before I got over my surprise enough to ask
Grundo what the message was, Mam dashed up to me
from the other side. "Oh, *there* you are, Roddy! We've
been hunting for you all over! Your grandfather wants
you. He's sent a car for you. It's waiting for you now
outside the castle."

My first thought was that this was an answer to my prayers. Then I looked up at Mam's face. She was so white that her eyes looked like big black holes. The hand she put on my shoulder was quivering. "*Which* grandfather?" I said.

"*My* father, of course," she said. "It's just like him to send a demand for you to the Chamberlain. I'm surprised he didn't send it straight to the King! Oh, Roddy, I'm sorry! He's insisting that you go and stay with him in that dreadful manse of his and I *daren't* refuse! He's already been dreadfully rude to the Chamberlain over the speaker. He'll do worse than that if I don't let you go. He'll probably insult the King next. Forgive me."

Poor Mam. She looked absolutely desperate. My stomach plunged about just at the sight of her. "Why does he want *me*?"

"Because he's never met you, and you're near enough to Wales here for him to send and fetch you," Mam answered distractedly. "He's told the entire Chamberlain's Office that I've no right to keep his only grandchild from him. You'll have to go, my love – the Chamberlain's insisting – but *be* polite to him. For my sake. It'll only be for a few days, until the Progress moves on after the Meeting of Kings. He says the car will bring you back then."

"I see," I said, the way you say things just to gain time. I looked at my fried egg. It looked back like a big, dead, yellow eye. Ugh. I thought of Grundo all on his own here, and Sybil discovering that he hadn't drunk her charmed water. "I'll go if I can take Grundo," I said.

"Oh, really, my love, I don't think…" Mam began.

"Listen, Mam," I said. "Your problem was that he's a widower and you were all on your own with him…"

"Well, that wasn't quite…" she began again.

"…so you ought to allow me to take some moral support with me," I said. As she wavered, I added, "Or I shall go to the Chamberlain's Office and use their speaker to tell him I won't go."

This so horrified Mam that she gave in. "All right. But I don't dare *think* what he'll say – Grundo, do you mind being dragged along to see a fearsome old man?"

"Not really," Grundo said. "I can always use the speaker in his manse to ask for help, can't I?"

"Then go and pack," Mam told him frantically. "Take old clothes. He'll make you go for walks, or even ride – Hurry *up*, Roddy! He's sent his same old driver who *hates* to be kept waiting!"

I didn't see why Mam needed to be scared of her father's driver as well as her father, but I drained my juice, snatched a piece of toast and rushed off eating it. Mam rushed with me, distractedly reminding me to remember a sweater, a toothbrush, walking shoes, a comb, my address book, everything… It wasn't exactly the right moment to start telling her of plots and treason, but I did honestly try, after I had rammed things into a bag and we were rushing up the steep path to the castle, with stones spurting from under our feet and clattering down on Grundo, who was bent over under a huge bag behind us.

"Are you listening to me?" I panted, when I'd told her what we'd overheard.

She was so upset and feeling so strongly for me getting into the clutches of her terrible old father that I don't think she did listen, even though she nodded. I just had to hope she would remember it later.

The car was drawn up in front of the main door of the castle, as if the driver, or Mam's father, imagined that I was staying in there with the King. It was black and uncomfortably like a hearse. The "same old driver", who looked as if he had been carved out of a block of something white and heavy and then dressed in navy blue, got out when he saw us coming and held out his big stony hand for my bag.

"Good morning," I panted. "I'm sorry to have kept you waiting."

He didn't say a word, just took my bag and stowed it in the boot. Then he took Grundo's bag with the same carved stone look. After that, he opened the rear door and stood there holding it. I saw a little what Mam meant.

"Nice morning," I said defiantly. No answer. I turned to Mam and hugged her. "Don't *worry*," I said. "I'm a very strong character myself and so is Grundo. We'll see you soon."

We climbed into the back seat of the hearse and were

driven away, both of us feeling a little dizzy at the speed of events.

Then we drove and drove and drove, until we were dizzy with that too. I still have not the least idea where we went. Grundo says he lost his sense of direction completely. All we knew were astonishingly green hills towering above grey, winding roads, grey stone walls like cross-hatching on the hillsides, grey slides of rock, and woods hanging over us from time to time like dark, lacy tunnels. Dad's good weather was getting better and better, so there was blue, blue sky with a brisk wind sliding white clouds across it, and sliding their shadows over the green hills in strange, shaggy shapes. Under the shadows, we saw heather darken and turn purple again, gorse blaze and then look a mere modest yellow, and sun and shade pass swiftly across small roaring rivers half hidden in ravines.

It was all very beautiful, but it went on so long, winding us further and further into the heart of the green mountains – until we finally began winding upwards among them. Then it was all green and grey again, with cloud shadows, and we had no sense of getting anywhere. We both jumped with surprise when the car rolled to a stop on a flat green stretch near the top of a mountain.

The stone-faced driver got out and opened the door on my side.

This obviously meant *Get out now*, so we scrambled to the stony green ground and stood staring about. Below us, a cleft twisted among the emerald sides of mountains until it was blue-green with distance, and beyond those green slopes were blue and grey and black peaks, peak after peak. The air was the chilliest and clearest I have ever breathed. Everything was silent. It was so quiet, I could almost hear the silence. And I realised that, up to then, I had lived my entire life close to people and their noise. It was strange to have it taken away.

The only house in sight was the manse. It was built backed against the nearest green peak, but below the top of the mountain, for shelter, though its dark chimneys stood almost as high as the green summit. It was dark and upright and squeezed into itself, all high narrow arches. You looked at it and wondered if it was a house built like a chapel, or a chapel built like a house and then squeezed narrower. There was no sign of any garden, just that house backed into the hillside and a drystone wall sticking out from one end of it.

The stone driver was trudging across the grass with our bags to the narrow, arched front door. We followed him, through the door and into a tall, dark hallway. He had gone somewhere else by the time we got indoors. But we had only been standing a moment wondering what to do now, when a door banged echoingly further down the hall and my mother's father came towards us.

He was tall and stiff and cold as a monument on a tomb. His black clothes – he was a priest of course – made his white face look pale as death, but his hair was black, without a trace of grey. I noticed his hair particularly because he put a chilly hand on each of my shoulders and turned me to the light from the narrow front door. His eyes were deep and black, with dark skin round them, but I saw he was a very handsome man.

"So you are the young Arianrhod," he said, deep and solemn. "At last." His voice made echoes in the hall and brought me out in gooseflesh. I began to feel very sorry for Mam. "You have quite a look of my Annie," he said. "Did she let you go willingly?"

"Yes," I said, trying not to let my teeth chatter. "I said I'd come provided my friend Gr— er… Ambrose Temple could come too. I hope you can find room for him."

He looked at Grundo then. Grundo gave him a serious freckled stare and said "How do you do?" politely.

"I see he would be lonely without you," my grandfather said.

He was welcome to think that, I thought, if only he would let Grundo stay. I was very relieved when he said, "Come with me, both of you, and I will show you to your rooms."

We followed him up steep, dark stairs, where his gown flowed over the wooden treads behind his straight back, and then along dark, wooden corridors. I had a queer feeling that we were walking right into the hill at the back of the house, but the two rooms he showed us to had windows looking out over the winding green hills and they were both obviously prepared for visitors, the beds made-up and water steaming in big bowls on the washstands. As if my grandfather had *known* I would be bringing Grundo. My bag was in one room and Grundo's was in the other.

"Lunch will be ready any moment," my grandfather said, "and you will wish to wash and tidy yourselves first. But if you want a bath…" He opened the next door along and showed us a huge bathroom, where a bath stood on clawed animal feet in the middle of bare floorboards. "I hope you will give warning when you do," he said. "Olwen has to bring up buckets from the copper." Then he went away downstairs again.

"No taps," said Grundo. "As bad as the bath-tent."

We washed and got ready quickly. When we met in the corridor again, we discovered that we had both put on the warmest clothes we had with us. We would have laughed about it, but it was not the kind of house you liked to laugh in. Instead, we went demurely downstairs, to where my grandfather was waiting in a tall, chilly dining room, standing at the head of a tall, black table.

He looked at us, pointed to two chairs and said grace in Welsh. It was all rolling, thundering language. I was suddenly very ashamed not to understand a word of it. Grundo looked on calmly, almost as if he did understand, and sat quietly down when it was finished, still looking intently at my grandfather.

I was looking at the door, where a fat, stone faced woman was coming in with a tureen. I was famished by then and it smelled wonderful.

It was a very good lunch, though almost silent at first. There was the leek soup, enough for two helpings each, followed by pancakes rolled round meat in sauce. After that, there were heaps of little hot griddle cakes covered in sugar. Grundo ate so many of those that the woman had to keep making more. She seemed to like that. She almost had a smile when she brought in the third lot.

"Pancakes," my grandfather said, deep and hollow, "are a traditional part of our diet in this country."

I was thinking, Well, at least he didn't *starve* my mother! But why is he so *stiff* and *stern*? Why doesn't he *smile* at all? I'm sure my mother used to ask herself the same things several times a day. I was sorrier for her than ever.

"I know this is an awkward question," I said, "but what should we call you?"

He looked at me in stern surprise. "My name is Gwyn," he said.

"Should I call you Grandfather Gwyn then?" I asked.

"If you wish," he said, not seeming to care.

"Might I call you that too, please?" Grundo asked.

He looked at Grundo long and thoughtfully, almost as if he was asking himself what Grundo's heredity was. "I suppose you have a right to," he said at last. "Now tell me, what do either of you know of Wales?"

The truthful answer, as far as I was concerned, was *Not a lot*. But I could hardly say that. Grundo came to my rescue – I was *extremely* glad he was there. Because Grundo has such trouble reading, he *listens* in lessons far more than I ever do. So he *knows* things. "It's divided into cantrevs," he said, "each with its lesser kings, and the Pendragon is High King over them all. The Pendragon rules the Laws. I know you have a different system of laws here, but I don't know how they work."

My grandfather looked almost approving. "And the meaning of the High King's title?" he asked.

It felt just like having a test during lessons, but I thought I knew the answer to that. "Son of the dragon," I said. "Because there is said to be a dragon roosting in the heart of Wales."

This didn't seem to be right. My grandfather said frigidly, "After a fashion. Pendragon is a title given to him by the English. By rights, it should be the title of the English King, but the English have forgotten about their dragons."

"There aren't any dragons in England!" I said.

He turned a face full of stern disapproval on me. "That is not true. Have you never heard of the red dragon and the white? There were times in the past when there were great battles between the two, in the days before the Islands of Blest were at peace."

I couldn't seem to stop saying the wrong thing, somehow. I protested, "But that's just a way of saying the Welsh and the English fought one another."

His black eyebrows rose slightly in his marble face. I

had never known so much scorn expressed with so little effort. He turned away from me and back to Grundo. "There are several dragons in England," he said to him. "The white is only the greatest. There are said to be more in Scotland, both in the waters and in the mountains, but I have no personal knowledge of these."

Grundo looked utterly fascinated. "What about Ireland?" he asked.

"Ireland," said my grandfather, "is in most places low and green and unsuitable for dragons. If there were any, Saint Patrick expelled them. But to go back to the Laws of Wales. We do not have Judges, as you do. Courts are called when necessary…"

He went into a long explanation. Grundo was still fascinated. I sat and watched their two profiles as they talked, Grundo's all pale, long nose and freckles, and my grandfather's like a statue from classical antiquity. My grandfather had quite a long nose too, but his face was so perfectly proportioned that you hardly noticed. They both had great, deep voices, though where Grundo's grated and grunted, my grandfather's voice rolled and boomed.

Soulmates! I thought. I was glad I'd brought Grundo.

At the same time, I began to see some more of my mother's problem. If my grandfather had been simply cold and strict and distant, it would have been easy to hate him and stop there. But the trouble was that he was also one of those people you *wanted* to please. There was a sort of grandness to him that made you ache to have him think well of you. Before long, I was quite desperate for him to stop talking just to Grundo and notice me – or at least not disapprove of me so much. Mam must have felt exactly the same. But I could see that, no matter how hard she tried, Mam was too soft-hearted and emotional for her father, and so he treated her with utter scorn. He scorned me for different reasons. I sat at the tall table almost in pain, because I knew I was a courtier born and bred, and that I was smart and good-mannered and used to summing people up so that I could take advantage of their faults, and I could see that my grandfather had nothing but contempt for people like me. It really hurt. Grundo may have been peculiar, but he was not like that and my grandfather liked him.

It was an enormous relief to me when we were allowed to get up from the table and leave the tall cold room. My grandfather took us outside, through the front door, into a blast of sunlight and cold, clean air. While I stood blinking, he said to us, "Now, where would you say the red dragon lies?"

Grundo and I looked at one another. Then we pointed, hesitating a bit, to the most distant brown mountains, lying against the horizon in a misty, jagged row.

"Correct," said my grandfather. "That is a part of his back. He is asleep for now. He will only arouse in extreme need, to those who know how to call him, and he does not like to be roused. The consequences are usually grave. The same is true of the white dragon of England. You call him too at your peril." The way he said this made us shiver. Then he said, in a much more normal way, "You will want to explore now. Go anywhere you like, but don't try to ride the mare and be back at six. We have tea then, not the dinner you are used to. I'll see you at tea. I have work to do before then."

He went back into the house. He had a study at the back of the hall, as we learnt later, though we never saw inside it. It was a bit puzzling really. We never saw him do any religious duties or see parishioners – there were no other houses for miles anyway – but as Grundo said, dubiously, we were not there on a Sunday or any other holy day, so how could we know?

We did find the chapel. It was downhill to the left of the house, very tiny and grey, with a little arch of stone on its roof with a bell hanging in it. It was surrounded in green, and there was a hump of green turf beside it like a big beehive, that had water trickling inside it. The whole place gave us an awed, uncertain feeling, so we went uphill again and round to the back of the house, where we came upon a stone shed with the car inside it. Beyond that, things were normal.

We found a kitchen garden there, fringed with those orange flowers that grow in sprays, and a yard behind the house with a well in it. The water had to be pumped from the well by a handle in the kitchen. Olwen, the fat housekeeper, showed us how to do that. It was hard work. Then we went out beyond the yard to a couple of hidden meadows. One meadow had a pair of cows and a calf in it, and the other had a placid, chunky grey horse.

By this time, our feelings of strangeness had worn off. We were used to being in new, unknown places and we began to feel almost at home. We leant on the gate and looked at the placid mare, who raised her chalky-white face to look back at us and then went calmly on with grazing.

I think her lack of interest irritated Grundo. He went into one of his impish moods. "I'm going to try riding her," he said, grinning at me.

"Your funeral," I said. To confess the truth, I almost looked forward to seeing Grundo in trouble with my grandfather. I was feeling mean, and depressed about my personality.

Grundo looks soft, but he is surprisingly wiry and this makes him a much better rider than I am. I have never got much beyond the basics. In a soft-hearted way that is annoyingly like Mam's, I am sorry for the horse for having me sit on its back making it do things. Grundo says this is silly. It's what horses are bred for. He can make most horses do what he wants.

He nipped over the gate and went calmly across to the mare. She took a quick glance at him and lost interest again. She took no notice at all when Grundo put his hands on her. She was not very tall. Grundo had no difficulty hoisting himself on to her back, where he sat and clicked his tongue at her to make her go. She swung her head round then and looked at him in astonishment. Then… I have no idea what she did then, and Grundo says he doesn't know either. She sort of walked out from underneath him. I swear that for one moment Grundo was sitting on her back, and for another moment Grundo was sitting up in the air, on nothing, looking absolutely stunned, and the next moment the mare was ten feet away and going back to grazing. Grundo came down on the grass on his back with a thump.

He picked himself up and came hobbling over to the gate, saying seriously, "I don't think I'll try again. You can see by all the white on her that she's very old."

That made me scream with laughter. Grundo was very offended and explained that the mare was old enough to have learnt lots of tricks, which only made me laugh more. And after a bit, Grundo began to see the funny side of it too. He said it felt very odd, being left sitting on nothing, and he kept wondering how the mare did it. We went scrambling up to the top of the hill behind the manse, laughing about it.

There were mountains all round as far as we could see up there. The peaks we had thought might be a dragon were lost among all the others.

"Do you think they really *are* part of a dragon?" I asked, while we went sliding and crouching down the other side of the summit. "It *was* rather mad, the way he said it." The thought that my grandfather might be mad really worried me. But it would certainly explain why my mother was so terrified of him.

"He's not mad," Grundo said decidedly. "*Everyone's* heard of the Welsh dragon."

"Are you sure?" I said. "He doesn't behave at all the way people usually do."

"No, but he behaves like *I* would behave if I hadn't been brought up at Court," Grundo said. "I sort of recognised him. He's like me underneath."

This made me feel much better. There was a huge, heathery moor beyond the manse hill, and we rushed out into it with the wind clapping our hair about and cloud shadows racing across us. There was the soft smell of water everywhere. And no roads, no buses, no people, and only the occasional large, high bird. We found a place where water bubbled out of the ground in a tiny fountain that spread into a pool covered with lurid green weeds. Neither of us had seen a natural spring before and we were delighted with it. We tried blocking it with our hands, but it just spouted up between our fingers, cold as ice.

"I suppose," Grundo said, "that the well in Sir James's Inner Garden must fill from a spring like this. Only I don't think this one's magic."

"Oh, don't!" I cried out. "I don't want to remember all that! It's not as if we can do a thing about it, whatever they're plotting to do." I spread my arms into the watery smelling wind. "I feel free for the first time in a hundred years!" I said. "Don't spoil it."

Grundo stood with his feet sinking into squashy

marsh plants and considered me. "I wish you wouldn't exaggerate," he said. "It annoys me. But you do look better. When we're with the Progress you always remind me of an ice-puddle someone's stamped in. All icy white edges. I'm afraid of getting cut on you sometimes."

I was astonished. "What *should* I be like then?"

Grundo shrugged. "I can't explain. More like – like a good sort of tree."

"A *tree*!" I exclaimed.

"Something that grew naturally, I mean," Grundo grunted. "A warm thing." He moved his feet with such appalling sucking noises that I had to laugh.

"*You're* the one who's rooted to the spot!" I said, and we wandered on, making for a topple of rock in the distance. When we got there, we sat on the side that was in the sun and away from the wind. After a long time, I said, "I didn't mean that about not wanting to remember Sir James's garden – it's just I feel so helpless."

Grundo said, "Me too. I keep wondering if the old Merlin might have been killed so that the new one could take over in time to go to the garden."

"That's an awful thing to think!" I said. But now Grundo had said it, I found I was thinking it too. "But the Merlin's supposed to be incorruptible," I said. "Grandad found him."

"He could have been deceived," Grundo said. "Your Grandfather Hyde's only human, even if he is a Magid. Why don't you try telling this grandfather?"

"Grandfather Gwyn?" I said. "What could he *do*? Besides, he's *Welsh*."

"Well, he made a fair old fuss to the Chamberlain's Office just to get you here," Grundo replied. "He knows how to raise a stink. Think about it."

I did think about it as we wandered on, but not all that much because, after what seemed a very short while, we saw that the sun was going down and looked at our watches and realised it was after five o'clock. We turned back and got lost. The moor was surrounded by green knobs that were the tops of mountains and they all looked the same. When we finally found the right knob and slid down the side of it to the manse, there was only just time to get cleaned up before tea was ready.

"I love this food!" Grundo grunted.

The table was crowded with four different kinds of bread, two cakes, six kinds of jam in matching dishes, cheese, butter and cream. Olwen followed us into the dining room with a vast teapot and, as soon as my grandfather had thundered out his grace, she came back with plates of sausage and fried potatoes. Grundo beamed and prepared to be very greedy. I had to stop before the cakes, but Grundo kept right on packing food in for nearly an hour and drinking cup after cup of tea. While he ate, he talked cheerfully, just as if my grandfather was a normal person.

My grandfather watched Grundo eat with a slightly astonished look, but he did not seem to mind being talked to. He even answered Grundo with a few deep words every so often. I was fairly sure Grundo was being this chatty so that I could join in and tell Grandfather Gwyn what we had overheard in Sir James's Inner Garden. But I couldn't. I knew he would give me that look with his eyebrows up and not believe a word. I seemed to curl up inside just *thinking* of speaking.

I was wondering how often my Mam had sat silent like this at meals, when Grundo helped himself to a third slice of cake, seriously measuring off the exact amount. "I have room for twenty-five degrees more cake," he explained, "and then I shall go back to soda bread and jam. Does Olwen do your cooking for you because you're a widower?"

At this, my grandfather turned to me. I could tell he was not pleased. It breathed off him like cold from a frozen pond. "Did Annie tell you I was a widower?" he asked me.

"She said she had never known her mother," I said.

"I am glad to hear her so truthful," my grandfather replied. I thought that was all he was going to say, but he seemed to think again and make an extra effort. "There has been," he said, and paused, and made another effort, "a separation."

I could feel him hurting, making the effort to say this. I was suddenly furious. "Oh!" I cried out. "I *hate* all this divorcing and separating! My Grandfather Hyde is separated from *his* wife and I've never even *seen* her *or* the aunt who lives with her. And that aunt's divorced, and so's the aunt who lives with Grandad, which is awfully hard on my cousin Toby. Half the *Court* is divorced! The King is separated from the Queen most of the time! Why do people *do* it?"

Grandfather Gwyn was giving me an attentive look. It was the sort of look you can feel. I felt as if his deep, dark eyes were opening me up, prising apart pieces of my brain. He said thoughtfully, "Often the very nature of people, the matter that brought them together, causes the separation later."

"Oh, probably," I said angrily. "But it doesn't stop them hurting. Ask Grundo. His parents are separated."

"Divorced," Grundo growled. "My father left."

"Now that's one person I *don't* blame!" I said. "Leaving Sybil was probably the most sensible thing he ever did. But he ought to have taken you with him."

"Well now," said Grandfather Gwyn. He sounded nearly amused. "The ice of Arianrhod has melted at last, it seems."

I could feel my face bursting into a red flush, right to the top of my hair and down my neck, because my grandfather had so obviously seen me the same way as Grundo did. So I was a puddle of ice, was I? I was so wrought up by then that I snapped at him, just as if he had been Alicia. "*You* can talk! If ever I saw a marble iceberg, it's *you*!"

Now he looked really amused. His face relaxed and he very nearly smiled.

"It's not *funny*!" I snarled at him. "I can see you made my mother terrified of you by behaving like this! Most of the time you'd make her think she wasn't worth *noticing*, and then you'd make *fun* of her!"

Then I gave a gasp and tried to hold my breath – but I couldn't because I was panting with rage – knowing that a strict person like my grandfather was bound to jump to his feet and order me thunderously out of the room.

In fact, he just said musingly, "Something of that, but Annie brought her own difficulties to the situation, you know." The mild way he said it surprised me. I was even more surprised when he said, "Come now, Arianrhod. Tell me what is really upsetting you so."

I almost burst into tears. But I didn't, because I suspected that Mam would have done and Grandfather Gwyn would have hated it. "If you must know," I blurted out, "there's a plot – in England – and most of the Court have been given bespelled water, even the King. The *Merlin*'s in it!"

"I know," he said. "This is why I asked for you to come here, before the balance of magic is disturbed even further."

For a second, I was thoroughly astonished. Then I thought, Oh! He's a wizard! And that made me feel much better. I could tell by the way Grundo's face snapped round to look at Grandfather Gwyn, and then went much pinker, that Grundo had had the same thought.

"Tell me in detail," my grandfather said to us, "every

word and sign and act that you remember."

So we told him. It took a while and Grundo absent-mindedly ate two more pieces of cake while we talked. He probably needed to. It couldn't have been pleasant for Grundo, having to describe what his mother did. Otherwise, I'd have called him a pig. Grandfather Gwyn leant forward with one forearm stiffly among the tea-things and seemed to drink in everything we said.

"Can you help at all?" Grundo said at last.

To our dismay, my grandfather slowly shook his head. "Unfortunately not," he said. "I am about to become vulnerable, in a way I very much resent, and will be able to do nothing directly for a while. You have just shown me the way of it. But there is something *you* can do, Arianrhod, if you think you have the courage. You will have to work out most of it for yourself, I am afraid. It is magic that is not mine to deal in, and it is something your mother never could have brought herself to do. But, if you think you are able, I can put you in the way of it tomorrow."

I sat in silence in that tall, cold room, staring at his intent white face across the plates and crumbs. Grundo looked to be holding his breath. "I – I suppose I'd better," I said, when the chills had almost stopped scurrying up and down my back. "Someone has to do something."

My Grandfather Gwyn *could* smile, after all. It was an unexpectedly warm, kind smile. It helped. A little. Actually, I was terrified.

# PART FOUR
# NICK

# CHAPTER SEVEN

✳

*I* sat down again after Romanov had gone. For some reason, I fitted myself carefully into the exact place I had been in before, with my back against the wall and my heels in the scuff marks. I suppose I wanted Arnold and Co to think I'd been sitting there all the time. But I wasn't really attending. I was shaking all over and I pretty well wanted to cry.

I was full of hurt and paranoia and plain terror that someone had wanted me killed. I kept thinking, But I *told* them in the Empire I wasn't going to be Emperor! They'd taken me there into those worlds and I'd signed things – sort of abdicated – so that my half-brother Rob could be Emperor instead. It didn't make *sense*.

I was full of hurt and paranoia too at the way Romanov had despised me. A lot of people had called me selfish. I'd been working on it, I thought. I'd looked after Dad and been really considerate, I thought. But I could tell Romanov saw through all that, to the way I really *felt*. And of course I still felt selfish, in spite of the way I behaved. All the same, I was *trying*, and it wasn't *fair*, and it wasn't fair either that Romanov had despised me for being ignorant too! I'd been working on that as well. I'd been reading everything I could lay hands on about magic and trying to get to other worlds – and trying every way I could to persuade the bunch of people who govern the Magids – they call them the Upper Room for some reason – to let me train as a Magid too. It wasn't *my* fault they wouldn't.

Then I thought about Romanov himself. I would never, if I lived to be a thousand, meet anyone else as powerfully magic as Romanov. It was shattering. I'd met quite a few Magids, and they seemed quite humdrum now, compared with the stuff I'd felt coming from Romanov. It was awesome, it was just not *fair*, for someone to be as strong as that. Razor-edge, lightning-strike strong. It shook me to my bones.

And those big cats shook me to my bones too. When I found they were *real*…

Hang on, I thought. This is a dream. You always put yourself through seriously nasty experiences in bad dreams. This is just a nightmare.

Then I felt a whole heap better. I looked up and saw that the overhead lights were getting stronger orange, while the gridded holes in the walls were growing pink. It looked as if the whole day had passed. Well, I thought, dreams do like to fast-forward things. I wasn't really surprised when, about five minutes later, Arnold came pounding up to me carrying his bag of tricks. His thick, fair face looked white and exhausted.

"Up you get. Time to go," he said. "The Prince's own mages handle security overnight."

I got up, thinking in a dreamlike way that it was rather a waste that we were all taking so much trouble to guard a Prince who was going to lose his Empire and be dead before long. How had Romanov known that anyway? But dreams are like that.

I was still thinking about this when we passed the first soldier. He looked at us enviously. "Poor beggars stay here all night in case anyone plants a bomb," Arnold remarked. Then we came up to Chick and Arnold said, "Time up. Hotel first or eat and drink?"

"*Food*!" Chick said, collapsing his sword to a knife and then stretching his arms out. "I'm so hungry I could eat that novice."

"I'd prefer a horse, personally," Arnold said and we went on round to underneath the pavilion. Dave and Pierre were already there, waiting. Arnold asked them too, "Hotel first, or food?"

"Food!" they both said and Dave added, "And wine.

Then some hotspots. Anyone know this town – know where's good to go?"

I watched them as they stood around discussing this. After Romanov, they struck me as simply normal people, jumped up a bit. I was a bit bored by them.

None of them did know where to go in Marseilles, as it turned out. Nor did I, when they asked me as a last resort. So we all went out through the guarded doors underneath the pavilion into the street and Arnold hailed a taxi. "Condweerie noo a yune bong plass a monjay," he told the driver as we all piled in. I think he meant, *Take us to a good place to eat*, but it sounded like Zulu with a German accent.

The driver seemed to understand though. He drove off downhill towards the sea with a tremendous rattle. Even allowing for the way the streets were cobbled and how old that taxi was, I think the way its engine worked was quite different from the cars I was used to. It was ten times louder.

But it got us there. Before long, it stopped with a wild shriek and the driver said, "Voila, messieurs. A whole street of eateries for your honours." Clearly, he had us spotted as English – or, considering Arnold and perhaps Chick too, not French anyway. The place he'd brought us to was a row of little cafés, and they all had big hand-done notices in their windows. SCARMBLED EGG, one said, and SNALES was another. LEG OF FROG WITH CHEEPS and STAKE OR OLDAY BREKFA said others.

We all cracked up. It had been a long day and it felt

good to be able to scream with laughter. "I am not," howled Dave, staggering about on the cobbles and wiping tears off his face, "repeat *not*, going to eat cheeping frog legs!"

"Let's go for the scarmbled egg," laughed Chick. "I want to know what they do to it."

So, in spite of Arnold saying he rather fancied the stake, we went into the SCARMBLED EGG one. We charged in, still laughing, and snatched up menus. I think the proprietors found us a bit alarming. They brought us a huge carafe of wine straightaway, as if they were trying to placate us, and then looked quite frightened when we all discovered we needed to visit the gents and surged up to our feet again.

There was only one of it, out in the back yard past the telephone and the kitchen, where a large fat French lady glowered suspiciously at us as we waited for our turns. I was last, being only the novice, so I had to stand a lot of the glare.

But when we came back to our table, things were almost perfect. We swigged the wine and ordered vast meals, some of it weirdly spelt and the rest in French, so that we had no idea what would be coming, and then we ate and ate, until we got to the cheese and sticky pastry stage, where we all slowed down cheerfully. Dave began saying that he wanted to look at the nightlife very soon.

"In a while," Arnold said. "I suppose I'd better take your reports first." He lit one of his horrible Aztec smokes and took out a notebook. "Chick? Any attempts to break through the East? Any threats?"

"Negative," said Chick. "I've never known the otherwheres calmer."

The others both said the same. Then Arnold looked at me. "How about your patrol? What's your name, by the way?"

They've finally asked! I thought. "Nick."

Arnold frowned. "Funny. I thought it was something like Maurice."

"That's my surname," I said, quick as a flash. "And I do have something to report. A fellow called Romanov turned up and he…"

That caused a real sensation. "*Romanov!*" they all shouted. They were awed and scared and thoroughly surprised. Arnold added suspiciously, "Are you *sure* it was Romanov?"

"That's who he said he was," I said. "Who is he? I never met anyone so powerful."

"Only the magical supremo," Chick said. "Romanov can do things most magic users in most worlds only dream of doing."

"He can do some things most of us never even thought of," said Pierre. "They say he charges the earth for them too."

"If you can find him," Arnold said wryly.

"I've heard," said Dave, "that he lives on an island made from at least ten different universes in at least seven different centuries. Went there to escape his missus."

"Sensible fellow," murmured Arnold.

"He escapes there to avoid being pestered to do magic," Pierre said. "I'd heard he was self-taught. Is that true?"

"Yes – that's the amazing thing about him," Dave said. "According to what I heard, he was born in a gutter on quite a remote world – Thule, I think, or maybe Blest – and he pulled himself out of poverty by teaching himself to do magic. Very unorthodox. But he had a gift for it and discovered things no one else knew how to do, so he charged high and got rich quick. He could probably buy our entire Empire now. And nobody'd dare say he couldn't."

"Yes, but," Arnold said doggedly, "was it really Romanov that Nick Maurice met?" He turned and puffed his awful smoke at me, staring through the brown clouds of it with big, earnest blue eyes. "If you were doing as you were told, you'd have been able to see his totem animal. What was it like?"

"I'd heard it was a sabre-tooth tiger," Chick put in.

"No, it was spotted," I said. "Not a tiger. A big, mean, hunting cat, sort of cream with dark grey blodges. It had tufts on its ears and sarcastic green eyes and he said it was female. It came up to my waist, easily. I was scared stiff of it."

Arnold nodded. "Then it was Romanov." I could see they were, all four, really impressed. "Did he tell you why he was there?" Arnold asked me. "Was he looking for the Prince?"

"I asked him that," I said. "And he seemed to think the Prince would make his own trouble, without any magical interference. When he was King, he said."

They exchanged worried glances at that. Dave muttered, "Could be right. By what I've heard, some of Romanov's island is thirty years in the future."

"They say he never bothers to lie," Chick agreed.

I was relieved. I hoped I'd given them enough to think of to stop them thinking any more about me. From the moment Arnold said he thought my name was Maurice, it was like a whole train of pennies dropping in my head. This was not a dream. It was *real*. I'd no idea how it happened, but I knew that somehow I'd done the thing I'd been longing to do and crossed over into another universe. A real other world. And when I did, I'd turned up beside those fliers while they had all been waiting for the novice to arrive, and they had thought I was him.

This meant that, somewhere back in that other London, there was the real Maurice.

If this Maurice was my age, he wasn't going to like having gone without breakfast and then finding they'd all left without him. He was going to go back to this academy he came from, or phone there, and *tell* them. If I was really lucky, them at the academy would just shrug and say serve him right for being late.

But I couldn't count on it.

What was much more likely, since this cricket match was a Test and going to go on for several days, was that the academy people were going to make arrangements for the real Maurice to get to Marseilles later that same day. Then they were going to phone someone in the Prince's Security team to say Maurice was on his way. In fact, it was just amazing luck that they hadn't phoned while I was sitting in that concrete passage thinking it was all a dream. I would have had a rude awakening. Perhaps it took them a long time to arrange the journey. But they could well have phoned by now. Or Maurice could even have got here.

It was probably only the fact that the mages had been starving hungry and gone off with me in that taxi without saying where they were going that had stopped me getting arrested a couple of hours ago.

They *would* arrest me. They'd do that in my own world if I accidentally got in among Security for the Queen. But this world was so paranoid that it had to have a charmed circle round a cricket field, and I'd got in on that too. These people were going to accuse me of magical terrorism or something. I *knew* they were. I had to get away.

But at that moment they were still sort of attending to me, even though they were now discussing totem beasts and the way the animals reflected a mage's personality. So I kept a humble, eager, novice-like look on my face. When they asked me if I thought Romanov's totem beast reflected Romanov's personality, I said, "Yes. It walked exactly like him."

They laughed. Then Chick said, puzzled, "But didn't he say anything else to you?"

I said, "He called me ignorant and went away in disgust." As I said it, I wondered if it was Maurice's academy that had sent Romanov to stop me before I did any acts of terrorism. But I saw that couldn't be right. Romanov had known my name. I hadn't told anyone here my name until just now.

"Just passing through, I suppose," Arnold said dubiously. "Odd though. I'd better report it as soon as we get to the hotel. Nick, you must be ready to give a detailed account to the Prince's mages."

"Sure," I said and thought that I'd better give them the slip on the way there.

Then Arnold said, "Call for the bill, Dave. *Ladeeshun* or whatever they say. Everyone got enough cash for this blow-out?"

The four of them began fetching out money. One glance was enough to show me that it wasn't anything *like* the couple of ten pound notes in my back pocket. Their notes were kind of white, with black writing on them, like legal documents, and the coins were vast heavy things that rang down on the table like church bells. I knew I had to get out *now*.

I stood up. I said, "I have to go to the gents again."

"Trying to get out of paying your share?" Pierre said, laughing.

The others laughed too and Chick said, "Hey, Nick,

you never told us what your totem beast is. Or is it a state secret?"

"No… It's a black panther," I said, edging off.

"Go on!" said Dave. "That would make you a high adept!"

"That was a joke," I said hurriedly. "Just a joke." And I marched off, followed by jolly shouts and more laughter. I felt bad. They were quite nice fellows really.

I didn't dare run, but I walked quite fast, down the passage past the huge Frenchwoman – she glowered at me again – and opened the door into the yard. It was a narrow door and I had to turn half round to get through it. That was how I happened to see the officer from the flier just coming in through the front door of the café. He was waving his cellphone and looking pretty agitated. You could see he had been hunting all over for us.

I shut the door very gently behind me and raced through the yard to the back entrance. There was an alley there full of rubbish bins. But no soldiers. Yet. I think the officer hadn't been sure enough of finding us to have the place surrounded. But I was sure he must have a squad outside the front. I ran.

I ran for my life, out of that alley and then through several others, always turning uphill away from that street when I could. That may have been a mistake. For one thing, it got steeper, so that there were steps in some places. For another thing, there were more and more people about, lovers walking, or people just sitting in doorways, so that when I began to hear shouts and police whistles and lots of feet climbing up behind me, I didn't dare run. The ones who saw me running would point me out to the police.

Then things got worse. Arnold's voice suddenly spoke, sounding like it was somewhere inside of me. *Nick, Nicholas Maurice. Come here. We want to ask you a few questions.* I'd forgotten they were mages. They were probably tracking me by magic.

Dave's voice spoke too. *Come on, Nick. Don't be a fool. Nicholas Maurice, there's a full security alert and you can't get away.*

My name's *not* Nicholas! I thought frantically. It's really Nichothodes Euthandor Timosus Benigedy Koryfoides. It was the first time I'd ever been glad of having this string of outlandish names. They seemed to cover up the voices. I recited them over and over again and climbed the hill until I'd no breath left and was hot as a furnace. I pounded up another set of steps, saying a name for each step, "Nichothodes – puff – Euthandor – puff – Timosus – gasp – Benigedy – pant – Koryfoides!" And the voices faded away as I burst out into bright lights, shops and crowds of people.

Thank goodness! I thought. I can get lost in these crowds!

It was proper city life there. Nobody spared me a glance as I went past tables on a pavement packed with people eating and drinking, and then crossed the road among a bunch of happy folk having a night out. They were all much better dressed than me, but nobody looked at me anyway. I got my breath back wandering along that side of the street, looking into expensive shop windows, and I was just beginning to feel safer when both ends of the road filled with uniforms. Police and soldiers were stopping everyone from leaving, and squads were coming down towards me asking everyone to show their ID.

I bolted up the nearest alley. There was some kind of big church up the other end and I stopped dead when I saw it. There were a couple of soldiers with rifles standing outside its door. Perhaps in this world you really could kneel holding the altar and shouting "Sanctuary!" and be safe. And they didn't want me doing that. I leant against the alley wall wondering what to do. I knew what I *should* do, and that was simply walk on into another world, or back into my own. But I couldn't seem to do that, however hard I pushed my shoulders at that wall, no more than I could do it when I'd tried at home. I didn't know *what* to do.

Then, Hang on! I thought. I spent most of today up a tree somewhere quite different. That should be safe enough, if I can get there. I'll try *that*.

So I looked around. And I could hardly believe my eyes. Paths to that wood, and to all sorts of other places, more or less radiated out from where I was standing. They looked dim and blue and at odd sort of angles to that alley, but they looked as real as Romanov had said they were. I bolted up the nearest path.

It was night there too and fairly dark, but before I had gone very far I could see the oval of turquoise light that was the cricket stadium. I took my bearings from that and trotted round and along into the wood. It was pitchy dark there, full of uncanny rustlings and birds hooting, but I refused to let that bother me and kept on trotting. I'll find that panther, I thought, then climb a tree and let her protect me. That should do it.

While I was shoving through the next clump of bushes, I smelt a butcherish sort of smell and heard the most tremendous grating and cracking, like teeth on bone, and I realised I had found the panther. It was the extra blackness under the next bush. But before I could say anything, she gave a hideous, fruity growl.

*Go away. Busy. Eating. MINE.*

I got out of those bushes fast. I could tell she would add a piece of me to her meal if I didn't leave her alone. There was no way that panther was a tame totem-thing. It shook me up and made me feel horribly lonely to realise that. I'd been relying on beastly protection. But as that wasn't on, I thought I'd climb a tree anyway and blundered on until I came to one that seemed easy to climb. I had my arms round its trunk and one foot up on the lowest branch, when I heard voices again.

*Nicholas Maurice, we know you're here. Come on out.*

I froze. I looked where the voices were coming from, and there were two things like shining yellowish ghosts drifting along among the trees about a foot in the air. They were over in the direction of the turquoise oval, but much nearer, following a path there. Inside the ghost-shapes I could just recognise Chick and Pierre. This was another thing I'd forgotten they could do.

I took a look down at myself. I seemed to be quite dark and solid. The only parts of me I could really see were my pale hands, clutching the tree. But for all I knew, Chick and Pierre looked dark and solid to themselves and *I* was the one who shone like a ghost to *them*. I didn't *know* enough, that was the problem. All I knew was that they hadn't seen me yet.

*Nicholas Maurice!* they fluted beguilingly.

*Nichothodes!* I said to myself and began backing gently away, reciting my names again. I backed, and crept, and bumped into several trees and a spiky bush, and watched the ghosts drifting along, more and more distant, until I backed right round behind the spiky bush and couldn't see them any more. Then I looked around and saw another path winding its dim, blue way up to my right, and I fair pelted up it.

This path was rocky and wet, with wet cliffs bulging up on both sides, and it was horribly uneven. I kept stumbling as I ran, but I didn't stop until the light from the turquoise stadium faded away entirely and I couldn't see it at all. I was looking over my shoulder, checking on it, when I whanged into a piece of cliff and fell down.

# CHAPTER EIGHT

*

*I* stayed down for quite a while. Here I was, I thought,
once again sitting in a state of terror and paranoia, only
this time was *worse*. Add to that the way my knee hurt
from ramming the cliff and the fact that my rear felt as if
I was sitting in a puddle and you have the recipe for true
misery. *And* it was dark.

There wasn't any way that I could see of getting
home to Dad. I seemed to have a choice of going back to
the wood and giving myself up to the ghostly shapes of
Chick and Pierre, or going on along this path, or choosing
another. There didn't seem to be any future in any of
those choices.

I felt vile. And guilty. Let's face it, I had deceived a

whole security team. I hadn't exactly *meant* to, but I had been so set on the idea that this was all a dream that I was having that I hadn't even *tried* to say, "Excuse me. I'm not your novice." Maybe this was because, underneath, I might have had a small sense of self-preservation which told me that, if I did, I was likely to be arrested and interrogated anyway. But I knew why I hadn't said anything really. It was because I had actually – really and truly – got to another world on my own, just as I'd been longing to do. And it was too good to spoil.

Now I was in a real mess. And so were the mages I'd deceived. It was no wonder that Arnold and Dave had been tracking me hard in Marseilles and that Chick and Pierre were in a trance searching the wood. They were in bad trouble. If they didn't find me, they'd almost certainly be arrested themselves.

I was not surprised someone had hired Romanov to terminate me. I was getting to be a real menace. It was for something I was going to do later, he said. Romanov must have known I was going to go from bad to worse – and all only because I'd set my heart on being a Magid. Magids were strong magicians. They guided the flow of magic from world to world. They were trouble-shooters too. Most of them were dealing with problems – really exciting problems – in several worlds at once, using all sorts of different magical skills to do it. I wanted to do that. I wanted it more than I'd ever wanted anything. But the people who ran the Magids – the Upper Room –

wouldn't let me. They wouldn't let me have any training. So it was no wonder I was blundering ignorantly around, getting into this sort of mess. Romanov had been right to despise me.

This set me thinking of Romanov again. I still had the idea he was more powerful than any Magid. Romanov, I thought. That's the name of the old Czars of Russia. And he probably was a Czar, a magics supremo, the magics Czar, the way we have drugs Czars in England. I wished I could *talk* to him about the mess I was in. I knew he could tell me how to get back to my own world.

This was where the odd thing happened.

It's hard to describe. It wasn't smelling, or feeling, but it was *like* both things. It was also like there was a tiny breeze blowing from the path ahead, as if thinking of Romanov set it off. But there was no breeze. The air was perfectly still and wet. All the same I could suddenly smell-feel that Romanov had gone along this very path on his way back to wherever his home was.

"He *said* come to him if anyone else came after me," I said out loud. "OK. I will."

I got up and began feeling my way along the path.

For I don't know how long, it was quite awful. It was so dark. I could see sky up above, between the rock walls, but it was almost as dark as the path. There were no stars in it – nothing – and it didn't help me to see at all. I could just pick out my hands, the right one trailing along the wet, lumpy rocks, and the left one stretched out in front in a shaky sort of way, in case I hit a spur or a corner of cliff. I didn't want to think what else I might hit. There were noises, squelshy sounds that made me sure my fingers were going to plunge into something big and slimy any second, and creaking noises, and dry flappings that were worst of all. Every time the flapping happened, the hairs on my neck came up and dragged on my collar as if it were velcro.

The ground was uneven too. My feet kicked stones I couldn't see, or staggered and slipped on slopes of rock. Several times I stubbed my toe really hard, but I never knew what I'd hit. I sloshed into puddles and crunched through muddy pebbles until my feet were soaked and sore and frozen, and I never knew what was coming next.

Then it began to rain. "That's *all* I need!" I moaned. It was cold, drenching rain that had me wet through in seconds, with water chasing down my face and bringing my hair down in sharp points into my eyes. My teeth started chattering, it was so cold. But, believe it or not, that rain was actually an improvement. The noises stopped, as if the creatures making them didn't like the rain any more than I did, and before long all I could hear was the rain drilling down, splashing in puddles and trickling off the rocks. And the fact that the rocks were so wet meant that they sort of picked up a glisten from the sky and the puddles glinted a bit, so I could see a bit of what was coming next. I pushed my hair out of my eyes and got on faster.

The rain slacked off to a drizzle at last and I began to think there was a bit more light. I could actually *see* the way winding ahead like a sort of cleft in the rocks, with all the edges just faintly traced in silvery blue. Then I began to hear noises ahead. Not the noises I'd heard before. This was a sort of booming and yelling.

I began going *very* slowly and cautiously, sliding my feet one behind the other and keeping one shoulder against the right-hand wall so that I could look round each bend as I came to it. There was something big and alive along there, yelling its head off.

After about three bends, I could hear words in the yelling. "We plough the fields and scatter the dynamite on the land!" I heard. And then, after another bend, "Good King Wencis last looked out – when did he *first* look out then? – on the feast of Stephen!"

I almost laughed, but I still went very cautiously, and the light kept getting stronger and the yelling went on. You couldn't call it singing. It was too out of tune. And finally I edged round another bend and saw the person making the din.

He was a skinny, white-haired old drunk and he was leaning against a bulge of rock singing his head off. When I peeped round the bend at him, he was yelling about "Rock of Ages, cleft for meeee!" and holding up a little blue flame in both shaky old hands. The flame lit his clothes shiny and blazed off the wet rocks and his wrinkled, yelling face. He held the flame higher up as I peeped at him and shouted, "Come on, come on, both of you! Or am I just seeing double? Come out where I can see all the pair of you! Don't *lurk*!"

I came round in front of him. There didn't seem any harm in him. I'd never seen anyone so drunk, not even my friends after they'd drunk all Dad's whisky. He couldn't have hurt anyone in that state. He had trouble just seeing me. He wavered about, holding the little flame out towards me, and blinked and peered. I'd been thinking this flame was some kind of outdoor candle, or a torch like Arnold and Co had used, but it wasn't. It was a little curl of blue light standing on his hands, blazing away out of nothing.

"I'm drunk," he said to me. "Night as a tute. Can't ever come this way unless I get drunk first. Too scared. Tell me, are *you* scared?"

"Yes," I said. I couldn't take my eyes off that little flame. It was one of the most extraordinary things I'd ever seen. "Doesn't that burn you?"

"Not at all, notatall, notatall," he shouted. He was too drunk to talk quietly. "Being of one substance with my flesh, you know, it can't hurt. Litchwight, I mean witchlight, they call it. Not even hot, dear lad. Not even warm. So, well then, out with it, out with it!"

"Out with what?" I said.

"Whatever you need or want, of course. You have to meet three folk in need in this place and give them what help you can, before you can get where you're going.

You're my third!" he shouted, waving his little flame backwards and forwards more or less under my nose, "so I'm naturally anxious to get you done and dealt with and get on. So out with it. What do you want?"

I should have asked him how to find Romanov. I see that now. A lot of things would have been different if I had. But I was so amazed by that little blue flame that I leant backwards to get its light out of my eyes and pointed to it. "Can I do that? Can you show me how to do it?"

He wavered forward from his rock, peering at me, and nearly fell down. "Amazing," he said, hastily getting his back to the rock again. "Amazing. You're *here*, but you can't do a simple thing like raising light, or do I mean lazing right? Whichever. You can't. Why not?"

"No one ever showed me how," I said.

He swayed about, looking solemn. "I quote," he said. "I'm very well read in the literature of several worlds, you know, and I quote. What do they teach them in these schools? Know where that comes from?"

"One of the Narnia books," I said. "The one where Narnia begins. Can you show me how to make a light like that?"

"*Tell* you," he corrected me, looking even more solemn. "I can't *show* you because it comes from inside yourself, see. What you do is find your centre – can you do that?"

"My navel, you mean?" I said.

"No, *no*!" he howled. "You're not a *woman*! Or *are*

you? Confess I can't see you too well, but your voice sounds like teenage male to me. Is that what you are?"

"Yes," I said.

"And a plumb ignorant one too," he grumbled. "Fancy not knowing – Well, your centre is *here*!"

He plunged towards me and took me completely by surprise by jabbing me hard just under my breastbone. What with that, and the blast of alcohol that came with the jab, I went staggering backwards into the rocks on the other side of the path. He overbalanced. He snatched at my knees as he went down, missed, and ended in a heap by my feet. The blue light seemed to splash all over the ground. Then it climbed one of his arms and settled on his shiny wet shoulder.

"Polar sexus," he said sadly. "That's where it is, polar sexus."

"Are you hurt?" I asked.

He raised his soaking grey head. "There is," he said, "a special angel appointed to watch over those under the inkerfluence of eight over the one. That, young man, is why I had to imbibe before coming here. It all hangs together. Now do you understand how to summon light?"

"No," I said frankly.

"Don't you even know where your solar plexus is?" he demanded.

"I thought you said polar sexus," I said.

He went up on to his hands and knees and shook his

head sadly. Water flew off as if he was a wet dog. "Now you're making fun of me. But I shall be forbearing," he said, "though mostly for the reason that I shan't get out of this place if I'm not. And I may add, young man, that your attitude towards the elderly is less than respectful. Polar sexus indeed!" He started fumbling around on the ground in front of my feet. "Where is it? Where did I put my damn light?"

"It's on your shoulder," I said.

He turned his face and saw it. He more or less put his nose in it. "Now you're having a joke on me," he said. "I shall be freezingly polite and ignore it, or we'll be here all night. Pick me up."

He smelt so disgustingly of booze that I really didn't want to touch him, but I did want to know how you made light, so I bent down and grabbed him by his sopping jacket. He didn't like that. He said, "Unhand me at once!" and crawled away backwards.

"You *asked* me to," I said. I was getting fed up.

"No, I didn't," he retorted. "I was merely seeking a way out of our dilemma by asking you to pick up my witchlight. If you can keep it alight when you have it, you will in fact be making it for yourself. Come on. Take it. It won't hurt you and I can easily make more."

Well, I wondered if he did mean this, but I went gently up to him and tried cupping the little flame in my hands. It didn't feel of anything very much. A bit warm perhaps, but that was all. I stood up holding it, really delighted.

Then it began to sink and fizzle.

"No, no! Ignore it," he cried out. "Think of something else quickly!" He scrambled himself up the rockface and somehow managed to stand up. Then he snapped his fingers and held out another blue flame, balanced on the palm of his withered old hand. "See? Now change the subject."

"Er," I said, trying not to look at the blue spark I was holding, "you said we had to meet three folks in need. Are you my first?"

"Of course not!" he said. "I don't need anything. I just want out of here, and you're my third, so I can go now."

"Who else did you meet," I asked, "before me?"

"A goat," he said. "I *kid* you not! Joke, joke, ha-ha! Lost its way, you know, and then there was an obnoxious child who said she was hiding from her sin twister – twin sister – and she only wanted me to promise not to give her away."

"What did you do about the goat?" I asked.

"What *can* one do for a goat? Turned it round and gave it a push on the rump, I think," he said. "That's a bit hazy, to tell the truth, but I know neither of them was half the trouble *you've* been. Do you think you've got it now?"

I dared to look down at my hands. There was a cautious little flicker there, about the size of a match flame. I tried willing it larger, but nothing happened.

"Sort of," I said.

He pushed off from the rocks and came staggering across to see. I swear the drink on his breath made the flame twice the size for an instant. "Yes, yes, you've got it now all right," he said. "No need for me to linger. Farewell, for I must leave thee, don't hang yourself on a weeping willow tree!" By then he was singing again, bawling out a tuneless tune and swaying himself round as he bawled. I thought he was going to walk straight into the rockface opposite us, but there turned out to be an opening there that I hadn't seen before. He plunged into it, turning it all blue-silver with the flame in his hand, singing his head off. "In his master's steps he trod," I heard, booming out of the rocky cleft. "Heat was in that very naughty word which the saint had printed! Print and be damned, I say..."

I giggled a bit and took another look at my flame. It seemed to have settled down quite snugly by this time, enough that it didn't seem to mind being moved across to my left hand so that I had my right hand free. I waited a bit to make absolutely sure it was going to go on burning, then I set off down the path again.

That part wasn't nearly so bad. It was such a help to be able to *see*. I got on quite fast. And when the drizzle stopped and the noises started again, I held the flame up towards where I'd heard them from and its blue light showed me that there was nothing there. It was all done to frighten people. So I began to stride on and even whistle a bit – and I was a bit more in tune than the old drunk, too – and my flame seemed to like the whistling. It grew bigger. After that I got a lot less nervous of it and began to play about with it, sliding it up my arm and then up past my ear to the top of my head. It burned a lot brighter on my head. I had an idea that I could probably slide it off into the air and have it floating in front of me, but I didn't quite dare do that in case I lost it. I kept it on my head and had both hands free. I even put my hands in my pockets to try to warm them and really strode out, whistling.

I strode round a corner and met my first person.

She was standing facing me in the path, but she wasn't really in the path at all. She was in a pale patch of light with scenery in it. The patch was just sort of *there*. It didn't light up any of the rocks around or the ground in front of it. She was my age, or perhaps a bit younger, and… well, you know how you have an idea of your ideal girl in your mind. She was mine. She had dark, curly hair that was blowing about in a wind I couldn't feel and really big, blue-grey eyes with nice eyelashes round them. Her face was thin and so was the rest of her. I remember noticing she was wearing an old-looking grey knitted sweater and leggings that went tight below her knees, but mostly I noticed she was much better-looking than I'd expected my ideal girl to be. But the chief thing about her was that she was one of those girls who look as if they've just grown, as naturally as… as a tree or… a hollyhock or something… as if she'd just *happened* somehow. I always fancy girls like that, even if they're older than me. It's my type.

I slowed right down and came up to her step by step. When I was near enough, I saw she was holding a scruffy bunch of flowers in one hand. They were not flowers picked for their looks. I don't know what most of them were, but I did see that one was a tall thing with blobby yellow flowers in steps down its stalk, and furry leaves. I noticed because a caterpillar dropped off it as I walked up.

By then, I was near enough to see that inside the patch of light she was standing somewhere quite high on a hillside. There was low blue distance behind her. And nearer than that, but still behind her, just on the edge of the slope, I could see a much younger kid – a boy – sitting sort of hunched over so that all I could see was his back. He didn't move, or speak, or even seem to know that I was there.

She knew I was there, though. She watched me walking up to her. Her eyes went to the flame sitting on my head.

"Oh, good," she said. "You're a wizard. I asked for a wizard particularly."

"I'm not really," I said. It was all so strange that I didn't feel shy or awkward, the way I would if I'd met her anywhere else. "I'm only just beginning to learn."

"Well, that *may* be all right," she said. "I asked for someone who could help in this situation, so you must be able to do what's needed. What's your name?"

"Nichothodes," I said. It seemed important to tell her my real name. "Nick, usually."

"I'm Arianrhod," she said. "A mouthful, just like your name. But I prefer people to call me Roddy."

I wanted to say that Arianrhod sounded much nicer than Roddy, but that seemed – I don't know – likely to annoy her, or – now I think back on it – more as if the conversation had to go another way. I went with the way it had to go and said, "What kind of help do you want?"

Her eyebrows came together anxiously. When I think back, I can see she was massively anxious the whole time. "That's the problem," she said. "I don't *know* how you can help. It almost seems hopeless. Our whole country is probably in horrible danger and nobody seems to know except me. And…" Her hand went back to point at the younger kid. "Grundoon of course. Sir James seems to have the Merlin completely under his thumb somehow. Or else the Merlin's turned bad. Sybil's in it too. I mean, I know the Merlin's quite new, and young, and a bit weak…"

"Hang on," I said. "Merlin is from King Arthur's time. An old man with a long white beard. He got locked away by a girl called Nem – Nemesis or something…"

"I dare say one was," she interrupted me. "A lot of the Merlins have had long, white beards. But this one's young. He's only just been appointed."

"No, Nemuë," I said. "That was her name. You mean

139

to tell me there's more than the one Merlin?"

"Yes, of course. It's an official post," she said impatiently. "The Merlin rules magics the way the King rules the country, except that it looks as if the Merlin's trying to rule the country too now. Or Sir James is and he's got hold of the Merlin somehow. Sir James is a really vile man, but the King never seems to notice, and he's got the King *and* the Prince doing what he says now."

"OK," I said. I couldn't really follow all that. "You want me to come and help sort your country out for you." I heard myself say this, sounding quite cool and efficient, and I thought, Who are you kidding, Nick? You are going to end up with this Merlin and this Sir Someone jumping up and down on your face! But what I thought didn't make any difference. The old drunk had told me the rules. I had to help Roddy in order to get out of this place. So I put out my hand and sort of pushed at the patch of light around the girl. And somehow it didn't surprise me that I seemed to hit solid rock just about the place where her odd bunch of flowers was. I was quite relieved actually. "No luck," I said.

Roddy sighed. "I was afraid of that," she said. "When will you get here?"

"Um," I said. "Where are you?"

She looked surprised that I didn't know. "I'm in the Islands of Blest, of course. How long do you think you'll be, getting here? It's urgent."

"I have to help two more people first," I said. "Then

140

I'll ask Romanov what to do and be right along. That's all I can promise."

She wasn't very pleased, but there didn't seem to be much either of us could do about that. "I'll see you soon, then," she said.

"See you soon," I agreed.

I turned sideways and squeezed past her patch of light. It was odd. The thing was like a flat disc with her inside it. When I was level with her, side on, all I could see was a curved line of daylight. When I was past that line, it was all gone. I looked back and there was nothing. I even went back to where I had been standing, but there was nothing there now, just black rocks.

"Oh, well," I said. I still don't know whether I was more disappointed or more relieved. It would have been wonderful to meet Roddy properly, in the flesh. But if I did, it would seem to mean having to deal with magic and politics in a place I knew nothing about, and I didn't feel up to doing that. So I went on, not knowing if I should chalk up one failure and try to help three more people, or if I really had agreed to help Roddy. And if so, did that count towards getting out of here? Perhaps, I thought hopefully, it was the thing I was going to do in the future that Romanov had been sent to stop me doing. Perhaps I could wait until I was grown up and then go to these Islands of Blest and sort them out then. Roddy would be grown up too then, and that struck me as a very good thing. I sort of smiled to myself and decided that I probably *had* promised to help her and it probably *did* count towards getting out of here, and I only had to put it off a few years and everything would be fine.

I think this made me careless. I was thinking so hard about it all that I almost walked straight past the place where the path forked.

Two steps further on, I replayed what I'd just seen: the light on my head glistening off a high promontory of rock with a dark path winding away on either side of it. I stopped. I backed up the two steps, and there, sure enough, was the promontory and the two paths. I'd simply gone off down the left hand fork without thinking about it. It had seemed to me that Romanov had gone that way. But when I stood in front of the promontory, I sort of *knew* he'd gone down both paths, both quite recently.

Since I didn't think even Romanov could be in two places at once, I reckoned he must have been along one of the paths first, then the other, and it was the one he'd used last that I needed. But I couldn't really tell which it was. I stood and dithered. And in the end I decided that I must have gone into the left hand path because I'd known unconsciously which was the right one. So I went that way.

This turned out to be a truly colossal mistake.

# PART FIVE
# RODDY

# CHAPTER NINE

✳

*T*he following morning, after Grundo had pigged out on bacon and eggs – well, I did too:the bacon was marvellous – Olwen brought us two heavy little knapsacks loaded with sandwiches. If I'd been on my own, I'd have asked to leave some of them behind. There were so *many*. As it was, I peered in at the several loaf-sized packages, thought of Grundo and wondered if there was enough.

Then my grandfather came in with a map and showed us how to go. "The place you are making for," he said, "is a ruined village where people lived before History began. You may recognise it by the small wood below it where a river runs. It is there they went to wash. The place itself is on the bare shelf just below the top of the hill. You will see the remains of the houses quite clearly. Be sure to visit each one."

He gave Grundo the map and went away to his study, to his mysterious work.

We set off, as he had told us, straight ahead from the front door. This took us round the top of the hanging scoop where the valley that led to the manse ended. We looked down as we walked on the grey road zigzagging up the green mountainside towards us. Beyond that, the valley coiled into blue-green distance without a house in sight.

"I wonder where his congregation comes from," Grundo said.

"Springs out of the earth, obviously," I said.

For some reason, this made us both shiver and we went a long way after that without speaking. It was a hot, blue day with only the faintest wind even up on the mountains where the map took us, the kind of day where there is a haze at the bottom of the sky, hiding the distance. It was quite hard to see the green and dun peaks as they wheeled slowly about us. The blue-black distance was only a suggestion. And it grew hotter and hotter.

"Dad must have forgotten to put the clouds back," I said. I was a little puzzled, because Dad is usually very particular to restore the weather systems to where they were before he moved them. I knew the King had wanted continuing fine weather, but there should have been signs by now – small clouds, gusts of wind – that Dad was beginning to bring the old weather back.

"The King probably ordered a heatwave until he's met the Pendragon," Grundo said. His mind was chiefly on the map. It was not like maps usually are. It was more like a little drawing of hills and mountains. Woods were put in as small trees and marshes were drawn as pools grown with rushes. I found it easier to follow than a real map, but Grundo kept grumbling about it. "How am I expected to follow an artwork?" he kept saying.

It took us the whole morning to get to the place – or maybe longer than that, I suspect. We trudged slantwise across hillsides where dark gorse stood above us blazing with yellow flowers smelling of vanilla, and beside crags, and up long slopes among pine trees, where the smell was sad and spicy. The only real incident was in a marsh strewn with black pools, where midges came out like smoke from a bonfire every time we trod on a tussock. Grundo got sick of the midges and went through an acre of fine emerald grass instead. The grass was growing on sucking mud. Grundo lost both shoes. We had to crawl for them and got very silly and laughed a lot and ended up covered with black, coaly slime. The slime flaked off in the sun as we walked on. By the time we reached the place, we had almost flaked back to normal again.

"It's unmistakable really," Grundo said, staring uphill at it.

It was like an accidental garden strewn with heaps

of regularly piled stones. Small rowans and hawthorns had grown up among the stones, along with heather and gorse, big bushes of broom and small shrubs of bilberry. In between, there was every kind of wild flower, from foxgloves and poppies and yarrow, through buttercups, down to speedwell and tiny heartsease. I was particularly enchanted with some flowers like dark blue trumpets nestling in sunny spaces and by the drifts of frail, wiry harebells. Blue is always my favourite colour. Grundo discovered ripe bilberries and was squatting eating them almost at once, while butterflies flitted across him in all directions but straight. Bees murmured everywhere and grasshoppers grated away all around.

"Let's have lunch before we explore," I said.

"Yes!" said Grundo, with his mouth all purple.

We sat down on the nearest sunny tumble of wall, just beside what looked like the ruins of a front door with very civilised steps up to it, where we ate an improbable quantity of sandwiches in peace and contentment filled with insect-sounds. I said the people who once lived here must have been very well organised.

"But what a long way they had to go for water," Grundo said, pointing to the little rustling wood down the hill, where you could just hear the distant trickling of the river.

"It didn't matter if they were used to it," I said. I had a sudden strongly imagined vision of that wood full of small pathways, some of them where children ran and laughed, others where sweaty men strode down to bathe, and others where women walked with baskets of washing, chatting and arguing. The part where the privet and blackthorn grew thickest and darkest, up near the waterfall, would have been – well – secret, somehow. I didn't know if this idea was correct or not, so I didn't mention it to Grundo. I said, "If you've quite finished pigging, we have work to do."

Grundo got up, groaning a little, and we went in among the houses. They were all just heaps of stone in rings or ovals, but you could see they had been houses because some of them were divided into rooms, and there were big slabs of stone in some that might have been tables. Or stairs. As we went from house to house in the hot, dreamy sunlight, with the butterflies darting and flitting about us, I kept seeing them all as well-built cottages, with stone walls downstairs and the upper walls neatly plastered. Each one would have had sliding shutters for windows, and a round, thatched roof like a hat on top. Most of them had small walled gardens at one side. But again, I was afraid I was being over-imaginative and I didn't tell Grundo this either.

He was poking around, grunting, wondering if people could stand up inside the buildings, and muttering that all the rooms were so tiny. "What does your grandfather expect us to find here?" he demanded. "Buried treasure?"

By this time, we were coming to the last and smallest house in the place. It was a ring of stones only a couple of feet high, off at the bottom end of the village, slightly aside from the other ruins. The grass inside the ring of stone was green even for this country and there were more flowers growing there than in any other spot. But I was thinking there were no dividing walls – this must have been a very humble cottage – when we were suddenly inside a perfect cloud of butterflies. They swept around us, all kinds, white, blue, small and brown, large yellow, big tortoiseshell, orange tipped, some almost red, and whirled on into the small ruin, where they sank in a quivering crowd towards the bank of yellow flowers to one side.

"Go with them," Grundo said with utter certainty. "They mean something."

We stepped inside on to the green, moist grass. And there the thing happened that my grandfather must have sent me for. It seemed to last for a second and to go on for a century – Grundo says a minute, I stood there like a statue for a minute, he says – and it is horribly hard to describe. So many things seemed to happen at once.

The first thing was that, as if someone had dealt me a thumping blow, I felt a terrible pain in my right hip. It hurt so that I could hardly stand up. And then, though I knew I was all the time standing in the sun in a ruin, I was in the house as it once had been. It was fairly dark, but extremely civilised and orderly, if you allowed for most things being on the floor, like knives and pots and cups and knitting, all laid neatly on the carpet. The reason it was arranged like that was because the woman lying on the low bed where the butterflies were had difficulty standing up. It hurt her to stand or walk. She had been ritually injured when she was fifteen because she was a powerful witch. A *very* powerful witch. She greeted me with dreadful, bitter joy. The village chief had smashed her right hip so that he could control her. She had never forgiven him. She had vowed never to pass on the knowledge her gifts had given her to anyone from the village. But the law is that you have to pass your knowledge on to *someone*. So, instead, she had searched the centuries and the millennia for the right person to pass her magic to. And she had found me.

She gave me her knowledge.

It was devastating. I had the knowledge all at once in a bundle – all she knew, all she could do, and her entire life with it. I felt like Mam's little laptop into which someone had suddenly downloaded fifty years' dealings in the world's Stock Exchanges. I staggered and limped and hobbled away from the small ruin, hardly able to see. All I remember is that the butterflies flew away as suddenly as they had come, spreading out as they went into a hundred different flightpaths. The only other thing I knew was that my hip hurt dreadfully.

I think Grundo was very frightened. He says my face was grey and my eyes like bright holes. He said, "Are you all right?" in the calm, quivery voice people use instead of screaming. When I didn't answer, and I couldn't – all

I could make was a queer, buzzing moan – he took a violent hold on my wrist and dragged me out of the long-ago village. He had to drag very slowly because I almost couldn't walk. My right thigh felt broken.

Down the flowery field we crept to the wood with the river in it. Grundo had to carry both our bags. He was probably wondering how we were going to get back to the manse. His first idea was to sit me down in the wood to recover, but that didn't work because my leg hurt too much to bend. So he cut through the dark corner past the waterfall and dragged me across the stepping stones and out on to the hillside beyond.

There it was as if we had passed an invisible boundary. The hurt in my hip stopped. It was just not there any more. "Oh, thank *goodness*!" I said. "Fancy being in that kind of agony all the *time*, Grundo!"

"Are you all right now?" he asked rather desperately.

"No," I said. My head seemed to be bursting, as if it had two brains in it. "I'm sorry," I said. "I shall have to lie down and go to sleep for a bit." And I flopped down on the grass and heather and more or less passed out.

Grundo says I slept for at least two hours. He sat anxiously beside me the entire time, not knowing what had happened to me and wondering what he would do if I never woke up again. He says I hardly seemed to be breathing most of the time. He told me very calmly, but I think he had been pretty brave.

I woke up suddenly – *pop*, like that – and sat up with

all sorts of strange new knowledge still sorting itself out madly in my mind, to find the sun quite low and both of us under a cloud of midges.

"Are you better *now*?" Grundo asked with great calmness. He was trying to scratch both legs, one arm and his hair at once, and he looked unusually pink and sweaty.

"Yes," I said. "Starving. Is there any food left?"

Grundo scrambled to tip sandwiches, cake and apples out of our bags. "Tell me what *happened*," he implored me.

I tried to tell him, while eating passionately. The odd thing was that I couldn't tell him what it was really *like*. I could only tell him what I'd learnt. "The woman who used to live in that house," I explained, "was a wizard and a priestess and a healer, a *very* strong one, very clever. She understood more about magic than anyone I've ever met. And..."

"But you *didn't* meet her," Grundo objected. "There was no one but us in that ruin."

"Yes, I did," I said. "She was lying in the place where the butterflies were." I saw her in my mind's eye as I said this, even though I knew Grundo was right and she had not been there. She was quite small and thin, very brown and rather wrinkled, and I could tell she thought of herself as old – but she wasn't, not even as old as Mam, and Mam is thirty-two, which is not old for people these days. She had hair like mine, black and curly, but hers was long and wild and a little greasy. And she stared up at me in bitter gladness, from the biggest, darkest, most vivid eyes I have ever seen. Her dry, brown mouth smiled, in spite of her pain. I felt as if I had known her for years and talked to her for months. She was *that* strong.

"She had bad teeth," I added. "The point is that her village tried to own her. The headman broke her hip to keep her and her magic with them, when she was fifteen and wanted to marry a man from over the hill. So she never married. She could hardly walk. And she hated them for it. And, although she did her duty strictly, and cured their diseases and warded them with magic and made their crops flourish and dealt with their enemies, she made a vow to herself that she would learn more magic than anyone else in the world and not tell anyone else in the village one syllable of what she learnt. Her assistants were all stupid anyway. They couldn't understand any magic deeper than wart-charming if they tried. But the trouble was, the rule is that you *have* to hand on your magical knowledge to *someone* or it stays around and destroys things. So she learnt and kept everything in her head, and when she knew enough, she searched all through the future to find someone to give the knowledge to. That's what Grandfather Gwyn sent me here for. So that she could find *me*."

"And *do* you know everything she knew?" Grundo asked. He sounded so disbelieving that I knew he was deeply impressed.

"Not yet," I said. It was unfolding in my head as I talked. I had a notion that I would be unfolding more of it for the rest of my life. "She gave it to me in a lump, you see, along with her bad hip for a while. It's all in lists, like files in a computer. Each file goes under a different flower. I think I'm supposed to learn which flower means which sort of magic and then access them when I need them. Lots of them are going to just sit there folded into a lump until I call them up. But I know some. Purple vetch is the first file, and that has all the time-magic in it, the stuff she needed to be able to search the future. And some really *strange* things!" I stared at these things, while Grundo stared at me staring into distant universes and huge, peculiar ideas I'd never thought of before. It was like looking down a whirlpool.

"Why did she choose *you*?" he growled. It was almost a complaint. Grundo felt left out.

"I think my brain matches hers," I said. "That's what she looked for, a brain, not a person. But she was glad I was well-intentioned too. She was going to die soon. Her hip had gone bad inside. And she really didn't tell anyone in the village her magic, I know. I'm pretty sure the place didn't last very long after she died. But I remembered to thank her. I told her that her knowledge was going to save more than just a village in *this* time."

"And will it?" Grundo asked eagerly. "Can you out-magic the Merlin now?"

I wondered. There was certainly stuff in my head that

would do that, but you had to learn what it was and how to work it first. "If I think very hard..." I said. "Let's walk back to the manse now. I still have to sort out just what I do know."

All the way back, in the mild evening sun, I was thinking, thinking. I kept discovering new flower-files I hadn't noticed before, each with more knowledge stacked inside them than I had ever dreamt existed. Once or twice, I annoyed Grundo by bursting out laughing. The first time was when I realised that all the magic we had learnt at Court was small and one-sided and incomplete. The reality was huge – and all the things our teachers said were complicated were really quite simple. And the other way round.

"Oh, good!" Grundo grunted when I told him. "I've always thought that."

Another time I laughed, I had to explain to him, "It was the kind of woman she is! Almost *all* the flower-headings are dry, twisty kind of plants, like thistles or brambles or teazles. Or gorse. That's a big file. There's not a juicy dandelion or a lily or a forget-me-not anywhere! She was *so* dry and bitter!"

"It's not *evil* magic, is it?" Grundo said anxiously.

"No," I said. "That's the odd thing! You'd think the way she hurt and hated, she *might* use bad magic, but she didn't. There are several evil files – privet, yew, ivy – but they're made like read-only. For reference, so you know what to do when someone uses black magic against you, and they all have the counter-spells with them, which are the only active ones. All the rest is just – well – clean knowledge. I don't know how she *did* it, considering the life she had!"

I kept having memories of that pain she'd lived with, like long blunt teeth clamped on the top of her leg, and she *still* did her duty and kept her magic white. It was enough to make me *swear* to be worthy of her gift, to use it *properly* or not at all.

My grandfather was outside the manse when we came round the last bend in the way, like a stick of charcoal on the grass in front of the house, watching for us. He did not move as we came across the top of the valley, except to take down the hand that was shading his eyes. When we came up to him, he said, "There is no need to tell me. I see you found what you went for. Tea is ready."

As we followed his upright black back into the manse, it came to me that Mam must often have been hurt or offended when he behaved like this. I wondered if *I* was. And I found I wasn't. It was his way. He had shown he was anxious by waiting outside for us. When he saw we had succeeded and that we were all right, he felt words were unnecessary because we all knew anyway. I wondered if I would ever be able to explain this to Mam. Or if she would believe me if I did.

Tea was magnificent again. I let Grundo enjoy himself and chat to Grandfather Gwyn and did not speak much myself. My head was still heavy and fuzzy with all that had been packed into it. Afterwards, I left Grundo looking at books in the tall, damp-smelling parlour and toiled away to bed. I suppose I undressed. I was in nightwear next morning. But all I remember is plunging into sleep.

# CHAPTER TEN

*

*I* slept very heavily. It was the kind of sleep people describe as "dreamless", except that it wasn't. All through it I felt that knowledge was unfolding in my brain. Then, around midnight, I seemed to have a dream.

I thought I lifted my head from my pillow because the bell in the little chapel was ringing. "I must go and see," I said to myself, "but I'm not used to this and I hope I get it right." So, while the small bell kept tolling out its silvery *ting, ting, ting*, I sorted sleepily through my new knowledge and used it to float out of bed, and through the window, where I sort of hovered round to the front of the manse. Everything was dark and gusty out there, but there was somehow enough grey light to see by. I could see that the arched door at the front of the chapel was open. People in dark clothes were coming out of the darkness inside it, riding horses, or riding other things much stranger, and coming slowly uphill in threes and pairs towards the manse.

There must have been a good fifty of them on their way by the time the chapel bell gave a final *tong-ting* and stopped. Their pale faces lifted expectantly then. My grandfather came out from behind the manse, riding the grey mare. He was not in his cassock, but all in black, tight-fitting clothes, except for his silky cloak, which had a white lining that billowed around the dark shape of him.

He spoke to the advancing people in the thunderous voice he used when he said grace. "I am summoned," he said, "but for no good purpose. Come."

He rode the grey mare straight forward, straight off the edge of the grass and into the air above the winding valley, and the other people followed him in a dark procession.

I had a moment when I knew this *had* to be a dream, and then another moment when it was fairly clear to me that my grandfather was not just a mere wizard. Then I was speeding after them through the air.

It was certainly *like* a dream for a short while. Blue-dark landscapes rushed underneath us, mountains heaved up, pale roads and glinting rivers coiled, black woodland swept up and swept behind, and every so often the clear yellow lights in houses flitted by far below. Those lights were like heaps and strings of jewels, and I got the feeling they were equally precious. But we did not stop for them, nor for anything else, even for the small flier that blundered across our way, chugging and roaring and no doubt full of people hoping they were imagining the sight of us, until we came to the dim shape of a castle on a knoll beneath. Then we swept down and around it in a grand curve, and my grandfather rode down the air to land on the turf inside the castle gardens.

I recognised the place as we came down, mostly because of the huge orderly cluster of tents, lorries and buses just outside the gardens to the right. This was Castle Belmont where the King's Progress was camped.

But we were not going to the camp. My grandfather led his riders silently on through the parkland until they came to the dark walls of the Inner Garden. There, at its gate, he turned and led them, much more swiftly, around outside its walls. I knew, for some reason, that this part was not my concern. I sat hovering in the dark air and watched while they circled the garden three times clockwise, faster and faster. My grandfather was always easy to see, on the white mare with the white lining of his cloak flapping and gleaming, so that on the second circuit it was easy to see that he was now carrying some kind of pale banner or standard. On the third circuit, most of the riders following him were carrying pale lights that bobbed and glimmered as they swept up to the gates, swept around in a great curve, and went noiselessly galloping and glinting round the walls in the opposite direction.

My innards gave a lurch at this, because this was widdershins. All that I had been taught by the teachers at Court said that this was the direction of bad magic. But the knowledge that was now in my head from the woman with the hurt hip reassured me about this. My grandfather was one of the few who were outside these rules, and the gates of the garden would not open to him until he had circled three times counter-clockwise as well.

Sure enough, on the third reappearance of the speeding procession, the gates sprang apart and the riders trotted sedately inside. They were not completely silent now. As I swooped down to follow them, I could hear thudding, and faint creaks and jingles from their harness, and the horses snorting as they recovered from the gallop.

I overshot them a little. I was not used to floating about bodiless. There was a tiny flickering among the bushes up beyond the first lopsided pool, and I assumed that was where the riders would be. But what I found there was a double ring of lighted candles. Sybil, Sir James and the Merlin were standing in strange attitudes inside it. The Merlin had his arms raised and bent as if he were pushing against a low ceiling.

"It's coming – coming at last!" he panted.

Sybil, who seemed to be heaving at an invisible rope, gasped, "I hope it's quick then. It's all I can do to hold it!"

Sir James didn't speak. His was the weakest magic

and it was clearly all he could do to keep up his part of the working. The candles glistened on his sweaty face and clutching hands.

The grey mare climbed the bank beside me and stopped. My grandfather sat on her back staring at the three magic workers with his face blank as marble and utterly scornful. "I am here," he said.

The three inside the ring of candles relaxed and puffed out great thankful breaths. "It's here," said the Merlin.

"Thank goodness!" said Sybil. "It took its time!"

Sir James, bent over, with his hands on his knees, gasped out, "They do, the big ones. Owe it to their pride, you know."

None of them looked towards my grandfather. I realised that they were unable to see him.

"You have summoned me," said my grandfather, "and had the temerity to bind me to your will. I hereby warn you that you are permitted to summon me three times only. You can bind me no further than that."

"It may be speaking," the Merlin said, with a strained, listening look. "Wasn't that some kind of a protest?"

"Oh, they always grumble, these strong Powers," Sir James cut in irritably. "Not used to bending their heads. Get on and instruct it, Sybil. I'm whacked."

I suppose I should have stayed to hear what Sybil was going to say. I wish I had now. But a great disgust took me. I felt quite sick that these three unpleasant people should summon my grandfather and call him "it" and give him orders, when they couldn't even see him, and barely hear him either. Besides, there was quite a bit of noise coming from the greensward near the gate where the other riders were, and I was curious to know what they were doing. I swooped back there.

They seemed to be enjoying themselves. Some of them were standing with their horses' reins hitched on one arm, chatting cheerfully while they prepared some kind of torches and lit them from their little glimmering lanterns. The rest of them were quite deliberately making footprints in the grass. One man in a tight dark hood was stamping hard, over and over. Another was tramping round and round in a clockwise ring, chuckling as the marks in the grass showed deeper and darker. Most of the others were encouraging their mounts to stamp or rear in order to leave hoofprints, and one man was leading two of the strange beasts back and forth in the moist ground near the pool, coaxing and whistling as grooms do to horses. The creatures hissed and rattled their wings and a peculiar smell came off them, but they obediently placed their two splayed feet over and over in the same places.

"Those are wyverns," my grandfather said, coming down beside me on foot, leading the grey mare. He did not seem in the least surprised or annoyed to see me there.

"And what are the rest of them doing?" I asked.

He actually chuckled. "Leaving prints. We are not allowed to lie, but we can mislead. Wait here." He unhitched the white standard from the mare's saddle and strode up the rise beyond the trickling pool – surprisingly nimble for the father of my mother – where he rammed the thing upright in the soft turf. It went in a good foot and stood there, fluttering. As far as I could see in the gloom, it was a long skull-shape on a stake, round which strips of leathery stuff were flapping. "I shouldn't look too closely if I were you," my grandfather said, as he came back and gathered up the mare's reins. "It is there as a mark and a warning." And he mounted the mare as nimbly as he had climbed the rise.

I did look. I stared at the thing, even though it was queer and horrible. It seemed a desecration to plant it in this garden of gentle magics. But then, Sybil had already spoilt the magic by bespelling its waters, and I supposed Sir James deserved it.

While I was staring, all my grandfather's people gave a great shout and rode at the mound where the warning was planted, whirling the flaring torches they had been preparing. It was as if each torch set fire to the very air around it. The whole mound was a great roaring bonfire in instants, with the standard in its blazing heart. It only lasted for seconds. I had a second's clear sight of what the standard really was. It was a stake that had been pushed through the rotting skull of a horse, and then through the skull of a human above that, and the flapping pieces were skin, raw and bloody, flayed from horse and human. I had to turn away.

More of the knowledge from the woman with the

smashed hip came to me and helped me while I was gagging. My grandfather was not a wizard. He was a great Power, and great ones are governed by strange rules. Power and pain go together, as the woman had learnt herself. And every fine, kindly thing is incomplete without a side that is less than pleasant.

"Fine, kindly thing!" I said aloud. "Grandfather Gwyn is fine all right, but *kindly*!" At that moment, I thought I never wanted to speak to my grandfather again.

Then I came to myself to see that the garden was filling with the white mist of dawn. Sir James was coming striding down the side of the mound, holding a bottle and a wineglass. The other two followed him, sipping out of glasses as they came. None of them seemed to see the hideous standard rearing up by their shoulders, but they saw the lawn by the gate well enough. The dew of the grass there was smudged green and trampled brown with footprints, hoofmarks and the shapes of huge three-clawed paws.

They rushed there and stared. After a moment, they actually danced with delight. "We've *real* power to draw on now!" I heard Sybil say.

The Merlin positively giggled. "Yes, and we can use it to lay in even more!" he said.

I was disgusted again and I left...

## CHAPTER ELEVEN

✳

*I* woke up in bed. It was bright morning and I was really worried. If Sybil and her friends could enslave Grandfather Gwyn, there seemed no reason why they should ever stop. No one and nothing was safe. I tried to convince myself I had merely had a peculiar dream, but I couldn't. I was sure it had all really happened.

To prove me right, there were only Grundo and me at breakfast and only two places set. "Isn't my grandfather here?" I asked Olwen when she came in with boiled eggs.

"He's away on business," she said, "riding the mare."

"So much for your idea of asking Grandfather Gwyn for help," I said glumly to Grundo when Olwen had gone.

"Well, he said he wouldn't be able to," Grundo answered, placidly tapping the tops of three eggs. "What's the matter? Why are you looking so desperate?"

I told him about what I thought had happened in the night. It can't have been pleasant for Grundo, hearing such things about his mother. He looked depressed. But he is used to Sybil. He ate his third egg in a resigned way and said, "There must be someone else you can ask for help. That's why he sent you to get all that knowledge. Think about it."

"You're right," I said. "I will." I sat watching him eat toast while I tried to open file after file in my head. *Teazle, Thistle, Ivy, Gorse, Bramble, Dog rose, Goosegrass*, I went through, and several other prickly or dour-looking plants that I didn't know the names of and only had pictures of in my head. It was odd. I knew each flower-file was crammed full of magical facts. I even knew roughly what was in each one, but it all stayed misty to me. Even the one I had used last night without realising what I was using – *red artemis: out-of-body-experiences* – had gone misty to me now.

In the end, I just ran through the scores of file-headings one by one, until one appeared that *didn't* stay misty. *Harebells: dealings with magical folk who are visible.* And a whole list of these magical folk: *dragons, Great Powers, gods, Little People, kelpies, boggarts, haunts, elves, piskies…* on and on. I hadn't realised there were so many. And there was, I realised, another whole file – *Mullein* – about dealing with magical folk who were *not* visible, which put itself alongside *Harebells* in case I needed that too. But the picture of a harebell was the one that was clearest in my mind's eye. For a moment, I distrusted it. It didn't seem as dry and thorny as the rest of the hurt woman's herbs. But though the pale blue bells of the flowers seemed almost juicy, I saw they grew on dry, wiry stems – as dry as anything in the other files. It seemed to be right. What we needed was one of the magical folks who could give us advice – someone *wise*.

I ran through the list of folk again. I expected the file to come up with *dragon* or *god*, but it didn't – and when I thought about it, I realised that someone big like that would make an enormous magical disturbance coming to talk to us. If Sybil didn't notice, the Merlin would. Realising that made me feel almost hopeful, in a way. None of the three conspirators had the least idea that Grundo and I knew they were up to something, and we needed to keep them from knowing until we knew enough to stop them. The list ran through my head and stopped. *Little People*. It was obvious, really.

Grundo put the last piece of toast regretfully back in the toastrack. "Got it?"

"Yes," I said. "Where do harebells grow?"

"There were lots in that ruined village," Grundo said, "but that's miles away. Wasn't there a sort of bank of them on that slope across the valley? I thought I saw some just before we saw your grandfather waiting for us."

"Let's go and see!" I said, leaping up. I was so pleased that I rushed out to the kitchen with the teapot and a pile of plates. Olwen looked very surprised. "We'll be back for lunch," I told her and went racing off after Grundo, who was already trotting out along the way we had taken yesterday.

But things are never that easy. There were only a few harebells growing by the head of the valley and I knew I needed thick drifts of them. It took us half the morning to find the right kind of sloping, sheltered hilltop where harebells grew in quantities. By that time, we were well into the hills on the chapel side of the manse. But at last we found the place, a small, warm dip full of a great bank of fluttering, pale blue bells. We sat down on the sunny edge of them, and I carefully picked five of the harebells and wound their wiry stems among the fingers of my left hand in the correct pattern. Then I called out the correct words from the file, three times.

And waited.

Our shadows had moved on the hillside over the dry grass quite noticeably before anything happened. Grundo had stretched out on the turf and then gone to sleep by that time. This was hard on him, because when a section of the harebell-covered hillside shifted gently to one side, he woke up with a jump and then didn't dare move. I could see him staring sideways across the freckles on his nose all through the rest of what happened.

As I said, a piece of the hillside shifted. It was as if

there had been an invisible fold in it up to then, which now straightened out to let a small person slip around the edge of it. The person had one hand up, pushing at the fold, and he was dreadfully out of breath.

"Your pardon, wise lady," he panted. His voice was husky and high. "You patient. Wait long."

I looked from him to the hillside. *Space is as a folding screen to the little people,* said the knowledge in my head, and it seemed to be right. There was obviously twice as much of the hill, folded to keep the place where the person lived out of sight. I tried not to stare at the fold, or at the person, too hard. If I had been standing up, he would have come about to my knees. Up to then, I had always thought that, apart from their size, the Little People would be like small humans. This was not so. He was covered with soft, sandy hair, which grew thicker on his head and around his pointy ears. Being so hairy probably accounted for the fact that he was wearing almost no clothes, just crossed belts on his long top half and cheerful red drawers on his lower part. I found it really hard not to stare at his legs. They bent the other way from human legs. But his hands and arms were very like mine, though hairy, and he had an anxious little face rather like a cat's, except that his eyes were brown. He wore a gold earring in one ear and kept flicking at it nervously. I expect I seemed horribly huge to him.

I didn't want him to think I had come just to stare. I greeted him politely in what the file said were the right words.

"You know *old* talk," he said respectfully. "Not necessary. Old talk hard for us these days. You wait, for they fetch me. I only one know speak your talk."

I looked at the harebells drooping from my fingers. "These are supposed to make me able to understand your language," I told him. "Why don't you just speak the way you usually do?"

He was very put out. "But I need learn! Practice," he protested. "I hear, I know more than I know to *say*. Please use own talk."

"All right," I said. It seemed unkind to say anything else. "I've come to you for advice really. Do you mind me asking you for help? Will you need anything in return?"

"No, no. No return. Just need to hear big person talk," he said, and hopped forward to sort of squat-sit in front of me on his wrong-way-bending legs. This put him so nearly out of Grundo's line of sight that Grundo had to roll both his eyes into the corners in order to see him. "Now you tell," the small person said, and clasped his nearly human-shaped hands over his wrong-shaped knees. His smell drifted over me, like the smell of a very clean cat. "Make long story. Speak slow. I hear and learn." He looked up at me, expectant and eager.

There is nothing that puts you off more, I find, than someone saying that. I explained very badly at first, and kept thinking that I'd better put it more simply, and then thinking, No, he wants to learn more words. I said most things twice in the end. And he kept nodding and staring at me brightly, and I thought despondently, I bet he hasn't understood a word!

But he had. When I finally faltered to a finish, he flicked his earring and looked sober. "Is bad thing," he said gravely, "they trap one so great as Gwyn. Strangeness is, they do without know who they got. Is using his another name maybe. The Strong all have names a lot. Stupids. Learn name from book and not know who meaning. And is most greatly bad that such stupids work great plot. A pause. I think."

With his furry elbows on his peculiar knees, he rested his chinless face in both hands and considered. I waited anxiously. Grundo seized the chance to roll his eyes back straight.

After a while, the Little Person remarked out of his musings, "Wise ones of my folk been say magics acting up. This why."

"And do they know…?" I began.

He held up his hand to stop me, sandy-pink palm forwards. "Still pause. I still think."

We waited. At length, he seemed to finish thinking. He took his face out of his hands and looked up at me, bright and whiskery. "I think two things you do. One not may work. Other fiercely danger."

"Please tell me anyway," I said.

He nodded. "Am do. But all mix together difficult. Like magics mix here in Blest. Blest magics all laid together close, over and under, like weaving. These stupids pull out threads. Come *could* unravel and that bad. If you do thing also in Blest, that might worse be nearly. You do first either thing, you do outside, that right. That secret. Or either yourself do thing so big it chance unravel, fierce also danger. You see? I know you understand."

I didn't. I had to think hard to get even some of this. "You're saying that magic is so interlaced here in Blest – right?" I asked. "That if I want to do it safely and secretly, I have to do something right outside this world? Or if I don't mind them knowing, I can do something so booming big *here* that it could untwist all the magics anyway?"

He seemed very pleased. "Booming big," he said, several times. "Word I like."

"Yes," I said. "But what things?"

He was surprised. "Why, head of yours full of old knowings! Why need ask? I humble new person. But I tell. Outside thing, you call on person walk dark paths. Paths outside all worlds. No one here know you do. But not may work. Blest thing, booming big thing, you raise the land. Violent dangerous. Maybe blow apart – blow in small mess bits – blow – what call?" He made rocking movements with one hand. "What *call*?" he repeated appealingly.

I had no idea what he meant this time. "Sway? Wave? Rock?" I suggested.

"*Balance*!" Grundo said deeply, unable to bear any more. "He means the balance of magic, you fool!"

The small person leapt wildly to one side, just like a grasshopper, he was so startled. "Man not dead!" he said feelingly. "He safe? Not. I think I go now."

"No, no, it's only Grundo. Please stay!" I said.

"Talk he growl like deep earth," said the small one. "Booming strong magic. I go."

And, to my great disappointment, he went. He flipped aside a fold in the harebell patch, slipped around it and vanished. "What did you have to interrupt for?" I said to Grundo.

He sat up and rolled his eyes to get the kinks out of them. "Because you were being stupid," he said. "He was trying to tell you that raising the land – whatever that is – is going to destroy the whole balance of magic here, and probably in most other worlds as well. That's why he was so anxious to make you understand. I think he meant only do that if the outside-path magic doesn't work. Whatever that is."

"Then we'll do the other thing— Oh, I *wish* you hadn't frightened him off!" I wailed.

"He'd told you what he thought anyway," Grundo said.

"Yes, but he wanted to practise his human language," I said. "You must admit he needed to. He'd have stayed for hours if only you'd kept quiet."

"Then we'd have missed lunch," said Grundo. "Come on. Let's go."

Always thinking about food! I thought. "Don't you

even feel how marvellous it is to have talked to one of the Little People?" I said.

"No, not as the main thing," Grundo grunted. "If you think like that, then you're treating him like something in a museum, not as a person. And I'm going back for lunch. Now."

Do you know, Grundo is right! I *was* thinking of the small person that way. Even though he gave us some excellent, if terrifying, advice, I still had to try hard as I followed Grundo across the hillsides *not* to think of the Little Person as something very rare and strange that I had been to stare and marvel at. I think it would have been easier to see him as a real person if he'd agreed to speak his own language.

# Chapter Twelve

✳

We tried to call help from the dark paths that afternoon. We sat in the grass above the manse while I called up the flower-files and thought through them to find the knowledge I needed. I knew it was there somewhere, but I was quite surprised to find it under *Mullein* as a branch of *speaking with the dead*. I suppose that put me in a bad mood. I hoped, very strongly, that the person I found to help would not be dead. That would be no help at all.

Then I was put out again, when I looked in the right branch of the file, to discover that the file names were not simply names of flowers, but quite often the plant you needed for most of the workings in the file. This ought to have been obvious from *harebells* this morning, but I didn't see it until that afternoon. It took practice to get used to the hurt lady's knowledge.

*A torch of mullein held in the hand is necessary for all the dark paths*, this branch said. And *could* we find mullein? We could not. I got more and more impatient, and underneath I was just so *anxious*, because while we searched about on the hillside and round the manse, Sybil and her friends were getting merrily on with their plans. We could be too *late*. I had only the haziest idea what mullein looked like anyway. Grundo knew. He had looked at the pictures in nature-study lessons because of not being able to read as well as me. He said he thought it looked a bit like evening primrose. But when he added that any old plant would probably do just as well, we very nearly quarrelled.

"Or try waving a turnip!" Grundo called over his shoulder. He went stumping off in disgust down to the chapel.

I ignored him and found rosemary and privet and ragged robin. Privet and ragged robin were two of those plants that my files had tagged as *Use only with great care*, along with briony, campion, hellebore and lily-of-the-valley. I was looking at them nervously, wondering what made them so dangerous, when Grundo came stumping back.

"There's a fuzzy plant covered with caterpillars against the back wall of the chapel," he said. "Come and look. I *think* it may be mullein."

It was, too. I knew as soon as I looked at it. It had pale, furry leaves and pale yellow flowers in clusters all down its stem and, as well as being covered in caterpillars, it was tall as a hollyhock. Grundo knocked the caterpillars off and handed me the flower with a Court bow. "There. Have you got them all?"

"I need dock," I said.

"By the chapel gate," he said. "A big bundle of it. And then?"

"Well, asphodel and periwinkle would help too, but I've got all the main ones," I said. "Let's go to the top of the hill. I need to face clear sky."

All the way up the hill, I could tell Grundo was brooding. When we got to the top, he said, "If doing this magic makes you like Alicia all the time, I'm not going to help you any more." He sat himself down facing towards the manse and humped his shoulders at me.

In the normal way, I'd have been furious with him for even thinking I was like Alicia, but my head was so full of what I had to do that all I said was "*Be* like that then!" and left him sitting there.

Oddly, as soon as I started the working, it was almost as if Grundo was not with me. There came a tremendous burst of energy from the bundle of plants in my fist, and from that moment on, I seemed to be alone on the top of the mountain, walled off from the world. This made me less embarrassed than I would have been if Grundo had been standing beside me. The spell was a rhyming one. The files told me what to say in the hurt woman's language, and then they told me what the words meant. I had to put the words into thoughts, and then into more words that rhymed. I felt really silly, waving a withering bundle of plants about and calling out, "Feet on the stony way, eyes that can't see, wizard man outside the worlds, come and help me!" Over and over. It felt pathetic. And futile.

I was quite sure it wasn't working, until I saw a dark space open in front of me. It felt like a window into emptiness at first. "Help me," I finished feebly. I nearly staggered away backwards when the darkness flickered blue, showing rocks and wetness, and someone came stumbling from around a corner towards me.

The first and most important thing I noticed about this person was that he had a little blue flame sitting on his forehead, the way our wizards do on important occasions. "Oh, good!" I said. "You're a wizard." But I was very nervous, because he was real *and* because he was somewhere else entirely.

I knew he could see me and hear me. But he didn't seem any too certain that he was a wizard. He mumbled something about being a beginner or just learning. My heart sank rather. He was more or less the same age as me. I could tell he was, although the blue flame distorted his face terribly. He looked demonic, with pits for eyes. But, I thought dubiously, perhaps this is how people from another world do look. In Blest, I would have said he was from India. I think. Anyway, he was dark and a lot taller than me.

Then I told myself that he *had* to be right. He was the one the mullein-spell had summoned, so he *had* to be. The flower-file was most insistent that the next thing you did was to get the person to say his or her true name. So I asked him his name, and he said it was Nichothodes. It sounded very foreign to me. And he was sort of frowning at me, as if he thought – rather like Grundo – that I was being very bossy and busy with my own troubles – which I was, but I couldn't help it. So I told him my name and tried to make a joke that we both had mouthfuls for names.

He still seemed dubious, but he said in a very businesslike way, "What way do you want me to help you?"

I explained or tried to. None of it seemed to mean very much to him, and we hit a snag almost at once, because he thought that the Merlin was a man with a long white beard from the days of some mythical king. I'd never heard of this King Arthur of his, but I said, "Well, a lot of the Merlins do have long white beards. The one who just died did." I tried to go on to explain how the Merlins kept the magical powers and worked with the Kings, who kept the political powers.

He didn't seem to understand at all. I got a feeling he didn't want to. I went on explaining, quite desperately, that the whole *country* was being threatened, along with the rest of the world, and probably other worlds with it. I see now that this was a foretaste of what happened every other time I tried to get help from someone, but at the time it seemed that it was because we were totally separate, me on a hill in Wales and he goodness knows where in the dark. I felt helpless and hopeless.

And he couldn't walk through from his dark place to me. He tried. He put out his hand and it was as if he had planted it against a glass wall. I could see his palm all flattened and white, with red lines in it.

"OK," he said. He seemed a great deal more cheerful about it than I was. He said he'd go and ask someone what to do. "Then I'll come back and try to help you and Grundoon sort it out," he said.

"Grun*do*," I said.

"Him too," he said cheerfully. "Where are you anyway?"

That made me feel as if the spell had let me down, because *surely* it ought to have let him know basic things like that. "I'm in Blest of course," I said.

"Then I'll see you soon," he said and went walking away past me, looming up blue and dark and then vanishing out of sight just beside me. The darkness stayed there for a moment, going denser and denser, and then faded back into the sky.

"That was a fat lot of good!" I said angrily to Grundo.

Grundo jumped a little and said, "Have you finished already?"

"Yes!" I said. I hurled my mashed bunch of herbs to the ground. "Powers preserve me from thick-headed, self-centred, cocky teenage wizards!"

"Wasn't it any good?" Grundo asked.

"Not a lot," I said. "*Now* what shall we do?"

Grundo gave a surprised look at the low sun and then at his watch. "We go in for tea, I think. That's the trouble with having tea instead of supper. The afternoon's so short. Anyway, your grandfather's back. I can see the grey mare in the field from here."

As we went sliding and crawling down the hill, Grundo seemed quite cheerful. I couldn't understand it. I was in a great state of gloom. All that hunting for flowers had been a total waste of time. The wizard boy was not capable of helping anyone. He was *stupid*. I wanted to blame the Little Person for suggesting the idea – but it was not his fault. He had no way of knowing I was going to get an ignorant idiot when I called. But that seemed to show there *was* no way to get help from outside. The only thing I could do now was to rejoin the King's Progress and find out as soon as possible what it meant to raise the land and how to do it. It was not something that was in my flower-files – I was sure of that. In the hurt woman's day it was not a thing anyone needed to do. They had little kings and small countries. Probably the magic of Blest had not even begun to be important for other places then.

In the manse, Grandfather Gwyn was waiting by the

tea table to say grace. At first glance he seemed as sombre and expressionless as ever, and maybe a little tired. One black eyebrow twitched impatiently as Grundo uttered cries of joy at the plate heaped with griddle cakes. But, after he had thundered forth a longer grace than usual, my grandfather looked at me briefly. There was just a flick of a smile for me, private between the two of us. Now, the smile seemed to say, you know some of my secret.

Yes, I thought, and some of that secret is that Sybil owns you for the moment. I can't tell you anything now. But I couldn't resist smiling back.

"That's better," my grandfather said as we sat down. "Arianrhod, you are too solemn. You should learn not to take things so hard. Your cause will be much better served if people perceive you as less tense and emotional."

Talk about the pot calling the kettle black! I thought. "Grandfather Gwyn," I said, "I have *reason* to be like this. I think Grundo and I should get back to the Progress as soon as possible."

"I agree," he said. "I have ordered the car for you. Be ready to start first thing tomorrow."

Grundo looked truly miserable. He had been enjoying himself thoroughly almost for the first time in his life. "In that case," he said, "could we have another plate of griddle cakes? I need to stock up."

My grandfather did his almost-smile again. "Certainly. And a packet to take with you when you go."

He was as good as his word. I think he always is.

When Grundo and I stumbled downstairs with our bags in the very early morning, my grandfather was waiting in the hall like a tall, black pillar, with a slightly greasy bag in his long, white hands. The hall was unusually sunny. The front door was open into the low sunlight and a melting green and gold distance beyond. The hearse-like car cut some of the light off as it came slowly crunching to a stop on the grass outside.

My grandfather passed Grundo the bag. "Olwen has put a packed breakfast for you in the car. Go in peace with my blessing."

He saw us to the car, but he didn't, to my secret relief, insist on a kiss or even try to shake hands. He just lifted one hand as the car started. The last we saw of him, he was turning, black and upright, to go back into the manse. The road tipped us down and round a corner almost at once, and all we saw was the green shoulders of mountains. I found I was sighing with regret as strong as Grundo's.

Olwen had provided the usual huge packets of sandwiches and cakes. We were eating for a good part of the long drive back and didn't pay much attention to the scenery – though I got the feeling we went a different way that was rather shorter. I certainly didn't recall the wide, sunny gorge we went through, or the full, grey river hurrying in the midst of it. But then, as Grundo said, until we spent these few strange days at the manse, neither of us had made a habit of watching the country as we travelled.

"You get trained out of it," Grundo said. "Scenery

just goes past and that's it."

We were both in a muddling mixture of regret at leaving and nervousness about what would happen when we were back with the Progress.

"I wonder what my mother will say," Grundo remarked. "I forgot to tell her I was going with you."

"My mam will have told her," I said. "And Sybil may have been too busy to be angry. You have to admit she's been hard at other things lately."

Our mix of feelings grew much fiercer as we saw the shape of Belmont Castle on its mound against the hot, blue sky. It had turned into a truly scorching day by then. I supposed that Dad was letting the weather stay fine still for the Meeting of Kings, but, as the car swept in through the massive castle gates and went winding up the gravel path past parched-looking trees, I began to think Dad might be overdoing things. He was on the way to causing a drought. It crossed my mind that this wasn't like Dad, but mostly I was realising that the driver was going to dump us at the castle door just where he had picked us up and wishing he wouldn't. Grundo looked at me. But we both knew now that it was no good trying to talk to this driver, so we said nothing while he drove in a smart circle on the gravel at the top and drew up with a crunch in front of the big double door of the castle. We said nothing but "Thank you" after that, when he opened the rear doors for us and plumped our bags down on the gravel. We stood clutching our packets of spare sandwiches and griddle cakes and watched the car drive away down the path, glimmering with the heat.

"He doesn't understand about the camp at all," Grundo said.

I agreed. In some way, that driver seemed to think that my grandfather's family was equal to the King's. We picked up our bags and humped them over to the steep way down into the camp.

And stood staring.

The field where the camp had been was empty. We could see old wheel-tracks and brown trodden paths and pale patches where tents had been, but not a sign of the Progress, not even the buses that usually went off last with us in them. Not a scrap of litter. Nothing. The field looked as if it had been empty for days.

"They've gone!" I said stupidly.

"They *can't* have gone long," Grundo said. "We've only been away three days and the King had to meet the Welsh King before they went. We'd better ask at the castle."

We left our bags and packets in a huddle overlooking the empty field and crunched over to the enormous front door, where we rang the polished brass bell-pull. We had to ring three times before there was any answer. By that time we were thinking that the castle was empty too.

Almost as we were ready to turn away, one of the halves of the double door was noisily unbarred and opened a little by a man in shirtsleeves. He may have been Sir James's butler. He stood half inside the opening looking annoyed at being disturbed. When he saw we were only children his face developed new sour creases. "Yes?" he said.

We both became very urgent in our best Court manners. "We're sorry to bother you," I said. "I'm Arianrhod Hyde and this is Ambrose Temple – Court wizards' children..."

"We were supposed to rejoin the Progress this morning," Grundo explained. "Can you possibly tell us...?"

"No use trying to join anything here," the man said, as if he didn't believe us. "Who are you trying to fool? The King left nearly a week ago now, right after he met with the Welsh King."

*Nearly a week*! I thought. This is *mad*! But I kept my Court manners and said politely, "Then perhaps you'll have a message for us from my parents. In the name of Hyde or Temple?"

"No. Sorry," said the man. He was obviously not sorry at all. "No one left any messages. Court just packed up and went."

I really could not believe this. My mother would always have left a note telling me the latest far-speaker codes at least. When I went to see Grandad Hyde in London, she usually hired a car for me as well, with instructions to follow the Progress even if it went somewhere unexpected.

While I was trying to think of a way to say this without accusing the man of lying, Grundo said, with great urgency, "Did they, by any chance, have another ceremony in the Inner Garden before they left?"

"They did," the man admitted. "Big do, for everyone to drink the waters. Went to it myself. What of it?"

"Just thank you," Grundo said politely.

I knew what had happened then. Mam had drunk the charmed water too and was now doing whatever Sybil wanted. And Sybil had always been only too ready to forget about me and Grundo. "Then have you," I asked the man, "any idea where the Progress is now? Please."

"*No* idea," the man said definitely and started to slide back inside the half-open door.

"Or where they were going?" Grundo put in quickly.

The man paused. I could see he was going to enjoy telling us. "Only know it was one of the big ports," he said. "King went to settle a dispute, where was it? Southampton? Liverpool? Somewhere like that. May have been Newcastle. Can't help you any more. Sorry." He slid inside and shut the door with a clash.

"You haven't helped us at *all*!" I more or less shouted at the closed door. "Grundo, he was lying, wasn't he?"

"I'm not sure. I think we need to know today's date," Grundo said.

"You mean," I said, "like the stories? More time's passed than we thought?"

Grundo nodded glumly.

We went over and picked up our belongings. There seemed no point staying here. We began trudging away down the hot gravel drive. About halfway to the gate, Grundo said, "I don't think they mean to do this thing with time, these people like your grandfather. Time's different for them. They probably just can't help it."

"That's all very well," I said, "but what shall we *do*?"

# PART SIX
# NICK

# CHAPTER THIRTEEN

✷

About five steps later, round the first bend in fact, was the weirdest city I'd ever been in.

I was in a crowded shopping arcade, surrounded by bustling, busy people. That was all I noticed at first, because everyone turned to stare at me. For a moment, I couldn't think what they were staring at, until I happened to see my reflection in the window of one of the big fancy shops inside the pillars of the arcade. I saw a sopping wet youth with a blue light standing up off the soaking hair on his forehead. *Anyone* would stare at that – particularly under the roof of a dry arcade.

I said "Damn!" and somehow managed to suck the witchlight into myself. I was not sure I was going to be able to get it back again, but I couldn't help that. The stares were really hostile. And it didn't help that everyone around me was really elaborately dressed. The women wore tight tops with loose sleeves and swirling skirts in bright colours, absolutely stiff with embroidery. The men had hip-hugging blouses and baggy trousers covered with embroidery too. I'd never seen so much embroidery in one place. The shop I could see myself in was selling rolls and rolls of differently embroidered cloth. I looked really out of place.

Get back and take the other path! I told myself. Quick!

But by that time I'd been swept along in the crowds quite some way, and jostled out towards the chest-high parapet lined with enormous pillars that seemed to separate the arcade from the street. I couldn't tell where the path was now. I'd just turned back to look for it, when everything went suddenly quiet and sedate, with almost no sound except hundreds of walking feet and music playing in the shops. It reminded me of the way everything goes law-abiding on a motorway when a police car drives past.

That was more or less what it was. The crowds drifted away sideways to make a clear space for two men in bright yellow who came slowly pacing through. They had embroidery too, in official-looking shield shapes, and more official embroidery on the fronts of their tall caps. The most noticeable thing about them, though, was the curly yellow sheepskin boots they wore from the knees down. It made their feet look vast. I remembered Dad once saying that you can always tell policemen by their boots. I'd never seen policemen who looked like this, but I knew at once what they were.

I also knew that I'd better keep out of sight. The best way seemed to be to cross the road, so I went on drifting towards the parapet with the rest of the crowd. I had a real shock when I got to the wall. It wasn't a road beyond it. It was a huge ravine.

It plunged down and down, hundreds of feet. And I could see it going up, quite as far, on the other side. What I had taken for the row of shops on the other side of the street was just one arcade in a whole stack of them, built one on top of another against the face of a cliff, rows of shops, rows of houses above and below, and rows of blank-looking factories lower down. Every so often, there were fancy iron bridges where people could get from one side of the city to the other.

Keeping half an eye on those slowly pacing policemen, I craned over sideways to see further. The place was all different canyons winding away in different directions, with more houses and shops stacked up the sides of them and more bridges between – as if the land here had cracked into a set of branching ravines and people had decided to live up the sides of them. It looked spectacular. There were huge cargo hoists, or perhaps lifts, in the spaces made by the massive pillars that held each layer of buildings up. Really complicated machinery, those were, painted in bright colours.

As the policemen paced slowly out of sight, I heard a sort of grinding and rushing coming from the depths below. There has to be a river down there, I thought, and I hitched myself on my stomach so that I could look down.

It wasn't a river, it was a train – two trains actually, like long silver bullets, coming smoothly into a stopping place far, far below. I watched tiny specks of people come milling out of the trains in the milky electric lighting down there.

By this time, I was really interested. Nobody seemed to be staring at me any more, so I decided to stay for a while. Two of the hoists across the way were working now, bringing the people up from the trains, and I told myself I'd look for the path when they'd stopped. I also told myself – knowing it was just an excuse – that the drunk had said I was supposed to help two more people on my way, and there were surely two I could help here. So I stayed hanging over the parapet.

Even if I hadn't been watching, I could have told when the hoists stopped at the level where I was. The crowd in the arcade suddenly doubled. I swung round to watch as it went in seconds from just busy to packed and hectic. People pushed past me both ways, treading on my feet and banging me with shopping bags. There was a roar of voices that made my head go round.

And I saw Romanov go past, only a foot away.

I leapt after him at once. I elbowed and pushed and barged and shouted, "Hey!" and "Excuse me!" and "Could you wait a moment, please?" whenever I thought he might hear me. He was quite easy to keep in sight because his jacket was white, with red and blue floral embroidery. Very few other people wore white. I kept him in sight for about a hundred yards, but I didn't catch up until we were level with one of the bridges. He had to slow down to turn out across it because he had two kids with him for some reason, and he wanted to make sure they kept with him. While he was stretching out to catch hold of the younger boy, I got near enough to tap him on the back of his embroidery. "Excuse me!" I panted.

He turned round and he wasn't Romanov. He wasn't even very *like* Romanov. His hair wasn't particularly dark and he wore glasses. Behind the glasses, his eyes were washy blue, and around the glasses his face was pale and haughty and thin without being jagged. He didn't even stand like Romanov. Romanov had had a sort of eager curve to him. This man was stiff and upright. And he was staring at me in utter outrage. I could feel my face flooding red as I stared back and wondered how on *earth* I'd managed to make such a mistake.

Then it got worse than embarrassing. The two kids grabbed my arms and they both began yelling. The big one had a voice that squawked and the small one went off like a train whistle. This made all the other people around start yelling too. That smaller kid was an utter brat. He kept pinching me, and twisting the pinches, until I'd had enough and I kicked him. At that, he screamed harder than ever and half the people near promptly grabbed me as well. In no time, I was sort of bent over under a heap of people and jerking about desperately to try to throw them off me.

Like that, I looked across and saw two pairs of yellow curly yeti-boots. I felt sick and dizzy, and I knew I was in real trouble then. "Look, it was a *mistake*!" I said.

Nobody listened to me. They all shouted at the policemen. Most of them seemed to be accusing me of picking the false Romanov's pocket, but there were other things they shouted that I didn't understand then. The brat kid went on screaming. The older kid squawked that I'd assaulted his brother. The false Romanov just stood there, looking outraged, as if simply touching him had been a crime. And there was an elderly blonde woman wearing pink and lilac embroidery which clashed horribly with the police uniforms, who grabbed a policeman by the arm and kept stabbing her finger at me, accusing me of nameless crimes.

Two more policemen arrived. They each took one of my arms and marched off with me, whatever I said. It wasn't far, just round the bend of the arcade, opposite the next hoist. They kicked open a door there and hauled me through. It was a police station. I could smell it was. There was a fellow with a moustache sitting behind a desk, looking very senior and important in lots more official yellow embroidery. He gave me a sarcastic glance and pointed with his thumb. The two policemen nodded and hustled me off into the depths of the place, where it was all carved out of the rock of the cliff. They kicked open another door there and threw me inside. While I was stumbling forward into the cell beyond, I saw the outside door burst open and all the rest of them come pouring through – false Romanov, both kids, pink lady and crowds more – all shouting accusations still.

Then the cell door shut with a bang and I couldn't hear them any more. There was a bunk-thing and I sat on it. There was a hole bored into the rock in the corner for a loo. Otherwise, there was nothing but walls that had been hacked out of rock and then whitewashed rather a long time ago. The only light came from a grille in the door and it was beastly cold.

I sat there trying to be angry for a while. But what I mostly felt was tired. I'd been having peculiar adventures now for more than a day and a night, and I suddenly found I'd had enough. I knew I was in bad trouble, but that didn't matter as much as the fact that I was exhausted. I lay down and went to sleep.

I must have slept for several hours. It seemed to be early evening when they came and woke me up. I suppose they'd meant to leave me there for long enough for me to get thoroughly intimidated, but if that *was* their idea, it misfired. You see, I am a total zombie just after I wake up.

It takes me half an hour even to get my eyes open. Ask anyone who knows me. I can't see, I can't talk properly, I can't do anything without help. The only thing I can do properly is think. And I know how to exploit my condition. I've had years of practice.

Anyway, the policeman fetching me shook me and shouted at me. If he did anything else, I didn't see because I couldn't get my eyes open. Eventually, he hauled on my arm and then poked my back. I stood up and walked into a wall. He pulled me straight and shoved me onwards. I wish I could have seen my progress to the front of the police station after that. I must have gone in zigzags. I kept hitting things and being pulled straight and then hitting something else. Two people kept shouting at me.

At length, they stood me still and I felt and smelt someone breathing into my face. "No, he's not blind. He's got his damned eyes shut," this man said. And he roared, "Open your eyes, Alph take you!"

I tried to explain. I meant to say, "I'm afraid I can't yet," but it came out as "Frayed auntie."

"What's *wrong* with you?" the policeman howled. "Is it some drug?"

"No, it's sleeping on an empty stomach," I said – except that it came out as "Nah, nah, empsa."

"He must be foreign," decided the second policeman.

"Yeh, yeh, yeh," I said, because that was true. "I've been a foreigner three times since yesterday," I added – or rather, "I'm before threems stay."

The second policeman, who was clearly the important one – he smelt importantly of some vile aftershave, like peaches boiled in burnt plastic – said fretfully, "I've never heard of this place Threems. Have you?"

"No," said the other one. "Do I write it down?"

"Name first," said Important. And he shouted at me, "*Name!*"

For some reason, I can always say my name. I said, "Nick Mallory," and it only came out a little slurred.

"Enter that and then search him," said Important. "Enter any ID or stolen property." I heard heavy footsteps and a creaking as Important paced away and sat down somewhere in front of me, and a pen scratching as the other policeman wrote. Then I felt him dig in my pockets. There were chinkings and exasperated noises. As far as I could tell, they'd found fifty-six p, my two tenners and my door key. I hoped they'd give the key back because Dad is always losing his.

"Foreign money," said the ordinary policeman, "and this flat metal thing. Could be a key."

"Keep it for analysis," said Important. "It might be a talisman."

"Wommy key," I said.

"But he can't have stolen this money here," Important went on, ignoring me, "because the revered Prayermaster was only carrying normal Loggia City currency."

"These notes are written in Loggian though," the other policeman said, puzzled.

"He probably stole them in some other world. Not a problem," Important said. "We'll deal with the serious charge *here* now. *You*!" he bawled at me. "Open your eyes!"

"Car do tha yeh," I explained.

"Write down obstructing the law," Important said. "And you, listen carefully." Because he thought I was foreign, he spoke very loudly to me and got louder and louder as he went on. "You have been accused of raising witchlight in a public place..."

So that's what the angry pink lady was on about! I thought.

"...and this is a very serious crime," Important boomed. "If proven, it means prison for life without option. The prison here is down under the railway lines. You won't enjoy it. So think very carefully before you answer my questions and tell me the exact truth. Are you a witch?"

"No," I said.

"But you know how to raise witchlight, don't you?" he yelled cunningly. "And that..."

"No, I don't," I said.

"...automatically makes you a witch. What did you say?" he howled.

"Don't. Can't. Never knew how," I said. By this time I was trying with all my might to speak properly. "Silly wom'n. Eyes bad. No glasses."

There was a bit of a silence at that. The ordinary

policeman said, "This is the fourth charge of witchcraft Mizz Jocelyn has laid this year. None of the others…"

"I know, I know," Important said irritably, "but the Prayermasters are after us to make our quota. What am I supposed to do?"

"Arress Mizz Jocelyn," I suggested.

"*Shut up!*" they both howled at me.

There was another silence. I could hear the pen scratching again and Important tapping away irritably on something. I supposed he was drumming his fingers while he thought how to prove I was a witch. By this time, my eyes were beginning to unstick. A very strong sense of self-preservation caused me to force my eyelids apart just a crack. I could see Important as a blur of yellow, lit sideways by distant sunlight. "Bellving field normal," he was murmuring. "Telepathic field up a bit – not much on its own. Power almost zero…"

My eyes shot halfway open without my having to try. The sun glinted off a set of brass and glass instruments, all little cogs and swivelling shiny rods, arranged in front of Important and all pointed at me. He was not drumming his fingers. He was tapping away at brass knobs and reading things off dials.

I knew I should be really alarmed, but I was still too sleepy. I simply sank back into my zombie state and concentrated on being only half awake. If his instruments were registering the way I am when I've just woken up, I wasn't going to interfere. Important's irritable face was coming clearer to me now. He was the one with the moustache. It was a huge, bushy one.

"Recent ritual barely shows," Important said. "This is completely inconclusive, damn it!"

"So we go with the vagrancy charge for now?" the other policeman asked.

"Seems like it," said Important. He started booming at me again. "You! Stand straight while I talk to you!" I did my best. I sort of re-slouched. "Better," he said, "but not much. Public Works will soon teach you proper behaviour. You've been lucky, very lucky. The honoured Prayermaster you attacked said he wouldn't prefer charges and your witch-readings are only high enough to be suspicious. One notch more and you'd be above the legal limit. You'd be on your way to jail by now. As it is, I'm only detaining you on a charge of vagrancy. This is what happens to anyone we pick up who's not carrying a Loggia entry-permit or Loggia currency. You're under curfew from this moment – understand? Are you listening?"

I nodded.

"Curfew," he said. "That means you must report to the Clerk of Public Works on Level Fourteen before sunset. Their office will assign you work in the cloth factories and give you somewhere to sleep. If you're found wandering any time after that, you get an automatic prison sentence. Understand?"

I nodded again.

"Right," he said. "I'm legally obliged to hand you this token. Here it is. Come on. Take it."

I put out my hand and he passed me a big round disc of some kind. I didn't look at it. I was staring at him and wondering if he ever breathed that moustache of his in. It was so big and fluffy, he could suffocate in his sleep. I wondered if I hoped he did. He was only doing his job, I supposed.

"This token entitles you to one free meal and one free night's sleep," he said. "After that, you'll have to work for a living like the rest of us do. Take him to the steps, Wright, and send him on his way."

"Don't I get my money and my key back?" I said.

"No," he said. "All vagrant property is forfeit to the city. Get going. You've only got an hour before sunset."

And I love you too! I thought, as the other policeman grabbed my arm and pulled me away to the outer door.

Outside, under the arches, the low sun glared in my eyes quite painfully from just above the opposite cliff. There seemed to be far fewer people around. Those who were around all looked fastidiously away as the policeman hauled me the few yards to the corner, where the massive tower was with the stairs and the lifts in it. The light was dim enough under it for me to be able to focus on the big fancy notices on its walls. LEVEL ELEVEN, one said. HAVE PASSES READY AT ALL TIMES said the next. And the rest had arrows pointing to LIFTS, STAIRS, MAIN SHOPPING ARCADE, CLOTH FAIR.

"Can I use the lift?" I asked the policeman.

"Lifts cost money," he said and pushed me towards STAIRS. "Get climbing. All the eateries on Fourteen will take your token, but you'll only have time to eat if you hurry. When the sun sets, you'll hear a hooter. If you haven't got to the PW Office by then you'll be liable to arrest."

A train came in down in the depths while he was talking, with a rush and a rumble and a wave of warm, smelly air. I thought how it must feel to be in a prison cell under those trains. I started climbing.

They were wide, elegant, cleanly cut stone steps, lit by fancy lamps overhead. I went up and up until I was sure that my feet would be out of sight of the policeman – if he bothered to wait and watch, that was – and then I stopped under a light and looked at the token. It was a big, white, enamel circle with blue enamel lettering on it. On one side it said Loggia City Public Works and when I turned it over it said 1 standard meal, sleep 1.

This is all it takes to make you an official vagrant, I thought. I put the disc in my pocket and went on climbing to the next level. Fairly naturally, I expected it to be Level Twelve.

Not a bit of it. The next notice I came to said →LEVEL ELEVEN A → *Residences 69-10042*, pointing to even grander stairs on the right, and the one further up after that pointed off to the left, saying ← LEVEL ELEVEN B ← *House of Prayer for Holy Jazepta, College of High Prayermaster.* The steps to this bit were brightly whitewashed, while the ordinary steps climbed on, straight ahead. It looked as if the levels were staggered up the cliff, not in straight rows as I'd thought. Level Twelve was quite a long climb further up and nothing like so exclusive. The stairs had hollows from people climbing them and the notice there just said ← SHOPS →.

My legs ached by then – you know how they do when you're short on sleep – so I wandered out on Twelve to take a rest. It was all small shops as far as I could see, spilled out like stalls into the arcade, very well-lit and cheerful and busy. I could see jewellery and veg, books and clothes, toys and bread. After that, the pillars got in the way. It was so cheerful there that I stood staring until I began to shiver. My clothes were still quite damp and I noticed the chill when I wasn't moving. I thought of dungeons under the railway and went back to the stairs.

I think Twelve A and Twelve B just said HOUSES and numbers, and Thirteen the same, though I was in a blur of climbing by then and didn't pay much attention, except to notice that the steps were much more worn and dirty by then and the lights on the ceiling weaker. But I snapped to attention at Thirteen B. The notices there said ← SEX and DRUGS →.

"That's frank, at least!" I panted. I wanted to stop and take a look, both ways, but I seemed to have been climbing for ages by then and I was starving hungry. With the luck I'd been having in this place, I knew someone was just going to have served me up my One Standard Meal when the sunset hooter would go and I wouldn't have time to eat it. So I put on speed, up really grotty steps that were cracked and crooked and filthy, with rubbish piled in the corners, and got up to Level Fourteen at last.

The first thing I saw there was a red and white enamel notice over the stairs to the next level. CAUTION it said, HIGH LEVELS OF RADIATION BEYOND THIS POINT.

"Oh, *fun*!" I said and I was glad I didn't have to go up there. The notices pointing each way along Level Fourteen said a whole list of factories, and the one pointing to the right added at the bottom, PUBLIC WORKS OFFICE, *Open Sunrise – Sunset*. "Right," I said and went that way. I could smell food along there too.

The arcade there was much lower and narrower, and it was held up by big square pillars that I could see were just meant to support radioactive Level Fifteen and the rest, and nothing to do with being pretty. The floor was black and sort of tarry. But the first thing I came to was a whole row of little caffs, crammed in together under the pillars, and those were all I could attend to by then. It was *hours* since those scarmbled eggs. I went along the row, looking.

That policeman had lied to me. Some of the caffs had menus in the windows saying "Fresh Scoppins, 3 tokes" or "5 bindals, 4 tokes" and several had stacks of coloured stickers showing you which factory they took tokens from, but only one had a notice saying "PW tokes taken here". So I had to go into that one.

It was a really depressing Greasy Spoon, one of those places where the windows are running with sweat from the cooking and lighted with raw, greenish strips that don't give any light. People were queueing for food at a glassed-in counter at the far end, where a dreary, fat woman in an apron was slapping food on plates and calling out things like, "You need another toke for bindals," and "Peslow's run out now." When they'd got their plates, the people sat wearily down at worn plastic tables to eat it. The only thing that seemed to be free was the drink people kept fetching from a spigot in the wall. It looked yellowish and a little fizzy.

I stood for a moment to get the hang of things. Everyone wore embroidery here too, only it was all shabby, with threads hanging out or pieces from other patterns darned in. Even the fat woman's apron was old embroidery.

She glared at me and jerked her chin. I held out my token. "This gets you nipling and colly or klaptico. That's all," she said, tapping the food-troughs with her big wooden spatula. "Which is it? Hurry up."

Klaptico looked swimmy and greasy and grey. Nipling was white and had a sort of look of mashed potatoes. It looked filling, so I chose that. She poured orange colly over it and then snatched my token away and stamped it with a huge black stamp.

"So don't think you can use it twice," she snapped,

sticking the token into the nipling like an ice-cream wafer. She handed me the plate, token and all. "Spear and spoon on the tray at the end."

The eating implements were a sort of spike and a mini-shovel. I picked up one of each and took my plate to a free table. All the other people sort of bent away from me as I went. Then they bent away again when I went to get myself a drink. Yes, I thought, working the spigot, I'm a vagrant. You don't know where I've been!

I was really puzzled by the drink. It tasted rusty and sweetish. "What is this stuff?" I asked the woman at the nearest table, as politely as I could.

She looked at me as if I was mad. "Water," she said.

"Oh," I said.

I turned back to my plate and took a look to see how other people were using their spike and shovel. They were spiking and shovelling, so I did that too. And after one shovelful I was wishing I'd had klaptico instead. Nipling was hot, like horse radish, and colly was another kind of hot, like salty chile. I had to keep going for more of the weird water, wondering each time if it was poisoning me, but I was so hungry that I ate every scrap. I swear I could taste nipling for the next twenty-four hours.

I put my plate and my glass in the bins near the counter and left, thankfully. Then feeling a good deal better but a bit fiery around the middle, I went along the black, blocky arcade until I came to a long brown building with hardly any windows and a large door covered with blue and white enamel notices. PUBLIC WORKS OFFICE. OPENING HOURS 08.00 – 16.00. DO NOT DISTURB NIGHTSHIFT UNLESS AN EMERGENCY. NO LOITERING. NO MONEY EXCHANGED FOR TOKENS, and scads of others. I stared at them all for a while until I saw one notice all by itself in the door jamb. INSERT PW TOKEN TO OPEN DOOR, it said and underneath it was a slit like a letterbox.

I thought, I don't want to do this. But I thought that Important was bound to have phoned up to this place and told them I was on my way. I thought of the prison under the trains. And I got out my nipling-coated token and posted it into the slit.

It went down with an almighty clanging crash. It made me jump.

It made me jump so hard that I realised that I'd been half asleep until then. I'd been doing what I was told like a zombie. Now I was wide awake all of a sudden, and quivering. And *angry*. Why should I be sent to work in a cloth factory like a slave, when all I'd done was mistake someone for Romanov? And I still hadn't found Romanov. I was supposed to help two more people before I could find him, and after that I'd promised to help that girl. Roddy. It dawned on me that I'd have to *mean* to help her or she wouldn't count as one of the people I'd helped. Instead, I was letting myself be stuck in this awful place. And that was stupid. Pathetic, really.

I turned away from the notice-studded door and ran back along the arcade, past the caffs, until I came to the stairs. I knew they'd look for me going down them. So I dived up the next flight, under the notice that warned about RADIATION.

# CHAPTER FOURTEEN

*

*M*y plan was quite simple. I was going to sit on those stairs, just high enough to be out of sight, until I heard the police come up. Then when they went back down looking for me, I was going to follow them and be behind them when they thought I was in front.

It didn't work out that way. That set of steps turned out to be quite short. There were no lights in the roof and the stairs were made of cracked and slippery white tiles. Unlike all the other flights, they curved, and as soon as I had climbed round the curve, and was feeling pleased that I was out of sight already, I saw sunset light up ahead. I realised I must have come to the very top of the cliff.

After that, I was too interested to stop. I wanted to see what was causing the dangerous radiation. I went on up.

The first thing I saw, before I was really at the top, was a tall, wire fence quite a long way overhead and another of those enamel notices fixed to it, beautifully lit by the flaring sun. AIRFIELD KEEP OUT. As I climbed slowly and cautiously up the last steps, I could see that the fence was actually on top of rows of small houses that backed on to the last piece of the cliff. The houses were all different and all sort of cottage-sized. After the buildings on the lower levels, they struck me as more like dollshouses or dog kennels, and the paint on them was blistered and peeling.

This must be where the poor people live, I thought. I went up the last few steps and saw the poor people.

There were crowds of them, all sitting out on the flat rock in front of the little houses. Every one of the grown-ups was working away at embroidery, so that the place sort of heaved and flashed as far as I could see both ways, with arms moving and needles catching the light. Kids were darting about, bringing things. Every so often, someone would say, "We need more number nine red," or "Bring me the one-two-five flower pattern," and a child would dart off to get it. There wasn't room to walk among the busy people and the spread-out cloths they were sewing at, so the kids mostly had to run along the very edge of the cliff. There were no pillars here and no wall. It looked terrifying.

I stood where I was or I would have trodden on someone, or put my big, dirty shoe in the middle of a bright flower pattern on one side, or a wreathing green-gold embroidery on the other. And I had hardly stood for a second when a plane of some kind took off from the airfield with a huge tinny whirring. I could tell it flew by quite different methods from the ones I knew. It zoomed right over our heads and I nearly fell back down the steps trying to duck. A boy standing with his toes curled round the edge of the cliff never even swayed. He gave me a jeering look.

I pretended not to see him and watched the plane go whirring away across the flat and sandy tops of all the cliffs. It looked almost like unbroken desert from up here, with just a few dark, wriggly cracks to show where the city canyons were. In the distance, where it seemed to turn into solid desert, I could see something shining orange in the sunlight. The plane seemed to be making for this shining thing.

"Do you mind if I ask you a question?" I said to the man beside my right leg. He was old, and I didn't really like to look at him, because he had a growth of some kind down one side of his face. It blocked one of his eyes and went on down to mix with his straggly beard.

He seemed quite friendly. He went on sewing away and said, "Ask away, lad," in what sounded like a strong country accent.

"Then, is the radiation from the planes in the airfield?" I said.

"No, no, that's from the sun," he said, and bit off his blue-green yarn and threaded his needle with more, all in one movement like a conjuring trick.

He bent to the embroidery again and a woman just beyond, sewing at the same cloth – only she was using golden green – said, "You shouldn't really be up here before sunset, my dear." She had a growth too, an oozy one, on her sewing arm.

"Yes, but they arrested me for a vagrant," I said.

"Ah, they do that," someone else said, from the flower embroidery on my other side. "They're always needing workers to make cloth for us."

By this time everybody seemed friendly. A lot of children who weren't fetching things at that moment came scampering along the edge of the cliff and balanced by the top of the stairs to stare at me. "Where are you from?" a girl asked me.

"Earth," I said.

They all laughed. "Silly!" said the girl. "*This* is Earth and you're not from here!"

"Yes, but," I said, "there are a lot of Earths. I think I've been on at least three lately."

"Ooh!" said a little one right behind me. "You mean, like Romanov?"

That made me jump. I came out in gooseflesh with excitement. "Romanov?" I said. "Has *Romanov* been here?"

"Yes, indeed," said the old man beside my leg. "He was here earlier today. He comes through quite often, you know – to gain altitude, he says. In the other worlds he goes to, the ground is higher than Level Eleven, so he comes in at Eleven and leaves from here."

"Romanov's been very good to us," said the woman with the growth on her arm.

"Surely has," the old man agreed. "He brings a new sunshield spell for us every time he comes by. My grandchildren can grow up without getting something like this." He left off sewing for an instant and tapped at the growth on his face. It sounded like someone patting a crusty loaf. "A good man, Romanov. Do you know him well?"

"I only met him this morning," I said. "At least – I *think* it was this morning, but it may have been yesterday. I'm trying to find him again. Do you know where he went?"

The old man shrugged as he sewed. "Back home by now, I'd think. You want to go back down to Eleven and go from there."

"You should go back down anyway, dear," the woman with the bad arm said. "The sun's doing you no good, even low as it is."

"You can do *ten minutes*!" the girl balancing beside me asserted. "Romanov *told* me."

Ten minutes, I thought. I want to find out everything I can in those ten minutes. I pointed up at the wire fence.

"How do they manage up in the airfield, if the radiation's that bad?"

A chuckle ran round everyone near. "They come up through trapdoors in fat white suits!" someone called out, three embroideries over.

"They do most of the flying by night," someone else said. "Loggia people do a lot by night. It's safest."

I looked over at the bright speck of the plane in the distance. It was coming down to land near the shiny things. "Brave pilot," I said.

"Oh, no. The planes are all protected," the old man said. "Prayermasters put spells on them."

"Oh," I said. "And what's that shiny place over there where the plane went?"

"Those are called xanadus," a kid behind me said.

"Though don't ask us why," the old man added. "They're the domes where they grow all the vegetables and suchlike."

"Nipling?" I asked.

Everyone laughed and groaned. "That stuff!"

While we were laughing, the sun went down. Just like that, it was blue dark. Lights came on the next second, fixed to the houses. To my surprise, everyone bent over the embroidery and went on sewing as if nothing had happened, including the old man, who was laughing so hard that the growth on his face jiggled. It looked like a rat clinging to him.

A second or so later, hooters sounded from below, all

over the city, lots of loud, howling noises like a herd of unhappy cows. That's it! I thought. I'm illegal now.

"That nipling!" the old man said, speaking through the howling. I could tell he was so used to the hooters that he hardly noticed them. "I tell you, they have a hard job *stopping* nipling growing! Comes up all over in their flowerpots, whatever they do. They keep trying to give it away. But we won't have it, workers won't touch it. I heard they feed it to the prisoners these days."

I shuddered. I could still taste the stuff. I thought of jail under the railways and a diet of nipling, and I suddenly felt very anxious indeed. "What do you think I should do?" I said. "You said I'd need to go down to Level Eleven, but I'll be arrested now the hooters have gone."

"They give you half an hour's grace," the woman with the bad arm said.

The old man chuckled again. "Didn't tell you that, did they? They like to keep you frightened in Public Works. But you'd be surprised how many curfew people seem to get held up on the stairs, getting back to their workhouses. I've known some who get delayed for whole nights." He raised his head for a moment. I think he was winking, but he did it with the eye that was mixed up with the growth and I wasn't sure.

"Thanks," I said. "Thanks for telling me."

"You're welcome," he said. "But before you go, do you mind if we ask *you* a question – me and my sons and daughters?" His hand went out, with the needle in it, and he wasn't sewing, for a wonder; he was pointing to the six other people round the green embroidery, including the woman with the bad arm.

"Fine," I said. "Go ahead."

I supposed he was going to ask me what I was doing here. I told you, I'm very self-centred. But he said, "This big square we're doing, it's a new idea of mine. It's not finished yet, but take a look at it. Think of yourself as a very rich man and tell me if you'd want to spend good money on it, and why."

Actually, I am pretty rich. *Very* rich really. But I was ashamed to tell him and I didn't think he'd have believed me anyway. I looked down at the square. I'd been admiring it out of the corner of my eye even before the sun set. Now the lights were on it, it was like something alive and growing, all greens and golds and coils that seemed almost to move. There were still white patches all over it where they hadn't embroidered yet, but I could see the main design and it was *fabulous*.

"It's fabulous!" I told them. "I'd pay a *lot*. It's one of the most beautiful things I've ever seen." It came into my mind that Dad would love it. He'd been talking about wanting something to hang on the wall of his study. He said he was sick of staring at a blank wall. If I could have thought of a way to pay for it and get it home, I'd have put in an order for it then and there.

The old man said, "Now, here's our question. If you

were this rich man, what would you do with our square when you'd bought it?"

"Hang it on the wall," I said. "Just have it there and stare at it. It would be different every time I looked at it, I know it would."

The old man banged his knee delightedly. "There, you *see*!" he said. It was clear they'd had a few family arguments about his new idea. Everyone else sewing on it glanced up at me and beamed, looking relieved.

"Well, it's good to know we're not working for nothing," the woman with the bad arm said. "I'd hate to think of it cut up for clothing." Then she called out to the smallest kid balancing beside me. "Sibbie, go down and tell him when there's no one about on Fourteen. But go careful. I don't want you ending up in a factory."

This made everything much simpler. I waved goodbye and followed Sibbie down the slippery tiled stairs to the bend. When she beckoned from the bottom to show it was all clear, I scudded down and across the tarry floor of Fourteen and went galloping away between the drifts of rubbish on the next lot of stairs.

There were a lot of people on the stairs below those, and more the further down I got. Voices and footsteps and loud music sounded from nearly every level I came to. What they'd told me was true: people did a lot at night here. I suppose it was safer not to come out in the sunlight, even on the lower levels.

When I met the first crowds, around the SEX, DRUGS

221

level, I was quite scared. But I noticed that there was not a single policeman about on the stairs. If I were them, I'd have patrolled the stairs all the time, but that must have seemed like too much hard work to them in those curly yellow boots. So I kept a look on my face that said, "I'm not important and I know just what I'm doing," and went on pushing and galloping my way down. Nobody even looked at me.

I went a bit more cautiously when I got to the *House of Prayer* notice. There was loud, droning chanting coming from there, which gave me a sort of fizzing feeling. Magic being done, I thought. Must be official magic. Go carefully. Anyway, my knees were aching by then. I went down the last flights very sedately and slowed right down when I got near Level Eleven. Easy to do. That last stretch was pretty crowded. I slid slowly down with my back against the wall and looked over people's heads at the Level Eleven archway below.

Before long, I saw a couple of policemen parade past down there, parting the crowd like butter. Good. I knew they wouldn't parade back for at least five minutes. I put on speed and hurried out under the massive arch, along the way that I'd been coming from when I'd thought I'd seen Romanov. I *still* couldn't see how I made that stupid mistake.

It was really lively along that arcade. People were laughing, talking, strolling along, listening to a group of musicians, applauding and rushing in and out of the brightly lit shops. Some of those were still selling embroidered cloth. I saw the identical patterns I'd seen being sewn up on Level Fifteen. But some shops seemed to have turned into dance halls or places to drink, and I had real trouble recognising the one opposite where I'd first come out. I worked out that it had been a bit along from one of the hoists, and in the end I was sure it must be the one where people were sitting out at tables, pouring drinks from big, fancy teapots and eating sticky cakes.

I looked for the path, sort of sideways-on from everything. And there it was, dark and steep and rocky, and glistening faintly with rain. It was just the shop that had changed. I shot into that path like a rat up a drainpipe.

I was in pitch dark the next second and stumbling about on that rocky surface, where I found myself sort of replaying in my mind those last instants before I shot into the darkness. It seemed to me that I had seen some familiar faces staring at me as I went. One was definitely Mizz Jocelyn, only she had changed for the evening from pink and mauve into beige and violent green. Another was a man in a suit embroidered like a flowerbed. He had this big, fluffy moustache, and it seemed to me that he could have been Important having an evening out in ordinary clothes – if you could call a bed of dahlias ordinary. There was another one too, a sharp-faced boy about my own age. I thought he might just have been that Prayermaster's elder son...

But they were there in that mad city and I was here,

now, in the path. I felt my way over to the left-hand wall and kept my hand trailing along the gritty, wet rockface until I felt the promontory that had divided the two branching paths. I swung round into the right hand fork there in triumph.

Or modified triumph anyway.

It was wet and pitch dark, and I couldn't seem to make another of those blue flames whatever I did. The drunk had only *given* it to me. He hadn't told me how to do it myself. I fumbled my way on, feeling less and less triumphant. I still had two people to help before I could get anywhere and, as soon as I remembered that, I began feeling really tired. I almost lay down on the wet rock and went to sleep. The only thing that stopped me was a strong notion that if I did, I wouldn't get up again. The slitherings and flappings were back again. They sounded hungry to me.

I tried singing, like the drunk. But that came out wavering and scared. So I tried to think about something else. I thought about Loggia City. What a crazy system it was, putting the people who did the embroidery right at the top where the sun would kill them. If they all died, the shops would have nothing to sell! I was really glad that Romanov was giving them sunshield spells. It proved that Romanov was a good thing and I was not making a mistake trying to find him.

I tried not to think of the way Romanov had despised me.

I thought about the girl, Roddy, instead. If she hadn't wanted me to deal with her politics, I'd have made a real effort to get through to her. She was quite something. I kept getting a sort of jolt every time I remembered the way she had stood balanced on that hillside. But she had looked at me as if I was a sort of tool and I didn't go for that. And I just couldn't see myself, not ever, doing anything about Kings and Merlins and suchlike. I'd gone out of my way, after all, not to have anything to do with ruling or rulers. No, that would have to wait for a few years.

On I went. I was trying to imagine what Roddy would be like in a few years' time, and getting a bit eager about it, when I noticed that the path had widened out a lot. Everything was just a little lighter and my feet echoed in a different way.

Damn! How am I going to know if a path I need goes off to the right? I thought. I got myself to the middle and sort of groped along there with one hand out in front.

And something groped back at me.

It sort of dabbed at me, whatever it was, wet and cold and desperate. It groped at my hand and then at my face. I went backwards with a shriek and sat down in a puddle. It had felt like a snake. But the thing shrieked and went backwards too. The ground shook under my behind. I sat staring, shaking all over. There was just enough grey light for me to pick out what seemed to be a couple of small trees, with the snake coiling this way and that down from them. I thought I must have walked into a forest.

"Oh, *please!*" said the forest – unless it was the snake. "*Help* me! I'm lost! I'm *stuck!*"

"What kind of a snake are you?" I said.

"I'm *not* a snake! I'm an elephant!" it said despairingly.

Elephants that talked now! I thought. But I'd already met a panther that I could understand, so why not? It was all one long, mad dream.

"It's more like a nightmare, *I* think," the elephant objected. "And I'm not exactly talking. You must be good at picking up four-legged thoughts. *Please* help me!"

I could hear its huge feet shuffling and grinding about just in front of me. It was in a bad state and it probably couldn't see me any more than I could see it. I was likely to be trodden on any second. I got up quickly. "OK, OK," I said out loud. "I'm supposed to help you anyway. Where do you want to go?"

"Not *this* way!" it said. "It's all so dark and I can't turn *round!*"

It began trumpeting then, ear-splitting squeals, and trampling in panic. I was terrified too. I thought it was going mad.

"*Stop it!*" I bellowed. "Shut up this moment or I won't help you!"

It shut up almost at once. I got the feeling it was used to humans yelling at it. "Sorry," it said meekly.

"That's better," I said. "Getting in a panic in this

place just makes it worse. Where are you from? How did you get here?"

"I was in the circus, outside the big top," it said, "waiting for my turn to go on, when all of a sudden there was this great whirling wind. All the tents came down or blew away, and people were screaming. I'm afraid I screamed too and ran away. I found a path that looked safe and I ran and ran, until it all got too narrow and..." It was starting to trample and puff.

"Steady, steady!" I said. "What did they call you in your circus?"

The trampling stopped. "Mini," the elephant admitted, sounding ashamed.

I couldn't help laughing.

"Short for Pudmini," the elephant said haughtily. "I'm a *lady* elephant."

"And I'm a gentleman human," I said, "and how I got here's a long story. My name's Nick – short for Nichothodes, if you want to know – and I'm on my way to see someone called Romanov. He'll be able to help both of us. So, if you just let me help you turn round..."

"I *can't* turn round!" Mini protested. "It's not *wide* enough!"

"Yes, it is," I said before she got too hysterical again. "Or I can guide you backwards..."

"I'm not *good* at going backwards!" she said frantically.

"Then we'll go forwards," I said, "very steadily and carefully." I managed to reach up, find her waving trunk and grab it. "Come along," I said. I made myself sound really firm, to disguise from both of us that I'd never handled an elephant before and hadn't a clue how you did it. "Forward carefully," I said, just as if I knew.

Have you ever tried to turn a panic-stricken elephant round in the dark, in a space that is probably too small, which you never saw before anyway? Don't try it. It's awful. I'd never have tried it if I'd seen anything else to do. You end up weak at the knees and ready to give up. I kept making soothing noises. Mini shook like an earthquake and squealed that she *couldn't* and I was hurting her trunk. I fumbled about and found one of her great thick tusks, but she didn't like that either.

"I've still got my harness on. Why don't you take hold of that?" she said.

I felt about again and found jingly leather somewhere on her huge face. It was all thick and wet and slimy in the rain, but I took hold of it and pulled her confidently sideways. This caused her to stick slantwise across the path. She nearly did go mad then. The noise was horrible. I was going, "Stop it, stop it, stop it! Or I'll go away and leave you here! Calm *down*!" and she was going, "Oh, I can't, I *can't*!"

"Stand *still*!" I screamed at her. "Where's the back of you?"

"Jammed right up against the cliff. I want to *kick*!"

"Well, don't," I said. "It won't help. What you need to do now is walk your front feet up the cliff this side until you're reared up, and then walk your back feet forward away from the cliff behind you. After that, you walk your *front* feet round to the left, so you come down facing the other way. Can you do that?"

"I don't *know*!" she said.

"You can," I said.

I'd never have got her to do it if she hadn't been brought up to trust humans. She'd been trained to stand on her hind legs and that helped too. But she kept losing her sense of direction halfway. I got her reared up twice with no end of rasping and elephant grunting, and twice she came down facing the wrong way. I only just dodged in time. In the end, I had to go right up to her and lean hard against her, and then keep her going the right way by walking my feet up and round on the cliff beside hers.

She went round sideways like a house tearing open. There was such a scraping and rending that I was sure she'd broken a tusk at least. Then there was a horrible moment when I was being ground against the cliff by her big, warm side. I was curled into a crouch with my face on my thighs and my knees crunching against rock. I felt her going the wrong way again and tried to uncurl to push her. And then uncurled again as if my life depended on it. Perhaps it did. And she went round at last. She came down quite lightly. Elephants can be pretty nimble when they want. And Mini did want. She was so glad to be loose that she went away down the path at a thundering gallop, while I slid down the cliff and sat in another puddle, quite sure that I'd lost both kneecaps and at least one big toe.

# CHAPTER FIFTEEN

✳

*M*ini stopped and waited for me about fifty yards on. I could see her enormous ears spreading anxiously against the dim sky as I limped after her.

"Are you all right? I haven't hurt you, have I?" She was a thoroughly considerate elephant. When I reached her, she said, "I'd prefer it if you'd take hold of my harness again. I feel safer that way."

I think that was considerate too. I grabbed hold gratefully and practically leant on her as we walked the last part. It turned out not to be far, just time for my knees to stop throbbing and my toe to start behaving normally. By that time, we could almost see the crags at each side of the path. Then a moment or so after that, we sort of came down sideways on to the rest of the world and out on to a wet, green slope, where Mini's feet went *suck, suck, suck* in the grass. And we were in wonderful, bright, pinkish light.

Mini went, "Oh! I've gone blind in one eye!" and started to panic again.

Her harness turned out to have been pink and scarlet, with silver decorations. Part of it was that kind of flat hat that goes on top of an elephant's head, and she had scraped it sideways on the cliff, so that it draped across her eye and one tusk. Her tusks, I was glad to see, had been banded with metal and neither of them had been broken.

"No, you haven't gone blind!" I told her. "Put your head down so that I can reach it."

She nodded her head down at once. She was really well trained. I hauled the whole wet, heavy lot of harness down across her face and her trunk so that it fell chinking down her legs and she could step out of it.

"*That's* a relief!" she said and blinked around with her big grey eyes. Elephants have ridiculously long, shaggy eyelashes. "It's sunset!" she said.

"Making my third in two days," I said, turning to look.

The sun was behind me, flaring pink and gold paths over sheets of water as far as I could see. The sound of water rippled and husked and whispered everywhere. Everything smelled of water, softly and strongly.

"Where are we?" Mini said.

"Romanov's place," I said. As soon as I was facing the water, I had no doubt of it. The water was all joined up to look like one sea or a huge lake, but the part on my left was clear blue like sea around a coral coast, with little waves frilling on white sand, and the part in front of me was muddy and rippling against rushes. Round to the right, the rushes were taller, but the grey water there was coming in fairly big waves and the rushes were blowing in a wind we couldn't feel. You could see the lines dividing the different kinds of water if you half closed your eyes. They rayed outwards towards the horizon like huge slices of pizza. Even the sun, setting in the midst of red and purple clouds, was divided into an orange part and a smaller slice that was much redder. It looked really odd. I remembered Dave saying that Romanov lived on an island that was made from parts of several worlds, and I knew where we were.

I also knew that if Romanov was here, then we were going to meet his big spotted cat any moment. I was suddenly not quite as glad to have got here as I had been.

"Oh, dear," Mini said. She was shuffling her front feet, and one of her back legs was rubbing up and down the other. She looked like an enormous, embarrassed schoolgirl. "Do you think there's anything to eat in this peculiar place? I'm so hungry."

I remembered reading somewhere that an elephant can be a match for a tiger. I swallowed a bit and said, "We'll go and ask. But if we happen to meet a whitish creature about so big…" I showed her with my hand halfway up my chest "…er, do you think you can, well, you know, sort of kick it? Or trample it, perhaps?"

"I *suppose* I could," she said doubtfully. "Is it fierce?"

"Yes," I said. "But it's all right if Romanov's with it. It does what he says."

"Oh, good," she said.

We turned away from the patchwork water and climbed the grassy rise to the high part of the island. My eyes were going this way and that, dreading the sight of that big cat. Mini's trunk flapped wistfully towards a big clump of trees in the distance, that were three kinds of green from the patchwork effect.

"I could eat those," she said.

"Romanov won't like it," I said. "Come on." We crossed a dividing line into yellower grass and pushed warily through some bushes – or I did; Mini trampled them, and if the cat had been in there we'd have known, and it wasn't – and came across the shoulder of the hill beside a high brick wall. I wasn't tall enough to see over it, but Mini was. Her trunk kept stretching out across the wall and then guiltily curling back. "Is the animal behind that?" I asked her.

"Only vegetables," she said. "They smell delicious."

Round the corner of the wall, I peered cautiously down at another piece of water. Deep blue water, this time. There was a long, low house by the shore there, sheltered by some pine trees. It looked really elegant, a bit like millionaire-dwellings you see on telly. I could see a diving board off one end, big picture windows and lots of clean new woodwork. And no big cat, to my relief. "Nearly there," I said and down we went.

As soon as we were on the flatter ground near the house, a crowd of hens rushed at us and nearly gave me a heart attack, running and cackling. They got in among Mini's feet and she was forced to stand still for fear of treading on them. "I think they're hungry too," she said.

Then a white goat came bounding up and nearly gave me another heart attack for a second, until I realised it was a goat. It was almost exactly the size the scornful cat had been.

"You want me to tread on this goat?" Mini asked dubiously.

I don't go for goats. I hate their smell and their mad eyes. *And* they have horns. "No, no, no!" I said, backing away. "It's only a goat." At that, Mini's trunk flipped out towards it, in an interested sort of way. The goat stared in what seemed to be horror and then galloped away yelling. "What did that?" I said.

"She's never seen an elephant before," Mini said. "*Do* find us something to *eat*!"

"All right," I said. Since it did seem urgent, I went over to the nice wooden door in the long side of the house.

I had meant to knock, but the door opened inwards under my fist. "Hallo?" I called out. No one answered,

234

so I went cautiously into the dusky corridor inside. It smelt wonderfully of new wood and it was very warm and quiet. There was a door to my right. "Hallo?" I said, and I opened it and looked in.

There was an empty, ultra-modern kitchen in there. This smelt of new bread and coffee, which, since I could still taste nipling inside myself, made me feel slightly ill. I shut that door and went on to the next one, straight ahead.

I opened that door on a blaze of sunset from big windows looking over the waters, and on a splendid smell of leather, wood and clean carpet. This room was a long, low, elegant living room – really *beautiful*, just the kind of room I'd like for myself – full of interesting comfortable sofas, low tables that caught the light, a long shelf of books, nice cushions, and almost no ornaments. Lovely. But there was no one in there either.

The corridor turned a corner then and ran through the middle of the house, with light coming in through slit-shaped windows in the roof. My feet went *splonch, splonch, splonch* on polished wooden floor as I walked down to the next door – broom cupboard – and the next – a very nice bathroom that was so up-to-date I didn't understand most of the fitments. The next door was on the other side. I opened it and it was pitch black inside. And I don't think I could have gone inside it even with the scornful cat after me. KEEP OUT! it said, like a smell boiling out of the darkness. Somehow, I knew it was

Romanov's workroom. I knew I had no business going in there. I backed off quickly and shut the door on the darkness.

That left just the one door, facing me at the end of the corridor. By this time, I was fairly sure Romanov was out, away in some other world, but I opened the door just to check.

There was a big, graceful bedroom beyond, where everything was square and white. Thin, white curtains blew inwards from the window just beyond the square, white bed. Clothes had been dropped on the white carpet, a leather jacket nearest to the door, a shirt beyond that, a pair of soft boots almost on the shirt, and socks after those. Then came underclothes, a towel and a wallet, and these led to suede trousers not quite draped over the white chair beside the bed. By the time my eyes had been led to the bed, I realised that Romanov was in it, asleep. I could just see a piece of his dark hair on the pillows.

I was horribly embarrassed and nearly backed straight out. You could see that Romanov had come home tired out and just thrown off his clothes and fallen into bed. I couldn't go and shake him awake and say, "I'm sorry, I've got a starving elephant outside." Could I? But that made me think of poor Mini standing outside in a crowd of hungry hens. I did know elephants needed a lot of food. I didn't know when she'd last had any.

All right, I thought. And if he turns me into a frog, I suppose she'll have to eat the trees. I swallowed, all the same, as I stepped over the suede jacket and on past the line of clothes. I leant over the bed. I put out a finger, but I didn't quite dare touch the hump that was probably Romanov's shoulder. Turn me into anything you like, but please don't *kill* me! I thought.

"Er – excuse me," I said.

Romanov rolled over. I jerked back. We stared at one another. He looked a bit more than just tired to me. He looked ill. An unhealthy sort of smell came off him. "Oh, not *you* again!" he said, thick and groaning.

"Are you all right?" I said.

"A touch of flu, I think," he said. "What are you doing here?"

"I came here with a starving elephant," I said. "Is it all right if I let her eat the trees?"

"No!" he groaned. He pushed his hand across his zigzag of a face, obviously trying to pull himself together. "An elephant? Seriously?"

"Yes," I said. "I met her stuck in those dark paths. Her name's Mini. I think her circus got hit by a tornado or something."

"Oh, God!" He held both hands to his face. "Just assure me you're not another of these bad dreams, will you?"

"I'm real," I said. "Honestly. So's the elephant."

"You keep turning up in my dreams with a parcel of children," he said.

When Dad had flu last Christmas, he kept calling

people in to tell them about the latest weird dream he'd had. I understood that. "That was flu," I said. "This is me for real. Have you got anything I can give Mini to eat?"

"I've no idea what elephants eat," he said and then pulled himself together again. "All right. Third shed along at this end of the house. Ask for elephant food while you're opening the door."

"Thanks," I said. "And your hens?"

"Bin of corn in the same shed," he said. "One bucketful poured on the ground."

"What about the goat?" I asked. "She need milking?"

I was not happy about that idea and I was very relieved when he said, "Helga? No, she's dry at the moment. Just find her some sweetcorn."

"And, er," I said, coming to the dreaded part, "what about your big cat?"

"In the forest over on the mainland," he said. "Takes care of herself."

I felt such a gush of relief at this that I went all considerate and helpful. I get like this with Dad, too, when he says I can have a day off school. "How about you? Can I get you anything? I know how to cook pasta."

Romanov shuddered. "No. I'll be fine. All I need is some sleep," he said, and he rolled over and pulled the covers across his face.

I tiptoed away out of the airy white bedroom and along to the front door. Mini loomed in front of me there, jigging anxiously inside the crowd of cackling hens. I'd forgotten how huge she was.

"Did you find any food?"

"Yes. It's under control," I said. "Follow me, troops, here comes the cavalry." I went marching away along the side of the house and the hens, like I'd hoped, rushed after me in a fussy gaggle – stupid things! – and left Mini free to follow me too.

The sheds were all new and clean and kind of stacked against one another and against the end of the house. When I got to the third, it was just a big garden shed really, and I had a moment when I thought that Romanov had said the first thing that came into his head in order to get rid of me. But I pushed the door open and said, "Elephant food?" and almost got trampled in the rush. The hens stormed inside yelling. Mini went, "*Oh, thank goodness!*" and nearly trod on me hauling out an immense bundle of leafy stuff with her trunk and then some sort of hay bale, while I was edging among hens to get to the wooden bin wedged in there among the stack of fodder. While I was unhooking the bucket from the wall and scooping up grain and Mini was going, "*Sugar* cane! My favourite!", the goat came dancing up too and helped itself to sugar cane more or less out of Mini's trunk.

I took the bucket and spilled it a fair distance off, away from Mini's feet, and looked up to see that goat chomping cane and staring at me like one of Dad's demons, while it made for the corn too. I had to bribe it with its own pile of grain. By that time, Mini's trunk was going out, curling round a bundle of fodder, pushing it into her funny triangular mouth and then going out for more, like clockwork. She really had been starving. Maybe the hens were too. They were all beak down, tail up and busy.

"Enjoy your feeding frenzy," I said and went along to snoop in the other sheds. There was a powerful-looking motor boat in one, that smelt piercingly of something that wasn't petrol. Garden stuff in the other. Then I noticed a door in the brick wall up the hill, so I went to take a look inside it.

Mini had said there were vegetables, but that hadn't given me the least idea of the garden that was behind that wall. It was vast. It was laid out in oblongs, with gravel paths between them, and there must have been every kind of fruit and veg there was, growing there, from every world there ever was. Just standing at the gate, I could see strawberries and apples and oranges, leeks, marrows, melons and lettuces, green droopy stuff I didn't know, and okra, and yellow things that weren't tomatoes. There were even flowers, away in the distance.

That was all I saw before the goat came romping up and tried to barge in past me. One thing I knew about goats: they eat anything they can get near, and I didn't think Romanov would be happy to find I'd let her into his garden. So I tried to shut the door on her. She pushed back. It must have seemed like Christmas to her, that garden. And she was strong. We had a mighty pushing match, me heaving from inside with my back to the door, the goat shoving madly from outside. It took me five minutes to get that door shut on her, and once I had, I was exhausted.

I did wander down a gravel path, but not far. I ached all over from the various things that had happened to me. My clothes were still damp and beginning to smell of mildew and, now the sun was almost down, I felt clammy. I felt as if I'd been without sleep for a week. So when I came to a tall stand of sweetcorn, I broke off a few heads for the goat, and I ate a few of the strawberries, because they were there, but they tasted of nipling to me, and then I gave up.

The goat was waiting outside. I had to slam the door and throw the corn at her in self defence. She snatched up a cob and stood doing her chomp-with-demon-stare act at me.

"I love you too," I told her.

Down by the sheds, Mini loomed with her trunk curled round leafy stuff and her eyes shut blissfully. The hens had guzzled and gone.

"I think I've done my bit," I said and I went into the house to find somewhere to sleep. There was one particular sofa I had my eye on. I felt about it the way that goat felt about the garden.

A telephone started to ring somewhere down the corridor.

I raced off to stop it ringing. I know the things Dad had said about what telephones did to his head when he'd had flu – and Romanov could probably *do* all those things that Dad had only threatened.

It was pretty dark in the corridor by then. It took me a minute to find the phone on a table down by the wall. I almost panicked before I found it. I kept imagining Romanov storming out of his bedroom casting spells to left and right and blaming me for not answering the thing.

I found it at last – it was an old-fashioned dial phone – and I fumbled up the receiver.

"*And* about time too!" said a woman's voice before I could say a word. "I don't know where you've been, Romanov, and I don't care, but I want you to *listen* to me for once!"

It was not a nice voice. To tell the truth, it reminded me of my mother's. Like Mum's, it had sweetness on top and beastly, grinding undertones beneath that made you squirm and want to get away. I could tell that this woman was in a really bitchy mood. And, as I always did with Mum, I tried to shut her up. "I'm sorry, madam," I said. "Mr Romanov is not available at this moment."

"But I'm his *wife*!" she said, cooing and grinding. "Fetch him at once."

"I am afraid I cannot do that, madam," I said. "Mr Romanov will not be available at all tonight."

"What do you mean, not available?" she demanded. And while I was wondering what I should say to that, because I could tell she was the kind of person who wouldn't let a little thing like someone having flu stand in her way, she luckily went on, "Who are *you* anyway?"

Then I was home and dry. "I'm just the caretaker, madam," I said. "Mr Romanov called me in to look after the elephant."

"Look after the *elephant*!" she exclaimed. "Is he starting a *circus*?"

"There do seem to be a number of animals here," I said, "but Mr Romanov's plans for them are a sealed book to me, madam. Perhaps you would like to call back when Mr Romanov can answer your query in person."

"I certainly will," she said. "Just tell me when that's going to be."

I said, "That's a little difficult to do, madam, but as he has only hired me for a week…"

"A *week*!" she said and then, "*Doh*!" just the way my mother used to when I'd got her really mad. I heard her end of the line go *clash, click, whirr…*

I couldn't help grinning as I laid the receiver quietly down beside the phone, so that she couldn't bother me or Romanov again, and crept off to the strange, futuristic bathroom. After that, I remember taking my clothes off and hanging them over warm pipes to dry, but not much else beyond the fact that the sofa I'd been eyeing up was even better than I'd hoped.

# PART SEVEN
# NICK CONTINUED

# CHAPTER SIXTEEN

※

*I* seemed to be dreaming about Roddy all that night. It must have been something to do with that house. Romanov said he'd dreamt about me in a crowd of kids, and in *my* dreams, Roddy was always with a whole bunch of children too. "I have to talk to you alone!" I kept saying to her, and she would give me a worried look and say, "Don't you understand? There's nobody else to look after them." Then I told her, "If we don't talk, the whole thing is going to overbalance." And she said, "It's the salamanders doing it." Over and over, in front of all kinds of scenery. It was crazy.

The phone ringing woke me up next morning. It rang and rang.

I woke up enough to give a deep, wild growl and shamble up the corridor draped in the towels I'd been using for blankets. I've told you what I'm like when I first wake up. I crashed into the table and knocked the phone off it. I left it on the floor and groped for the receiver until I found it, then I shook it a bit to shut it up. When that didn't stop the noise, I put it to my ear and gave another wild growl.

"Is that you this time, Romanov?" said the horrible woman's voice.

"Graah!" I said.

"No – listen to me," she said. "I've tried and I've tried to be forgiving, and God knows I've tried to live on the pittance you give me…"

I groaned. Probably that was exactly what Romanov would have done, because she thought I was him. She went on and on. It was all about how difficult it was to keep up appearances without more money, and how people stared at her because she had to wear the same dress twice – all that stuff. It got up my nose completely. "Why don't you earn some money of your own then?" I said, except that it came out as, "Wumunumumen?"

"*What*?" she said. "Romanov, are you *drunk*?"

"No, I just haven't had any coffee yet," I said, or rather, "Jussuffcuffya."

"You *are*!" she said, almost triumphantly. "Romanov, I'm seriously worried about you. You could have had a scintillating career here. The world was at your feet when you *deserted* me and took yourself off to that island. I didn't understand you then, I don't understand you now. I hear you're planning to open a circus. Frankly, it doesn't surprise me that you've started drinking too. You must come back at once and take your place among decent people with the right outlook on life before you fall apart completely. You *know* I can look after you. I can *help* you, Romanov. I think you're in with a bad crowd – I didn't like the sound of that caretaker you're employing at *all* and I'm sure that elephant is just a cry for help..."

It was around then that I tried to stop her by putting the receiver back on the telephone, but it did no good. Her voice just went on trumpeting out into the corridor, on and on, all about what a weak character Romanov was and how he needed a good woman to help him. I sat on the floor and listened for five minutes or so, thinking it was really no wonder Romanov had left her and wondering how to shut her up. I was too sleepy to think properly, but I could tell that her voice was coming streaming in by magic from somewhere across my right shoulder. Everything was done by magic here. That gave me a sort of idea, and I sighed and picked the receiver up again.

She was angry by this time. She was going, "Romanov, will you *answer* me! If you don't, you can be sure I shall do exactly what I said. I can manipulate magic too, you know. If you stay this obstinate, I shall lay my hands on all the power I can get and I shall make you *sorry*. It may take me years, but I shall *do* it and then you'd better look out! I am sick to *death* of your attitude…"

Squawk, squawk, squawk, I thought, while I carefully traced the line her voice was coming in on, and when I had it, I sort of turned the line on round, like you turn the hands of a clock to point to a different hour. Her voice went fuzzy, and then faint, and then turned into a whisper with gaps in it, and finally it stopped altogether. I could tell she was still talking, but now she was doing it in quite the wrong direction, yelling away into the sea somewhere, and the corridor was peaceful again.

Beautiful! I thought and slouched off in my towels to look for my clothes.

They were dry, but stiff as cardboard. While I was unbending them from round the pipes, I got the feeling that the plumbing had gone more normal than I remembered, but I still couldn't see properly, so I wasn't sure. And when I shuffled my way into the kitchen, that seemed different too – smaller, probably. But I need four cups of coffee before I turn into a real human being and I gave the coffee priority. I hunted by smell. I'm good at that. I found a tin of coffee and a jug and a strainer, and while I was hunting down the kettle I could hear singing on the range – this range was a shiny black sort of stove with a fire in its middle, which I certainly didn't remember from last night – I discovered a newly baked loaf in one of its ovens.

Doing well, I thought and sniffed around for the butter.

That hunt took me to the window above the sink, where the butter dish had been put into a bowl of water to keep cool. While I was feeling about for it, the window flew open and something sticky and pliable came through it and tried to take hold of my face. I jumped backwards. I nearly screamed. It was such a shock that my eyes actually came right open. My heart banged and I came up to normal human standard in a flash. This was just as well, as it turned out, but at the time I was really annoyed. Being sleepy is my *luxury*, and the sticky thing was only Mini's trunk, anxiously probing in case I'd died in the night or something. I swore at her.

"You went deathly quiet inside the house and I didn't know where you *were!*" she said.

"I was *asleep*, you fool!" I snarled.

"Oh!" she said. Then she went into her nervous schoolgirl act. I could hear one of her back legs rubbing shyly against the other. "I'm terribly sorry, but I'm…"

"Hungry," I growled. "God! You ate a whole shedful last night!"

"The goat ate quite a lot too," she said apologetically.

"All right, all right, all *right!*" I said and I stamped out through the door – the door now opened straight out of the kitchen, confusingly – and along the house to the shed, which was about as empty as a shed could be. There was one wisp of something left. The goat was in there polishing that off as I came. "Out!" I said to her.

She turned round, chewing, ready to give me a cheeky look. Then she saw the mood I was in. I swear I saw that goat change her mind. She went trotting meekly outside and left the place to Mini and the hens.

I slammed the shed door shut. "Elephant food," I said. "Hen food. Food for goats while you're at it too." When I opened the door again, the place was stacked to the ceiling, so full of hay and branches and big cattlecake things that I had a hard job getting to the corn bin. "Right," I said as I scooped corn up with the bucket, "keep this shed full like this in future or I'll want to know the reason why. That clear? It makes no sense to have to keep opening and shutting doors. Let the elephant help herself."

Then I fed the hens and, still angry and yearning for coffee, stamped back to the kitchen. On the way, I spotted an egg laid in the flowerbed by the house wall and I scooped that up. Odd, I thought. I clearly remembered that last night this wall was neat stone and nice pale wood. Now it seemed to be white-painted plaster. But I was wanting my coffee too much to bother about it.

I went in and put the egg in the butter bowl – Romanov might fancy it, I thought – and got my coffee at last. I didn't take nearly as long having breakfast as I'd meant to. Somehow being properly awake so soon had thrown me off line. I felt urgent and still angry. I cut myself a doorstep of bread with masses of butter and went along to see Romanov while I was eating it. I thought I'd better tell him how I'd turned his wife off.

His square white bedroom didn't seem nearly so airy this morning. The window looked smaller. And I could have sworn that the spaces between his thrown-down clothes had almost halved since I was last in there. Romanov looked worse by light of morning. His hair was sticky with sweat and his face looked dreadful because the brown tan of it had gone yellow on top of greyness. He didn't move or open his eyes as I leant over him.

Well, I thought, not too happily, flu usually gets worse before it gets better. "Want any breakfast?" I said. "Or can I find you an aspirin?"

He just turned over fretfully and didn't answer. There was no way I could think of to get a doctor to him, so I just went quietly out again and shut the door.

My foot kicked the telephone on my way down the passage. I picked it up, jingling, in a buttery hand. It was a toy telephone, red and blue plastic, and there wasn't even a flex in the wall or anything joining it to the yellow plastic receiver lying on the table. I stared at it a moment. "Cordless phone?" I said. "Heavily disguised mobile?" But I knew it wasn't either of those. It was a toy. "That's magic for you," I said when I was in the kitchen hunting for a basket. "It's all magic in this place. You just have to take a firm line with it, I suppose."

I went out with the basket to see if the hens had laid any more eggs. They had. Eggs were hidden in all sorts of cunning clumps and crannies. I kept finding them.

"Oh, good!" Mini said, looming over me with her ears lifting anxiously. "I'd been so afraid of treading on one of those. What are they for?"

I looked up at her, meaning to explain about eggs, but I happened to see the garden wall beyond her. It was definitely lower now, and its bricks were old and crumbling away in places. It was also much nearer the house than I expected. "Mini," I said, "has it struck you that this place is getting smaller?"

"Oh, it *is*," she said. "It's only a hundred steps over to the trees this morning. I'd been meaning to ask you why."

"I think it may be because Romanov's ill," I said.

Mini wasn't attending. Her ears and her trunk were both lifted towards the sky, somewhere behind the house. I craned round that way. The house was in my way, but I could hear something, a sort of whirring.

"What is it?" I said.

Mini's eyes, wonderful grey, clever, innocent eyes, turned to meet mine. "Some kind of a flying machine," she said. Her thick, grey eyelashes fluttered nervously. "It – it doesn't feel good."

"Is it coming here?" I said.

"Yes," she said. "I think so."

"In that case," I said, "come and put yourself in front of the door to the house. I don't think we want whoever it is going inside. Not with Romanov ill."

# Chapter Seventeen

❊

After a bit, from where we stood, with Mini across the house door and me with my head just about touching the lowest bit of her grey, wrinkled stomach, I could see the flier too, across her huge rump and the corner of the roof. It was just passing from a whitish slice of sky to a blue one. It crossed the line that divided the two sorts of sky with a kind of a blip, which seemed to slow it down. At any rate, it took longer than I expected to cross the blue slice, and when it came to the next line, there was another blip as it crossed into a slice that was all bulgy grey and silver clouds and went doggedly whirring across those. It took so long that I kept hoping it wasn't coming here after all. But that was too much to hope, of course.

Five minutes later, it circled deafeningly in over the house and came down at the top of the hill, beside the garden wall. It was like a helicopter without the big rotors, white and quite small. Mini curled her trunk up in disgust at the smell that came off it. The hens ran for their lives. I clutched my basket of eggs and stared at big numbers and letters on its pointed tail, and the goat came wandering up, chewing, and stared too.

"I bet it's Mrs Romanov," I said as the whirring stopped. "I made her really annoyed this morning."

A door popped open and two boys in embroidered jackets jumped down on to the grass. A man followed them out in a more stately way and stood staring around for a moment, tugging his embroidered coat down and putting his gold-rimmed glasses straight, before he snapped a curt word to the boys and they all three began walking down the grassy slope towards the house.

My stomach sort of jumped. This was that Prayermaster I'd mistaken for Romanov in Loggia City, with his two kids. They must be here to have the law on me. I wondered if I could get Mini to kick their flier to bits so that they couldn't drag me off back there.

"No, I will *not*!" Mini said. "What do you take me for?"

Then I'll just have to throw eggs at them, I thought, watching them as they came. They were just like I remembered them. The Prayermaster had that stiff, self-righteous look, the look you learn to know and dread in teachers at school, and the boys were just as bad. The older one was dark and smug and saintly. The younger one was the ratty little sneak with fair hair and a pointed face who had pinched me and twisted the pinches.

They all three looked up at Mini and down at the goat, and then shrugged and looked across at me. The Prayermaster unclosed his disapproving mouth to say, "Nick Mallory." I nodded. I suppose he had got my name from the Loggia City police. "The unclean one," he said, "known as Romanov – I take it he is inside this house."

Unclean yourself! I thought. "What do you want to know that for?"

"Naturally, because we are here to eliminate him," the Prayermaster explained, as if he was saying something very obvious to someone very stupid. "Kindly stand aside from the door and remove your animals as you go."

I stared into his cool, straight face and his stern, grey eyes inside their gold-rimmed lenses and I wondered all over again how on *earth* I'd managed to mistake him for Romanov. And the way he put his explanation made me very suspicious. "Just a moment," I said. "Did you by any chance offer Romanov money to eliminate *me*?"

They were so surprised that I knew I'd guessed wrong about that. Ratty's little mauve face gaped, but he changed it almost at once to a jeer. The older boy blinked and stared. The Prayermaster looked stunned, and then appalled and pitying. "That you should think such a thing of me," he said, "that you should imagine that I would have money dealings with an unclean one, shows that you stand in serious need of guidance and correction, my boy. I shall take you to Loggia City and show you your errors shortly. Meanwhile, stand aside from that door."

"But you did put some kind of spell on me, back in Loggia, didn't you?" I said. "You must have done. It's the only explanation."

The Prayermaster's face went stony. "Moderate your language before me," he said. "Cleanse your mouth. I did no such filth. That which I did was wholly lawful and this I freely admit to. It is my custom, as it has been for years, to raise up correct prayers daily for one to come to me who could lead me to the place where Romanov hides. Yesterday, my prayers were answered, when you came. And having found you, I then set Joel here..." he laid a fatherly hand on the elder boy's head "...to watch for your escape and lay bonds upon you to lead us to this place. But this was all done in purity and in the proper form." He closed his mouth into a straight line and gave me a hard stare.

"In other words," I said, "you did do something, but *spell* is a dirty word."

He glared at me. The two boys flickered glances at one another. They were loving this.

Mini blew a sigh through her trunk. "I don't understand."

"Never mind," I thought at her. "They're nutters." I was interested that none of those three seemed to know

Mini had said anything. It seemed as if she was on some wavelength that they weren't picking up. "Then I'm sorry to sound offensive," I said, "but I think it was a dirty trick whatever you call it. You got me arrested for no reason at all. And what's Romanov done to harm *you*?"

Both boys spoke up at this. Little Ratty said, "He's vile, strong vile, and he hides away here where we can't get at him."

Joel said, "Shut up, Japheth! Romanov doesn't pray properly, and he's got at the workers with his anti-prayers so that they keep asking for more money. Isn't that right?" he asked, turning his face up sweetly to Daddy Prayermaster.

The Prayermaster nodded and patted Joel's head again. Ratty Japheth muttered, "Know-it-all. Pet-boy!" but the Prayermaster pretended not to hear.

"Well, so they *should* ask for more money!" I said. "They're the ones who have to sit out in the radiation sewing these pretty flowers you lot wear all over your clothes."

The Prayermaster did me his look of sorrow and pity. "You have no true understanding," he said sadly. "When we have done with Romanov, it will be my pleasure to have you in our Prayer House for proper instruction."

The boys flickered another glance at each other at this, full of glee. I could tell it would be their pleasure too. With steel toecaps probably.

"Just try it!" I said. "I'm bigger than either of you.

You'll be lucky to come away with the right number of fingers."

Joel sniggered. Ratty Japheth said, "Ah, but *you'll* be under the prayer. *We* won't."

The Prayermaster just stood there as if it were no concern of his. I said to him, "Little sweethearts, your sons, aren't they? And I don't think much of you as a father either!"

He ignored this. "Move your animals," he said, "and stand aside from that door."

I said, "Well, I suppose I *could*, only I don't see what good it would do you. Romanov's not here. Didn't I say? I came all the way here for nothing, just like you lot did."

The Prayermaster took no notice of that either. He put his hands up by his shoulders, palms out towards me, and said, "Let the prayer be answered that opens all portals!"

There was a fairly strong feeling of pushing. The goat swayed with it. I found it quite hard not to take a step backwards into Mini. Mini swayed too, but this turned out to be because she had spotted another egg in the flowerbed. Her trunk shot out straight, fixed on the egg and curled up holding it. Very politely and gently, she put it in my basket with the other eggs. "One you missed!" she told me proudly.

To say the Prayermaster was put out would be putting it mildly. He took his hands down and goggled. The boys gawped. I don't think they have elephants much in Loggia City. But I think that what really got to the Prayermaster was the way Mini seemed immune to his kind of magic. He could see he was up against a mountain of passive resistance here. He went thoughtful.

But he was not the kind to give in. He stepped back, humming and intoning things under his breath that I couldn't quite hear, and his hands came out and made a careful shape in the air. I tried not to think about that shape, but I was fairly sure that it was the outline of me, basket and all. He gave me a stern but kindly look as he finished. "You do not seem to understand," he said, "that the longer you deny me entrance here, the worse it will be for you. You are now under the prayer, Nick Mallory. Remorse and despair grip you - and will grip you harder the longer you abide. I propose to take a turn round this abomination of an island. When I come back, I believe you will have thought better of your intransigence. Come, boys."

He cupped one of his large, well-kept hands round each boy's head and pushed them in front of him towards the other end of the house. But he let go after a few steps and strode on in front, up the slope in the direction of the trees. He was one of those who always has to stride in front. The boys turned back towards me.

"He's *not* our father!" Joel said. "Thank all the powers! We're just his two best prayerboys. So!"

"And we don't like you," Japheth added. I could tell I had really annoyed them by thinking they were the Prayermaster's sons.

I was going to say something about the way they all deserved one another, related or not. I had my mouth open ready to say it, when Japheth trod on another egg that I'd missed. His embroidered legs shot out from under him. He landed on his behind with an eggy *smish*.

I laughed. I couldn't help it. It was wonderful. Poetic.

Japheth's reaction was anything but poetic. His mauvish little face went a sort of grey-purple and he stared, glared – worse than glared – at me as he got up. It was nearly a mad look, the sort of look you'd imagine a murderer giving his victim just before he brought the axe down. It almost frightened me for a moment.

"Now I *really* hate you," he told me, in a soft little voice that sent quite a shiver down my spine. "You just wait."

"I'll do that," I said. I was nearly twice his size after all. "You'll still look an idiot."

He didn't answer. He just turned round, with his backside all yellow, and stalked away after the other two.

I sprang into action the moment they were out of sight. I don't know about remorse and despair, but I was ready to bet that the Prayermaster was simply using that guff to cover up his next move. I knew he was going to walk round the house and look for another way to get in. And the window was open beside Romanov's bed.

"Quick," I said to Mini. "Guard the door while I'm inside."

"All right," she said. "Are they really wanting to kill

the person in the house?"

"Sure of it," I said. "Don't let them in whatever they do."

I whipped underneath Mini and through the door, dumped the eggs on the kitchen table and whirled round to shoot the bolt on the inside. *Rattle, clap*. That felt better. I didn't bother shutting the kitchen window then, because Mini was faithfully in front of it, making the room quite dark. All the same, the place seemed smaller again than it had been. I simply pelted out and along the corridor to Romanov's bedroom. That seemed smaller too, and it smelt a bit dank, but the main thing was that there was nobody else in there yet except Romanov himself. I'd got there in time. I slammed both halves of the window shut and banged the latch until it was down so tight that I couldn't get it up again.

Romanov groaned and rolled over at the noise, but that was all right.

I raced out and into the bathroom. That was suddenly quite tiny, and the little window high in the wall didn't seem made to be opened anyway. I charged across the corridor to the room that was probably Romanov's workroom. I opened the door to it, but I couldn't go in there, any more than I had been able to before. It was dark in there anyway. I hoped that this meant it didn't have a window, but to be on the safe side, I slammed the door shut and dragged the telephone table over in front of it. Then, hoping that whatever kept me out would at least

263

hold the Prayermaster up a bit, I rushed back towards the living room. As I remembered, the walls there were mostly windows, great wide ones, and he'd only have to smash one to get in.

Before I got there, an evil white face with horns and a beard came round the corner at me. I nearly screamed. I jumped several feet backwards. Then I swore. It was that goat. It must have whizzed indoors after me.

"Keep away from me," I said to it, "or I won't be responsible for what I'll do!"

Then I went into the living room. I had to stop for a second and stare. The shelf of books was the same, but all the sofas were gone, including the one I'd slept on. In their place there was a set of moth-eaten old armchairs standing about on a floor of old bare wood with dingy rugs on it. There were still a lot of windows, but they weren't the nice, pale-wooden modern ones I remembered. They were a sort of job lot. There was one rickety long one with lots of small panes, one big tall one that was just a sheet of glass surrounded by new white wood, and about six small crooked ones that would have looked better in one of the sheds. And they all had different fastenings, none of which worked very well. I rushed round them hammering them shut and wedging the worst catches with books. The one that was a big sheet of glass really worried me though. It was so easy to break. But when I pushed my head against the glass and squinted downwards, I saw there was a sheer drop from it to a piece of water that looked like real deep ocean. Big white surf was breaking against the walls of the house down there. So perhaps it was all right. Unless Prayermasters could fly, of course.

I turned round to discover that the goat had followed me. It looked at me. I looked at it. And I realised I'd gone and shut myself into the house with it. I knew goats smell strong, but I hadn't known before that when they're indoors they *reek*. Or it was more of a stench, really.

"All right," I said. "But if you eat any of these books, Romanov will probably kill you." I knew he would. They all had leather covers and titles like *A True and Faithfulle Historie of the Travels of Jehan Amberglaffe*. My Dad is always paying fortunes for books like those. He doesn't let me touch them.

The goat looked slyly aside from me and started eyeing up an armchair.

"Yes, have that instead if you have to," I said.

Then I remembered the kitchen window and raced off to shut that. The goat had been in the kitchen first. The stone floor was all covered with crumbs from the loaf it had snitched off the table. But Mini, bless her heart, was still standing outside. I took a look out under her grey wrinkled belly as I made that window fast. The hens were pecking about in the grass again and the flier was still there above them on the slope, but there was no sign of the Prayermaster or his boys.

Perhaps, I thought, while I hastily crawled around the

flagstones scooping up handfuls of loaf crumbs, they're all in one of the sheds doing dangerous incantations. So the next thing to do is go and stand in Romanov's bedroom and incantate back at them. I threw the breadcrumbs into the range-fire and set off that way again.

Before I'd even reached the door, I heard the hens shrieking and flapping outside. Then I heard the last sound I would have expected – the violent, tinny whirring of the flier. They were leaving. Or pretending to go. It had to be a trap.

To tell the truth, I felt a bit of a fool. I leant over the sink and peered under Mini's wrinkly, grey tum – which moved out of the way as I got there, as if Mini was as surprised as I was – and the rotor-thingy on the flier's pointed end was definitely spinning, and its front end was cocked upwards ready for take-off. Its door was still open, though, and Japheth's skinny shape, all covered in bright red embroidery, was tearing along the hillside beside the garden wall, arms waving, obviously terrified he'd be left behind.

That was astonishing enough. Even more astonishing, there was a new person there. He was an elderly man in tweeds, and he was just stopping on his way down to the house to look over his shoulder at the flier. He had a sort of ex-army look, this new man. I wondered if he'd somehow frightened the other three off. Anyway, he watched, and I watched, while Japheth went rushing up to the open door of the flier and scrambled up through it, and then got it jammed in his hurry to close it and had to open it again, so that it was still partly open when the flier took off in a tremendous, whirring swoop and then went fairly belting, and wagging about as it belted, away across the waters on the other side of the garden.

The ex-army man shrugged and came on towards the house again, sort of staggering as if he was exhausted.

I suddenly recognised him by the way he walked. It was the drunk who had given me the blue flame. I said, "Oh, *no!*" and wondered whether to keep the door bolted and lie low.

He was outside the door the next second. I heard him say, "*Come* on, elephant! *Out* of it now! Move over!" and I heard Mini politely getting out of his way. She really was much too polite and humble for an elephant. After that, he was banging on the door and shouting, "Hallo, the house! Anyone home? Open *up*, dammit!"

And I behaved just like Mini. I suppose it was those military orders. I unbolted the door and stood aside while he came stumbling in.

"Somebody here," he said. "Good. For Pete's sake have you got any *coffee*? I'm out on my feet and dying of a hangover." And he pulled a chair out from the table and crumpled into it, with his elbows on the table and his face in his skinny old hands. "Coffee!" he croaked imploringly. "*Black* coffee!"

I know how it feels to need coffee. I'm like that every morning. I shoved the kettle on to the hot part of the range and began looking for the other things. "Coming up," I said.

"Thanks," he sighed. His tweed suit was sopping. He was steaming as he sat there. His face was sort of bluish-white and he was so exhausted that he never looked at me, or even at Mini, who was peering in through the door at him. But he seemed to feel he had to explain himself. All the time I was making the coffee, he was bringing out little sentences, in jolts, by way of explaining. "Not usually like this," he said. "Fact is... I have to get drunk before I can walk the dark paths... can't see them sober... never could... Shaman stuff not my strong suit... Worn off now... head like a treadmill... Took so *long*... Hadn't bargained for Romanov's island being in the past... Cunning stuff... Ten years or more behind the times, this place is... though I believe parts of the island may be in the future too... Must be why Romanov knows what's going to happen... Have to ask him how it's done... Pay him too... Please remind me to ask him what his fee is this time... Thanks, lad. *Thanks.* You're a hero."

I pushed the biggest mug I could find, full of strong coffee, into his hands and he drank it scalding hot without stopping to breathe. Then he held it out for more. He drank the second lot slowly, in sips, without speaking, and steamed, and turned a slightly better colour. When I'd given him the third mugful, he sat up a bit straighter and asked, almost alertly, "What was that flier doing outside that went off in such a hurry?"

"I don't know why they went off like that," I said, "unless they were afraid of you."

"Could have been," he said. "Depends who they were."

"It was a Prayermaster from Loggia City and his two boys," I said. "They wanted to kill Romanov and they used me..."

"Then that explains it," he interrupted. "We Magids have been trying to keep the Prayermasters in line for centuries now."

"You're a *Magid*?" I asked. I was delighted. I'd met three Magids in my life and now here was another one.

"For my sins," he said, dismissing the whole thing. He rubbed at his little moustache and frowned at his coffee in a tired way. "What's Romanov been doing to stir them up? I wish he wouldn't *do* this – keep stirring people up. Not that I can stop him, of course. Far more powerful magic than any of mine. All I've got is moral pull. Better use that, I suppose. Lad, you wouldn't have anything to eat, would you? My stomach's just reported in starving."

I looked at the basket on the table. "Eggs?"

He shuddered violently. "Not eggs, not after two hundred quidsworth of booze! I couldn't! Anything else?"

"Well," I said, "the goat's just eaten the bread, but..." On the off chance, I reached back and opened the oven where I'd found the loaf. And there was another one in there, to my great relief. Magic at its best. "Here's another loaf," I said.

I found him a big hunk of cheese in a cupboard and brought the butter out of its bowl and put them in front of him. He eyed it all a moment, speculatively, rather like the goat had wondered about the armchair, and then he suddenly snatched the loaf and a knife and ate. And ate. And finished the loaf. Neither of us talked until he'd done.

By this time he looked a lot better. I found him staring at me rather piercingly. He had eyes that looked at you so firmly that you couldn't remember what colour they were, just how they looked at you. All I knew was that his were red-rimmed.

"Now," he said. "You, lad. Has Romanov taken on an apprentice at long last?"

"No," I said. "Or… well, I was hoping he'd take me on, but… I didn't know how to get home, you see, but when I got here, Romanov was ill, so I couldn't ask him anything."

"*Ah!*" he said. He raised a finger at me triumphantly. "Got it! Placed you. You're the lad I gave the magelight to. Did it help at all?"

"It was great," I said, "but I couldn't get it back again after I sent it away."

I got the piercing look again. "You from Earth, by any chance?"

I nodded.

"Thought so," he said. "Earth people always have trouble raising magelight. Something in the climate, I suppose. Mind telling me your name?"

"Nick Mallory," I said. "But I'm not really from Earth…"

"Yes, but according to your Dad, you were born there," he said. "Your mother was pregnant with you when he married her, he tells me." And while I stared at him, he added, "He told me all about you while I was getting drunk enough to go after you. Cost him two hundred pounds, I'm afraid. But he didn't mention you were so large and striking-looking. Accounts for me not recognising you before. Expecting someone smaller. Well, at least this means I don't have to pay Romanov to find you." He stood up and held out his hand in an old-fashioned, courteous way. "Pleased to meet you, Nick. My name's Hyde, Maxwell Hyde."

"Oh," I said. "Er. How do you do." I was gobsmacked.

# CHAPTER EIGHTEEN

✳

When I got my senses back, I wanted to ask Maxwell Hyde a hundred things. But he was so tired he was swaying about.

"Later," he said. "I have to sleep, lad. Just a couple of hours and I shall be right as rain. I don't need much. Just a couple of hours."

So I took him along to the living room. I'd forgotten the goat. It had eaten half an armchair and it looked up at us cheekily with a strip of carpet dangling out of its mouth. "Damn," I said.

Maxwell Hyde said, "I'm not having *that* in here!" and he took hold of the goat by one of its horns and its backside and ran it into the kitchen. There was a good deal of clattering and bleating in there, but he got the front door open somehow and kicked it outside. I was impressed.

Meanwhile, I was dragging together the two armchairs and a stool to make him a bed. I draped a carpet over it all to hide the part the goat had eaten, and it made quite a respectable place to sleep.

"Thanks, lad," Maxwell Hyde said, coming back, wiping goat hairs off himself. "I'll be with you again for lunch. Tell Romanov I'll talk to him then, if you would." He climbed into my contraption and, as far as I could see, went to sleep on the spot. He was snoring when I shut the door.

I went along to Romanov then, but I couldn't tell him anything. He seemed to be unconscious. His face was ash-coloured and covered with little clusters of sweat. The illness-smell in the room was stronger than ever. I tried to open the window for him, but I'd shut it too firmly and I couldn't budge it. So I went away. I didn't know what else to do.

Lunch, I thought, and went to the kitchen. There were eggs, of course, but Maxwell Hyde hadn't seemed to fancy those and he'd eaten all the cheese. I hunted around and I couldn't find any pasta, which is the other thing I know how to cook, and I got rather anxious. I wanted to do things right for Maxwell Hyde. Dad thought so much of him. *I* thought a lot of him too, because he was a Magid and helped secretly run the universe, and I could tell he was the sort of person who expected proper meals to turn up regularly whatever else was going on.

And I was even more anxious about Romanov, in a horrible, nagging way. I was sure he ought to be in hospital. But there was no way to get him to one. And then I was almost equally anxious about that Prayermaster. I kept expecting him to turn up again. I was sure he had flown away just to tempt me outside so that he could knock me out with a well-aimed prayer and then go after Romanov.

I made more coffee and sat at the kitchen table drinking it and staring at the chinking, glowing fire in the range. It was odd. The fire never seemed to need fuel and it never occurred to me to look for any. It glowed comfortingly orange and black and red between the bars, and it helped me think somehow.

Strange that Maxwell Hyde had turned out to be a Magid and come looking for me. I supposed he meant to take me back to Dad. In a way, I was relieved, because that *definitely* meant I'd have to wait before I did anything to help that girl, Roddy. But after that dream I'd had, I wasn't sure that I was allowed to wait – and that made me nervous *and* excited in about equal shares – and it also made it awkward if Maxwell Hyde was determined to run me back home the way he had dealt with the goat. It was funny the way I always had to call him by both his names – Maxwell and Hyde – in my mind. If I thought of him as Mr Hyde, I found I was calling him Dr Jekyll.

If I tried thinking Maxwell, it made me think of silver hammers...

It was here I realised that my thoughts had gone all small and silly. It is maddening the way your mind sheers off into silly ideas when you try to think seriously – or I know my mind does. I got up in exasperation and went outside. I was too annoyed with myself not to.

The island was definitely smaller. There was only a short bank between the house door and the garden wall, and the trees had moved closer. There was an odd, ragged look to everything, so that I could actually see the lines between the different slices of grass, raying inwards towards the garden. The garden wall was mostly made of stone now, with low, tumbled-down places in it. Mini looked huge beside it. She snatched her trunk back guiltily as I came outside and stood swinging it, rubbing one back leg up the other, looking really embarrassed.

"What are you doing?" I said.

"Nothing," she said.

The goat distracted me then by bouncing up to me as if it thought I wanted it there. Besides, I realised that there was a mass of food in that garden. Maxwell Hyde could have strawberries for lunch. I went to the rickety gate in the collapsing wall and forced it open. And stood staring dismally. It was like a small, tangled allotment in there, with bushy apple trees round the walls and weeds everywhere. While I stared at it, the goat bundled in past me and began eating barren-looking Brussels sprouts just as if it wasn't full of loaf and armchair. Mini's trunk snaked slyly over my shoulder and fastened on a green apple in the nearest tree.

"I love these things," she said, "even though they give me a funny tummy."

I suddenly remembered – from telly, I think – that elephants have quite delicate digestions. And I was furious. It was everything, really, from the phone call first thing in the morning onwards. But I took it out on Mini.

"*Leave* it!" I shouted at her. "You *stupid* elephant! You'll ruin your stomach! And I'll have *you* ill as well as everything else! Anyway, it's stealing!"

She was really hurt. Her trunk whipped back and she gave me a shocked look. I shall never forget the way those wonderful grey eyes looked at me. "I thought you were *kind*," she said. Then she turned round with that sudden nimbleness that elephants can produce and went away.

I felt beastly. All I could think of to do was to wade in among the weeds and search moodily for anything I knew how to cook. There wasn't much. I found brown-edged lettuce, little greenish tomatoes on a starved vine and a handful of rubbery plums. I was just coming out with this sorry lot bundled up in my sweatshirt, when Mini came galloping back again.

"Oh, do come! I've found something horrible! *Please* come!"

Her ears were folding and unfolding, her trunk was tossing and she was trampling from foot to foot. Her eyes were beginning to roll. I could see she was in a right state. "OK," I said. "With you in a second."

I charged into the house, dumped the veg and even remembered to shut the door against the goat. Then I followed Mini at a run to the other end of the island. It was only about a hundred yards by then, across line after line of different kinds of grass.

Mini stopped beyond the clump of trees, shaking all over. "Down there," she said. Her trunk gave a short jab in the right direction. "I can't go down there again! I *can't!*"

The island was quite high above the waters on that side. I had to go over a steep, grassy lip and down two sloping shelves of crunchy, white pebbles to get near the sea. Mini had left deep sliding footprints in them, going down, and even deeper ones going up. It was easy to see why she had gone here. The slice of water facing the pebbles was a lovely tropical green-blue, rocked by calm ripples. Warm air blew off it. Just the place an elephant would choose to swim. Except...

I stopped dead.

Someone else was in the water, rolling gently in the shallow ripples. He was brown and red and shiny. At first I thought he was alive and trying to roll out of the water. He worked about so. Then the ripples turned him so that an eye stared at me out of a cracked, gold-rimmed lens. Above and below the eye was a horrible red and white mess. Then I hoped he *was* dead. No one should be alive with his head smashed like that. The clear water was red-brown around him in clouds. Lots of little flies were sort of sizzling this way and that on him as he rolled. And he rolled the other way, letting me see the embroidery on his back all chopped open and red, and a white glimpse of shoulder blade as the flies went down on him again.

I made myself creep a step nearer. My foot knocked wood, and I looked away from the Prayermaster for a moment to see the spade and the axe that had done this to him lying on the pebbles. The metal parts were red and gummy, with hairs sticking to them. I thought of Japheth running to the flier covered in what I'd taken for red embroidery. I gagged. I couldn't help it. I'm ashamed, but I'm no good at this kind of thing at all. I made one frantic scramble into the water to touch the Prayermaster's staring, tepid face and knew for sure that he was dead. Then I went crashing and crunching up the pebbles until he was out of sight, and threw up. By the time I crawled up over the grass lip with the taste of sicky coffee in my nose, I was shaking worse than Mini.

"*Is* someone dead there?" she asked.

"Yes," I said. "Dreadfully. Let's go somewhere else. There's nothing we can do until Maxwell Hyde wakes up."

We went back to the sunny place by the garden wall and I sat there like a sack. Mini kept curling her trunk half round me, then taking it away. I think she was making sure I was still alive.

After a long time, I said, "I'm sorry I yelled at you. I was in a bad mood."

"I know," she said. "You keep having to feed people. I – er – I'd eaten a lot of apples anyway before you came out."

"That could be a mistake," I said. I watched the hens pecking about for a while and then I said, "There's a triangle of sea near where we came in that had a tropical look. You could have your swim there."

"I've lost the urge," she said sadly.

We were still there when the house door opened and Maxwell Hyde came out looking very much awake. He was all trim and neat and shaved, though his clothes still seemed damp. "Can't you pull yourself together?" he said to me. "You're filling the air with doom and gloom. You *and* the elephant. What's wrong with you?"

"I'll show you," I said. I got up and reached up to give Mini a pat. "You needn't come," I said to her, "unless you want to."

"Thank you," she said. "I think I'll go and have that swim instead."

"You do that. But," I said, "don't drown or anything. I can't stand any more."

She curled up her trunk and opened her mouth in amusement. "Elephants float beautifully," she said and went lumbering off.

I took Maxwell Hyde in the opposite direction, not very willingly. I could feel my feet dragging. He gave me one of his keen looks and said, "Can you understand what the elephant's saying then?"

"Yes," I said. "Can't you?"

He shook his sprucely combed grey head. "No, I can't. It's not precisely a universal gift, lad. Has she told you what Romanov wants with an elephant, then?"

"He doesn't," I said. "I mean, she isn't his. I met her stuck in the dark paths. She belonged to a circus, but it got struck by a storm – it sounded like a tornado from what she said – and she ran away in a panic. She was my third person needing help, like you said." I'd been trying to think who the second person was that I had helped after Roddy. I knew it had to be someone in Loggia City but I couldn't see who.

"I *see*," he said. "That's a weight off my mind. I'd been puzzled to death why Romanov could possibly need an elephant. So you can understand animal speech?"

"Not the goat," I said. The goat was coming down from among the trees as I said this. It had a spray of leaves sticking out of its mouth and curiosity all over its face.

"Goats," said Maxwell Hyde, "are a special case. Mad as hatters, all of them. Now where is this thing we've come to see?"

"Down here," I said and led him off down the pebbles, and pointed with my head turned away. "Down in the water."

"My God!" he said. Then, after some crunching about, "This is horrible! Hacked to death with a *spade*!" There were watery, shingly sounds. I guessed he was dragging the Prayermaster out of the sea, but I still couldn't look. "Nothing much to be done except hope he died quickly," he said, coming back up beside me and swallowing a little. "Who was he?"

"The Prayermaster from Loggia City who wanted to kill Romanov," I said. By this time, I was swallowing too.

"I thought I recognised the embroidery," Maxwell Hyde said. "Biter bit, eh? All right, there's no need to stay here if it makes you throw up. Come back to the house. There's something I want to ask you about there."

I set off thankfully and came face to face with the goat at the top of the shingle. "Oh, lord! It won't – won't try to eat *him*, will it?"

"I don't think they're carnivores, but we'll make sure anyway," he said and he did the horn-and-rump hold on the goat again and ran it back to the sheds before it could so much as bleat. "Go and find some rope," he said to me. "Bound to be some in these sheds."

I looked into the shed nearest the house, expecting the smart motor boat. It was just a pathetic old punt now, but there was a coil of rope hanging on the wall beside it, along with garden tools, a saw and two empty hooks. "I think the spade and the axe came from there," I said, handing Maxwell Hyde the rope.

He was looking a bit irritable because the goat was jumping up and down under his hands, but he said quite coolly, "Bound to have come from somewhere near. Wrap one end of that round the creature's neck – quickly."

I managed to put a loop of the rope more or less in the right place and then watched, fascinated, while the loose end wrapped itself round the rest of the rope and tied itself into a firm knot.

"Thanks. Phew!" said Maxwell Hyde, standing up rather breathlessly. "Active, *smelly* beasts, goats are." He walked off towards the house. I looked back uncertainly, but the other end of the rope was tied somehow to the shed door and the goat had already run out almost to the whole length of it. Impressive. "I must say," he said, "that I did wonder a bit at that child running to the flier all covered in blood like that, but I was a bit tired just then."

Of course it had been blood. I felt a fool, thinking it had been embroidery.

"Who was flying the machine?" Maxwell Hyde asked me.

"It must have been the other prayerboy. Joel," I said. "Unless they had a pilot with them."

"Could have been a boy," he commented. "Went up in a surge like an amateur, full throttle, wagging about and so on. And where was Romanov in all this?"

"He was in bed. He's awfully ill," I said protectively. "I know he was because I was running around inside shutting windows in case the Prayermaster tried to get in." I heard myself saying this and, for the first time, I wondered about myself. I had been looking after Romanov and protecting him ever since I got here, and yet Romanov had seemed ready enough to bump *me* off for money if he'd decided I deserved it. I wondered if it was magic, a protective spell perhaps, but I didn't really think it was. I think I just admired him. I said, again protectively, "They really were wanting to kill him. They called him unclean. But all he'd done was give the embroidery workers stuff to block the radiation."

"So that's what annoyed them," Maxwell Hyde said thoughtfully. "Right. I have my own witness that you were locked inside with an elephant in front of the door, and I didn't spot any blood on you, so you're clear, I think." He opened the door and I followed him into the kitchen as he said, "But I only have your word for Romanov."

"I can tell you write detective stories," I said.

He turned round at me in a way that made me almost back out again. "I am also a Magid," he said, "and it is my job to look into this." He was full of authority. I felt as if I'd made a loud joke at a funeral. Then he relaxed a bit and said, "But I want your opinion about this first." He led me to the living room, where he opened the door and said, "Well? What's going on here?"

I gawped a bit. It was like another shed in there now. The walls were warped, grey boards with green mossy stuff at the bottom, and there were holes in the splintered old wood of the floor. I could see water glinting and lapping through the holes. All the windows were crooked and draped with cobwebs, and as for the two chairs I had given him to sleep on… Well, it was lucky I'd draped a rug on them. They were two rotten old deckchairs, and the canvas in one was quite perilously split.

"I think it must be because Romanov's so ill," I said.

He frowned at me.

"The island and everything else have been getting smaller and messier ever since I came here and found him," I explained. "He must be too ill to sustain the magic or something."

"That's most unlikely," Maxwell Hyde told me sternly. "The island and its contents have to be self-sustaining or he'd never be able to go away. My guess is that it all ought to draw energy from each of the worlds it's part of. Not much from each, to keep the balance. Cunning stuff. Romanov is good at it, lad. Where is he? We'd better look into this."

"Along here," I said and took him to the bedroom.

It was awful in there. It had become a tiny, poky room with thick walls, dribbling wetness and covered with black flecks of mildew. It was a fug of sickness. Romanov looked like a corpse laid out on the narrow bed, almost as bad as the Prayermaster. His cheeks had sunk in and his hair had got pasted to his head with sweat, so that his face was a sharp, grey, zigzag skull. I was relieved when I saw he was still breathing.

"*Faugh!*" said Maxwell Hyde.

I made for the window to get it open – or try to – but he barked at me, "*Stop!* Stand just where you are and don't move!"

I stood still, more or less treading on Romanov's suede jacket. "What has he got?" I asked.

"Let's find out," Maxwell Hyde said. He leant over and, very delicately, touched Romanov's sweaty forehead. He grunted, but Romanov never moved. Then, to my surprise, Maxwell Hyde took his fingers away, rather as if he were running them along an invisible line of string, and felt across through the air until he was all but touching my forehead. "Thought so," he muttered and felt away again, back to Romanov.

"What is it?" I said.

"Look," he said. "Or can't you see it?"

I could see it as soon as he told me to look. There was a blurred line of filthy-looking greyish-yellow light stretching between Romanov's head and mine. It was really nasty. It made me almost want to throw up again. "Yes, I can see it," I said.

"How often did you touch him?" Maxwell Hyde asked sharply.

I thought. As far as I could tell, I hadn't. "I don't think I did," I said. "I didn't quite like to. I mean…"

"Well, that's something to be thankful for at least," Maxwell Hyde said. "He could well be dead now, if you had." He stood up straight and stared me in the eye. "I'm going to want a detailed report from you, of everything you've done since you vanished from London, my lad. But, before you do *anything* else, you're going to oblige me by going and joining the elephant in the sea.

Take all your clothes off, leave them on the beach for me to delouse, and go right under. There's nothing like salt water for cleaning black magic off. If you find the elephant's in fresh water, don't go in there. Find a piece that's genuine sea. Go on. I'm going to be busy working on this end while you bathe."

I crawled away, feeling as if I'd been convicted of leprosy. I wondered if I'd ever like myself again. Even the sight of Mini on her side in crystal blue water, spraying her own back through her trunk, failed to cheer me up.

"Is that water salt?" I asked her.

"Very," she said merrily. "It makes me sneeze."

I tasted it untrustingly, and it was. Very. It practically skinned my tongue. In fact, it was so salty and so easy to swim in that I wondered whether Romanov had included a piece of the Dead Sea at this point. Mini was so delighted to have me in the water too that I began to feel quite a bit better quite soon. We churned about and threw swathes of water at one another. She rolled and I splashed.

Eventually, I looked up to see Maxwell Hyde on the grass, going carefully over my clothes. He was blowing into my shoes as I got out and went up to him.

"That's better," he said. "Clothing's clear. Let's look at you. Turn round. Raise your arms. Bend down so that I can see the top of your head. Right. Fine. You're clear too now," he said, handing me a ragged old towel. "Get dry and get dressed."

He walked away. "Is Romanov OK?" I called after him.

"He will be," he called back. "Don't be long. Lunch."

When I got to the kitchen, he was standing over the range stirring a vast pan of eggs. My miserable lettuce and manky tomatoes had been turned into a halfway decent salad, and there was another new loaf to go with it.

"I thought you didn't want eggs," I said, scratching at my salt-sticky hair.

"That was this morning," he said. "Dig me out a tray and some cutlery. I'm hoping Romanov will be up to eating some of this."

When everything was ready, I offered to take the tray in to Romanov, but he wouldn't let me. "I'm not letting you near him," he said. "Don't you understand? Someone laid a pretty vicious working on you, designed to destroy Romanov and get you blamed for it. I *think* I've scotched it, but I'm not taking any chances." He carried the tray off to Romanov himself, along with a vast pot of tea and an enormous mug, and came back looking pleased with himself. "*That* seems all right," he said. "Got his appetite back. Get eating, lad. While you're getting yourself round this lot, I want a detailed account of exactly what you've been up to since you were standing by my elbow in London."

So I told him. Maxwell Hyde interrupted me several times, and insisted on going back over what I'd just said and making me tell it again. The first time was over the magic I'd done with Arnold, Chick, Dave and Pierre, to make the cricket stadium safe.

"Oh, I get you!" he said, when I'd explained again. "*That* world. English Empire over most of Europe and paranoid over the Russian-Turkish bloc. Well, one thing's certain and that's that this anti-Romanov stuff wasn't put on you *there*. Half their paranoia is because their mages aren't any good, if you ask me. Typical slipshod working, the one you had your hand in, lad. Why are you looking so doleful?"

I was feeling bad about those four mages again. "I got them into bad trouble," I said. "Arnold and them. Pretending to be a novice that way. I could tell they were in trouble by the frantic way they were hunting for me."

Maxwell Hyde gave a sigh. "Probably. I'll check up – have to anyway – but, frankly, I don't see what else you could have done without being shot as a spy. You played it right by instinct, as far as I can see. Go on."

I did and he interrupted me again to ask about the black panther in the wood, and again to ask me about when the mages were looking for me there. "Misty, were they? Now, think carefully. Would you say they were only partly there, while you were *really* there?"

"That's what it seemed like," I said. "I didn't know if they could see me or not. That's why I went up the dark path, to get away from them. But I sat down then and decided in the end that I'd better go and find Romanov."

"Now, hang on," Maxwell Hyde said. "You told me Romanov seemed to despise you and you were obviously pretty scared of him. Exactly *why* did you think Romanov was the man to consult? Did it feel like a compulsion at all?"

"It could have been," I admitted. "I know it seems odd, when I knew he'd been offered money to get rid of me, but I think I went because he was *excellent* really. He was a hundred times better than Arnold and his lot. And I could pay him too. Besides, wasn't that spell already *on* me, from when Romanov came to find me? He was ill before I got here."

"We'll consider that in the right place," Maxwell Hyde said. "Could have been overkill, you see. Carry on."

I went on, until I came to where I met Maxwell Hyde himself. He made faces there. I think he was ashamed of being so drunk. Then we both heard a sudden humming at the back of the kitchen and whirled round. There was a large fridge standing there, working away.

Maxwell Hyde bounced up. "Ah," he said. "Romanov's feeling better." He looked inside the fridge with appreciative noises, and fetched out a big piece of cheese and a cluster of strawberry puddings. They had strange writing on the cartons, but they tasted like strawberry mousse to me. We both had one and he took one through to Romanov.

I was glad of the interruption. I was still having such a mixture of feelings about meeting that girl Roddy – or I was embarrassed, or *something* – that I wanted to leave her out of it altogether. Now I had time to work out how not to mention her, so I sat and stared at the range and thought. It wasn't a range any more, really. It was a white thing with doors and no sign of a fire. Nothing like so comforting.

Then Maxwell Hyde came back and went on listening to me, with his leather-patched elbow on the table and his sharp, soldierly chin in his hand. I went on seamlessly to my time in Loggia City, then to meeting Mini, and then to the end, and didn't mention Roddy at all. Maxwell Hyde nodded and grunted a bit, but he didn't interrupt.

"Right," he said, when I was up to the place where the flier took off. "Plenty of food for thought there. Some of it I'll need to think about a bit. But there are two things that spring to mind straightaway. First, about just when this anti-Romanov working was put on you. I wondered about the Prayermaster doing it for a while. It's their kind of thing. They do a lot of dirty work under the name of prayer. But the more I think about it, the more I'm convinced that it was done in London, by this person who sent you off. Under my nose too." He sniffed in an irritable way. "Says volumes for how nervous I was," he said. "I should have spotted it. Anyway, does that make sense to you?"

I nodded. It did seem likely.

"Then you've got an enemy," Maxwell Hyde said. "Someone who dislikes you as much as he dislikes Romanov. Any ideas?"

All I could think of was that this enemy was something to do with my real father's Koryfonic Empire. We discussed that for a bit, but in the end Maxwell Hyde shook his head sharply.

"No," he said. "Won't wash. Person has to have it in for Romanov even more than for you. I'll check with Romanov, of course, but I'd take a strong guess that he's never gone near that Empire. Got more sense. Anyway, to get on to the second thing. I'd be interested to know at what point you moved back ten years. It took me all night to suss out how to do that, even after I'd discovered I'd have to. When did you realise?"

"I didn't," I said. "I just went here. But..." I thought about it. "It could have been when the path forked," I said doubtfully. "Something was a bit wrong then – but I don't know."

"Any idea *how* you did it?" Maxwell Hyde asked. I shook my head and he sighed. "No, it was all blind instinct, I suppose," he said. "Ah, well. The nasty part seems clear enough though. The Prayermaster gets you to lead him to Romanov and arrives here with these two boys. Whereupon they do him in. Any idea why?"

I thought of the implacable, schoolmaster face with its gold-rimmed glasses and found the corners of my mouth pinching in. "If you'd met him, you'd know. They must have hated him, really *hated* him." Maxwell Hyde shot me one of his looks. "They were horrible kids," I said. "I've no sympathy for them either. But think of the worst schoolmaster you ever had."

Maxwell Hyde winced a bit. "Right," he said. "Right.

Prayers and beatings, you think? So we have two vicious young killers loose with a flier, who know how to find Romanov." He sprang up again. "I'll just go and warn him, I think."

While he was gone, I ate two banana puddings and a chocolate one and felt better. It looked as if Maxwell Hyde hadn't noticed that I'd left out meeting Roddy, and he was definitely not suspecting me of murder any more, though I think he'd wondered. This was a relief.

"I've let Romanov know," Maxwell Hyde announced, coming back, "and he says he'll alter this island as soon as he can, so they can't find him again. But the mystery thickens about this enemy you both have. He's never touched your Empire, so it can't be that. And he had no connection with you whatsoever before yesterday. So we're stuck there too. But I said we'd get rid of the Prayermaster for him. Come along."

He went to the outside door and beckoned with the folded sheet he was carrying. I swallowed and went with him, wishing I hadn't eaten those extra puddings.

That side of the island was already further away. We'd walked nearly three hundred yards before we met Mini, hanging around beside the goat. Both of them looked miserable.

"My tummy's funny," Mini explained sadly.

"How many apples *did* you eat?" I said.

"Two whole treefuls," she admitted.

"Then you know who's to blame," I said. "Try filling

up with hay. What's wrong with the goat?"

"She doesn't like being tied up," Mini said.

"Tell her my heart bleeds," I said.

I hated the next bit. I had to go crunching down those pebbles and help wrap the sheet round the Prayermaster. It was horrible, even though I tried not to look. Banana was sort of coming back up my nose before long and I had to go and sit on the grass.

Maxwell Hyde came up to join me. "My idea," he said, "was to sling this fellow – and the murder weapons – further along this coast, so they'll end up in the world the beach really belongs to. A nasty puzzle for the people there, I'm afraid, but it won't be nearly as much bad luck for them as it will be for Romanov, if we leave everything here. A murdered corpse always brings vile bad luck on the spot where it happened. Trouble is, Romanov can't remember where he got this section *from*. I'll have to think a bit."

I nodded and swallowed, and after a bit I began to feel better. I looked round at Maxwell Hyde, sitting upright, with his thin, businesslike hands clasped round his damp, tweed knee, intending to ask how his thinking was getting on. He looked round at me at the same moment.

"No," he said. "Doesn't add up. I told you to help three people on the way. Your story only has two, even if you count the elephant as a person and the second one as the old chap with the tapestry. Or do you count the Prayermaster too?"

I could feel my face slowly going as fiery as the middle of the vanished kitchen range. I said, "Well, it *may* have been him."

His look got twice as keen. I could feel it on the side of my face. "Come clean," he said. "What was the third?"

"Er," I said. "There was this girl – but maybe it isn't, because I haven't helped her yet. Arianrhod, but she said to call her Roddy. She was in some place called Blest, you see, and I said I'd go there after I'd seen Romanov."

There was silence. All I could hear were several different kinds of sea breeze hitting the trees. I thought it was ominous.

"Well!" said Maxwell Hyde. "Well, I'm blessed! No pun intended. Fair, was she, or dark?"

"Dark," I said. "About my age."

"*Well,*" he said again. "I was about to point out to you, my lad, that you seem to have unfinished business, but this clinches it, I think. What did my granddaughter ask you to do?"

"Your *granddaughter*!" I yelped.

He nodded. "Has to be. Unusual name, magical heritage, prefers to be called Roddy, lives in Blest. My eldest granddaughter. QED."

"You mean," I gulped, "that you're from this place too?"

"That's right." He chuckled, quite suddenly.

"But how come…" I began.

"How come I publish mystery stories on Earth?"

he said. "I publish on Thule, Tellans, lots of places too. Everyone in those places is apt to go on about how convincing my alternate-world setting is, but of course it's only Blest. Quite ordinary to me – and to Blest people, worse luck. I hardly sell at all in Blest. Sales so bad, in fact, that I thought I'd make use of my Magid skills to turn a penny or so in other worlds. What did she want – Roddy?"

He had this way of spearing you with the last little thing he said. I wriggled a bit and said, "There's this plot. The Merlin seems to be in it and she wanted outside help."

Maxwell Hyde narrowed his eyes. It was as if he were looking at this Merlin fellow from a long way off. He shook his head. "She's wrong, of course. She has this little way of getting wrought up, our Roddy. The Merlin's young yet, but he's a deep one. They all are. Maybe up to something Roddy got the wrong end of the stick about. Bound to be. She's only a child. Right. I'll speak to your father," he said, getting up. "Let's get this Prayermaster seen to then."

"What do you mean," I said, getting up slowly, "speak to Dad?"

He turned round on his way down the slope. "Well, he's obviously got to see that you're in one piece before I carry you off to Blest, hasn't he?"

I stared at him. He looked up at me seriously.

"Look," he said, "you've not only got unfinished business, lad. You've also managed to do something I can only do with difficulty, when drunk. *Plus* you've had conversations with animals and held off a Prayermaster when he tried to put you under the prayer. *Not* things most people can do. I consider it my duty, before you try something that kills you or harms your world, to take you home to Blest with me and give you a little basic training. Right?"

"Does the Upper Room want you to?" I asked eagerly.

"Huh!" He went crunching off down the pebbles, talking over his shoulder. "Magids have a free hand mostly in what they do. We do what needs doing. Come along now."

# PART EIGHT
# RODDY

## CHAPTER NINETEEN

*

*I*t was very hot. Grundo and I sat in the shade of the castle gate, drearily discussing what to do. Even if we could *get* to Liverpool or Southampton or Newcastle, we didn't know which and we had almost no money.

"We have to get to somewhere where people know where the King is for certain," Grundo said.

"That's not so easy," I said. "He changes his mind all the time. *And* they change the far-speaker codes every day. The only ones we've got are long out of date. We can't even call them up and ask."

"Your other grandfather found the Progress easily enough," Grundo said.

"That's because he's a Magid," I said. "I wish we

could go to Grandad in London, but that's almost as far away as the port cities. We could call my grandmother up, though. Let's go back to the castle and ask to use their far-speaker."

We trudged all the way back up the winding drive, where we rang at the shiny brass bell-pull again. We rang several times. After that, Grundo heaved up the huge iron knocker and knocked. No one came. It was obvious no one was going to come.

"It stands to reason," Grundo said miserably, as we trudged down to the gate again. "A nasty man like Sir James is bound to have nasty servants. They don't want to know, do they?"

It was a horrible feeling. We sat limply in the shade of the gate once more, completely at a loss.

Eventually, Grundo said wistfully, "I wish I had relations we could go to. Have *you* got any who might be nearer than London?"

"I don't know," I said. "I mean I do have the Dimbers, but I've never met them. They're Dad's family, you see, and Grandad is divorced from my grandmother. They may not want us."

"How near do they live?" Grundo asked.

"How far is Gloucestershire from here?" I said.

Grundo was galvanised. "You're *hopeless*!" he said. He dived for his bag and brought out a map book. "Gloucestershire's practically next door. We may even be *in* it here!" He leafed furiously through the book.

"Whereabouts in Gloucestershire?"

It was my turn to dive for my bag. I fetched out my address book and found Hyde. That was wrong, because my grandmother had refused to change her name from Dimber. I turned to the Ds and discovered that I really knew the address quite well. Mum made me send them a letter every New Year and cards on their birthdays. "Dimber House, Sutton Dimber," I read. There was even a far-speaker code, for what good that did us.

Grundo searched the pages of his map book with a slow, studious finger. The maps didn't bother him, but the writing on them did. "Got it!" he said at last. "And this castle's on the same page. Roddy, it's only about forty miles away! We could walk there, if we had to."

"It would take *days*!" I said. "Walking's slow."

"Then let's go out on the road and find a car to give us a lift," said Grundo.

We repacked our bags and set off. I was still dubious. "I warn you," I told Grundo, as we came out into the blazing road, "they may be very peculiar, if my Aunt Dora is anything to go by."

"Your father's not peculiar," he said.

"That's because Grandad brought him up," I explained. "They wouldn't let anyone male stay with them beyond seven years. That's why Dad and Grandad had to leave. But Grandad once said that he'd had as much as he could take by then. The Dimbers are hereditary witches, you see. And that's all I really know."

301

Grundo sighed enviously. "When I grow up," he pronounced, "I shall take care to have three really peculiar families at least. I want crowds of mad relatives."

We toiled on between hot hedges, arguing how Grundo could possibly achieve this. As we came to the junction with the main road, I remember I was saying, "Three peculiar wives mean three bigamies or three divorces. Can you stand that?" Then I said, "Hang on."

On the shady corner where the roads met, my eye was caught by a blue drift of speedwell flowers. Instantly, my mind was full of a wood in winter and of a hanging swathe of creeper crowded with grey puffs of seed. *Old man's beard*, I found myself thinking, or *Traveller's joy,* and I could feel another of the hurt woman's flower-files opening. *Journeys and expeditions*, this one said, *cross-refer to spirit travelling and shape-shifting*. I didn't think we needed *that* reference, but speedwell flowers were in there, under ordinary journeys, and I realised they were not called *speedwell* without a reason. It was a simple spell for a safe and lucky journey, and I knew we needed that. *Best performed where three ways meet*, it said, and we had that, because the main road went off hot and shimmering in two directions and the castle road met it to make the third way.

Grundo put his bag down and waited expressionlessly while I picked seven of the juicy little flowers. If I hadn't been concentrating so hard on the flower-file in my head, I might have noticed a few danger signals from Grundo then. Grundo was trying to be civilised, but he was deeply jealous by now. From his point of view, I had had all the luck – all the magics, all the interesting relatives – and he had had nothing but being allowed to tag along. It wouldn't take much more to make Grundo dangerously annoyed. And when Grundo was annoyed, he was liable to do strange things with his back to front magic.

But I was far too hot, blinking sweat out of my eyes while I concentrated on translating the rhyme into modern language, and I didn't think of Grundo. I carefully threw one small flower in each of the three roads. Then I threw three more while I said, "Journey flower, speedwell fair, keep us safe and speed us there." Finally, I threw the seventh flower down the road we had to take.

Then I did look at Grundo, but all I saw was that he was white in the heat. His face was freckled on top of his freckles with transparent beads of sweat. "Do we have to walk?" he said.

"I think so," I said.

Grundo grunted and we started walking.

The spell took a while to work. Our feet got hot and sore. Heat came blasting up off the road. Everything shimmered: green shimmers from the humpy green hills on one side and grey quiverings above the long stretches of green-gold wheat on the other. The near-black trees beyond the fields were hazed and motionless in the heat, and unreal puddles glimmered in the distance up the road.

Grundo gave up at the next crossroads. He said he

was probably going to die before my spell worked and sat down in the whippy dry grass by the signpost. I got out the last of the griddle cakes and waved them at him enticingly, but he said he wasn't hungry. I was just putting the packet away again when the first cars we had seen came howling and clicking between the dusty hedges, three of them, one after another. We jumped up and waved.

Everyone in those cars waved cheerfully back and they drove past without stopping.

"Now I *shall* die," Grundo said.

We really knew so very little about hitching lifts – and you should have heard what Grandad said to me later about how dangerous it was! – but we went on waving and cars went on passing, until at length one did stop. It had a notice in the front that said DOCTOR. The man driving it leaned out of his window and asked, "Is this a medical emergency or just a friendly wave?"

We rushed up to the car and explained. He looked serious. "Sutton Dimber's well outside my practice," he said, "but I'll do what I can for you. Climb in and I'll see if we can catch our area nurse."

He drove us to a village clinic. All I remember about that drive is that we tried opening the windows and the wind that blew in was hot. But I remember his car screaming into the clinic forecourt just in time to catch the nurse climbing into her little green car. The doctor passed us on to her and went screaming off again.

The nurse was rather a strict lady, as you might expect, and she thoroughly disapproved of the way we were wandering about the country on our own. She said we were on no account ever to do it again. Sutton Dimber was out of her way too, she said, but she drove us into the nearest town, sweating our way between shimmering hedges, while she talked about all the wells and reservoirs that were drying up and shook her head about the drought. She was probably a bit of a snob. When we told her how we had been left behind by the Royal Progress, she turned a great deal more friendly and stopped talking about the drought.

"Then it's no wonder you're both so ignorant," she said. "Haven't had a chance to learn, have you? Look, I can't do much for you – I've got an old man with a bad leg to see to – but I'll show you the place in the Square where you can catch the Dimber bus. Have you got the money for the fare?"

We counted the money we had and it turned out to be just enough.

"Then ask the bus to drop you outside Dimber House," she said. "You'll get to it before you get to the village and you'd only have to walk the mile back." And as she drove into the Square, she said, "There's the stop. Wait right outside the Chequers Inn or they won't know you're waiting. There's one due at two thirty, any minute now." She stopped and we opened the doors to get out. "They *are* expecting you? The Dimbers?" she said.

"Well, no," I said and started to explain.

She clicked her tongue. "*Oh*, dear! Then I'd better call them up and warn them when I get to my old man," she said. "You really can't just land on people like that, you know. You're not the King."

"We k*now*," Grundo growled, but she didn't hear and drove away.

But she did warn the Dimbers. When we finally got out of the hot, rumbling bus – which was worse than a bus in the Progress because I swear it visited every tiny spot in Gloucestershire and sat and rumbled by village greens in sweltering heat, waiting to connect with other buses - I saw my Aunt Judith anxiously waiting for us outside Dimber House. I knew it must be my aunt because she was about the same age as my Aunt Dora. I could see her even before we got off the bus, because the house stood above the road, all by itself against the sky, and Judith was at the top of the six foot drop down into the road, standing in the bare garden above the wall.

Dimber House was unexpected. From the name, I'd expected it to be big, but it was quite modest. It was tall and narrow, with lots of dark windows, and it looked as if it had escaped from being one of a row of houses in a town. It was not exactly forbidding, but it was strange, standing all by itself in the middle of the country. It was built of row upon row of different dark bricks, ending at the bottom with small deep red ones like tiles, that Aunt Judith said were Roman bricks. She said this showed that

Dimber House had been there continuously, just like the Dimbers, for nearly two thousand years. "And we go back much further than that," she added.

But that was after we'd got off the bus. When she saw us getting off, Judith came striding along the wall calling out, "*There* you are! Come this way, my dears!" and pointing to the nearly hidden steps that went sideways up into the garden. It was a great relief to know she knew we were coming. She watched us anxiously as we climbed the steps, clutching a mauve, handwoven shawl around her in spite of the heat. I could see she was an anxious person. She was tall and thin and long-faced, with long, dark hair that had a lot of grey in it, and she was serious and kind and still rather good-looking, in an arty way. She welcomed us at the top of the steps with a thin, cold hand and a very nice smile.

"I hear the King went off and left you. What an *awful* thing to happen! You're entirely welcome to stay with us, my dears, until we've got in touch with your parents. I'm sure that won't take long because they must be madly worried about you. The trouble is, nobody seems to know where the Progress *is* just at the moment. But it's only a slight snag. You'll see."

She led us up the brick path to the house, talking away. I looked around as we went. Apart from a bush of lavender and a box tree cut into a round ball, there was nothing in this garden. It was all tufty grass. How odd, I thought. I'd always thought that witches cultivated herbs and were generally bowered in fertility. And I tried not to exchange looks with Grundo. I knew that a certain similarity to Grandfather Gwyn's manse could not have escaped him. It was a relief to find a searingly bright, cherry-pink rose climbing over the front porch.

There were squeals and barking coming from behind the house. Grundo says he thought the Dimbers kept pigs. But the sounds cut off when we went into the front part of the house. It was all quiet and stone-flagged and dark in there, and it went up in shallow steps.

"Oh, mind the steps!" Judith cried out, too late. "These are mine," she added apologetically as we both banged into upright wooden looms. The whole dim hall was lined with weaving machinery and smelt like new carpets. There was a spinning wheel ready to be fallen over at the far end. Grundo only just saved himself from it. "This is my trade," Judith explained as she opened the door beyond the spinning wheel. "I sell quite well actually. It always surprises me. Put your bags down on the stairs there and come on in. Here they are, Mother."

"Come in! Come in! Let me set eyes on Arianrhod at last!" my grandmother shrieked from the kitchen. "Where is she? Oh, *there* you are! Aren't you *tall*! Come in, come in, let me look at you, and the boy too."

My grandmother's name is Hepzibah Dimber – but she shrieked at me almost at once that I was to call her Heppy – and she couldn't have been more different from her daughter Judith. She was quite small, a head shorter than me, and she would have been plump if she hadn't worn very obvious corsets which made her look like a tight little bolster. On the top half of the bolster she wore a shiny orange blouse with a flouncy bow, and on the bottom half a short, tight, black skirt. Where Judith had bare feet shoved into wide, arty sandals, Heppy wore stockings with shiny black hearts on them and shiny brown shoes with three inch heels. She trotted towards us, beaming, waving plump hands with several rings on each finger. Her hair was dyed a sort of apricot and her mouth was painted a shiny red.

The minute I saw her, I knew I was a snob – worse than the district nurse. I was ashamed of myself, but it was true. It came of being brought up at Court – and at Court most people consider Sybil pretty vulgar. I now saw that Sybil was refined compared with Heppy. Heppy was the most vulgar woman I'd ever seen. I was amazed that my soldierly, well-bred Grandad Hyde had ever married Heppy. That was the marvel, not the divorce. And it was only my Court training in manners that made me able to smile back at her and kiss her scented, powdered cheek as if I liked doing it. It was awful. I felt like a cold little bitch. But it was the truth.

Grundo got off more lightly. He only had to shake hands. But his eyes widened as his nose approached the flouncy bow and his fingers felt the twenty rings.

My grandmother took us both by one arm and pulled us over into the best light. "Let me look at you," she kept saying. I thought her eyes must be very bad, because the kitchen was one of the brightest rooms in that house. Sunlight streamed in through several windows, and it was all most cheerfully decorated with bright handwoven rugs and knitted cushions, and a big table with a most impressive red and white tablecloth all woven with little figures and flowers. Judith blushed when I looked at it admiringly, and admitted that she had made it. "Then it's no wonder you sell a lot of weaving!" I said.

Meanwhile, Heppy was peering up into our faces and saying, "Well, well, well! She favours you a bit, doesn't she, Judith? Same anxious look about the eyes. And what strong witchcraft! If it wasn't for all this strange stuff she's got in her head, I'd take her by right to be our third witch here. That'd solve a few problems, eh?"

This took my attention back from the tablecloth with a jolt. I realised that Heppy's eyes were not bad at all. She had just brought us into the sunlight in order to exercise her divining powers. She was a very strong witch indeed.

She gave a huge cackle of laughter when she saw I understood this. Then she looked regretful. She twisted her mouth until there were lines all round her lipstick. "Pity," she said. "That stuff in your head's set you on quite another path, Arianrhod. Shame I didn't get to you first, my girl. Now what about you, little man?" She peered intently at Grundo. "Called Ambrose, are you?"

"I'm usually called Grundo," he said.

Heppy gave another cackle of laughter. "Very fitting,

with a growl for a voice like that! But what's wrong with you? You're all back to front!"

"Dyslexia," Grundo said bitterly.

"Don't believe in it," she told him. "It's just a fancy modern word for mixed up. You turn yourself rightabouts and you'll be fine. What's your mother doing to let you get so scrambled in the first place? Who *is* she? Oh, I see. It's that Sybil Temple. Always was a greedy, selfish wifty-wafty, that girl. Trust her to mix a child up! You ought to be living with your father, my boy."

I wanted to *shake* Heppy. Grundo was shamed and embarrassed and shifting from foot to foot. "Nobody knows where my father is," he muttered.

"Ran away from her, ran away from Court," Heppy said. "I know. You should go and find him. It doesn't do a child any good, being dragged round the country after the King all the time, if you ask me. That goes for you too, Arianrhod."

"Er – Heppy, could you call me Roddy?" I said. "I do prefer it."

"Whatever for? That's a *boy's* name!" she squawked. "You ought to be taking up your true heritage, my girl, not trying to be someone else."

I felt my face flooding hot with annoyance. I knew it would take very little for me to have a real row with my grandmother. I didn't like her. And I had a feeling she didn't like me either.

# CHAPTER TWENTY

*

*L*uckily, before things got any worse for me or for Grundo, a kettle whistled over on the stove and Heppy went trotting and clacking over there to make tea. She shortly came trotting and clacking back carrying a vast teapot in a knitted cosy. Grundo and I watched her tottery high heels both ways in nervous fascination. We expected her to tangle with a rug and trip at any moment, but she never did. It was like a miracle.

Judith, meanwhile, was setting the table and laying out covered plates of small sandwiches. "These are only cucumber," she apologised. "We'll do better for supper."

"*Tea!*" Heppy shrieked. "*Tea's up!*" The nearest I can get to describing my grandmother's voice when she screamed is a parrot imitating a steam-whistle. We heard a lot of her screaming later, but I never found a better description.

Her voice must have carried out into the back garden with no trouble at all. They could probably hear it a mile away in the village. The back door burst open almost instantly and, almost before it had hit the wall with a *crash*, two small girls bounded in, followed by a large, curly, yellow dog. A black cat, which had been snoozing on a cushion up to then, woke up and bolted. Grundo said later that the cat's behaviour was highly significant. "And sensible," he added.

One of the small girls was wearing baggy trousers and a white vest. The other was in a trailing, shiny, pink tea-gown which almost certainly belonged to Heppy. Otherwise, you would never have told them apart. They both had the same light brown hair falling in twists to their shoulders, and the same pale, pert little face with huge blue eyes.

There was a brisk minute of pandemonium. The dog barked. Heppy screamed, "Shut the *door*, Ilsabil! *Isadora, you've been at my clothes again!*"

At the same time, Judith was saying, "These are my twins. This is Isadora and this is Ilsabil. Girls, come and meet your cousin Arianrhod and her friend Ambrose."

*Also* at the same time, the twin in trousers screamed, "Oh my *God*!" and backed dramatically against the wall. "It's a *boy* in here! Don't let it near me!" She made fending motions at Grundo. But the twin in the silk dress put on a sickly, gushing smile and glided up to Grundo with both arms out. "A *boy*!" she cried, in a deep, actressy voice. "Let me *at* him!"

Then, just as I was thinking, in a slightly stunned way, that this behaviour was the way you told these twins apart, the one in the dress recoiled from Grundo with a scream. "*Mother!*" she howled. "*How* can you let a great rough *boy* in here?" Instantly, the other twin put on the sickly, gushing smile and undulated up to Grundo, stretching her arms out and yelling, "A kiss, my lover, a *kiss*!"

Grundo's face was a study and I didn't blame him.

"Shake hands with your cousin!" Heppy screamed.

They didn't, of course. Shaking hands would have been too normal for these twins. Ilsabil sank to her baggy-trousered knees. "Oh, my!" she yelled, "have you *really* spared time from Court to come to our humble house?" while Isadora swished her pink dress and said, "Of course, when I come to Court I shall outshine everyone there."

"That could be true," I said. "And you might not like it."

Neither twin listened to me. They hurled themselves into chairs round the table shouting, "*What's for tea?*" and dragged the covers off the plates. "Oh!" screamed one of them, "I *hate* cucumber! I'm *allergic* to it!" while the other one yelled, "*Cucumber*! I *love* it!" Again, just as I was thinking this was another way to tell them apart, they swapped roles, and the one who hated cucumber shouted, "Snatch! Seize! I'm going to eat all these *delicious* sandwiches *myself*!" Meanwhile, the other one whined, "Moth-*ther*! I can't eat *this*! I'm *electric* to cucumber!"

"Allergic, dear," Judith said anxiously. "And I don't think you are."

"Yes, I am," whined the twin.

"Yes, she *is*," whined the other one. "She fizzes all over."

It was like this the whole time. At first, I tried telling myself that all the children at Court had to be so well behaved that I'd forgotten what normal little girls were like. That may have been true, but I very soon decided that Ilsabil and Isadora had never been normal in their lives. Neither of them was the same person for more than two minutes. Neither of them seemed to care what she did or said, as long as it fixed everyone's attention on her.

Judith watched them all the time with an anxious, pleading smile.

Heppy gazed at them proudly. "Aren't they a caution?" she said several times. Then she asked Grundo, "Can you tell them apart?"

"No, and I've given up trying," he said. "I'm calling them both Izzy."

"Pathetic!" squealed both twins. "*Per-thetic*! Izzy, izzy, is he stupid!" This was followed by, "Mother! I'm very hurt and insulted!" from one twin, and "Oh, gorgeous boy! He's calling me Izzy!" from the other. And then the same thing the other way round.

I had hoped to talk to Judith about Sybil and the Merlin. Judith seemed to be the calm, sensible one in this family, and I was sure she could give me proper advice. But it was hopeless even to try during tea. The Izzies kept everyone's thoughts and ears on them the whole time.

"They're very excited at seeing you, you see," Judith explained, in her anxious, apologising way. "They've heard so much about you and their Uncle Daniel and the Progress."

The moment everyone had finished tea, the Izzies jumped down and rushed shrieking to the back door. They were stopped there by an even louder shriek from Heppy. "Wait! Take Ambrose and the dog with you and play in the garden. We have to show Arianrhod the Regalia."

"Oh, *why*? I want to see it too," shouted Ilsabil.

"Stupid stuff!" Isadora proclaimed, with a toss of hair and chin. "I wouldn't go and look at it if you paid me."

Then of course they did it the other way around, excep that Ilsabil added, "Regalia – such boredom!" with a deep, world-weary sigh.

As for Grundo, he positively scowled at being told to play with the Izzies. I think the only thing that reconciled him to it was the dog. Grundo has always wanted a dog, even more than I have, but the Waymaster's Office forbids pets on the Progress. He went out into the garden with one hand on the dog's curly back, while Heppy and Judith took me past the looms and into their front room.

Good! I thought. Maybe we can talk now.

It was one of those hushed rooms with a lot of upright antique furniture and books in glass cases. It looked as if it were very rarely used, but now I come to think of it, they must have used it every day. Somehow, they must have managed to make the Izzies take care in there.

"Phew!" Heppy said, as the quiet of it closed in around us. "I can hear myself think again! Roll on the day when we have to turn one of those girls out!"

Judith looked anguished. "There always have to be three Dimbers," she explained to me, "one from each generation and no more. In seven years' time, there is going to be the most *agonising* choice. We've no idea whether we'll keep Isadora or Ilsabil on as our third. How *do* you choose between identical twins?"

"Time enough to choose," Heppy said. "Don't buy trouble, Jude. And as I always tell her, Arianrhod, it was just as agonising in *my* day, when we had to choose between Judith and Dora." She chuckled. "And I'd complicated things by going and having your father before either of the girls. That's just as unheard-of as twins in our family, I can tell you."

"What would have happened to my father," I asked, "if Grandad hadn't taken him to London?"

"Oh, he'd have been packed off over the hill where we usually send the boys," Heppy said. "There's a family of male witches with a farm there. It's where the husbands come from usually. I was unusual, falling for Maxwell.

317

And, while we're on this, I'll tell you straight, Arianrhod, this is quite a problem, you bringing the boy with you. You yourself are welcome for as long as you care to stay, but seven days is all I can house a male stranger. What would you like us to do for you?"

"Well," I said, "you've been awfully kind and I don't want to cause a problem. If you know how to find where the King is, Grundo and I will rejoin the Progress as soon as we can."

Heppy looked up at her tall daughter and Judith, as usual, looked anxious. "Huh!" Heppy said. "You can't find them either, can you? Thought so. Those wizards are keeping the King secret again, aren't they?"

"I was told one of the ports," I said.

Heppy swept that aside. "They could be anywhere. No, your best bet is to go to your grandfather in London. Maxwell can do the finding for you. He's good at it. Judith, when you've a moment, will you get Maxwell on the far-speaker? If I speak to him, we'll only end up shouting at one another."

Judith smiled at me. "Of course. But first…"

"Yes, yes, she has to be shown the Dimber Regalia. It's her right as a female of the family." Heppy, upright and barrel-shaped, bustled across the room. One wall was dark oak panelling. I watched as she laid one chubby, much beringed hand on a particular place in the wooden squares. "Now you'll see," she said over her shoulder. Then she worked magic. It was nothing like any of the magic I had in my head. It was reverent magic, very old and very practised, and it sent a shiver up my spine. I felt another shiver as two doors, that had not been there in the wall before, came creaking open like a cupboard. Inside, something blazed. There was a sweet smell, of old wood and new flowers.

Judith put an arm round my shoulders and pushed me gently towards the open space. "Our vessels of virtue," she said softly. "Full of beauty and power."

I found myself gasping. Inside the wooden space, laid out on red velvet, were cups, bowls, plates and jugs of gold and silver. All were most exquisitely made and wonderfully elegantly shaped. Some had patterns raised in the metal – patterns that I knew meant something, except that the meanings were just out of reach somehow – and some had small clusters of sapphires and pearls set into them. One of the most beautiful was a great cut-glass goblet with a base of gold filigree that grew around the glass like part of a flower. The centrepiece was a majestic, flat chalice with golden handles, that had tiny running patterns on every part of it. Around it were old, old cups, worn lopsided with use. I could see everything was immensely old and full of power. And it all felt alive. The life in the things seemed to pour out of the cupboard and scintillate on all the elegant, shiny surfaces. While I was trying to decide which vessel was the most splendid – the crystal goblet, the chalice, or maybe the small, strange one like a vase, irregularly dotted with bulging pearls and sapphires – their sheer aliveness seemed to cause two little gleams of light to go dancing over them. They looked almost like eyes.

"Aren't they something?" Heppy said warmly.

At her parrot-voice, the eyes vanished, but the sense of warmth and strength stayed. The things felt so safe and so strong that I had no doubt that they would help me when I tried to explain about Sybil and the Merlin.

"They're the repositories of our strength," Judith said raptly, clasping her hands gawkily to her chest. The shine from the vessels was gold and silver on her face. It made her look quite beautiful for a moment.

"And," Heppy said, "believe it or not, we use them every day."

"Yes, every day, for whatever needs working on in our jurisdiction," Judith said. "We're working at slaking this drought just now. And there seems to be a little imbalance in the magics here at the moment that we're trying to put right."

"And you use everything in here?" I asked.

"Not all at once, of course," Heppy said. "But according to which day it is and where the moon is. We give them all a drop of blood every time we use them. This is why we can't have men around. Can't you feel how secret and how *female* they are?"

To tell the truth, I couldn't. The strength that came out of the space lined with red velvet did not feel to me particularly much to do with women, or men either. But I did my best not to say this. "They are – quite wonderful," I said. "Quite the most strong and beautiful..." Then my worries got the better of me and I burst out with "Oh, Heppy, Judith, *how* do I go about raising the land?"

"Good *Lords*!" Heppy banged the two halves of the cupboard shut and the cracks in panels where they had been vanished at once. "Heavens, child, don't *say* such things! In front of the Regalia too! Don't even *think* them! Whatever put that notion into your head?"

"You really shouldn't know about that," Judith said reproachfully. "Come and sit down, my dear, and tell us what made you say that. I can see you're dreadfully anxious about something, but I feel sure you have to be over-reacting."

I could see they were both going to treat me as an over-fanciful child. I sighed. But I sat down all the same in the upright chair Judith guided me to and tried to explain. I was so worried by then that tears were trying to push themselves out of my eyes, and I could hear my voice shaking as I talked.

And it was no good. Heppy simply laughed comfortably. "No, dear. You've got the wrong end of the stick somewhere. The Merlins are always for good and Court wizards are chosen for their loyalty. What you're talking about just can't happen in Blest. We're the most stable of all the worlds. You misunderstood something grown-up, dear. That's all."

"It's so easy," Judith explained soothingly, "to hear

three adults talking in the dark and to imagine all *sorts* of queer things. No wonder you went on and had bad dreams about it. If you'd overheard them in daylight, you'd have felt quite different."

"But you said yourselves that the magics were unbalanced," I said desperately. "And Grandfather Gwyn told me…"

"*Hush!*" Heppy said sternly. "We don't mention That One here. And he's someone you can't be expected to understand, not for years yet. You go and play in the garden, Arianrhod my dear, and don't trouble your head any more. Judith will get on the far-speaker to Maxwell for us and we'll have you all sorted out before bedtime. You'll see."

I left Judith dragging a far-speaker out from among the looms and went dejectedly out into the back garden. It was almost as empty as the front, just grass - where Grundo was sitting with his arms round the dog and wearing his most faraway look - and some wire netting around it.

The Izzies were cavorting around the grass. "Pathetic!" said one.

"This boy is per-*thetic!*" said the other. "Fancy not understanding us Dimbers!"

When they saw me, they left off trying to provoke Grundo and began doing handstands up against the wire netting. "*You* understand us, don't you?" Isadora said. She was rather muffled because her dress had turned upside down with her. I pretended not to hear and looked anxiously at Grundo instead. He just looked vague. He had had tons of practice in ignoring Alicia after all.

"Our family *never* stays married," Ilsabil proclaimed, clattering the netting with her feet. "It's against our rules. Anyway, I'm thinking of joining a circus."

"We *invented* single parent families," Isadora said, from inside her dress. She came down, tangled in pink silk. "Our customs go back thousands of years," she added breathlessly, "but I shall never marry. Boys are too pathetic. So are circuses. I shall be a great actress."

"I believe you," I said, as Ilsabil came down in her turn.

Ilsabil went upside down again with a twang almost immediately. "I shall marry a rich wizard," she declared, "and wear lots of jewels and lipstick. Then I shall kick him out and keep his money after seven years. Because *I'm* going to be chosen for Dimber third, not Isadora— *Ouch*!"

She ended in a scream and a collapse when Isadora rushed at her shrieking, *"No you won't!"* and shoved her hard in the stomach.

"Filthy little *witch*!" Ilsabil yelled. They fell on one another and fought energetically. The pink dress tore with a noise like a gunshot.

Grundo, I could tell, neither heard nor saw any of this. I thought at the time that he had simply tuned the Izzies out, the way he does with Alicia or Sybil. It never occurred to me he might be up to something.

# CHAPTER TWENTY-ONE

*

*I* found out what Grundo had been up to in the middle of that night. But before that, Judith had rung London at least twenty times. She came away from the far-speaker looking more anxious each time.

"I can't understand it," she said. "I'm getting the engaged signal every time!"

"Don't worry so," Heppy said. "Dora's probably calling that vile man of hers. That Jerome. Or Maxwell has some crisis on. Try again early tomorrow. And I'll try telepathy after that. I'd try it now, only it always annoys Maxwell so when I do it. I always seem to catch him at an awkward moment." And she cackled with laughter.

Of course, Judith did worry. She was that sort. She set

about cooking supper with her long, kind face all tense and wrinkled. I offered to help her, but she wouldn't hear of it. Children didn't help in that house. So I went away and defended Grundo from the Izzies instead.

They had discovered how to victimise him by then. One would twirl in and poke him, chanting, "Long nose, long nose, oh, pathetic long nose!" and the other would come sweetly undulating up on the other side and ask in a babyish little voice, "Forgive me asking, but where *did* you get all those pretty freckles from?" Then, of course, they would swap roles.

Grundo couldn't handle this at all. He was looking desperate when I came up. I took hold of an Izzy in each hand and shook them, quite roughly. "If you little freaks do or say one more thing to Grundo," I said, "I shall turn you both into *fleas*. Don't think I can't. So leave him alone. Now."

They twisted round and stared up at me innocently. "But men are fair game," Isadora said.

"*Heppy* says so," added Ilsabil.

"And *I* say not," I said. "And I say that *you* are ignorant, badly brought up little witches, and I've got hold of you, so you are going to do what *I* say, not what Heppy tells you. Understand?"

Their little pink mouths opened charmingly. "Oh, but..."

"But nothing," I said. "Don't try and charm *me*. *I* don't think you're sweet. I think you both need spanking." I banged their heads together, not quite as hard as I wanted to, and stalked away.

I could feel them staring after me with hatred. I spent the rest of that evening expecting them to take some horrible revenge on me. But, to my surprise, they treated me almost with respect. I don't think anyone had ever told them off before. They didn't like it, but it seemed to have made them think.

All the same, I think they put something slimy in Grundo's bed that night. Poor Grundo. He was given a little room in the attic next door to the Izzies. I was given a grand guest bedroom halfway down the house. It had a wonderful high brass bedstead with knobs on its brass rails and a whole bank of pillows, and it was covered with an enormous patchwork quilt.

"Be gentle with the quilt," Judith said. "My great-grandmother made it – your great-*great*-grandmother, that is. It's quite fragile these days."

"It's beautiful," I said, because it was. I looked at the big windows. They had brass curtain rails threaded with big brass rings. The curtains hanging from the rings were as beautiful as the quilt, but newer. "Did you weave the curtains?" I asked. "They're lovely."

"Well, yes, as a matter of fact I did," Judith said. She went away with an anxious, apologetic smile, as near to being pleased as I had seen her.

I settled down under the ancestral patchwork and fell straight into sleep. I was tired out. And it seemed to me that I had another dream after a while, of the same kind that I had dreamed at Grandfather Gwyn's. I thought I floated out from under the quilt and through the window and sped off across the countryside. Dim, blue fields and dark copses unfurled beneath me for miles, until I arrived at Belmont Castle and whirled through the grounds to the Inner Garden. This time, I didn't go into it. I sort of roosted on the wall, looking down into the garden's moist, quiet spaces. Grandfather Gwyn's horrible horse-standard was still there. I could see it as a white streak at the corner of my eye while I examined the garden.

It was spoilt. The lawns were drying out, making trees droop and bushes wither, and the waters did not seem to be running freely anywhere in the conduits and cisterns. Where the waterfalls poured into the pools, they made a strange, harsh tinkling, quite unlike the earlier deep, singing gurgle. Some animal-heads had stopped running entirely. But this was only the outer sign of what Sybil had done. When I looked more closely – in a way it was feeling as much as seeing – I found a yellow-white ghostly layer of rottenness over everything. It covered the lawns and the flowers, and was particularly disgusting where it draped and glopped over the trees or oozed down the waterfalls.

I wasn't wrong about this! I thought in my dream. After what Heppy and Judith had said, I had been almost distrusting my own memories, thinking perhaps that I *had* made a mistake, or imagined Sybil talking to Sir James and the Merlin, and possibly that I had only dreamed that they had summoned Grandfather Gwyn here. Now – at least in my dream – I knew it had been true.

Then I turned my head and saw someone else standing sadly on the wall beside me. She towered above me, tall and slender in a dress that blew about without any wind to blow it, and her long hair blew across, almost like tendrils, to touch me. It was the touch of her hair that had made me notice her. Even so, I was not sure at first that she was really there. I could see right through her, to trees and stars in the sky. She was just a sort of whiteness faintly across these things, like a cloud. Then she looked at me with huge eyes and I saw that she *was* real. She seemed to be about my age, but I was fairly sure that she was older than the garden and more real than I was.

"This used to be one of the strong shrines," she murmured. "It anchored the land." She sighed. She beckoned me to watch and reached down underneath Sybil's layer of rottenness, where she took hold of the good part of the garden that still lay down there and pulled gently. She drew it out, all the power and virtue and goodness that was left, as if it was a huge, mossy cloth covered with faint, running glimmers, and draped it dripping around her shoulders. It smelt wonderful, of rain and woodland and deep, clear waters. "I have to take it back for a while," she mused as she pulled it round her. She seemed to be thinking aloud, but she was speaking to me too. "It will cause a strong imbalance."

While I was waiting for her to say more, somebody called my name from inside the guest bedroom and I had to leave in a hurry. This is the way when somebody calls you by name. I went with such helter-skelter speed that the dark country teemed and whirled underneath me and I landed in the brass bedstead with a thump. I was quite giddy when I sat up. But, this time, I knew I was awake. I could feel the frail squares of the quilt under my fingers and hear the brass rails rattle, both on the bed and above the curtains.

"Who's there and what do you want?" I asked slurrily.

Someone said, "Ah, she did hear!" in a satisfied way, and several other someones said, "We are. We need to speak to you."

There was light coming from low down at the side of the room, gleaming and yellowish. I never found out where the light came from. I looked in the morning and there was nothing. I blinked in the low, golden glow and stared. There was a most peculiar creature perched on the brass rail at the end of the bed, looking at me with glistening, pinkish eyes. He was big, at least as big as the curly dog asleep downstairs, and he had a protruding front and long, fluted, trailing parts, like wings. Hand-like parts gripped the brass rail and a face-like, bird-like part stared at me. What struck me as most peculiar, though, was that he was wholly transparent. I mean, I could see through him, just as I could see through the lady I had just met, but where she had been like vapour or a cloud, he was like a balloon full of nothing, and faintly pinkish all through. Without that low-down light, I would not have been able to see him at all. The same light, I saw suddenly, glistened on a whole row more of the creatures clustered along the curtain rails above. These ones seemed to be smaller and they were all sorts of different shapes.

"Who are you all?" I said.

"I am the person who inhabits the Dimber chalice," the big one said gravely. "The people on the curtain rails inhabit the other vessels of the Regalia. We have inhabited these vessels and worked magics at the bidding of the Dimbers since we were first summoned, hundreds of years ago. We want to know if this is wrong."

"Yes, is this slavery or not?" chirped one of the ones on the curtain rail.

"The boy told us it was," sang another.

"We used to be free folks," another chimed in, "until we were summoned and bound by magic."

"So is this wrong?" the big one enquired. "The boy says that it is. He told us that in this day and age there are laws that forbid one person to imprison another, or to force people to work unless they have agreed to do so. He says the Dimbers are acting unlawfully in this. Would you agree?"

Oh, dear! I thought. Now I knew why the Regalia had felt so much alive. I also knew why I had seen those two little spots of light, so much like eyes. They *were* eyes, Grundo's, looking in. He had been spoiling for trouble anyway, and it must have been the last straw when he was sent away to play with the Izzies while I was shown the treasure.

"Let me get this straight," I said slowly. It was difficult to think. Half my mind felt as if it was still with the Inner Garden. "Grundo told you that you've been enslaved by the Dimbers, is that right? So now you have to live in the chalice and the other things and do magic when they tell you to. How did they get you to live in the things?"

"By spell and ritual," said the big creature. "One day I was free and floating in my hedgerow, and the next, I was haled into the chalice and my power was at the command of Eliza Dimber. It was the same for the others, with different Dimbers."

"We had no choice," twittered the ones on the railings. "The spell laid on us was strong."

"But that was a long time ago, wasn't it?" I said. "The laws might have been different then. And I'm not sure it was slavery. They do reward you, don't they?"

The creatures on the railings burst out twittering again, like a row of birds. "They give us blood," one sang, and another sang, "But blood is not our proper food!" Another piped, "What is a reward? We never asked to work." A small one answered, "Reward is living in a vessel of glory," and others twittered him down with, "Freedom is better!" A medium-sized one chanted, "But we would be dead by now, but for the spells and the blood."

"This is all true," the big one said, staring at me solemnly, "but the boy said it was slavery because no one asked us first."

"I suppose that *is* right, in a way," I felt forced to agree. "But why did you come to me?"

"The boy has unbreakable protections round his room," the medium-sized one chanted from the curtain rail. "We can't get in."

This did not surprise me. If I were next door to the Izzies all night, I would make sure no one could get into my room too. It surprised me slightly that Grundo could do this, but then Grundo never seems to know what he can do until he does it. All the same... "I don't understand," I said. "If Grundo has already told you all this – did you come to me for a second opinion or what?"

"He advised us to speak to Hepzibah or Judith Dimber," the big creature told me, "but they have never known that we exist. They were asleep and we couldn't get them to hear us. And we need to know whether we should proceed now with the rest of the boy's advice."

"Oh-oh!" I said. "What else has Grundo told you?"

"To leave the treasure and stop doing the Dimbers' bidding," chirped a small one from the curtains.

The rest burst out twittering at that. "Good advice!" or "Bad advice!" or "No one has ever advised us before!" and "No one has ever *noticed* us before!" came from a dozen transparent, pulsing throats. It was like a tree full of sparrows until the big one took charge again.

He frilled and fluttered his trailing bits, in a way that reminded me exactly of Judith clutching and resettling her mauve shawl. The rest all stopped twittering when he did this. "Looking to the future," he said, "viewing what is to come, we think we should take the boy's advice."

The smaller ones all went crowding this way and that along the curtain rails, looking very anxious indeed. I saw their point. I saw where all this had been leading now. If I was booked to be enslaved to one of the Izzies, I would be terrified. "I see," I said. "It might not be so bad. They seem quite kind to their dog."

The big creature just looked at me out of sad shining pink eyes.

"Yes," I said, "but – if Heppy and Judith don't know you exist, they won't understand it if you leave. It seems a bit hard on them. What is it that you actually *do* for them?"

"Secret ceremonies with me," the big one said, "and appropriate rituals with all of us, for the health of the land and its magics, in this part of the country. Our belief is that both Dimber ladies have power enough of their own to do this without us."

But they love that treasure, I thought. They revere it. If these people leave, the Regalia's going to be like the Inner Garden after the lady on the wall took the goodness away.

"Look," I said. "Your problem is really Ilsabil, isn't it? Or Isadora?"

None of the creatures spoke, but there was a terrible tense stillness about the way they perched that showed me I was right. They were dreadfully loyal, though. None of them would say a word against any Dimber. How can I handle this? I wondered. Oh, *blast* Grundo! What a perfect revenge he's taken!

"I think what you need," I said, "is some way of making them realise that you're people and just as alive as their dog."

This caused a perfect storm of cheeping and chanting. It was like having the dawn chorus in my bedroom.

"If only they *knew*!"

"We've served so long, but they all think of us as *things*!"

"Just to be *thanked* for once!"

"And so we *are* people, just as you are!"

"They can't *see* us, they can't *see* us or hear us!"

"We want them to *know*!"

They made me lose my thread. "What were you before you were made to inhabit the Regalia?" I asked them.

"Merely some of the folk who live in the land," the big one told me. "You people never seem to see us, but there are crowds of us everywhere. In summer we sway and sing, and climb ladders of hot air…"

I missed the next bit because a flower-file suddenly opened in my head. You took your time! I thought crossly, but it was all there, under *Mullein* again. *Invisible beings of the day: very potent transparent folk existing in crowds all over the land, idle and joyful, can be commanded but should be entreated with politeness as, when annoyed, they can cause storms, floods and droughts. Cross-refer to Bad Magics: enslavement.* She had known them well, the hurt lady.

"It was high summer," the big creature was saying, when I started listening again, "and it was a great shock to me when the spells were cast and I was hurled from my bed in the warm air into the cold, gold chalice. I admit that my existence has been useful since…"

*Should be entreated with politeness*, I thought. And they're very loyal really. "Look, wouldn't you rather help the Dimbers of your own free will?" I asked.

"Certainly," said the big creature, frilling his trailing parts. "It is not the work we object to. We would like to be *asked* to do what we do."

"Politely," muttered someone on the curtains.

"Of course," I said. "So this is what you should do. You mustn't really leave, you must just leave the Regalia for a day or so, until the Dimbers realise that you exist. I'll help. I'll tell them that you're really people that they didn't know they'd enslaved. Then when they start talking to you, tell the Dimbers that you're quite willing to go on working for them, so long as they ask you politely *first*. Tell them that slavery is wrong. Do you think that will do it?"

This was exactly what they had hoped I would say. They told me so in chorus, singing and twittering and chanting, and thanking me over and over again. I settled back to sleep, smiling a little smugly, because it seemed to me that I'd done everyone a favour. I'd scotched Grundo, helped these strange invisible folks, showed Heppy and Judith that there had been a dreadful mistake all these years, and possibly even forced the Izzies to be polite to something for once.

It didn't work out like that at all.

# Chapter Twenty-Two

*

$T$here must have been an early morning ritual. I was woken by Heppy screaming. She screamed like a parrot, on and on and on. I sprang up in my nightclothes and rushed downstairs to the stiff living room. Grundo came tumbling and yawning down after me, wearing nothing but his trousers.

The cupboard in the panelling was open. I saw at a glance that the Regalia inside was lifeless. It was still beautiful, but it was lacklustre, simply cups and plates and vases, with nothing special about them, except fine workmanship. It could have been merely the Crown Jewels.

Heppy was in front of the cupboard, dressed up to the nines in a blue satin two-piece, jumping up and down in her high heels and screaming. Judith was wringing her hands under a lovely lace shawl, and the Izzies were there too, sitting in two corners looking scared and almost subdued. They were wearing frilly yellow dresses with yellow bows in their hair, and I had no idea which was which, even less than yesterday.

Mainly I thought, Oh, dear! I think this was an important ceremony!

"*Look!*" Heppy shrieked, pointing a dramatic arm at the cupboard. "The virtue's *gone! Somebody's stolen all our power!*"

"No, no, they haven't, Heppy, honestly," I said. I took a quick look around. The big creature was sitting on one of the open cupboard doors, looking sorrowful and anxious. His frilly parts were almost trailing in Heppy's face, but I hadn't seen him straightaway because these strange beings were truly extremely hard to see by daylight. The rest were perched around the room, roosting beside vases on the mantelpiece, on the long-case clock and on top of the glass-fronted bookcases. "They're all here," I said. Heppy just went on screaming, so I shouted, loudly and slowly, "Heppy! THEY'RE ALL HERE! All the folks that inhabit the Regalia are SITTING HERE IN THIS ROOM!"

"What do you mean?" Heppy bawled at me.

"The power in the Regalia!" I said. "It's because long-ago Dimbers put spells on these invisible people and forced them to live in the treasure and – and empower it for you. They don't look like us, but they're alive. They're people too, just like we are. Honestly, Heppy. Judith, can't you see them? They're perched all over the room. They've been enslaved to the Regalia for centuries…"

Heppy was looking so thunderous by then that I began to falter a bit, but I tried to keep going.

"They came to see me in the night," I said, "because they'd realised that they'd never been *asked* to do what they do. But they're ever so loyal and they didn't want to leave. They were just upset that you treated them like *things* instead of people. So I suggested…"

Heppy screamed. Her screaming up to then had been nothing to the way she screamed now. She screamed. And she screamed. Then she cursed. Then she yelled, "Are *you* telling me, little madam from Court, how to deal with my *own Regalia*? The – the *cheek* of it!"

"All they want is for you to ask them nicely," I said desperately, but I don't think she listened.

"The cool, barefaced *cheek* of it!" Heppy screamed. And she went on screaming, "The *cheek* of it!" with occasional shrieks of, "*Judith*, have *you* ever heard the *like*? In all my *days*, I've never *seen* such ingratitude! My own flesh and blood too!"

She was an almost continuous background to Judith, who was anxiously trying to ask me to explain a bit more. I did my best, but it was not easy, because I wanted to keep Grundo out of it and I very much *didn't* want to tell the Izzies' mother that it was the Izzies the Regalia folks were afraid of. Judith just could not seem to understand.

And Heppy was not giving herself a chance to understand anyway.

"But *why* did you tell the treasure it was enslaved, dear?" Judith asked me patiently. She just couldn't seem to think of it as *people* living *in* the Regalia, whatever I said. "What made you suddenly do this?"

Grundo suddenly spoke up, in his calmest, deepest voice. "She didn't. It was me. I talked to the Regalia first. I told them they were enslaved. And they are."

That set Heppy off again, worse than ever. She was so angry that she practically danced. "*Get out of my sight!*" she screamed at Grundo. "Go and get dressed. Pack your things." She glared at Grundo, pop-eyed with rage, until Grundo turned white and fled. "I'm not having that boy in my house one moment longer!" she screamed. "He's going! Going this very morning! *And you!*" she shrieked, turning on me. "You sneaky little traitress! You're going too!"

"I am not a traitress or a sneak," I said. I was almost as angry as she was. "I was simply trying to deal in an honourable way with people who came to me for advice. You're just not *listening* to me!"

"You chilly little sneak!" she screamed. "I take you in and you go behind my back!"

"I *had* to!" I shouted. "You can't see them and I *can*!"

"*And* you're a liar!" she shouted back. "Judith, put them both in the car and drive them to Mrs Candace. *She* can sort them out. I've had enough of them."

And this was more or less what happened, except that Judith anxiously insisted we were to have breakfast first, because it was a long drive. She insisted on the Izzies coming too. "You're too upset, Mother," she said. "They'll only bother you."

While Heppy was arguing that her own dear twins never bothered her in the slightest, it was only *some people*! – glaring at me – I tried to apologise to all the transparent creatures sitting sadly about in the room. "I'm so sorry," I said. "I don't seem to have done any..."

That was all I managed to say before Heppy rushed at me and shoved me out into the hallway. "*I'll* talk to them! It's *my right!*" she yelled.

At least she was beginning to admit that the creatures existed, I thought while I was chewing toast I didn't want. The Izzies were grinning secretly at one another and only pretending to be scared by then. I hoped very much that they might begin to believe in the creatures too, but I simply couldn't tell. They seemed to take Heppy's word for most things, so if Heppy believed... No, all I could hope was that they would not be too rowdy in the car, and that was probably too much to hope for anyway.

The car lived in a niche carved in the wall below the front garden, and it was quite new and modern. That surprised me. I had expected any car that Judith drove to be sort of handwoven, if you see what I mean. We all got in. Judith made me sit beside her in the front, which meant that Grundo had to sit in the back between the Izzies. I'm not sure, but I *think* this may have been Judith's quiet way of punishing Grundo for abusing their hospitality. He looked very white and sulky between the two frilly yellow dresses.

I probably looked much the same. As we rushed between hedges along the hot, white road, I felt thoroughly in disgrace. I thought I *had* abused the Dimbers' hospitality really. It came to me that the honourable, *sensible* thing to have done last night was for me to have gone and woken Judith or Heppy up and tried to show them the folks perching on the rails, or at least explained about them. But, I had to admit, this would simply have meant we had the row in the night instead of this morning. Heppy would have screamed just as loudly then. Because – and this was the thing niggling and pinching at me – Heppy did not like me any more than I liked her. It was a horrid fact. You are supposed to get on with your own grandmother, and I didn't. The reason I had not tried to wake even Judith up last night was that, as soon as I saw the strange being perched on my bed-rail, I knew I was about to go one up on Heppy. It had given me a feeling of triumph, almost like gloating. And that was horrible.

I felt so bad about it all that I just had to talk. "Who is Mrs Candace?" I asked.

"Pathetic!" said one of the Izzies. "Not heard of Mrs Candace!"

"My dear!" said the other Izzy, in a fine, affected voice. "Mrs Candace's Mrs Superwitch and she can *skin* you with her eyes, my dear!"

"Be quiet, dears," Judith said in her mild way. "She's the Lady of Governance, Arianrhod, if you know what that means."

"No," I said. "I'm afraid I don't."

"She doesn't know everything then, Miss Courtly Knowitall," jeered an Izzy.

"Actually, my dear, she's just plumb ignorant," the other joined in. "Be kind to her. It's just her upbringing."

It seemed to be me they had their knife into today. Not surprising. I turned round and said, in a low, menacing voice, "I said something about fleas last night. And I meant it."

They gave me mean looks and shut up.

"The Lady of Governance," Judith said, just as if there had been no interruption. "Yes, I suppose you might not know. The Court and the Progress concentrate almost entirely on the male side of magic, don't they? The Lady of Governance is the female counterpart of the Merlin. She's as powerful as he is, but she doesn't usually concern herself with State magics. She controls the more domestic things. This one, Mrs Candace, makes a point of monitoring us hereditary witches – in the nicest possible way, because after all we're all busy with the health of the land – and I suppose that's why Mother thought of her."

This was complete news to me. Up till then, I had supposed the Merlin was on his own. Maybe, I thought, Sybil doesn't know about Mrs Candace either! Then this could be a good thing, instead of a total disgrace. I was grateful to Judith for giving me something else to think of beside my failings as a granddaughter.

I sat and thought about a counterweight to the Merlin as I stared out of the window and Judith drove. After a while, I realised I could see the wild relatives of the creatures from the Regalia. They were almost completely transparent and had no colour at all. They were all over the place and they looked completely, utterly happy. They purred in the heat with peacefulness. They sat and swung in hedges, or lazed in hovering crowds over the ripening wheat, or blurred into dancing distance against hills and woodland. Yesterday, I would have taken them for heat haze, but today I saw they were of all shapes and sizes, although none was as large as the creature from the chalice.

I watched them tumble and fly among the grass by the hedges in the wind from our wheels and wondered why I could suddenly see them now. Perhaps all the information from the hurt lady had expanded that part of my brain – but it felt more as if I had simply only needed to know they existed in order to see them. But how did Grundo know about them? How did he spot them in the Regalia?

I asked Grundo during the sweltering break when Judith bought more motor fuel, while the Izzies danced around us both calling names.

He looked surprised. "I've always been able to see them," he said.

We got back in the car. Grundo seemed to be holding his own in the back against the Izzies, but there were moments when the struggle tipped the Izzies' way and their voices rose in a waspish whine. "*Per*-thetic boy! He's all in a shell. He's an oyster!"

"Not an oyster, my dear. A snail. All ooooozy!"

If it got any worse than this, I said, "Fleas!" over my shoulder. Judith simply pretended not to hear.

It was a long, long drive. At lunchtime, we stopped on a baking village green for prettybread from the local baker. It wasn't very nice, stale and tough. The Izzies took one bite of theirs and then announced they were slimming, so Grundo ate it all, while the Izzies turned cartwheels all over the village green. A row of fascinated children turned up and stared at the Izzies' frilly yellow knickers, until a big woman came out of the Post Office and sent them all indoors.

Judith didn't seem to notice any of this. Nor did she pay attention when we all got back into the searingly hot car seats and the Izzies discovered there was no prettybread left. She just said, "Well, it wasn't very nice, dears," and drove on.

The rest of the drive was full of complaints from the Izzies. They were too hot, they were starving and it wasn't *fair*. On and on, while the country turned to smooth green hills with lines of trees at their tops, and very straight white roads. Then there was blue distance and a narrow spire against the horizon.

"There's Salisbury," Judith said. "Nearly there." Then, much to my surprise, she spoke quite sternly to the Izzies.

"Mrs Candace is a very old lady, dears, and she can do Heppy and me a lot of harm if we annoy her. So I must ask you to behave really *beautifully* while we're there. Can you do that?"

"But, my dear, I *am* beautiful," replied one Izzy.

The other whined, "Old ladies are so *boring*. Can't we stay in the car?"

"No," said Judith. "She'll be very disappointed not to see you."

It must have been misguided mother-love that made Judith say that. We finally stopped at a house on the outskirts of Salisbury, that was almost hidden by high evergreen hedges, and walked stiffly up the path behind the hedges, where Judith pushed open a green front door into a cool, elegant house and stepped inside, calling, "Mrs Candace! It's Judith Dimber. You were expecting us, weren't you?"

"Yes, my dear. I'm in here," an elderly voice called back.

We trooped into the room, where Mrs Candace was sitting elegantly on a low chair beside a table full of tea-things. She turned. She had the most beautiful small head loaded with thick ,white hair, and amazingly shapely legs in silken stockings. The dismay on her face when she saw the Izzies nearly made me laugh. "I didn't know you were bringing the twins, dear," she said. I realised that the affected voice the Izzies kept using was an imitation of Mrs Candace. She was so old fashioned and well bred and well spoken that she did sound almost affected.

"We knew you would just *love* to see us!" one Izzy said. It was almost an exact imitation. Mrs Candace winced.

The other Izzy said rudely, "And who's *he*? We don't allow boots in the house."

She pointed at the man standing by the table holding a teacup. He was a pleasant-looking elderly man in a shabby linen jacket. He was wearing green rubber boots. He looked down at his boots and then at the Izzy and seemed rather startled, but he didn't say anything.

"Oh, yes," Mrs Candace said. "May I introduce Salisbury? We were just consulting about your problem, as it happens."

"Salisbury?" said Judith.

"That's right," Mrs Candace said. "Salisbury the city."

"Oh!" Judith wrapped her shawl around her in a flustered way and introduced Grundo and me. Obviously, the idea of speaking to a city in green rubber boots was too much for her.

The Izzies had no such problems. One of them said, "That's *stupid*!" and the other agreed, "No one can talk to a *town*." And they stared rudely at Salisbury.

Judith, as usual, pretended not to notice. She said, "I can't stay very long, I'm afraid. It's such a long drive."

"You'll stay for a cup of tea," Mrs Candace stated. "Then I shall make sure you get home much faster than you came. More tea and perhaps some cake," she said to the air.

We all sat down politely on little padded chairs, except for the Izzies, who wandered about, pulling and prodding at everything in the elegant room. A fat grey cat that had been peacefully asleep on a stool only just escaped on to a high cabinet in time, where it stood with its fur bushed, staring down at the Izzies in horror. Mrs Candace looked up at it anxiously. But Judith simply pulled her shawl closer round her shoulders and went on explaining how Grundo and I had been left behind by the Progress.

A teapot and a big cake cut into large, squashy slices came floating through the room. The Izzies left off trying to reach the cat and stared. Grundo's eyes followed the path of the cake with interest. I screwed my eyelids up against the daylight and found I could just see the shapes of four transparent, birdlike creatures guiding the teapot and the cake down on to the small table beside Mrs Candace.

"Don't even *think* of it!" I whispered fiercely at Grundo.

He shot me a guilty look and grinned. Then he worked some magic. It is often hard to tell when Grundo is working magic. He doesn't move and his face hardly changes. But this time, I had no doubt. It jolted me. I jumped as if I'd had a bad fright and so did Mrs Candace. I rounded on Grundo to tell him to behave.

But, just then, one of the Izzies succeeded in grabbing the cat's dangling grey tail. The cat squawked. The cabinet rocked and all the delicate china inside it rattled. And, to my surprise, Judith sprang up and more or less shouted at the Izzies. "Isadora, stop that at *once*! Come *here*, both of you!"

The twins, looking as surprised as I felt, wandered sulkily towards her. "It's booooring here!" Isadora moaned and Ilsabil said sweetly, "But we're being *ever* so good, Mother. We *promised*!" Then, as usual, they did it the other way round.

"You are not being good at all!" Judith snapped. Her face was most uncharacteristically red and angry. "Say sorry to Mrs Candace and then we'll go home. I do apologise," she said to the rest of us. "We really must leave now. It's such a long way."

She began pushing the Izzies out of the room. Both of them leaned backwards. "But I want some *cake*!" Ilsabil protested.

"You're not getting any. You don't deserve it," Judith said. "We're going straight home and you're going to have another long talk with your grandmother."

Both Izzies burst into loud tears. We could hear them wailing and yelling even after the front door had slammed behind them. We could hear them through the opening and shutting of car doors and the sound of the engine starting. We went on hearing them until the noise of the engine had died away into the distance.

"Well!" said Mrs Candace in the final silence. "What was *that* about?"

"Grundo?" I said.

Grundo went pink. "They had a spell on Judith," he

growled, "so that they could do whatever they liked and she would never notice."

"And you took it off?" Mrs Candace demanded.

"Not quite. They had it on Hepzibah too," Grundo explained. "I had to put a spell on *them*, to make what they were doing obvious to Judith – and Hepzibah too, I hope, once they get home. It was difficult. It took me the whole drive to work it out."

"*Well*!" Mrs Candace said again. "In the normal way, young man, I would give you a good talking-to. It is not allowed to tamper with people's personalities. That's black magic. But in this case, I concede that it was richly deserved. Still, it seems hard on poor Judith to have to take to the road again without even a cup of tea. I'd better do what I promised her. Help yourselves to cake. I won't be long."

She stood up – with an effort. She was old and creaking. Salisbury passed us cake, gravely and silently, and the cat came down from on high and sat across Grundo's legs, purring. The cat knew who to be grateful to all right. I bit into squashy cake while I watched Mrs Candace bring several pieces of empty air together and then sort of pleat it in her twisty old fingers.

"Find them a way through a suitable otherwhere," she murmured, "and then bring their road to it and fold it like a fan, so that they only touch the road at the tops of the folds..."

I found I knew this spell, or one so like it that it made no

difference. It was under *Travellers' joy: mundane journeys.*
It was one of six ways to shorten a road. I wondered, as
I watched, if Mrs Candace knew the other five too. And,
before I had quite finished my cake, I realised that Judith
was nearly home already with her carload of yelling Izzies.
Mrs Candace was good at what she did. She was even doing
something the flower-file in my head had not mentioned:
unpleating the road behind the car as it travelled, so that
no other cars would get caught in the spell. That impressed
me.

"There!" Mrs Candace sank down as if it had tired her
to take so much off the journey. Salisbury sat down too at
last, cautiously, and the low chair groaned underneath him.
He passed her a cup of tea. She smiled at him and turned
to me, still smiling. I saw that she had once been ravingly
beautiful. "That seemed the least I could do for her," she
said. "Now, what have you two been up to that Hepzibah
Dimber couldn't handle?"

I didn't want to talk about it, so I said, "Grundo?"

Grundo explained about the invisible beings in the
Regalia.

"Hm," said Mrs Candace. "Oh, dear." A plate of cake
came up beside her and jiggled invitingly. "*Thank* you,"
she said carefully as she took a slice. "I do make a point
of thanking them," she said to Grundo, "though it's not
always easy to know how to reward them. There are,
however, quite a number of minor magicians who treat
their captive folk very badly. And I assure you, I had *no*

*idea* that the Dimbers didn't know they were using them. I see I must start looking into all that. But there is more," she added, looking at me.

I nodded and, once again, tried to explain what Sybil, Sir James and the Merlin had done.

Mrs Candace listened attentively, with her head gracefully bent, and I had real hopes that she believed me until she said, "Ah, no. You can't have it right, my dear. This Merlin is very new and young, so new that I haven't met him yet, but he'd be simply incapable of the kind of treason you describe. If he *was* capable of it, he wouldn't be the Merlin, do you see? I think you must have misunderstood some new idea of his."

"The Little Person believed I was right," I said despairingly. I knew I *had* to make Mrs Candace understand. She was the one who counterbalanced the Merlin. "He took it very seriously and he advised me to raise the land."

"On *no* account!" Mrs Candace said sharply. "*What* a thing to suggest! I'm surprised he even mentioned it. The Little People are usually so wise – though they can be mischievous. Perhaps this one was or perhaps he didn't realise you were only a child. You see, my dear," she went on, leaning forward and staring earnestly at me with her enormous, almond-shaped, pale green eyes, "the magic of Blest is most intricately interlaced with itself – the hugely old, the old, and the newer *and* the most recent – so that each part supports all the others. What you're suggesting is pulling up the very foundations. This would make it all come loose or perhaps even blow it apart. And we can't have that, because Blest magic keeps the magics of several hundred surrounding worlds in their right places. Do you see?"

"But if Blest magic went all rotten..." I began.

"Oh, I grant you," she said. "If *that* happened. But it hasn't. Unless somebody was superhumanly clever at keeping it from me, I'd know. I can *feel* there's nothing wrong."

The far-speaker on the table beside her chair began warbling for attention. Salisbury nodded at it and spoke for the first time, in a gently rumbling voice, like bricks grating. "I got through to London at last."

Mrs Candace smiled sweetly at him and picked up the speaker. "Hallo, is that Maxwell Hyde?... Oh, it's Dora, is it? Is Mr Hyde there?... Well, tell him as soon as he comes in that I've got his granddaughter here with me and I'm proposing to send her... Yes, Arianrhod, and she has a friend with her, Ambrose Temple... No, no, just tell him they'll be with you this evening. Salisbury's going to see to it now. Nothing to worry about."

She put the speaker down and smiled. "There, that's all sorted out."

It wasn't, but she was not to know that.

# PART NINE
# NICK

# CHAPTER TWENTY-THREE

*

*I* couldn't get over the way my father let me go to Blest with Maxwell Hyde. Dad was still in the London hotel when we got back – me pulling Maxwell Hyde and Maxwell Hyde keeping up a long, grumbling moan about how much he hated the dark paths. The people from the conference had left days ago, but Dad said he'd had to stay because he'd lost his front door key again. He took it quite philosophically when I explained that my key was still in the Police Station in Loggia City, and just said that he'd phone a locksmith from the hotel.

See what I mean? In the normal way, Dad falls over his own brain not to admit that anything supernatural can happen. It must be his defence against all those demons he writes about. But now he not only admitted the existence of other worlds and a Magid who lived in one of them, but he let me go there with him.

"That man Hyde cost me over two hundred quid, getting him drunk enough to go and find you," he said to me. "Let him teach you a few tricks. I want *some* return for my money."

I knew this was Dad's way of telling me he'd been worried sick when I suddenly disappeared from beside him in the hotel corridor. I was quite touched. I was still in a state of shock about it after he'd bought me some extra clothes and Maxwell Hyde gripped me by one arm and walked downhill into Blest with me.

Going between worlds the way Magids do it means walking down a hill that is mostly grass, with patches of tarmac and misty bits every so often. Each misty bit seems to be between other worlds. I looked sideways along the grassy stretches and saw that the dark paths led away there in all sorts of directions. I was very interested, but Maxwell Hyde didn't seem to know the paths were there.

Then we stepped on to tarmac again in front of Maxwell Hyde's London house, and I was very excited and nervous for a moment. Now we're going to meet Roddy! I thought, and the prospect of all those foreign politics made me feel a bit sick. But Roddy wasn't there. We were in a street of tall, Londonish houses that were all much smarter and better painted than any London houses I knew.

"That's because no one knows when the King is going to turn up and see them," Maxwell Hyde explained as he unlocked his own glistening green front door. "The Council sends you an order to redecorate if they think you're getting dingy."

That struck me as fascist. "Do they tell you what colours to paint it too?" I asked. It helped to cover up my nervousness.

"No, no," he said. "They leave that to the owner – though I daresay they'd object if I decided on murals of naked women or some such."

The London buses in Blest are bright blue. One roared past behind us as we went into the house. They use some kind of fuel that smells quite different from diesel but just as bad.

"Hallo! I'm back! Brought a visitor!" Maxwell Hyde shouted, stamping his feet on the doormat.

It smelt quite different from an Earth house indoors. Sort of spicy. Maxwell Hyde's daughter and her boy Toby hurried down the hall to meet us. The daughter is called Dora. She keeps house for him and she is quite potty. She dyes her hair bright red and wears layers of coloured clothes like a native of Peru, all different patterns and hung all over with dangly beads and stuff. Most of them were charms. Toby was younger than me and seemed quite normal, except that he behaved as if he was frightened. He had this way of hanging about as near as he could get to anyone bigger than him, as if it was safer like that. He was very pale, with almost-red hair.

"Oh, you've brought an Asian friend!" Dora exclaimed.

A lot of people on Earth think I'm Indian too, or Greek. It annoys me, but I'm used to it. Maxwell Hyde told Dora firmly that I was from another world, but she didn't listen. She *kept* asking me about the exotic magic of the Orient. She was obsessed with Eastern magics.

"Don't mind her," Maxwell Hyde told me, when Dora had gone off, talking loudly to herself, to find us some lunch. "She's never got over being turned out of her mother's house. Sad really. Wasn't equipped to cope."

There wasn't any lunch. Toby had to be sent out for what they call prettybread. Prettybread is a bit like a fat pizza with onions and things baked into it and frizzled cheese on top. Part of Dora's dottiness was that she was always forgetting to buy food. She kept having to send Toby out – and me too, once I got used to the way food was here – to buy cheese or cakes or tea for her. People in Blest drink tea all the time and they eat cakes with it far more than I am used to. Half the shops are kept by people who look Chinese, selling fat brown packets of tea and sixty kinds of sticky cakes. Coffee has to come from a chocolate shop and is much more expensive.

Luckily, Maxwell Hyde grows vegetables in his back garden. Most people in London do, just as if they lived in the country. This meant that there was nearly always *something* to eat (though the night there was nothing but beetroot nearly killed me). And one of the first things Maxwell Hyde did was to rush out into his garden to see how things were coming on there. He grows dahlias in among other flowers around the lawn near the house and the veg down the other end. The dahlias weren't up yet, just cabbagey clumps sitting in hard, dry earth, but you wouldn't believe how proud he was of those clumps. He got a hose and watered them at once.

After lunch, he took me into the main room and, with Toby leaning against him and peering under our elbows, he showed me a map of the Islands of Blest. These were – the way everything is in Blest – like and not like what I was used to. Their Islands are *almost* like the British Isles, but not really quite, as if someone had given the whole lot a big push from the direction of France and then stood on Ireland and pulled so that they stretched. Wales and Cornwall were a lot bigger and Scotland was not nearly so frilly.

"You'll find the eastern coast of England has straightened out from your point of view," Maxwell Hyde remarked. "Higher above sea level here."

There wasn't much of Norfolk or Lincolnshire there actually, and Yorkshire seemed rather slender too, but that was made up for by the south coast being much nearer France, so that the Isle of Wight was one of the Channel Islands. Then I spotted one big difference.

"Don't you have any railways?" I said.

"What are railways?" Toby asked.

"Trains," I said. "Chuff-chuff."

"No, just roads and canals," Maxwell Hyde said. "Our industrial history is quite different from yours. You never discovered cokale."

"You what?" I said.

"Cokale. Chuff-chuff," said Toby, and laughed. That was my fault for taking Toby for a fool. He wasn't, not by any means, but I'm no good at telling, with people younger than me.

Maxwell Hyde told me all about their different history then, until my head went round. All I really remember is that their King never settled down in one place, but went round in an enormous Progress most of the year. I think this goes back to the fact that Blest has a hundred times more magic than we do. In the old days, the King was supposed to keep the magic in the land healthy, by visiting every corner of it. These days, the Merlin and someone called the Lady of Governance look after the magic for him, but the King still travels.

I suppose I really remember this because Maxwell Hyde happened to say that Roddy travelled with the King, because her parents were part of the Progress, and I thought of what she had said about this Merlin of theirs. It was disappointing to hear that Maxwell Hyde didn't even know where the King and the rest of them were at that moment.

"What's the matter?" Maxwell Hyde asked me.

I didn't want to go on about Roddy. I was embarrassed.

So I said quickly, "Those mages. Arnold and them. I think I got them into bad trouble…"

"Oh, the Plantagenate Empire. I remember," Maxwell Hyde said. "Good thing you reminded me. I'll go and take a look in a couple of days when we've settled down here."

We settled down almost at once, into a regular routine, and nobody talked about Roddy any more. I *think* I was glad. After breakfast every day, as soon as I'd had enough coffee to get my eyes open, Maxwell Hyde gave me lessons in magic. That was terrific. I was really glad to be taught about magic at last, even though so much of it seemed to be just learning rules. I supposed there had to *be* rules or things wouldn't work, but after that short talk I'd had with Romanov, I couldn't help being a bit suspicious – you know, that the rules only applied to a small part of it all, and once I'd learnt enough, I'd know that the rules wouldn't work with the rest.

But I did try to learn the rules. And here was a strange thing about magic. Some things I could do standing on my head, and the other half I didn't think I'd *ever* be able to do. There was never any middle ground, no things I could *almost* do. And it was the same with theory: some of it obvious and the other things I just couldn't *begin* to understand. Maxwell Hyde set me exercises in theory to do for the rest of the day, while he went away to his study and rattled away at his laptop thingy, writing a new detective story. Very familiar. My dad does that too.

I used to sit there chewing Blest's version of a ballpoint pen and really envying Toby. His school was over for the year and I could hear him playing outside with the other kids in the street. He was quiet as a mouse indoors, but outside you could hear him for miles. He used to come in all smoothly sweaty, laughing, while I got up from my theory feeling as if I'd put my head through Dora's coffee mill.

The weather got hotter and hotter, which didn't make theory any easier. And there was another difficulty too, that made me wonder if I was as mad as Dora.

"This is becoming a regular drought," Maxwell Hyde said, anxious about the precious dahlias. "I suppose Daniel knows what he's doing. It made sense to have fine weather for the King's meeting with the Pendragon, but if he doesn't call it off soon, I shall have to have a word with him."

I was very interested to learn that this Daniel was Maxwell Hyde's son and Roddy's father. He was chief weather wizard to the King. Magic ran in that family, like anything.

Anyway, it got so hot and dry before long that the streets shimmered. Dora tried to do her father a favour and water the garden for him. She got out the hose and unrolled it. I saw her out of my window, standing pointing the nozzle at a flowerbed and muttering away to herself. But no water came out because she'd forgotten to hitch it to a tap. Toby came in from the street and quietly fixed it and turned the tap on. Water came squirting out all over Dora's shoes. She looked astonished.

That was typical. Toby was always quietly covering up for his mother's dottiness.

By then, my other problem was really bothering me. I kept seeing these transparent creature-things drifting about. They were all sorts of shapes. It almost seemed as if the long thin ones didn't like the heat and came indoors to get cool. They floated around the bedroom while I was working, where I could only just see them, but there came to be more and more of them every time I looked. The rounder kind seemed to love the heat. They sat in the road in clusters, going gently up and down like people in a swimming pool. The ones with stranger shapes seemed to follow Dora around. This was what really bothered me. They were what she muttered to.

I didn't dare say a word about them until the morning Maxwell Hyde made another attempt to teach me to raise witchlight. "Slowly," he said. "Steady. Think of the energy under your breastbone filling your hands with light."

I almost did it. I almost got it. Then one of the transparent things came bumbling along and sat on my hands instead. I could see others crowding in at me from all sides of the room. I tried to shake the thing loose. "Get off!" I said, flapping my hands. "Get *out* of it!" Then I know my face went as red as last night's beetroot supper. "I – I – I..." I went.

"It's all right," he said, calmly smiling. "The invisible folk are always attracted to magic-working. Take no notice of them."

"We don't have them on Earth," I said defensively.

"Yes, you do," he said. "I can always see them there, even though I can't see them here at all on Blest. It seems to work that way. Carry on."

I tried to carry on, but I'd lost it by then. And I think I was too busy giving relieved looks at the floating creatures to concentrate. I couldn't help asking, "Why do they like Dora so much?"

"She's hung with charms. Lives in a stream of half-spells, poor girl," he said. He sighed. "Always trying to prove she's as good as her sister Judith, I think. I hoped she'd snap out of it – and she did for a while after Toby was born. Then she got divorced and that made her as bad as ever."

Twice a week, Dora got dressed up in black and lots of clattering jet beads and an enormous round hat and went out for the evening. The first time I saw her dressed up, she said, "I'm off to my magic circle," and looked past my left shoulder in her dotty way. "Would you like to come too, Nick?"

"Not unless you fancy taking all your clothes off and galloping round in a ring," Maxwell Hyde said, quickly and warningly. Toby looked dreadfully ashamed.

"Er – perhaps not tonight," I said. "Thanks all the same, Dora."

"It's the most releasing and natural experience," Dora said reproachfully. "You're like all Orientals – you spend far too much time watching your tummy button. Be liberated. Try it. My group is full of wonderful people."

"Yes, yes, off you go," Maxwell Hyde said. And after she had gone, he told me, "You may not believe me, but Dora is the *sane* one in that group. I'd better look in on them soon. After I've had a go at the Plantagenate Empire, I think. They sometimes get up to very silly, harmful stuff."

He went to see the Plantagenate Empire two days later. He gave Toby and me some money and told Toby to show me London. Then he walked out into the street and vanished beside the bus stop. Toby and I got on a bus at the exact same spot.

# CHAPTER TWENTY-FOUR

＊

*B*lest London was quite a bit different because they'd never had the Great Fire. There were thatched cottages in Mayfair and the parks were all in strange places. Toby and I had great fun, in spite of the baking heat. I told Toby that I didn't want to see historic buildings, like the Houses of Parliament and so on, and he said we couldn't anyway because the parliament was in Winchester and not very important in the first place. So we saw the circus that was permanently in Piccadilly, and waxworks that really moved, and their London Bridge that had houses on it and tourist shops. They have the Tower, oddly enough, and a Tower Bridge that opens for shipping, though it doesn't look anything like ours on our Earth, and lots more boats on the Thames than in our London. Their ice creams taste a lot different.

Because it was so hot, we went back by waterbus. Toby showed me the ground where the hurley team he followed played. They didn't have football. Hurley is much more dangerous. Toby followed the Vauxhall Vampires and two of them broke their necks at it last week. Vox Vamps, you say, or just Vamps, like we say Wolves or Hammers.

I liked Toby a lot. It was a new experience for me. I wasn't used to liking someone so much younger than me.

We got home to find that Maxwell Hyde had just come in too.

"That was quick!" I said.

He gave his little soldierly grin. "Ah, I'm an old hand, Nick. I went straight to the head of things and made enquiries at the Academy of Mages. Told them I was the Magid looking into the recent infiltration in Marseilles." That made me laugh. He looked solemn. "It's absolutely true. I am and I was. And they told me, without any beating about the bush. Those poor fellows did get into some trouble, I'm sorry to say. They were removed from any Royal Security that night. But nobody thought it was their fault. They were just blamed for not noticing you weren't the right novice. Inefficiency and so on. And because fully-trained mages are much in demand, all four of them have found new jobs already. Charles Pick and Pierre Lefevre now work in France, and Arnold Hesse and David Croft are in Canada for Inland Security there."

You can't imagine how relieved I was to hear that.

"Where's Canada?" Toby asked.

"A part of North America," said his grandfather. "In some worlds, Europeans settled quite a lot in…"

He never finished that explanation. Dora suddenly dashed in, white as a sheet. She slammed the living room door and stood with her back to it, shaking. "Don't go into the garden!" she gasped. "I went for a lettuce."

"What did it do? Bite you?" Maxwell Hyde asked.

She shuddered. "No. I never got that far. There's a white devil on the lawn. With *horns*!"

"*What*?" said Maxwell Hyde. "Are you *sure*?"

Dora shuddered some more. "Oh yes. It was quite real. I know I lose touch quite often, but I always know when something I see is real. It was eating the dahlias."

At this, Maxwell Hyde thundered, "*WHAT*?" and set off for the garden like an Olympic sprinter. Dora got whirled aside and Toby and I pelted past her, full of curiosity.

In the baking garden, the white devil looked up from a flowerbed with a leaf fetchingly dangling beside its beard, saw Maxwell Hyde and came prancing towards him, obviously delighted to see him.

Maxwell Hyde stopped in his tracks. "Nick," he said, "do I, or do I not, know this goat?"

"Yes," I said. "It's Romanov's. It must have followed you somehow." I did wish it was Mini instead. I suddenly, hugely wished Mini was there. It was like being homesick.

"But *why*?" said Maxwell Hyde. The goat was frisking around him, making playful scything motions with its horns. I could see the rope we had tied round its neck and the frayed end where it had bitten it through.

"It's fond of you," I said. "You conquered its heart by taking hold of its horn and its rump and rushing it about."

Maxwell Hyde managed to grab the bitten end of the rope. "Pooh!" he said. "I'd forgotten the way goats smell." He tried to snatch the leaf hanging out of the goat's mouth, but the goat deftly swallowed it as his fingers reached it. "I hope that dahlia poisons you – it was my Red Royal Button," he said. "What was its name? I forget."

"Helga," I said.

The goat tried to bite a lump out of his trousers. He took it by the horns and held it off. "Helga, the goat from hell," he said. "I think it's starving. Toby, go and tell your mother to ring up the nearest animal feed merchant and order a ton of goat food. Nick, get to the garden shed. We need a stake, a mallet and the strongest clothesline you can find."

"Wouldn't a chain be better?" I suggested.

"Yes, but I'm going to use magic as a temporary measure," he panted. The goat was getting strenuous. "Hurry *up*!"

It turned out to be a violently busy evening.

Toby and I hammered the stake into the lawn – not

very easily. Toby hit me on the toe with the mallet, so I took it off him, but the earth was so hard I could hardly get the stake to go in. But that may have been because I kept missing it with the mallet. When I got it sort of in, Maxwell Hyde wrestled the goat over and we tied her to the stake where she couldn't eat dahlias.

This happened three times, because every time Maxwell Hyde walked away, the goat lunged after him and the stake came out of the lawn. Toby got her to stay put in the end by finding her a lump of stale prettybread. After that Maxwell Hyde hammered the stake in himself.

We had just finished when a motorised cart drew up at the front door, piled high with nourishment for goats. Toby and I staggered backwards and forwards through the house with bales of hay and sacks of nugget-things. One of the sacks burst. We dragged it all out on to the lawn, where Maxwell Hyde surrounded the goat knee deep in food and she weighed into it just as if she hadn't already eaten half a bed of flowers and most of a prettybread.

"There. What did I say?" he said. "She was starving."

It seemed to me that this was a permanent condition with that goat, but I didn't say so.

The shock of meeting the goat seemed to have put Dora in touch with reality much more firmly than usual. She objected – just like an ordinary person – to the hall and the back room being covered with wisps of hay and rolling nugget-things. She made Toby and me clear it up. While we were doing this, the phone rang. At least, it wasn't quite a phone. In Blest they call the things far-speakers and they work mostly the way a phone does, except that they go off like an old-fashioned alarm clock at first. This makes you jump out of your skin. But if you don't answer them straight away, they go on to make a horrible, strangled, warbling sound, which is worse.

Dora gave a shriek and went to answer it before it got to warbling.

As soon as she did, she gave another shriek and held the phone-thing out as if it was contaminated. "Toby! It's your father! Come and talk to him."

Things got difficult then. It turned out that Toby's dad was insisting on his rights as a parent. He wanted Toby to come and stay with him. Dora refused to let Toby go near him. Maxwell Hyde had to tear himself away from watching Helga guzzle and talk to Toby's dad too. While he did, Dora sat on the old sofa at the side of the hall and kept saying, "If you let Toby go near that man, I shall go mad, Daddy, I really shall!" In between, she said, "Don't forget it's my magic circle again tonight. I don't want to take my bad feelings there."

I thought we were never going to get any supper. I went away and had a bath instead.

When I came downstairs again, the hall was full of drifting transparent creatures – the slender, wavy kind that seem to like emotions – and everything seemed to be settled. Maxwell Hyde was going to drive Toby over to his dad for the day on Friday. He said I should come with them so that I could see the country. Dora seemed to think that between us we could save Toby from his father, so that was all right.

I was sent out for some sticky cakes to celebrate and, to my great relief, we had supper. Afterwards, Dora decked herself out in her black outfit and the rest of us settled down peacefully.

Toby and his grandfather had a complete ritual in the evenings. Everything happened in order. First, they turned on the media and sat in two special chairs to watch it. The media was *like* television, except that it looked more like a picture frame on the wall and only ever seemed to show news or hurley games. If you wanted soaps, you read a book. If you wanted music, you went to a concert or put on a cubette. I read a book because the news was always dead boring and I didn't understand hurley.

The hurley came first. I heard dimly behind what I was reading that the Vox Vamps had lost their third game in a row and were sacking their manager. Sounds familiar, I thought, and read on. It was quite a good book that Maxwell Hyde had recommended. I was deep in it when I heard, "Today the King himself met with Flemish trade officials in Norfolk, in an effort to solve the currency dispute..." and I looked up vaguely, hoping they were showing their King.

The King was in the picture as I looked. He was kingly and tall, with a neat beard, and there was a young fellow with him who was the eldest prince. They were walking across some flat grass, where, in spite of the bright sun, you could see it was very windy. Their coats were flapping, and so were the coats of the businessmen walking to meet them. I had a moment, looking at all those grey suits, when I thought I was back home on Earth. But as the wind blew the coats aside, I saw they all had different bright linings – quite unlike businessmen on Earth.

I was going back to my book, when the camera – or whatever they use on Blest – went panning round the rows of smartly dressed people in the background. I went on looking because I thought I might spot Roddy there. But they all seemed to be adults. The newscaster said, "Negotiations have been interrupted twice today by a dispute among the Court wizards…"

"Hey, what's this?" said Maxwell Hyde.

"The dispute was only settled when the King agreed to accompany the wizards to an undisclosed site elsewhere in England," the media said. Then they went back to a hurley game.

"What site? What *is* this? What are they *up* to?" Maxwell Hyde jumped out of his chair and rushed to the far-speaker.

He was gone for about half an hour. He came back looking displeased and rather puzzled, saying, "Well, *I* don't know. Daniel seems to be in a meeting about it. They couldn't contact him and I had to get on to the

Chancellor's Office instead. Some fool of a clerk who didn't really know anything. She seemed to think that it wasn't really a dispute, just some idiot suggestion from that stupid cow Sybil – those are my adjectives, by the way; the young lady gave me official-speak and gave almost nothing away, if she even *knew*, which I doubt. All she really knew was that the King has nothing to do with it, whatever it is. Storm in a teacup, by the sound of it. Get the boardgame out, Toby."

So they went on to the next bit of their routine, which was this game the two of them played every night. It was really passionate. They sat facing each other over a small table with the board and pieces on it, as tense as people could be – and if you couldn't tell by their faces how tense they were, you could tell by the number of transparent creatures who came crowding around them. Both of them were ready to kill to win.

They'd offered to teach me this game, but I couldn't understand the rules of it any more than I could understand hurley. I watched them a bit, out of politeness, but all it did for me was make me homesick for my computer games. My computer wouldn't work in Blest anyway. They use quite a different system. I went back to my book.

I'd read about a chapter, and Maxwell Hyde had moved on from low moaning, because Toby seemed to be winning, to his usual unfair attempt to persuade Toby to be kind to his poor old decrepit grandfather, when Dora came back.

Dora sailed into the main room with her eyes wide and dreamy and a silly smile on her face. But such a blast of terror and pain came in with her that all three of our heads whipped round. She was carrying some kind of creature by its tail.

All I saw of it was a mistiness and a blur, because Maxwell Hyde jumped up and slapped the thing out of her hand. The table went over with a crash and the creature bolted under the big cupboard. "*Dora!*" he said.

She gave him a bewildered look. "It was only a salamander, Daddy."

"Whatever it is, it's a sentient creature!" Maxwell Hyde told her angrily. "You've no business carrying it around like that!"

"But we've *all* got one in the circle!" Dora protested. "They're to enhance our magic."

"Are they now?" he said, and he took her by one rattling black sleeve and led her to his chair by the table, which Toby had just put upright. "Sit there," he said, "and write me out the names and addresses of all the people in this magic circle of yours." A piece of paper appeared in front of Dora. Maxwell Hyde unclipped the pen from his top pocket and pushed it into her hand. "Write," he said.

"But *why*?" Dora looked up from under her hat at him. She really did not seem to understand.

He barked at her, "*Just do it*! NOW!" and rattled the paper angrily under her nose.

She went white and began writing. Meanwhile Toby,

who had been collecting dropped game-pieces, picked up one that had rolled near the cupboard and asked, "Shall I try to tempt the salamander out?"

"No. Leave it," Maxwell Hyde said curtly. "Poor thing's mad with terror anyway. Nick, go to the cupboard under the stairs and fetch out any baskets you can find with lids to them."

"But won't it set fire to the house?" Toby asked as I was opening the door.

"I'll surround it in a field of water. Keep writing, Dora. Get on, Nick," Maxwell Hyde said. "This is urgent."

# CHAPTER TWENTY-FIVE

✳

*I* found a lunch basket, a smelly fishing creel and a fancy thing with raffia flowers on it. "Will these do?" I asked. Maxwell Hyde was leaning over Dora counting names and addresses. "Perfect," he said, not looking at me or the baskets. "This is only eleven, Dora. And you make twelve. There has to be thirteen of you, hasn't there? Who's your head wallah?"

"Oh, I forgot Mrs Blantyre," Dora said and wrote again.

Maxwell Hyde more or less snatched the paper from under the pen. "Come on, boys," he said. "Follow me. Bring the baskets." He marched out of the house into the warm, dark blue evening and slammed the front door behind us. "Luckily," he remarked as he strode down the street with us hurrying after him, "all these silly people live within walking distance. I think we'll start with Mrs Blantyre. Evil old biddy."

I gave Toby the fishing creel to carry. "What are we doing?" I asked Maxwell Hyde.

"Rescuing salamanders of course," he said. "Before they set half London on fire. Before anyone gets a chance to torture them. Two things you should both know," he went on, swinging round the corner in the direction of the Thames. "One, salamanders are not native to this country. Most of them come from Morocco or the Sahara. So it follows that someone has deliberately imported these. Probably in appalling conditions. And two, salamanders, if hurt or frightened enough, give off an extremely strong discharge of magic. If the witch tormenting them is like Dora's lot – an idiot – then the magic almost instantly becomes a violent burst of fire. Do you see now why we're in such a hurry?"

We did. We half ran behind him, baskets bumping, down that street and the next, until we came to a nice little house in a quiet mews. Maxwell Hyde hammered with its little brass knocker. The door was opened, after quite a while, by an old lady with loopy hair, who peered at us sweetly over little half-moon glasses.

"Evening, Mrs Blantyre," Maxwell Hyde said. "I've come for your salamanders, please."

Mrs Blantyre blinked, very, very sweetly. "What salamanders, dear?"

"I haven't got time for this," Maxwell Hyde said. And he raised Magid power. He looked just the same, but he suddenly became quite awesome. He stood there as strong as a great mountain, or a huge natural disaster. I looked on with interest. It was more or less what I used to do when I was small and older kids tried to bully me. "I'll have your salamanders," he said. "Now."

She took one look and trotted away into her house. She came back again a few seconds later holding a tiny cage that exuded dim light and blasts of panic and horror. "Here, dear. I can't think why…"

Maxwell Hyde took the cage and tipped the three terrified, misty occupants into the fishing creel. "Tell them they're safe now, Toby. Make it strong. Where did you get these, Mrs Blantyre?"

"I can't think why…" Mrs Blantyre said again.

"*Tell* me," Maxwell Hyde said. "You might as well. I'll find out anyhow."

Mrs Blantyre looked sweetly hurt. "If you really insist. They come from a dear little junk shop out in Ealing, dear. Tonio's Curios. They only cost sixpence a dozen. I can't think why…"

"*Thank* you," said Maxwell Hyde. "*Good* evening, madam. So she'll have bought twenty-four," he told us as we hurried away, "to go round thirteen. Elevens into twenty means that most of the others are going to have two each. *Damn*!"

As we hurried on to the next address, Toby began to

have trouble. The salamanders were still terrified and still heating up. The creel started to stink of hot fish. I took it off him and raised it up to my face, where I tried to give the poor things a shot of the power that had conquered Mrs Blantyre. "It's all *right*," I said. "We've rescued you. You're going to be *safe* now. It's *OK!*"

They *sort* of believed me. It was interesting. They had proper thoughts, like Mini, tiny desperate thoughts, and they understood me. They simmered down a bit and Toby took the creel and took over soothing them again.

It was fairly hectic. We rushed from house to house in the dark and Maxwell Hyde intimidated person after person into giving up terrified, despairing salamanders. We filled the creel and the lunch basket with them and began on the raffia basket, which began smoking and crackling almost at once, until I more or less shouted at it. And twice Maxwell Hyde had a real row on a doorstep, when someone pretended they had only got one salamander and he knew they had two. They shouted after him that they were calling the police.

The twelfth house we went to was on fire. Rolls of orange-tinted smoke were coming from its downstairs windows and the fire engine was clanging its way down the street to it as we got there. The front door of the place crashed open. An old fellow came staggering out, shouting "Help!"

Toby and I dived to catch the two salamanders that shot out with him. Toby got his, but I was carrying two

382

of the baskets and I missed mine. It streaked down the nearest drain and vanished. It's probably still around in the sewers somewhere.

"I only dipped them in water!" the old fellow said indignantly to Maxwell Hyde. "That's all I did – dipped them in water!"

"Then you deserve all you get," Maxwell Hyde said. "I hope your house burns down. Come along, boys." He took the lunch basket off me and we went marching home with our twenty-two salamanders. They weighed nothing at all. If it wasn't for the misty glow coming from them, and the smell of fish and hot raffia, you'd have thought the baskets were empty.

At his own house, Maxwell Hyde went marching straight on through to the garden. "Fortunate about this heatwave," he said. "It's an ill wind. They'll be warm enough among the bushes for now. Tell them they'll be safe as long as they stay in this garden, Nick."

"Won't the goat...?" Toby began.

"I imagine she's got *some* sense," Maxwell Hyde said. "Heartburn won't be in it, if she tries to eat a salamander."

The goat came to the end of her halter and watched with interest as we tipped the baskets gently on their sides and opened the lids and little glowing lizard-shapes came tiptoeing out, and stopped dead still for a second like tiny lighted statues, and then whizzed suddenly into hiding in the flowerbeds. They look very like lizards, but they have whorls and curlicues coming from their heads and backs, made of sort of dots of light. They're really elegant, like very small ghostly dragons.

"I don't see how *anyone* could be cruel to those," Toby said as we went back into the main room. I didn't answer. I was busy hoping we could go on to phase three of their evening routine now, which was mugs of cocoa, followed by bed. All those witches had exhausted me.

The first thing we saw in that room was Dora, still in her hat. She was sitting on the sofa with her salamander stretched along her knee. You could see it very clearly against her black satin skirt. All its fire-dot curlicues were gently vibrating. I'd never seen anything so obviously purring. Dora looked up at us with a worried, guilty smile. "I did very wrong, didn't I?" she whispered. "It's *sweet!*"

Toby's white, tense face relaxed and he went away to make cocoa.

"Her heart's in the right place really, you see," Maxwell Hyde said to me out in the hall. "She just gets influenced by people. Come upstairs and help me turn out the dirty washing. I think we're going to need the laundry hamper for the next bit."

"Whatever for?" I groaned.

He explained as we tramped upstairs. "Tonio's Curios. We have to get the salamanders they're selling *out* of there before Mrs Blantyre gets on the far-speaker and warns this Tonio. I put a prohibition on her to stop her, but she'll have wriggled out of it by morning. Dreadful old witch. Like one of those sweeteners that gives mice cancer."

So, after a quick cup of cocoa, we loaded the big hamper into the back seat of Maxwell Hyde's car, and Toby squeezed in beside it, and we drove out to Ealing. It was midnight by then. Clocks were striking all over London as we set off.

Cars are different in Blest. They go with almost the same sort of clockwork chugging as the flier I saw in Loggia City, and they turn out to make me horribly carsick. I kept swallowing and tasting cocoa all the way, and staring urgently at dark houses and then dark hedges in order not to think about how I felt.

It was quite a way. Ealing in Blest is pretty well in the country. We stopped at the end of a village-like street and – well – sort of *attended* to what was in the air. Almost straightaway we could feel the solid misery of hundreds of salamanders that were shut in somewhere much too small for them. All we had to do was to drive gently in the direction the misery came from – until it was nearly unbearable really – and we found the place. It was in a back street, facing open fields, with just one distant streetlight up along the hedge to show us the garage doors with heavy padlocks on the ground floor of a tumbledown old house.

The feeling of panic and despair was so strong from behind the garage doors that we all worked as fast as we could. Toby and I wrestled the hamper out, dumped it in front of the doors and opened its lid, while Maxwell Hyde did swift Magid work on the padlocks. He had those doors open in no time. We could see the salamanders then, as well as feel them. They were near the back, in two cages, each about the size of an Earth television set, and there were literally hundreds of them in both cages. The cages were glowing and pulsing as the salamanders crawled and scrambled and climbed over one another, every one of them desperate to find more space. Toby made a dart for them and hit a table with a statue on top. I stopped as I was plunging after him and caught the statue in my arms as it fell.

"*Wait!*" whispered Maxwell Hyde and made his blue witchlight for us.

Just as well he did. The garage-space was packed with old furniture, and every piece of furniture had statues and jugs on it. The salamander cages were on an old piano by the back wall, just beyond a collection of dented coal scuttles, with several firescreens in front of that. The noise you could make falling over all that didn't bear thinking of.

My legs were longest, so I climbed over to the back taking big, high steps and grabbed the nearest cage. The salamanders inside it were so frightened that they seethed about, with a noise like sand blasting on to metal. As I tried to pass the cage to Toby, my hair frizzled and the cage got almost too hot to hold. I whispered to them that they were OK now, but I think they were too frightened to attend. I sort of tossed the cage to Toby, who shoved it at Maxwell Hyde, who sort of juggled it down on to the grass outside. The second cage was even hotter and noisier, and the grass made a sort of frying sound when Maxwell Hyde dumped it beside the hamper. I think he had to work some magic so that the hamper didn't catch fire. Then the two of them opened the cages and tried to tip the salamanders into the hamper.

Only about half of them went in. The rest surged up over the sides and across the lid and ran away. One ran up Toby and curled frantically round his neck. Toby made a strangled squealing sound, trying not to yell as it burnt him. One ran up Maxwell Hyde's trouser leg. He jerked and stamped and made faces in the witchlight, trying his hardest to stay quiet as he passed me the cages to put back on the piano. Toby got the hamper shut, although he was still squealing. While I was making long, careful strides over things I could barely see, I heard footsteps creaking on boards up above and voices overhead. I dumped those cages and made it out through the garage doors again in such a panic that I swear I levitated. I don't remember touching the floor once. Lights came on in the upstairs windows as I shot outside. I dived on the hamper and heaved it, single-handed, into the car, and Toby rushed in after it, trying to wrestle the salamander off his neck. Maxwell Hyde plunged into the driver's seat a second later and we drove off like rally drivers.

I looked back as we roared up the road to see that

Maxwell Hyde had somehow managed to padlock the garage doors again. Light was now shining out of the cracks round the edges of them.

"What happens when they call the police?" I asked.

"Nothing. Most people can't see salamanders," Maxwell Hyde said, with his teeth clenched. "Police won't admit to their existence. Damn it to hell! Is my trouser leg on fire, Nick?"

"No," I said.

"You could have fooled me!" he said. "*And* we've left Hertfordshire – or is this Middlesex? – infested with the things!"

We had a fairly eventful drive back. The salamander came out of Maxwell Hyde's trousers half a mile later and I had to catch it before it got mixed up with the pedals. That was when I discovered that the floor of the car was thick with the creatures. Half the ones that got away must have bolted inside the car because it was warm and seemed safe, and they *kept* getting under the brake and the accelerator and the two other pedals that Blest cars have, and I kept having to pull them out. My hands were all burned before long. Maxwell Hyde cursed as he drove, a blue streak, calling down all sorts of horrible things upon witches and junk-shop owners and salamander smugglers, and kicking out at salamanders as he swore. It was hardly surprising that the salamanders inside the hamper stayed upset enough to make the hamper smoke and crackle. When I looked round to tell Toby to calm them down, I found he was asleep with his head on the hamper and the salamander that had been round his neck curled up on his ear.

I sang to the wretched beasts. It was the only thing I could think of. I sat there trying to sing every soothing song I knew. I went through "Golden Slumbers" and "Bye Baby Bunting" and "Away in a Manger," at which Maxwell Hyde stopped swearing and started choking with laughter, so I tried Scottish songs with lots of soothing swoopings, but those didn't work so well, so I went back to "Golden Slumbers" because that seemed to work best.

"Golden slumbers," I hollered, "bless your eyes, *Smiles* awake you when you rise!" The Beatles knew a thing or two. The more I sang it, the more salamanders crawled out of the upholstery and the door pockets and came and sat on me. By the end of our journey I was under a pile of them, all of them with their fire-dot curlicues vibrating and fibrillating, purring their misty little heads off. The ones in the hamper weren't quite so happy, but at least they seemed to have calmed down.

Back in London, Maxwell Hyde drew up in front of the house and made the front door spring open of its own accord. I climbed stiffly out of my seat and went up the steps, and the salamanders all jumped off me and ran like a moving fiery mat in front of me to the back door, where I let them out into the garden. Then I went back and helped him wake Toby and heave the hamper along to the garden too. When we opened it, bright twinkling salamanders ran out and about in such quantities that Helga had to skip this way and that to avoid them.

"How do we feed them all?" I croaked.

"We don't. They live on the sun's energy," Maxwell Hyde said. "Or so I'm told. I hope I was told right." He sent Toby up to bed and Toby took his salamander up with him. I made more cocoa.

"Have we got all the salamanders in the country now?" I rasped, when Maxwell Hyde came back from putting the car away. I was still hoarse from all those "Golden Slumbers".

He blew on his cocoa and shook his head. "By no means," he said. "We've just spoilt one tiny corner of the trade, I'm afraid. Some of the rest we'll pick up when houses catch fire here in London. Ditto in other parts of the country. But I suspect we're also going to have to raid a few warehouses later this week. Tomorrow I'll try and find out just how they're coming into the country. Get some sleep first, though."

# CHAPTER TWENTY-SIX

✳

We had salamanders everywhere the next day. They were all over the garden and all over the roof too. Several hundred of them came indoors, where they coiled up in every unexpected place they could find, provided it was warm. About the only place they didn't get to was the kitchen stove – Dora's salamander had taken the stove over and it spat sparks at the others to make them keep off – and round Toby's neck, because *his* salamander spent the day there, but they got everywhere else. I kept having to push them off my notebook and shake them out of my clothes. They climbed on the far-speaker, where Maxwell Hyde worked away in his shirtsleeves, sweating and phoning freight companies to see which of them imported apparently empty crates from hot countries. He sat on salamanders more than once.

Around lunchtime, he took a break and drank a cup of tea with me out on the baking lawn. I was looking up at the salamanders vibrating all over the roof. If you half closed your eyes, you could take them for a heat shimmer – them and the transparent people both. The transparent folks were obviously very interested and came drifting up in droves. The goat was beginning to look almost nervous.

I said it was lucky there was still this heatwave.

"Well, yes," Maxwell Hyde said, staring up at the roof too, "except that it's all so dry. It would only take one spark from one frightened salamander— What *really* makes me angry is that importing these creatures is so cruel and unnecessary! If the fools doing it simply want to raise some extra power, why don't they tap busy roads or power-lines? Or there are hundreds of power nodes in these islands. They don't *need* to torment living beings."

"Have you found where they're coming from?" I asked.

"Not yet," he said. "But I will." And he went back to making calls.

After supper that evening, he had his answer. The salamanders were being brought in by air from some place in Egypt that wasn't a place on Earth – or at least, it was nowhere I'd ever heard of. The next cargo flight from there came into London Airport late on Saturday.

"Nick, Toby, pencil in a sleepless night on Saturday,"

he said gleefully as he turned the media on, starting the evening routine. "And remind me, one of you, to buy another couple of laundry hampers."

The media came on and reported that a barge on its way to Manchester had suddenly burst into flames. A lorry going to Norwich had done the same, and Bristol city centre was on fire. Maxwell Hyde watched, champing the pencil he'd been taking notes with all day. "They're being sent all over the country," he said. "Why? Who needs extra magic in all these places all of a sudden?"

"I hope the salamanders on the barge got to land," Toby said, putting one finger gently on the salamander lying along his shoulder.

"So do I," said Maxwell Hyde. "By the way, that salamander stays *here* when we go to see your father tomorrow."

Toby's face went white and mulish, but he didn't make the fuss I would have expected. I suppose that said something about what his father was like.

His father is called Jerome Kirk. He was living all by himself these days, in a farmhouse somewhere just south of the main chalk hills – the Ridgeway Downs, was the name of them in Blest. I wouldn't have called it that far from London, but Blest only has a couple of big motor roads and even those wind about like anything. In order to get to Toby's dad before lunch, we started at what felt like dawn to me. I still hadn't got my eyes open when they bundled me into the car.

For the first part of the journey I grumped to myself that, if they weren't going to have railways, then the least they could do was build a few good motorways, and worried about feeling car-sick. Then my eyes came open and I felt better. I even began admiring the way the green land lifted out of the milky white heat haze, into a row of hills like a long spine across the middle of the country. The road snaked along under rows of dry trees, keeping the spine of hills in the distance, until we turned into a narrow lane, and then down more narrow lanes, and arrived at the farmhouse crouching among a lot more trees below the hills on the south side.

We unstuck ourselves from the car seats and went and knocked at the unpainted front door. It was a gloomy, yellow old house, and it seemed amazing how anywhere could be so dark inside on such a blazing bright day. It had glum stone floors and low ceilings with lots of beams that didn't seem to have been painted, or even dusted, for about half a century. There was dust and clobber everywhere. Toby's dad kind of prowled about in it with his back to us most of the time. He was a big man with a big, bushy beard and a big, veiny nose and rather small, weepy eyes. He had a big belly too, but the chief thing I remember – probably from seeing his back so much – was his bent, baggy legs in bent, baggy trousers. I kept thinking that when he took those trousers off at night, he probably leant them against a chair and they stood up by themselves in the same bent shape.

I think Jerome Kirk was supposed to be an artist, but there wasn't much sign of it. One small room had an easel and paints and things in it, but they were all covered with dust like everywhere else.

He didn't seem all that glad to see us. "So you came," he said. "I didn't think you would."

Toby didn't seem exactly over the moon either. He said, "Hallo, Dad," in a subdued way. Jerome Kirk showed his teeth in a savage smile of welcome – I suppose it was welcome – and gave Toby a clout between the shoulders. Then he went on his prowl, while we stood there.

After a bit, he prowled back carrying a big earthenware jug. "You must be thirsty," he said. "This is my own home made perry. Want some?"

Maxwell Hyde and Toby said, "No, thank you," in chorus, but I was so hot and so thirsty that I said, "Yes, please!" I thought, while Jerome Kirk poured me out some into a dusty glass, that Maxwell Hyde muttered something like "Not really advisable," but I didn't see why until I took a big, thirsty swig.

The stuff was not just horrible. It was like being carsick. It was like the times when you burp wrong and your stomach juices come up into your mouth. I wondered if I was poisoned.

Luckily, Jerome Kirk poured himself a big tankard full and wandered off again, jug in one hand, drink in the other. "…outside and look at my orchard," his voice came echoing back.

We followed him out through his kitchen, where I seized the chance to pour the glassful down the sink and replace it with water. Toby got the giggles. Maxwell Hyde coolly got them both a drink of water too and we went outside into knee-length grass and clumps of nettles.

There were a lot of fruit trees there, but they weren't up to much. They were old and bent, with branches missing and a few pale little apples or wormy plums on the sick-looking boughs that were left. Dad would have had a fit. He cherishes his fruit trees. And Maxwell Hyde looked as if he agreed with my dad. He went wandering off with his mouth turned down at the ends. The thing I was most interested in out there was a rickety table with things on it covered with cloths and wasps circling. It looked like lunch.

But obviously not yet. Toby just quietly disappeared, so I went wandering down the slope of the orchard, avoiding nettles and drinking my water, and wondering what we were supposed to do now we had come all this way to be here.

Down at the end, in soggy green grass, Jerome Kirk suddenly appeared and cornered me against a giant tangle of blackberry bush interlaced with nettles. He did it really expertly. All through the talk we had, I was weaving this way and that, trying to escape and hitting a huge, thorny branch if I went one way and a mixture of nettles and thistles if I went the other. If I found what seemed a way to slide out, Jerome Kirk just wandered nearer and cut the way off. By the end, I was backed right up against the tangle, getting prickled all over. I was really upset. Usually, I pride myself on being able to duck out of anything, but he had me completely caught.

"I was going to speak to Toby," he said, "but you'll do even better. Seething with talent, aren't you? What are you doing going around with Maxwell Hyde?"

"He's teaching me," I said, sliding to the right and hitting thorns. I slid left and got nettled. "I needed to learn about magic."

Jerome Kirk spat into the blackberry bush. "Bloody Magid," he said. "They can't stir a finger without permission from Above, these Magids. Brown-nose puppy dogs. You'd be far better off coming in with us instead."

"Er," I said, trying another slide into thorns. "Coming in with who?" The thorns brought me up short and I was forced to stare at the red veins in his nose and at his dirty beard. I thought he must be the last person in Blest I'd ever want to join up with. I felt sorry for Toby for having the man as his father. I mean, by all accounts, my own father was pretty awful too, but I'd never met him. I felt a gust of pure thankfulness that I had been able to choose Dad instead. "What do you mean?" I said.

He leant towards me and began speaking eagerly, waving the jug in his hand in circles, and I leant backwards, trying to get out of range of the yucky smell of the perry from the jug and from his breath.

"We're an association," he said, "but we don't name ourselves. We just exist and gather strength and numbers. Now the Merlin's put himself at our head, we're really going places. We're going to clear these islands of the old-school-tie entrenched magics, and the wimps and Magids and brown-noses that crawl along with them, and we're going to bring in new energies, new people, the *small* magic users who are never given a chance under this present regime. You're young. You need to join our new order. You don't want to be throttled by their stupid *rules*!"

He went on like this for quite a while. Every so often, he seemed to go on a prowl, but he only *seemed* to. He was really moving in to pin me down closer each time. I stood there licking at sweat gathering on my top lip and felt truly trapped.

Then he said, "*Think* about it. We've already discovered a whole new source of power. Salamanders! How about *that*? You'd never get any of the old guard finding an idea like that, would you?" He leant towards me, gathered his tankard and his jug into one hand, and tapped the side of his big, veiny nose at me. I stared. I had never seen anyone do that before, not outside the telly, not for real. "And that's only one of the new ideas that are coming through," he told me. "I know. I'm in their inmost councils. They asked me to live here and keep an eye on the old magics in case they get out of hand. That's a fact. And I'll tell you another thing." He tapped his nose at me again. "We're almost ready to show our hand. You don't have long to decide. *Think* about it. And if you want to join us – and you will, of course – just give me a nod before you go. Right?"

I was backed into the bush by then. I said, "Right," feebly.

He nodded and, to my immense relief, he turned his baggy back and prowled away.

All I could think of after that was to find Maxwell Hyde and tell him what Jerome Kirk had said about salamanders. It seemed urgent to me, if they really were getting ready for a revolution or whatever. And I could see that it tied in with what Roddy had said. But I couldn't find Maxwell Hyde anywhere at first, and when I did, he was at the rickety table with Jerome Kirk and Toby. They were waiting for me to begin lunch.

Lunch was a bit of a trial. It was cold meat and bread, which was all right, but there was this great swimmy dish of home made pickle in the middle, and the wasps really went for that. I kept trying to show Maxwell Hyde I had something urgent to tell him, but I couldn't sort of get through to him. We were all too busy dodging wasps.

Before the end of lunch, Maxwell Hyde and Jerome Kirk got into an argument about politics and, as soon as they started, I thought, Stupid! What am I worrying about? Tell him on the way home! Toby slipped away the moment the argument began. I was sick of the wasps, so I slipped off too.

I went the way I thought I saw Toby go, across the road and uphill from the house. There was a path there, winding up on to the hot hillside, so I went that way, twisting about among head high bushes, until I came out on a steep grassy bit where the path forked.

There I stopped. It came to me with a sort of *thump* that Jerome Kirk had not been lying when he said he lived near the old magics. There was a wood up to my right. It was dark, hot and rustling, and made of very upright old trees. I found I was staring at it nearly with terror. Whatever was inside that wood was very old, very strong and – well – awesome. I simply could not bring myself to go near it. If Toby had gone there, he was a lot braver than I was.

I took the left fork instead. It went veering along below the top of the hillside. There was a bit of a breeze up there that rattled the dry wiry ends of the grass and shook hot smells, almost like spice, out of no end of dry wiry flowers. Insects hummed or hopped, but none of them were wasps and it was blazingly, strongly peaceful there. If I looked down, all I could see were woods and fields into blue distance. If I looked up, there was blue, blue sky and, against it, the green hilltop which sort of peeled back in places to show hard whiteness, like the hill's bones.

It came to me as I wandered on, and more and more whiteness peeled out of the green turf, that I must be walking westwards along that spine of chalk downs that I had seen from the main road. In that case, I thought, the whiteness was like bones, the backbone of Blest. I kept looking up at it as I walked. And after nearly a mile, I came to a place where more turf than usual had peeled away, into a sort of humpy cliff. The humps fell into a most definite shape. There were two long pieces with a slight gap between and, above and back eastward of those, a big bulge and a sort of hollow in the midst of the bulge.

I was thinking of bones. I thought to myself that this bit really almost looked like a huge skull. An enormous animal skull, with huge jaws, many times larger than an elephant's skull. And I imagined to myself that this creature – a really immense creature – was lying all along the hillside just below the top of it, mostly buried in chalk and turf.

Then I got all excited, thinking it really might be a dinosaur skeleton. Yet I almost didn't want to scramble up there and look, because I *knew* I would be disappointed when it turned out to be just a chalk cliff. But I did climb up. And the nearer I got, the more like a huge head the thing got. By the time I was level with the end of the part that looked almost like jaws, I could see dents in the top one, like nostrils, and when I edged nearer, there were faint patterns on it that were nearly like scales, white on white. Then, if I looked up to the hollow in the bulging part, I could have sworn it was an eye socket with the eyelid down over it. There was even a stony sort of fringe to it, like chalky eyelashes.

"Hell's bells!" I said, out loud. "I think it really *is* a huge fossil!"

"WHO," said the hillside, "ARE YOU CALLING A FOSSIL?"

I fell several yards down on to the turf. It gave me such a shock. And the whole cliff thrummed and heaved and then buckled as the huge jaws moved, and it more or less threw me off. I looked up to find that the place that I had thought was an eye socket had opened. A vast, green eye was looking down at me.

I don't think I *could* have moved. I managed to say, "What *are* you then?" My voice came out as a squawky whisper, but I was too interested not to ask.

"THE WHITE DRAGON OF ENGLAND," the huge head answered. "DO PEOPLE NO LONGER SPEAK OF ME?"

"Yes," I said hurriedly. "Oh, yes. They do." After all, I had heard of such a creature on Earth, and it stood to reason that there was one on Blest too, with all the magic they had there. "But not very often," I said, to be truthful. I was looking back along the hillside as I said this, and now I could see very plainly where the green turf humped upwards over the shape of the enormous body. If it comes out, I thought, I am dead. Its tail must have stretched right back into the woods. "Er," I said, making stupid conversation for all I was worth, "you've been here a long time, haven't you?"

"FROM THE BEGINNING," it replied. The hillside

shook and blurred with its voice. I could feel it through my entire body. "I SLEEP UNTIL I AM NEEDED. DO YOU HAVE NEED OF ME?"

"Not really," I said. "Well, no – no, not at all really. I just came along here by accident really."

The vast green eye blinked, shut, open, shut. I hoped it might be going back to sleep, but I could tell it was thinking. I could feel, almost hear, great slow, grinding thoughts going on in the huge head.

The eye opened again. "I AM NOT WOKEN BY ACCIDENT," said the earth-moving voice. "NOTHING I DO IS EVER ACCIDENTAL. I AM NOT CALLED FORTH LIGHTLY."

"Oh, I quite understand," I said. You say such silly things when your brain is cancelled out by terror. "I – I'm not here to call you forth. Honestly!" I began to back away down the slope, very gently and quietly, but I had to stop when the hillside blurred again and pieces of chalk and turf and earth began to drop all round me.

"WHEN YOU DO," the great voice announced, "REMEMBER THAT I WILL NOT BE PLEASED. MANY PEOPLE WILL HAVE REASON TO REGRET THAT YOU CALLED ME. GO NOW."

Nothing would have possessed me even to *try* to call that thing out.

I went, staring upwards the whole time at that vast green eye watching me all the way down to the path. It turned in its socket to watch me as I trotted shakily back the way I had come. My knees trembled. As soon as I had got beyond where that eye could possibly turn far enough to see me, I sprinted - I fair pelted - between hot gorse bushes, and I did not stop running until I came down to the road and saw Toby and Maxwell Hyde standing by the car. I trotted up to them, streaming with sweat. Maxwell Hyde was looking grim. Toby, for some reason, was looking rather like I felt. I supposed they were annoyed with me for keeping them waiting.

"Sorry to be so long," I said in an airy, artificial way. What had just happened was something I didn't think I would ever be able to speak about. "Went further than I meant to," I said.

"Get in," said Maxwell Hyde. "Both of you."

We got in and he drove off. He had been driving for miles before I recovered. I kept thinking, *That thing! That huge thing!* Lying under the turf, just waiting. Too true that people would regret it if it ever came out.

When we were nearly back to London, Maxwell Hyde spoke, in a very dry voice. "Toby," he said, "I think we shall have to cut the connection with your father. He's in with a bad crowd, I'm afraid."

Oh! I thought. My mind had been so blown by that dragon that I had clean forgotten the talk I had had with Jerome Kirk. But it looked as if he had been fool enough to try to enlist Maxwell Hyde in his group, so I wouldn't need to tell about it after all.

"Yes," Toby more or less whispered. "He talked to me too."

"Is that why you're looking so devastated then?" Maxwell Hyde asked him.

"No," Toby said. "That was the wood."

"What about the wood?" his grandfather said snappishly.

"I don't know," Toby said. "There were tall people. I didn't know if they were really there or not. They were scary."

"Scary how?" Maxwell Hyde asked. "Diabolical, you mean?"

"No. I wondered if they were angels," Toby said. "But they kept asking me if I was ready yet and I didn't understand. The wood asked me too, you see."

This gave me the idea that Toby had had an experience at least as terrifying as mine. I could tell he was relieved when Maxwell Hyde just made that "Hm" noise that people do when they have no idea what someone is talking about, and didn't ask any more. He bent his head towards me instead and said, "And you talked to the good Jerome too, did you, Nick?"

"Yes," I said. "He's in with whoever's getting the salamanders."

Maxwell Hyde went "Hm" again, but this time in a nasty, considering, grim way. I could tell by the way he glared through the windscreen that he was thinking about what I'd said all the rest of our drive through London. It was getting to be dusk by then. As he parked the car, he said, "Well, we won't talk about that any more. I'm starving. Too worried about munching on a wasp to eat much lunch."

I suppose we were all tired, but we were a bit pathetic really. We couldn't wait to get indoors and get back to the evening routine. Dora was standing there, wringing her hands, not because we were so late, but because she had remembered to buy seven kinds of cheese and cooked some potatoes, but she couldn't work out how to turn it into a proper supper. We didn't care. We sent salamanders shooting in all directions as we rushed to the table and ate cold potatoes with slices of cheese. Then we pounded into the main room and turned on the media for the tail end of the hurley report.

Maxwell Hyde and Toby got out their game then. I settled down on a chair at one side and opened a magic theory book with a sigh of relief. I was really ready for a bit of quiet boredom. Dora sat on the sofa rustling through a magazine called *The Meaning of Dreams*.

They were well into the moaning stage of the game and I had read the same page four times without getting any of it into my head, when Dora sprang up from the sofa and screamed.

The room was suddenly full of soundless men riding tall, soundless horses. A soundless wind came with them. It fluttered my book and tore Dora's dyed hair sideways. She sort of grabbed at her hair as she screamed and clapped one hand down to keep her skirt from blowing up round her waist. The same wind billowed the cloaks of the horsemen. There were far more riders in among us than the room could possibly have held, and yet they were all definitely there. The one nearest me was carrying a thing like a battle standard, except that it was really just a rough stake with the skull of a horse skewered on to it, and pieces of raw, bloody horse-skin blew out from it in the wind. I stared at it and felt ill.

The rider in front was on a white horse and he was all in black except for the white lining in his flapping cloak. "I apologise for this," he said. I ought not to have been able to hear him through the noise Dora was making, but I could hear him perfectly. He had quite a strong Welsh accent. "You must forgive me," he said, leaning down to Maxwell Hyde. "I am constrained by an enchantment to do as I do."

He reached out and took hold of Maxwell Hyde round his waist. He lifted him up as easily as you would lift a kitten and slung him over the white horse face down. Maxwell Hyde said, "*What* the…?" as he was lifted and then stopped as if he had passed out.

Toby was the only one of us who behaved at all well. He jumped in front of the white horse and shouted, "*Stop it*! Put my grandfather *down*!"

"I wish I could, young man," said the rider. Then he rode forward just as if Toby was not standing there. The table, the game-pieces and one of the chairs went all over the floor when Toby had to fling himself out of the way, and the horsemen rode away out of the room, taking the wind with them. They didn't ride through the wall. They sort of rode away in the space they were in and took that space and Maxwell Hyde with them.

Dora's screams seemed even louder once they were gone. "He's *taken Daddy*!" she shrieked. "That was Gwyn ap Nud! He's Lord of the Dead and he's taken Daddy!"

She made such a noise that we almost didn't hear someone knocking on the front door.

# PART TEN
# RODDY AND NICK

# CHAPTER TWENTY-SEVEN

*

*M*rs Candace, besides being very old, is a bit crippled and has to walk with a stick. She didn't come any further than her front door with us. There she shook hands with Grundo in a very formal, old-fashioned way and kissed me goodbye. I flinched a bit as her dry old mouth brushed my cheek, not because it was an unpleasant feeling, but because that one small touch somehow told me that it was her right hip that was the crippled part of her. It was just like the hurt lady in the ruined village. And I thought, Do all women with strong powers have to have a ruined hip then?

"Go with Salisbury, my dears," she said. "Everything's arranged."

We followed Salisbury's striding, green rubber boots outside and along the street. By the time we got to the corner, the boots had been joined by two big, smooth-haired retrievers, a black one and a golden one, frisking sedately on either side of Salisbury. Grundo was delighted. "Are they yours?" he asked, staring up at Salisbury's tall face.

Salisbury nodded. "I am never without a dog or two," he said. "They have owners, of course."

"Um," said Grundo. "I think I see."

However it was, the dogs came with us all the way to the edge of town, weaving to and fro, the way dogs do, until we came to a space in front of quite a tall little hill, whereupon they began weaving more widely. One cocked a leg and peed on the tire of a square, brown, old car that was parked there.

"Don't you do that, you dirty brute, you!" someone shouted from the hill.

It really was a very odd little hill, if you looked closely. It seemed to be made of buried houses. You could see windows and doors and bits of walls half hidden under the grass, piled on top of one another all the way to the summit. Halfway up, where a tree leaned over a buried doorway, an old tramp was sitting on a turfy doorstep.

"Can't you keep your bleeding dogs in order?" he yelled at Salisbury, in a high, cracked old voice.

"Easily," said Salisbury. "They never foul my streets. This is my brother," he said to us. "Old Sarum."

We gaped up at the tramp. He got up and climbed nimbly down the hill. He was wearing rubber boots too, only his were black and cracked and mucky, and a coat and trousers so old that you couldn't tell what colour they had once been. Beside the tall Salisbury, he looked almost like a gnome. His half bald white head barely came up to Salisbury's waist. He grinned a wicked grin, with crooked teeth in it, right in Grundo's face, and said, "*Elder* brother, I'll have you know. I had my charter before *he* was built or thought of. And I *still* send a Member to Parliament in Winchester. I'm a rotten borough, I am."

"My brother is not so attached to his buildings as I am," Salisbury explained. "This is why he is able to take you to London."

Old Sarum's face contorted dreadfully. First, it went a long, long egg-shape and his lower lip stuck out so that we thought he was going to cry. Then it crunched together short with a snap, like an angry nutcracker. "Attached!" he said. "That's a joke! How could anyone be attached to a heap of old ruins? I tell you, it's no fun being a rotten borough. Got no people left, have I?" He wheeled round to look petulantly up at his tall brother. "Have you got any guarantee," he demanded, "that London's going to let me in? Well, *have* you?"

"Get them to the outskirts," Salisbury said. "Then parley."

"You get on to him then and make sure he's expecting me," Old Sarum retorted. "I don't want to uproot myself all that way for nothing, do I?"

"If he won't let you in, they can always go the rest of the way by bus or taxi," Salisbury said, turning away on one green rubber heel. "But I'll let him know. Get going."

"Oh, all right, all right," Old Sarum grumbled. "I'm only a rotten borough. I do your dirty work. Come on, then," he said to us. "Don't just stand there. Or don't you want to get to London?" He shambled to the old brown car and hopped up into its driving seat. "Get in, get in," he called out of the window. "This is Salisbury's pride and joy, this vehicle. He saves it for the Bishop or the Candace woman usually. We're *honoured* today, we are."

Grundo and I exchanged a look as we hurried to open the polished brown door to the back seat. Neither of us was quite sure what a rotten borough was, but Old Sarum certainly smelt as if he were rotten. The whiff as he hurried past us was faint but nasty. Inside, among the shiny brown leather upholstery, it was really quite strong – or not so much strong as filling the space with a rotten sort of persistence, like a blocked drain on a hot day. And this *was* a hot day. Grundo and I wound down the car's yellow-tinted windows as fast as we could. They would only go about halfway downs and, because of the brownish-yellow tint, looking out through them was a very odd experience. Through the lower half, the figure of Salisbury, walking away among the houses with the two dogs, seemed lit with unnatural thundery sunlight. Through the open part above, everything looked too blue by contrast. And the smell was still just as bad.

"Dogs' dos," Old Sarum muttered as he started the engine. "Won't let them foul *his* streets, oh no! So they come and do it on me all the time. I tell you, it's no fun being a rotten borough."

He kept on like this for most of the journey. We had no idea if he was talking to us or just muttering, so we slithered back into the shiny seat and said, "Mm," and "Oh?" and "Really?" from time to time, in case Old Sarum got offended, and tried to get the wind in our faces to counteract the smell. It did not help that it was a hot wind.

I think Old Sarum took a strange route. Grundo says he did, anyway. There seemed no reason, even to me, why we should before long find ourselves driving past Stonehenge.

"*Look* at that!" Old Sarum exclaimed pridefully. "Take a good, long look. *There's* real stonework for you! *That's* how to treat stones! And to think, in the old days, that all of it used to be mine! Enough to make you cry, it is."

We leaned over to that side to look. Grundo said politely, "You must have owned an incredible amount of magic once, then."

"Magic!" said Old Sarum. "That's beyond magic into thaumaturgical transcendental, son! I could weep!"

Grundo said more polite things. I couldn't speak. The sight of that compact ring of great stones, huge and small at once, and dense with strength through the queer thundery windows, did strange things to the inside of my head. I raised myself higher, so that I could see it above the glass in its proper strong greys, and discovered that some of the way I was feeling seemed to be due to the fact that Stonehenge had triggered one of the hurt lady's flower-files. *Briar rose: places of power.* But I found that the knowledge was all swimming away from me, rotating like a wheel, in spinning spokes of wisdom. At first I thought that this was because I didn't really need to know about Stonehenge. Then I realised that it was because this place was not *in* the file. The hurt lady's knowledge went back to the days before Stonehenge was made. This made me feel so odd that I had to clutch one of the straps beside the window and shut my eyes until we had gone past.

After that, we seemed to work our way on to the main London road, but whenever we came to a town, we left that road and zigzagged between dusty hedges on small, white lanes, and only came back to the main road after we had passed the town.

"Have to give them a wide berth," Old Sarum muttered. "Don't want an argument. Don't want all that about You can't come through *me*, you rotten borough! Oh, it's no fun, I tell you."

Back on the main road, we rumbled along beside dark trees, with a long green line of hills over to our right. Around the time sunset was growing up the sky behind us, Grundo and I both found our heads being snatched round towards that line of hills. There was something there. Back into my head came *Briar rose: places of power*. This time it was odder still. Some of whatever power it was had evidently been old when the hurt lady made her files, but some of it was not there, and new, and quite as strong as Stonehenge.

"What's that?" Grundo asked, rather dizzily. "Over that way."

"Can't say, I'm sure," Old Sarum answered. "Some old stuff, nothing to do with me. I'm only a rotten borough."

We drove and the feeling died away gradually, almost reluctantly, as if something might have been trying to get our attention. Sunset blazed all round the sky. And quite suddenly the car began to zigzag around in the road and Old Sarum started to shout. "Gerroff, *gerroff*! Gerroff my windscreen, damn your eyes!"

We stopped with a squeal and a dreadful jolt.

"One of you get out there and kill this thing, whatever it is! Bat or whatever," Old Sarum commanded. "I can't see a thing with it there."

Grundo and I looked past him at the windscreen, but as far as we could see, there was nothing there but yellow-tinted glass and some flies stuck to it.

"Get it *off*!" howled Old Sarum.

We sighed and climbed out into the dusky road, where all at once everything was smelling of dew and damp hay. "I think he's gone potty," Grundo grunted under the noise of the car drumming and throbbing beside the hedge.

"Or he was potty to start with," I agreed.

We edged along to the front of the car. There still did not seem to be anything wrong with the windscreen, until we reached the long, brown bonnet and leant over to look. Then the thing clinging to the windscreen-wiper flinched away from us and tried to scuttle up over the top of the car. Grundo made a grab – with a touch of magic to help – and caught it by the filmy veiling along its back. He held it out to me in both hands, quivering and all but invisible.

"What do you think it is?"

"Kill it, come on!" Old Sarum ordered, leaning out of his window.

It was alive and terrified and bewildered. It was also beginning to glow faintly. "No, don't," I said. "I think it may be a salamander. They're rare."

"Ouch – it's getting hot! I think you're right," Grundo agreed. "What's a soothing spell, quickly?"

I began a spell for him and he took it up too as soon as he remembered it. We bent over the quivering salamander, while Old Sarum watched ironically. "It's vermin," he said. "That thing can set fire to a house, you know."

"Yes, but it won't now," I said. "I think you can let it go into the hedge, Grundo."

"It doesn't want to go," Grundo said. "It's foreign.

It's lost. It's escaped from somewhere horrible and it doesn't know where to go to be safe."

"Speaks to you, does it?" Old Sarum asked sarcastically. "Don't trust it. It's just vermin. Throw it in the hedge."

"Not speaks, exactly," Grundo said, "but I think it's telling me the truth. Roddy, we'd better take it to your Grandfather Hyde and ask him what to do about it."

"Good idea," I said, although if Old Sarum hadn't been there setting me a bad example, I might have been sarcastic too. I felt really envious of the way Grundo could understand the salamander.

As for Old Sarum, he did his ghastly face contortions again, going long and egg-shaped and then snapping into a nutcracker bunch. "It's your funeral," he said, as Grundo climbed into the car, tenderly holding the salamander. "*You're* the ones that'll fry and sizzle when it sets this car on fire, not me. I don't burn easy."

"Then that's one good thing about being a rotten borough, isn't it?" I said, climbing back in too. After the fresh dewy evening, the smell in the car was beastly.

"True, but Salisbury's going to be pretty peeved when I come back and tell him his car burnt up," Old Sarum retorted. He started the car moving and grumbled for the next ten miles. "Tell him I never *got* to London and he'll *do* me. Lose my charter and my MP, I shouldn't wonder. And I *hate* the smell of burning. Sets all my bricks on edge."

"Just shut up," Grundo whispered. He crooned the

soothing spell to the salamander until it climbed up his arm to his shoulder, where it sat pulsing out pleasure. What with my envy about that and the smell and the way Old Sarum was grumbling, I didn't want to be in the car at all. I turned and stuck my face out of the open half of the window.

After a while, when the road was nearly dark, I realised that there was a white horse alongside, keeping pace with the car. I looked up to see that there was a rider on its back, whose flapping black cloak showed a white lining. "Oh!" I said.

Grandfather Gwyn leaned down to the open half of the window. "They have called me out for a third time," he said, "to carry away a great many more people. In some ways, though, this is good news. If they try to call me again, I am free to summon *them*. But I am sorry about the rest of it."

Before I could answer, he clicked his tongue to the grey mare and she went surging off up the road ahead.

Grundo stared. "He went faster than this car!" he said. "What did he say? I didn't quite hear."

"Something private," I said. For some reason, I did not want to tell Grundo how very anxious this had made me. Sybil was Grundo's mother, after all, and she had just done something new. I wanted to get to my lovely, safe, soldierly Magid of a Grandad Hyde more than anything in the world just then. Grandad would know. He would be able to tell me what Sybil and her friends had done this time. I wished he was here telling me *now*. Every time Old Sarum slowed down for a corner or a crossroads, I wanted to scream at him to drive *faster*. When he slowed down and stopped just outside London, I almost did scream. "Drive *on*!" I shouted.

"Can't do that," Old Sarum said. "This is London. Got to negotiate, don't we?"

To my utter exasperation, he turned off the engine and climbed out of the car. I flung my door open and jumped out too. After a moment, Grundo got out as well, leaving the salamander curled up on the seat. The smells of a hot city night, a hot country night and Old Sarum flooded round us. Hedges rustled behind us. In front, the headlights of our car blazed down a suburban road lined with streetlights and glistened on two enormous shiny things planted like roadblocks in front of us.

They were shoes. It took us a moment to see that they were shoes.

Our heads turned slowly upwards and we saw London, vast and shadowy, towering against the purple city sky. "What are *you* doing here?" he said to Old Sarum.

London had the strangest voice. Part of it was like the groan and clatter of thick traffic, and the rest was a chorus of different voices, high, low, and tenor voices, voices with very upper class accents, bass voices speaking purest Cockney, overseas voices, and every grade of voice in between. It was almost like hearing a huge concert.

Old Sarum whined and bowed and rubbed his hands together. In the headlights, his face went through extraordinary contortions. "I'm only a rotten borough, your honour, and I mean no harm. Not wishing to trespass in any way upon your honour's precincts, but I was *given* this mission, see. I'm to drive these two here, take them to the Magid. I knew that might be pushing it a bit, your honour, but what's a poor rotten borough like me to do when people in high places start giving orders? No offence in the world..."

"Who gave you your orders?" chorused London. He had his shadowy head bent, listening to Old Sarum, but even in that dim light he seemed to have the strangest face. It was like the framework of a strong, noble face with other faces stuck into it. Part of one cheek was shifty. The end of one eyebrow and part of his mouth seemed to leer. One of his eyes seemed to be glass. At least, his left eye caught the light differently from the right one. A tarry, bricky, city smell blew off him, with a touch of stale river mixed in.

"It was that Candace woman, your honour," Old Sarum whined. "What she tells Salisbury, Salisbury does. Nothing to do with me, except that I got roped in to do the dirty work. *As* usual."

"Mrs Candace," orchestrated London, "used to be a great beauty. I knew her well. She held salons in Berkeley Square. Then she married an Italian Count."

"Yeah, but he died and she gave all that up," Old

Sarum said. "Lives in Salisbury now and bosses the country from there."

"I know," London rumbled. "And you should speak of her with proper respect."

"All the respect in the world, your honour," Old Sarum protested. "Anything you say. But I don't have to tell someone who straddles a great river like you do that humans are just water under your bridges. Water under all your bridges. Mrs Candace, these two young 'uns with me, they're all the same. They come, they go. You live on. Even I live on, your honour."

"We grew up for and by means of humans," London thumped out. He sounded like hammers on a building site.

"Well, speak for yourself, your honour," Old Sarum whined. "All humans mean to me these days is they let me send one of them off to argue in Winchester. What I'm trying to say, your honour, is that it's nothing to you what humans come or go. So you might as well let me take these to the Magid."

"On what grounds?" chorused London.

I began to feel increasingly uneasy. It wasn't just that I was frantic to get to Grandad, or even that we were standing in the road being argued over by two cities. It was because now that I had learnt to see the near invisible creatures like the ones who inhabited the Dimber Regalia, I could see – and hear – them here too. They were being drawn here by the argument. The hedges behind were full of stealthy rustlings and small blinks of light. Bluish shadows were stalking in from the rear of the car. These felt different from those I had seen earlier today. I realised that the ones I had seen by sunlight were the lazy, harmless creatures of the day. These, now, were the people of the night. And very few of them were friendly.

Grundo had seen them too. His head kept turning towards the hedges as the argument went on.

At length, London said, in a distant sort of city buzz, as if he were considering, "I've no objections to the humans entering. When have I ever prevented that? I suppose they can take a bus or a taxi."

"We've no money!" Grundo called up at him anxiously. "We used it all yesterday."

I don't think London heard him. He suggested in chorus, "Or they can walk."

Old Sarum sent a contorted glance towards the hedges and the shadows in the road and stuck his lower lip out. "As to that, your honour, I'm not sure they would be safe. I was told to keep them safe, meaning no disrespect."

"I have never guaranteed safety," London replied, "or wealth either."

"No, and your streets aren't really paved with gold neither," Old Sarum retorted. "*I* know. It's not *your* fault some humans get rich and have a lovely time and some has to doss on a doorstep or get robbed. Nothing to do with you. But we're not talking about that, your honour. We're discussing about me driving them to a particular doorstep like Mrs Candace *wants* me to. Is that too much to ask?"

There was a long pause. London appeared to be listening to something in the distance, the sing-song of a fire engine or an ambulance perhaps. We certainly heard something like that, followed by clocks striking, while we waited. Then, finally, his vast figure straightened a little. His chorus voice sounded amused.

"I have been under orders too," he told us. "Even me. It seems that time was needed to penetrate certain magical defences. The enchantment was absolute while it lasted, but I can let you go now. Get in your car and drive where you want to go." He lifted one huge, glossy shoe and stepped over the nearest row of houses into the next street. Before he lifted the other foot, he stood astride the houses and gave a rumbling chuckle. "I shall be with you all the way, of course."

He was too. We climbed quickly and thankfully back into the car and Old Sarum drove on through the city. And every time I glanced out of the open half of the window, I saw London's huge shadowy figure wading among the houses beside us.

It seemed to take an age to get to Grandad's house. I was mad with anxiety all the way. I knew that if Sybil was able to order London to hold us up while Grandfather Gwyn carried out her orders, then she had grown hideously powerful and we *had* to tell Grandad.

But it never occurred to me what she had done. Old

Sarum drew up outside the house at last with a fine shriek of brakes and I jumped out and rushed to the front door. While I clattered away at the knocker, I could hear Old Sarum going on at Grundo. "Oh, I don't do it to be thanked. I'm just the dogsbody, I am. You rush away too. Don't mind me, I'm only a rotten borough…" And Grundo was trying to make himself heard, saying, "But we *do* thank you. We're very, very grateful. Hey, let me get the salamander out before you drive away…"

Long before the door was opened, Old Sarum had driven away and Grundo had joined me on the doorstep with the salamander on his shoulder. I clattered the knocker one more time and the door was opened at last by my cousin Toby.

Toby is always a pale boy, but just then he was chalky, with a dazed sort of stare to his eyes. Behind him, I could hear the most dreadful yelling and sobbing noises. Dora, I thought.

"What's happened?" I said. "What's wrong?"

Toby gulped. "Grandad. He was carried off just a minute ago. Mum says it was the King of the Dead who took him."

The inside of me seemed to pitch downwards into somewhere icy. "I shall kill Sybil," I said. "Quite soon."

# CHAPTER TWENTY-EIGHT

*

*I*hadn't expected Roddy to be quite so overbearing. I suppose she was upset about all the things that had been happening, but then so were we. The way Maxwell Hyde had been taken – just like that! – seemed to hang over us all like nervousness and horror. It was almost as if something awful was *going* to happen. Instead of it just having happened, if you see what I mean.

I was picking up furniture and game pieces and trying to calm Dora down while I did it. Salamanders were rushing about and transparent creatures were bundling this way and that in droves. I was saying, "Hush, you'll upset the salamanders. Hush, it doesn't *help* to yell," when Roddy came striding in with Toby and another boy behind her.

She stood staring about. You'd think her eyes were weapons. They sort of snapped dark fire. Otherwise, she was just as I'd been remembering her, with that look of having simply grown, like a tree or something. She had a fabulous figure, even in baggy old trousers and an old grey sweater, quite thin, but all beautifully rounded, and she smelt nice too, even from where I was on the floor. My heart began beating in little rapid bangs. My legs felt weak and I could feel my face flushing red and then draining white again.

But part of the simply-grown thing with Roddy was that she never even thought she might have that sort of effect on people. In fact, she didn't care *what* effect she had. She said, "This place looks as if a bomb hit it! And there are salamanders *everywhere*. Haven't any of you thought of the fire risk?"

That was enough to start my heart beating normally, if you count angry thumping as normal. And I could pretend that any strange colour in my face was due to groping under the sofa for game pieces.

"You!" she snapped at me. "What's your version of Grandad's disappearance?"

I stood up. It helps to be tall enough to loom a bit. "What no 'Hallo, Nick, fancy seeing *you* again!'?" I said. "Shut *up*, Dora."

"Yes, be *quiet*, Auntie," Roddy said. "Of course I remember you, but this is urgent."

"Gwyn ap Nud," I said. "I know him because we

have him on Earth too. Just rode through here and hauled Maxwell Hyde up on his horse and left."

At this stage, Dora decided to stop screaming and turn social. She surged off the sofa with tears on her face, saying, "My niece, Arianrhod Hyde, and her friend, Ambrose Temple, Nick. Nick is Daddy's Oriental pupil, Roddy dear."

This attempt at Courtly graces misfired rather. I said, "I am *not* Oriental! I've *told* you!"

Roddy snapped, "He prefers to be called *Grundo*! I've *told* you!" Then she whirled round on me and demanded, "Haven't you *any* idea where Grandad's been taken?"

Obvious, I thought. Land of the Dead. But she was in such mood I didn't say so. "I could try some divining," I said. "I've got pretty good at that."

"You do that," she commanded and whirled round on poor Dora again. "Auntie, Grundo's very tired and hungry. Could you find him some supper? And I'm afraid we'll both have to stay the night, unless the Progress is very near. Can you find Grundo a bed? Could he go in with Toby?"

I looked at this Grundo. He was a strange-looking kid with a hooked nose and a faceful of freckles, slightly older than Toby. He didn't look particularly tired. He and Toby were giggling together because they both had a salamander sitting round their necks.

It was never any good commanding Dora. Maxwell Hyde had always been pretty careful not to, not if he wanted anything done, that was. She stared at Roddy and then went into wet mode, sinking on to the sofa and wringing her hands. "But I couldn't think of anything to go with the potatoes!" she moaned.

"Oh, *God*!" Roddy said. "Grundo has to eat *something*!"

I saw she was going to start snapping commands at Toby next and Toby had already had a pretty tough day. He was looking wiped. "Through here," I said and led the way to the dining room where the cheese and the potatoes were still on the table. I fetched out more plates and knives and found the pickle.

Grundo stared a bit and said in a strange grunty voice, "I'm not sure I can manage cold potatoes after all that cake with Mrs Candace."

"There's plenty of cheese though," Roddy said coaxingly, pulling out a chair for him. "Sit down and try to eat a bit anyway."

She was like that all the time with this Grundo. To other people, she was all, "Grundo must have this, Grundo mustn't go without that," and with Grundo himself she was as if she was his caring elder sister – or his very fussy mother, more like. You'd think Grundo was the only person in her world. It annoyed me. I wanted to tell her to forget Grundo and get a life. Anyway, the sight of food had its usual effect on me. I sat down, scooped up pickle and began a second supper. Toby came and sat beside me and started eating too.

"What are you *doing*?" Roddy demanded.

"Eating," I said.

"But you're supposed to be divining for where Grandad is!" she said.

"I will when I've got my strength up," I said soothingly.

Roddy was disgusted. "I asked you for help. You're – you're obstructionist!"

"And you," I said, "would get on a bit better if you stopped being so uptight and domineering." I'd never seen anyone look so outraged. She was too angry to speak. Toby shot me a look that said he was going to laugh any minute and probably choke on a potato. So I said to Roddy, "Oh, come on, sit down and get something to eat yourself."

She stared at me like a queen on a particularly haughty day. "I tell you," she said, "there's a *conspiracy*."

"I agree," I said. "I believe you. But that doesn't mean you have to stop eating. And while you eat, we can work out what we ought to do about it. That make sense?"

She dragged a chair out reluctantly. "Sit down, Grundo. The most important thing is to find out where the King's Progress is at the moment."

"They're still in Norfolk," Toby said. "It was on the morning media."

"Oh," said Roddy. She seemed a bit daunted for a moment. "I *must* get in touch with my parents!" she said. "I know! Grandad's bound to have Dad's latest speaker code, isn't he?" She was pushing her chair back again to go to the far-speaker as she said it.

Grundo settled that. "Sit down," he said. "Nick's right. No one in the Progress knows we know anything, so you need to be careful what you say. You could get your parents into trouble. We need to decide what to do first. You're not the only one who's had a shock, you know."

The power of the Grundo! She listened to his quiet growly voice and she sat down again at once. Actually, he was quite a nice kid. I discovered that as soon as we got talking. Not that this helped when it came to us deciding what to do. I was pretty stumped, to tell the truth. With Kings and politics in it, and powerful people like the Merlin, and Maxwell Hyde pretty probably dead, I didn't see what kids like us *could* do.

"I wish we could ask Romanov," I said.

# CHAPTER TWENTY-NINE

✳

*N*ick is the most maddening person I ever knew. If you try to make him do anything, he just goes kind of heavy at you. But perfectly polite. He gets a sweet look on his altogether too handsome face and refuses to budge. What made it worse was the way I seemed to feel him pushing at me all the time, in a warm, moist, eager way that I didn't understand and didn't want at all. I nearly threw one of Aunt Dora's vile, bruised-looking potatoes at him several times.

We did get things talked through in the end – though Nick didn't help by bleating every so often that we ought to talk to Romanov. I'd never heard of this Romanov, so I took no notice, and we did get our priorities straight at last. We had to find where Grandfather Gwyn had taken Grandad and let my parents know what was going on.

After we cleared the food away, Nick finally got down to some serious divination magic. I didn't feel too hopeful of it. His method seemed to be to spread a whole lot of books and maps on the living room floor and surround these with bowls of ink and water and different sorts of weights on strings – all of it in danger from twenty inquisitive salamanders – and sit hunched over it with Toby and Grundo squatting beside him and a crowd of the transparent folk hovering over their heads. The boys kept giving him advice. Aunt Dora put in her bit by sitting on the sofa and calling out things like, "Are you sure you know what you're doing?" and "Is that how they do this in the Orient, dear?" and "Daddy won't be pleased if you spill that ink!"

I couldn't have worked like that, but Nick seemed quite placid. No doubt it helped that he was also basking in admiration. Grundo was in a fair way to thinking that Nick was the most marvellous person he'd ever met. I don't think any boys Nick's age had ever treated him like a human being before. Boys at Court were always too lofty, or else nervous because Grundo was a magic user, or both. As for Toby, I could see he had been Nick's worshipper for weeks.

I began seriously to believe I had bungled that working in Wales – or why else had the spell sent me an amateur wizard with a swelled head? Oh, well, I thought and went and found the far-speaker in the hall.

Grandad had one of those useful codepads, where you punch the name of the person you want and it springs open to show you the code. Hoping hard that he had kept it up to date, I punched in Daniel Hyde. It duly sprang open and the code *looked* right. Court codes are usually two letters and three numbers. This said DH145, so I dialled that.

It rang for quite a long time and was finally answered by a high, breathless voice saying, "Court Weather Office."

The relief! I was so glad to get through that I hardly noticed or minded that the voice was the voice of Grundo's odious sister, Alicia. She was a royal page after all, and one of their duties was to take calls when everyone else was too busy. "Oh, Alicia!" I said. "Could I speak to Dad? This is Roddy and it's urgent."

She knew my voice too. She giggled unpleasantly in her usual way. "So you've turned up again!" she said. "Where are you? I thought we'd left you safely stuck away in Wales."

"No," I said. "I'm in London now and I need to speak to my father at once. Could you get him to the speaker, please?"

She giggled even harder. "No," she said. "I can't."

"Do you mind telling me why not?" I said.

"Because he's not here," she said. "He hasn't been here for ages now. We expelled all the dissident wizards two weeks ago."

I had that pitching downwards feeling inside again, but I said, politely, "Then perhaps you can tell me where he is now."

"*Wouldn't* you like to know!" Alicia said. "He's where nobody's ever going to find him again. And your mother's there too. And you know, Roddy, you really have no business ringing this number, because you're not a member of Court any longer. I shouldn't really be speaking to you." There was true triumph in her voice. I could tell she had been looking forward to telling me this from the moment she heard my voice on the speaker. "Both your parents have been impeached for treason to the Crown, you see," she explained.

"Thank you *so* much for telling me," I said. "Who's seeing to the weather then?"

"Well, nobody at the moment," she said, "but I expect a new appointment will be made as soon as the King has abdicated."

"Oh," I said. "*Is* the King going to abdicate?"

"I didn't tell you that!" she said hastily. She sounded quite frightened.

"Of *course* not," I said. "Alicia, you've been so good telling me all this. Now tell me what happens to Grundo, please."

"Oh, is he with you?" Alicia asked coldly. "I suppose you'd better send him back to Court. Not to Norfolk though. We're moving first thing in the morning and we won't get to— Oh, what a nuisance that child always is!

Send him to Salisbury Plain the day after tomorrow. He can always wait if we're not there yet. Goodbye, Roddy. *So* nice talking to you." She rang off.

I stood and stared at the whirring earpiece. I felt dead. All I seemed to be able to think was that it was no *wonder* the weather had been so hot all this time. Dad couldn't have had a chance to change it. Then I thought – viciously – that Alicia had always been a liar if she thought she could hurt my feelings and get away with it. This simply could not be true. I slammed the receiver back, slapped the codepad shut and punched in Annie Hyde instead, furiously. Mam would surely tell me that none of it was true.

Mam's code was AH369 currently. But all I got when I dialled it up was a mechanical voice saying, *The owner of this code is no longer in Court. The owner of this code is no longer...*

I put the receiver back and stared at my grandfather's dark, shabby wallpaper. *Both* my parents seemed to be gone. Grandad was gone too, the King was about to abdicate, and no one seemed to realise that there really was a conspiracy. Who could I tell? Who could possibly help? I couldn't tell Grandfather Gwyn because he had been ordered to take my Grandfather Hyde away, with the help of London himself. Who else could I *tell*?

I thought of Mrs Candace. She was pretty powerful. She might not have believed me this afternoon, but she'd *have* to believe me now.

I snapped the pad again. If she was Lady of Governance, Grandad would surely have her number. Yes. He did. It was there and I dialled it. And it rang and rang and rang. I allowed for someone with a crippled hip. I let the call go from whirring to bleeping. I allowed time for her to lever herself out of her chair, and time to limp slowly across a big room. I allowed time on top of that. But still no one answered the speaker.

I put the receiver slowly down and stared at the wallpaper again. After a bit, as an experiment, I dialled the code for Salisbury again. Just the code. I didn't get whirring this time, just silence. I got silence for so long that I was going to give up, when a strange, heavy, unechoing voice answered.

"Salisbury here."

"Oh," I said. "Thank goodness! Look, I've been trying to call Mrs Candace, but she doesn't answer – this is Arianrhod Hyde, by the way. Is Mrs Candace all right, or asleep or something?"

"I regret to say," replied Salisbury's heavy voice, "that Mrs Candace is no longer with me. She was removed from her house earlier this evening."

"Who?" I said. "Who took her?"

There was a short silence. Then Salisbury said, "The son of Nud, I believe. I was ordered not to interfere. I am sorry."

"That's all right," I said. "If even London had to obey orders, there was nothing you could do. Do you know where she was taken?"

There was another short silence. Then he said, "No."

"Thanks anyway," I said. I cut the connection and stared at the wall some more. Then, as a last resort, I snapped the codepad open to Hepzibah Dimber and, rather reluctantly, dialled that number.

That whirred and bleeped and bleeped too. It rang for so long that I began to think I would be glad even to speak to an Izzy. But it's Friday night, I thought as I rang off. Maybe they've all gone out. But it was so late by then that I didn't believe it.

After a while, I went back into the living room. As I came in, Nick looked up and said, as if he was quite surprised, "Maxwell Hyde's still alive! That's certain."

"But he's not anywhere we can *find*," Toby added.

Grundo said, and I could see it was part of an argument they had been having, "It *has* to be outside this world. Your results don't make sense any other way."

Dora gazed at me and said brightly, "Anything the matter, dear?"

"Oh, no," I said. "Nothing at all. My parents have only been expelled from Court, the King's only going to abdicate, and Mrs Candace and the Dimbers have only been kidnapped too. Nothing wrong at all."

The boys' faces turned up to me. Nick said, "Wow!"

"Is that all you can say?" I more or less screamed.

Dora, who seemed not to have heard a thing I said, beamed kindly. "You know, dear, you need to discharge all the adverse vibrations," she said. "Sit down here and have a good cry. It does wonders."

"Does it indeed?" I said rudely. "Thank you very much!" Then I sat down in the nearest shabby armchair and burst into tears. As one boy, Grundo, Toby and Nick all became exceedingly embarrassed and turned their backs on me. I really wanted to scream then.

# CHAPTER THIRTY

✳

*I* had Grundo sleeping on the couch in my room that
night. Everyone agreed that Roddy had better have
Maxwell Hyde's room, and Toby's room didn't have a
couch. Lucky Toby. Grundo must be the most restless
sleeper in all the universes. When he wasn't turning over
and over and jangling the couch springs, he was either
snoring like a football rattle or shouting out in his sleep
that everything was back to front and he couldn't *do*
it! He kept waking me up. And whenever he woke me,
the feeling of nervous horror came back and I lay and
worried.

I knew we had to find Romanov and ask him what to
do. With Maxwell Hyde gone, and from what Roddy said,

I could see things in Blest were going down the plughole fast. Romanov would know what to do. He had real power. I could even sort of feel the weird non-direction I ought to go in to find Romanov, but I couldn't even start to go that way. It was the same as the way I couldn't walk into another world. I seemed to need somebody else there to help or give me a push before I could do it.

In the end it got light. I could hear birds singing and salamanders scuttling to get to the places where the sun would shine first. By then, Grundo was sleeping as peacefully as a log of course, but I knew I wasn't going to be able to sleep now. I swore and got up.

And it was an odd thing. Instead of being nine-tenths asleep and unable to open my eyes like I usually am, I felt quite sharp and awake. Maybe it was because I'd been practising being awake all night. I collected my clothes and dressed downstairs in the kitchen. While I was making coffee, I looked in Dora's mirror with the rabbits round it, expecting to see that I had giant, droopy black bags under my eyes, but I looked normal. Just grumpy.

My coffee was poured out into a mug ready to drink when the doorbell rang. That was when I discovered I was in a really bad mood. The doorbell rang twice more while I was going along to answer it. Then someone battered away with the knocker.

"All *right*!" I shouted. "All right, all right, all *right*! Do you expect me to *teleport* to the door or something?" I wrenched the door open.

Two quite small girls were jigging about on the doorstep, both in little pleated sailor-dresses. The one on the left was in blue trimmed with white and the one on the right was in white trimmed with blue. Otherwise I couldn't tell them apart. When they saw my angry face they flung their arms round one another and stared at me over their shoulders with identical soulful looks.

"He must be Grandad's pet ape," said the blue one, and the white one said, "I *love* them when they're angry!" and sighed ecstatically.

"You've come to the wrong house," I said.

"No, we haven't," said the blue one. "We want Mr Maxwell Hyde."

"He's our grandfather," the white one explained. "I'm Isadora and this is Ilsabil and tell him it's urgent."

"He isn't here," I said. "He's been kidnapped."

We all stared at one another blankly for a moment. Then the Ilsabil one said, as if she was about a century old, "They're such liars, these boys."

"We must search the house," Isadora agreed.

They unwound their arms and started to walk inside, one on either side of me. I put out both my arms and stopped them at neck level. "Just a moment," I said. "How come you're trying to visit your grandfather at five-thirty in the morning? There's been jiggery-pokery for weeks now. How do I know Maxwell Hyde really *is* your grandfather? He never said a word about you."

"Now you've hurt our feelings!" Ilsabil said tragically.

"He never said a word about *you*, whoever you are!" Isadora said. Then, as if they had given one another a secret signal, they both shoved mightily at my arms. I shoved back. I could feel them using some sort of witchcraft to get past me. That didn't bother me particularly, though it made me more suspicious than ever. I went on shoving back. The one on the left sank her teeth into my forearm and the one on the right kicked my shins.

"*Let us in!*" they screamed.

By this time, I was sure they were another part of the conspiracy, that was trying to storm Maxwell Hyde's house. I took hold of them by a skinny arm each and tried to bundle them back into the street.

"We'll wake everyone up in all the houses!" Ilsabil threatened.

"We're being assaulted!" Isadora screamed. "Help! *Child abuse!*"

I suppose it was not surprising that the noise woke everyone except Dora – Dora is even harder to wake than I am. Grundo turned up at my elbow, buttoning his shirt. "Oh, God! It's the Izzies!" he grunted. "That's *all* we needed!"

The Izzies stopped yelling and fighting in order to exchange weary looks across me. "It's per-thetic again!" said one.

"Fetch Roddy," commanded the other.

"I'm here," Roddy said sleepily from behind me. "What are you two little beasts doing screaming on the doorstep at this hour of the morning?"

"Roddy, this huge Indian boy is *hurting* us!" Isadora whined.

"You probably deserve it," Roddy retorted. "Why are you here? Did Judith bring you?"

One twin promptly went sweet and gentle and the other crisply efficient. "My dear," the gentle one said sadly, "Judith has *vanished*. So has Heppy."

"We begged a lift from Mrs Simpson," stated the efficient one. "We are so resourceful."

Then they did it the other way round. I felt as if my eyes were crossing.

Roddy sighed. "You'd better let them in," she said to me. "I've been afraid this might have happened."

I let go of the Izzies willingly. They immediately twinkled in past me on tiptoes, wafting their arms this way and that like ballet dancers.

"What have you done with your dog?" Grundo boomed at them as they wafted past him.

"With the vicar," an Izzy said over her shoulder, wafting. "*Food*," she added, in tones of deep longing.

"She wanted to keep us too," said the other, "but we slipped away. *Kitchen*," she added yearningly.

They broke into a gallop and rushed to the kitchen. By the time we got there, they had found every packet of cereal in the place and were busily pouring vast heaps of breakfast food into bowls, along with all the milk there was. Puffed rice had gone all over the floor and they had upset my coffee in it. I dourly got a cloth and mopped it all up, while Grundo put the kettle on again.

"We'd better have toast," Roddy said irritably. "It's no good expecting any sense out of those two until they've fed their horrible little faces."

She was very pale, with blue patches under her eyes, as if she hadn't slept, and she seemed tenser than ever. I did wish she was not so tense all the time. That is the unexpected trouble with love affairs, I thought as I made more coffee. You can fancy a girl like mad, but more than just the *look* of her comes into it. You find yourself having to allow for her *personality* too. At five-thirty in the morning.

"They're your cousins, are they?" I said, nodding at the Izzies as they guzzled.

"Yes," she said. "Dora's sister's twins. They're awful."

At least she had the sense to see that, I thought. None of that blood being thicker than water nonsense with Roddy. It seemed to be one thing we had in common, even if it wasn't much of a basis for a love affair. I was rather surprised, as I put the coffee on the table as far away from the Izzies as possible, that I still meant to have a love affair. It was not as if I'd had any encouragement.

Around this point, Toby put his sleepy face into the kitchen, saw the Izzies and went pale. "Oh, no!" he said. "Not *them* now! I'm going to see to the goat." And he went.

Grundo chuckled. "A hundred per cent vote against,"

he said. "Here's some toast and you're to *eat* it, Roddy."

"Did I say I wouldn't?" she snapped.

"No," he grunted. "You *looked* at it." He waited until Roddy had taken a mouthful and turned to the Izzies. "Now, tell us. How did Heppy and Judith vanish? When?"

Isadora looked up from filling her bowl for the fourth time. "We need more milk and some toast first."

"You've had all the milk," I said.

"Then our lips are sealed," said Ilsabil.

"No they are not," Roddy said. "One of you is to make some toast while the other talks." She took a large bite of toast. "Or fleas," she said with her mouth full.

The Izzies exchanged gentle, angelic looks. "We don't understand," said Ilsabil, "why you aren't nice to us."

"*None* of you responds to our great charm," said Isadora.

"*What* great charm?" I said. "If you want people to be nice to you, *you* have to be nice to *them*. Are you going to tell us what happened or shall I bang your heads together?"

They stared at me haughtily. After a bit, Ilsabil flounced up and made sulky efforts to cut bread.

"We don't really know," Isadora said, quite as sulky. "It was just before supper and we were in the garden. Heppy and Judith were being *boring*, making a fuss about trying to talk to the Regalia, so we stayed outside. And we thought we heard a horse whinny inside the house.

And Heppy shouted a bit, but she does that a lot. We thought she was shouting at the Regalia again, so we took no notice…"

While Isadora was saying this, Ilsabil was looking from me to Grundo and then at Roddy, with a sweet, helpless smile, waiting for one of us to come and make toast for her. None of us took any notice.

"It sounded like quite a lot of horses," Isadora said, "but not for very long. We couldn't understand it. Then we got hungry and came in for supper and Judith and Heppy weren't there. They weren't anywhere in the house and supper was still *raw*. We got *so* hungry! When it was dark and they still hadn't come back…"

Toby came into the kitchen. Ilsabil was still gently waving the breadknife above the loaf. Toby pushed her aside and packed the grill with doorsteps of bread with cheese on them. "The goat's almost eaten through her stake," he said as he worked.

"I'll go and look in a moment," I said. "Go on, Izzie."

"We sort of knew they weren't *going* to come back," Isadora said. "And we were so hungry by then that we found Heppy's purse and went down to the shop with the money, and on the way we remembered that Mrs Simpson always goes to London Airport over Friday night to collect the new tea when it's fresh…"

"See how resourceful we are," Ilsabil murmured.

"Except about making toast," Grundo said. "So you went off and just left the dog, didn't you?"

"No, promise," Isadora said. "We changed our *clothes* and went to the vicar and told her what had happened and said we had to go to Grandad because he's a Magid…"

"*And* left Jackson with her, so *there*!" said Ilsabil. "She wanted to keep us too, but we told her Mrs Simpson was giving us a lift to London…"

"Then we had to run and we *just* caught Mrs Simpson before she drove away," Isadora said. "And she sighed and said 'Jump aboard then' and we did."

"But we never had any supper because it was such a rush," Ilsabil said, with a wistful eye on the cheesy toast.

To do them justice, both twins were looking quite upset, though it may have had more to do with missing supper than losing their mother, to my mind. "What do you make of it?" I asked Roddy.

"Every magic user who might have been able to stop Sybil seems to have gone," she said. "I'm willing to bet that all the other hereditary witches have been taken too."

"You think we should check?" Grundo asked.

"What's the point? We should be *doing* something!" she said, twisting her hands together. "Only what should we *do*?"

"Find Romanov," I said.

She rounded on me. "You *keep* bleating that!"

Allow for personality, I told myself, but I thought if I had to do much more allowing I might run out of patience. "For one thing," I said, "I was told Romanov has more magic than anyone in several universes – he's

449

a sort of magics Csar – and for another thing, he knows your grandfather quite well…"

Her annoyance faded down into surprise. "You never said that before!"

I *didn't* say that she had never given me a chance. I took a long breath and said, "That's why I think he'll help."

"So how do we find him?" she demanded.

I'm so glad you asked me that question, I thought. "Um," I said. "He doesn't live in a particular world. He has this strange island that's made out of bits of several different universes and I sort of know the direction…"

She sighed. "In other words, you can't find him."

"I didn't say…" I began.

Toby interrupted in his quiet way. "The goat," he said. "You said she was Romanov's goat."

"That's *it*!" I shouted. I jumped up and chairs crashed on the tiles all round me. The only wonder was that even this didn't wake Dora up. "Let's go!"

# PART ELEVEN
# RODDY AND NICK

# CHAPTER THIRTY-ONE

✳

*I* could not *believe* it when the Izzies turned up! It seemed like the last straw, even though it was more proof that I wasn't imagining the conspiracy, since it made it clear that Heppy and Judith had really vanished too.

Then the Izzies insisted on coming with us to find this Romanov person. We should have simply dashed off and left them, while they were busy pulling strings of cheese off their toast with their teeth. But they shouted to know what we were doing, and Nick took entirely the wrong line with them. He told them they had to stay behind and explain to Dora. He said they were too young to go on the dark paths. You would not *credit* the whining and arguing and winning persuasions this led to from the Izzies. When that didn't work, they followed it up with double yelling. At least that gave Grundo time to eat a proper breakfast.

When he and Toby had finished eating, I gave in. I said, "All right, you can come." They instantly stopped whining, wiped their greasy hands on their sailor suits and flung their arms round me, exclaiming that I was the most marvellous cousin in the *world*! I pushed them away. "On condition that you stop acting about and *behave*," I added. They looked wronged and hurt and saintly. "Just stop trying to twist everyone round your greasy little fingers," I said.

"Yes, cut the glamour," Nick said. "You're like a couple of ageing filmstars. You could be sixty instead of six."

"We're *not* six!" Isadora exclaimed – if she was the one in white. "We're nearly *nine*!"

"Whatever," said Nick. "I've had enough. Let's go."

We all bundled out into the garden, at the precise moment when the goat bit through the last of her stake with a snap. Nick dashed over and caught hold of the stake at both ends, so that the chain fastened to the goat's neck couldn't slide off it.

"Now, Helga," he said, "we want you to take us to Romanov. Romanov, Helga. All of you think very hard about this goat taking us back to her owner."

Helga leered up at Nick with her evil goat's face and

chewed her cud, quite unmoved. We stood round her, panting and trying to *will* her to obey Nick. I tried to find a spell among the hurt woman's flower-files that would help. But that woman knew goats. I found, under *Teazle, to drive sheep without a dog*, and *to call cattle*, and *to influence a pig*, and after further searching I found *to teach a dog to obey*, *to call a hawk to the hand* and even *to tame a feral cat*, but not a single thing about goats. So I dropped that idea and looked through journey spells instead. I found the *speedwell* spell and the one Mrs Candace had used, and a whole string of magics called *journeys in the spirit*, none of which seemed quite right. The trouble with ordinary journey spells was that they were just that – spells for travel in country that you knew – and the spirit journeys meant that you left your body behind. I gave up and found one called to *bless a journey* instead.

And while we waited, I couldn't help noticing that it was the most heavenly day, one of those days with a milky look over the blue sky, where everything seems to be holding its breath for something marvellous to happen. Beyond the hazy chimneys around the garden, I could hear the huge, hushed mutter of London. The lawn we were standing on was grey-green with dew, marked all over with the faint, green footsteps of salamanders. In the distance, a silvery clock was striking the half hour, up and down the scale, as if London was singing encouragement to us.

By then, Nick was putting out instructions to the goat so strongly that I was actually getting mental glimpses of a flat, green shore where the sea was divided into big triangles of differently coloured water. As the clock finished striking, Helga sighed. Then she ducked clear of Nick and bounced sharply away, pulling the chain taut with a rattle.

"All hold on to me and to one another," Nick said. "Don't let go."

We each snatched hold of the nearest person. Grundo grabbed Nick and I took hold of Grundo's shirt. Behind me, one of the Izzies said, "You'll disarrange my *pleats*!" and as she said it we were off at a run, diagonally across the dewy lawn. I just had time to think what fools we looked, rushing through the garden in a line behind a goat, when we were not in the garden any more. We were plunging down a steep, earthy path that very quickly became a short tunnel. Some Izzy squeaked that it was *dark*. Then we came out into the queerest and most terrifying place I had ever seen.

It was like the sky on a summer night. It was dark and blue, but with light in it somewhere, so that it was not totally dark, but there were no stars. The terrifying part was that this sky was all round us, above and below, in an immense, dark blue void. In front of us, stretching away into distant distance, was a line of bright islands. They were just hanging there, like unstrung beads, or huge stepping-stones, for as far as we could see. Each island was a slightly different shape from the others, but each shone out in various greens and golds and blues, blazing a path across the void. And each one was only about ten feet across.

As I got to the end of the tunnel, the goat jumped to the nearest island, which dipped and swung and swayed under her, quite hideously.

"I can't do that!" I gasped. I was giddy just to look.

"Interesting, though," Nick panted, scrambling on the earthy edge of the tunnel. He sounded just as scared as I was, but he said, "They must be universes. It's just the way a goat would see things."

The goat galloped on across the island and he had to jump after her. The island positively plunged under his weight. I had to jump then, because Grundo leapt after Nick, and the island not only plunged again, but went jogging around sideways when the other three jumped on to it. I couldn't stand up. The awful thought was that if I overbalanced, I'd simply fall into that empty, blue night and go on falling. It was too much for me. I went on one hand and both knees. Clinging to Grundo's shirt for dear life, I scrambled across a surface rather like roughened glass. If I looked down through the glassiness, I saw dim seas and continents, mountains and rivers, and had to shut my eyes. It was truly horrible to have to open my eyes and stand up at the edge of the island, and then to make that jump across nothing to the next island.

It was only just near enough for me to jump to. I was

sure it was too far for the Izzies and Toby. I whimpered to Nick, and he hauled on the goat and stopped her on the dipping, jogging, slippery surface, while I stayed standing up and held out my arms to catch first Isadora, then Toby, and finally Ilsabil. Ilsabil nearly slipped off backwards. My heart banged in my throat and my arms felt weak as I grabbed her wrists.

Worse, I looked back the way we'd come as I steadied her. It was hard not to. And the line of luminous islands stretched back into the distance that way too. There was no way to tell which one was Blest. There was no way to tell which direction to go in. If it hadn't been for the goat, we would have been completely lost out there. The Izzies were making little squeaks about it. Toby's teeth were chattering. I think we were all shaking. But the goat dashed off as soon as Nick stopped hauling on her chain and leapt to the next, slightly nearer island, and we had to go too.

We took the next few islands at a fairly swift pace, leaving a line of them bucking and twirling behind us, and trying not to think about falling off. And Nick and the goat suddenly went down inside the next one. Oh, good! I thought. We've arrived! In the greatest possible relief, I went hurrying down another tunnel on Grundo's heels.

"Hell!" Nick said from in front of me. "This is wrong. *Wrong*, Helga!"

We were in a library, the lot of us, surrounded by the smell of wood and books. I could have cried. The thought of having to come out of here and jump across islands again was almost more than I could take.

It was a dark, low-beamed place, full of dark books, so I didn't see straightaway that there were people in it. Then someone beside us said, "Who on earth are *you*? How did you get here?"

We all whirled round to find a lamplit table in an alcove just beside us. There were open books and pages of notes spread on the table. Four boys of about Nick's age were sitting there with pens in their hands and looks of slightly condescending amazement on their faces – Nick has the same superior look: it must go with that age-group, I think. These boys were wearing suits of fairly new-looking pale suede, which had blotches of ink and dinner and chemicals down the fronts, quite disgustingly, and the blotches were as new-looking as the suede.

"Mistake," Nick said to them. "We're just leaving."

"But why the goat?" asked one of the boys. "Do tell."

"You probably need a goat and a pair of twins for a transport spell, where they come from," another said.

"Did you say *spell* or *smell*?" asked the third.

The fourth boy, who was rather spotty and looked even more superior than the other three, stared at Nick with his eyes narrowed. "You know," he said, "it's that false novice who tried to get near the Prince in Marseilles. I recognise the psychic profile. Fear not," he said to Nick. "I shan't give you away as long as you tell us how you got in among Security like that."

"That was a mistake too," Nick said, jangling at Helga's chain to get her to move. But she was interested in the papers on the table and would not budge. "Get that paper out of her reach," Nick said. "She eats anything she can get near."

"What – books too?" asked the boy in the outside seat.

"Feed her Fusek's *Panmagicon* then," suggested the boy beyond him. "I've had a bellyful of it. Give the goat a turn."

He was leaning over and wagging a big, leather-covered book in the goat's face, when a door at the end of the room clashed open and a big, fat man with a beard strode in. He was wearing a suede suit too, but his was dark and shiny with age, and extremely tight across the front. Over it, he wore a flowing black robe. You could see at a glance he was a teacher. From the smug look on the spotty boy's face, I could tell that he had somehow fetched this man.

"What is going on here?" the teacher demanded, in a big, rumbling voice.

Nick shot me a desperate look. I looked back in equal desperation. Toby and Grundo seemed stunned. We all stood there, wordlessly.

To my surprise and gratitude, the Izzies summed up the situation and took a hand. "Oh!" Isadora cried. "I just *love* tight, fat tummies!"

"But not with a *beard*!" trilled Ilsabil. "Get him to shave that beard!"

Both twins twinkled up to the teacher and flung their arms round him. Ilsabil put up a hand to stroke his beard and cried out, "Yuk! *Bristles*, my dear!" while Isadora nestled her face against his tight, suede-clad stomach, murmuring, "Ooh! *Fatness!*" I could feel both of them fairly pumping out glamour spells.

The teacher, who had been starting on some kind of spell of his own, was entirely disconcerted. He stepped back a pace and gave an uncertain laugh. This gave the rest of us the moment we needed to pull ourselves together and start urging the goat to leave. Leave! I thought. *Leave* here!

"Come *on*, Helga!" Nick said. "Romanov!"

Helga raised her head at that name, kicked up her heels and galloped back the way she had come. Nick was jerked after her. I grabbed Nick, Grundo and Toby snatched a twin's arm each, and Grundo twined his hand painfully into my hair. We rushed in a bunch into a dark tunnel. Next second, we had popped out on top of this world, where Helga was already jumping to another island.

"Thanks, you Izzies!" Nick panted, as the island dipped and swung.

Somehow that void was worse the second time. I suppose it was because I knew what I was in for. The bright islands seemed so tiny, and they pitched and joggled so. I tried to ignore them and keep my eyes on the goat's white rear, unerringly skipping across the gaps ahead of me. Goats are a strange shape behind, almost as if they have a coat-hanger just above their tail. But it made me dizzy every time Helga's hooves hung in mid-void in front of me. I tried staring down at the vague landscapes inside the islands instead and this was worse. The more closely I looked, the more the landscape seemed to pull me in. I found my knees sinking into the glassy surface and the hand I was resting on plunging downward on to a green-brown continent.

"This is awful!" I said.

Nick, ahead of me, having to use both hands on the stake and being towed like a water-skier from island to island, ought to have been hating it even more, but he said, "Oh, come on, Roddy. It's a unique experience."

I could hardly believe it when there was a grunt of agreement from Grundo and another from Toby. One of the Izzies said, "We may be the first humans ever to do this."

It was a shock to find them all braver than me. After that, I tried to stand up and look straight ahead, and I really did not know which was worse – crossing the slippery, dipping islands, or the awful moments when I had to jump, into nothing and over nothing, on to the next island – though the very worst moment was when I almost didn't land on one and nearly took the others with me. The journey seemed to go on for eternity.

Then it was suddenly over. The goat gave out a goatish yell, kicked up her white heels and went down head first like a duck into an island no different from any of the others. We all galloped down a green-lit tunnel behind her, past a wood, where a huge, spotted cat sat staring contemptuously out at us, and then we were there.

# CHAPTER THIRTY-TWO

✳

*I* knew we were there when I saw Romanov's spotted cat. The way she twitched just the end of her tail at us was positively jeering, but I was too relieved to care. I just felt a moment of great regret that I couldn't have my black panther waiting about outside my home world in the same way, and then we were on Romanov's island. I'd never been so glad of anything in my life. Those islands were amazing, but they were also *scary*. Roddy looked awful, ready to faint. She knew better than the kids what a horrible, risky thing we had just done.

The Izzies kept squawking about why were the sea and the sky in stripes.

I bent down and undid the chain from Helga's neck.

"Oh, do shut up," I said as the goat went trotting away over the hilltop. "This place is made of a lot of different places, that's all."

"You ought to be nice to us," one of them said. "We saved you from the fat man."

I didn't answer. It had suddenly occurred to me – almost like an inspiration – why that goat had taken us to that library in the Plantagenate world. Maxwell Hyde had been there, that was why! And that goat thought the sun shone out of Maxwell Hyde's fundament (as my dad would say), so she had gone there to look for him.

"Answer me!" snapped one Izzy. "*Speak* to us, Nick!" cooed the other one.

"Fleas," Roddy said, loudly and violently.

The twins gave a gasp of terror. It may have been because of this strange thing Roddy said, but I think it was more because Mini came trampling over the top of the hill just then, with her ears spread and her trunk eagerly stretched out. I'd forgotten how big she was. In fact, she seemed huger than I remembered, and gnarlier, and more positive somehow. The Izzies screamed and ran away in two directions. Roddy sat down as if her legs had given way and Grundo and Toby sort of dodged in behind her. But Mini took no notice. She lumbered straight up to me and stopped, with her legs trampling excitedly and her trunk sort of feeling at me, this way and that, over my face and my front and my sides, like an eager, grey snake.

"Nick!" she said. "It really *is* you! I've missed you so much!"

I got in under her trunk and between her tusks – they had smart new golden bands round them that looked magical in some way - and hugged as much of her face as I could reach. "I've missed you too, Mini," I said, out loud. "Like being homesick for you."

Her trunk curled round my shoulders. It was like a hug. "Me too!" she told me. "I waited and waited, all these ten years!"

"Ten years?" I said.

"It is," she said. "I counted. Last time I saw you was when I'd eaten all those apples. After you went, Romanov had to use some of his magic to make me better. And that was ten years ago now."

I could still hardly believe it. "You really had ten years here? It's only been about three weeks for me." This explained why Mini seemed so much bigger. When I first met her, she must have been quite a young elephant and she was full-grown now.

Behind me, Toby and Grundo were discussing us. "That elephant's really talking to him," Toby observed.

"Yes," Grundo answered. "She's got a voice like a plummy old aunt, but I can't quite hear the words. Can you?'

"Who are those sober, intellectual boys?" Mini asked me.

This made me giggle. There were times when Toby

and Grundo were like two old men. I turned round and introduced everyone. "This is Mini," I said, "my favourite elephant. Mini, that's Toby, this is Grundo, and Roddy's the girl on the grass. The twins over there are Isadora and Ilsabil, but don't ask me which is which."

"Pleased to meet you," Mini said, politely swinging her trunk.

This made the Izzies start backwards dramatically, but Roddy got up and said, "Pleased to meet you, Mini." So all the girls could understand Mini. Interesting.

"Is Romanov here?" I asked.

"Yes, he's just got back from somewhere," Mini said. "He's in the house."

We all went over the hill together and down towards the house. It looked splendidly well-kept now, made of pale wood and crisp, blue stonework, with wide windows. The goat was outside the smart, white front door, in a huddle of hens, bleating fit to burst. As we arrived, Romanov came out, wiping his face on a towel, to see what was the matter. We all stopped and Roddy murmured, "I see what you meant now." It was the effect Romanov had. He was at full power. He fair sizzled with it. Otherwise, he looked just the same, a lean and energetic dark zigzag, and not at all as if ten years had passed.

"You again," he said to me. It was flat and unwelcoming. "I dreamt ten years ago that you came back with a crowd of children."

"When you were ill," I said. "That may have coloured

your dreams. We need help…"

The goat was butting at Romanov and stamping and bleating. "Just a moment," he said. He put both hands to Helga's head. After a second, he moved them along her sides. "Oh, you are in trouble," he said to her, "but it's all right now." He took her by one horn and started to lead her away along the house.

"What's the matter with her?" I said.

"She's in labour," Romanov said over his shoulder. "Going to have her kids any moment. You feed the hens for me, will you, while I get her bedded down in the shed. The rest of you go indoors and help yourselves to a drink in the kitchen."

The Izzies clasped their hands and looked ecstatic. "Baby *goats!*" said one. "We're coming to *watch!*" said the other.

Romanov looked back at them out of one eye in his zigzag profile. "No," he said.

That was all. But it shut the Izzies up completely. They turned and followed Roddy into the house, as good as gold.

I went along to the shed and Mini sauntered companionably beside me. Then she stood watching while I gave the hens their corn. One of her back legs began to rub up the other. I took the hint and made the shed provide elephant food too. Really, I might never have been away – I felt so much at home here. I could hear Romanov in the next shed, heaving straw about and talking soothingly to Helga. I felt the fizz of him setting some kind of magic on her too, probably to ease the birth for her. This is the life! I thought. But Romanov was obviously going to be quite a time with Helga, so I went back to the house.

The kitchen was all airy and wide and up-to-date this time. About the only thing in it that I remembered was the big wooden table. When I got there, Toby and Grundo were busily finding interesting food and drink in the refrigerator and Roddy was going on at the Izzies.

"If either of you little beasts says one more thing to upset Grundo," she was saying, "I shall do something so bad that you won't know what's hit you!"

Grundo didn't seem upset to me. He was putting armfuls of potted puddings on the table and the expression on his face was one of greedy joy. Nor did the Izzies look to be upsetting him. They were seizing puddings as they arrived and stacking them in two heaps, one for the kind they knew they liked, and the other for the kind they'd never seen before but hoped to get to like shortly. Behaving like normal girls for once, I thought. But that was Roddy for you. She'd just had a bad experience and her reaction to any sort of upset was to fuss about Grundo.

"And don't eat all the good kinds," Roddy scolded. "Grundo's entitled to eat a sweet he enjoys too. And Toby," she added as an afterthought.

"Roddy," I said, "aren't you entitled to something

you like yourself? Or is it all for Grundo?"

A mistake. Her face flooded pink-red, her eyes flashed like dark stars, and she whirled round on me. I'd have been in trouble then, if Romanov hadn't come quietly up behind me. "One moment," he said. "Something's wrong here."

We all jumped, because we hadn't heard him come in, and stared nervously at him. He looked, very intently and keenly, from one to another of us. Toby said, scared but brave, "Is the goat all right?"

"Yes," Romanov said. "She wants to be left to do it by herself." And he continued looking from face to face – except that, by this time, he was darting his look between Roddy and Grundo. Roddy seemed plain puzzled. But Grundo, the fourth or fifth time that look stabbed at him, shifted from foot to foot and began to colour up, in blotches between his freckles, until he almost seemed as if he had measles. "Are you going to tell us what you're doing or shall I?" Romanov asked him, in a cutting, conversational way.

Grundo's lips seemed to stick together for a moment. He worked them loose and said in a gluey sort of grunt, "I – I will."

"Go on then," Romanov said, flat and unfriendly.

"I – I…" Grundo went.

"He's not doing anything," Roddy interrupted. "Don't pick on him."

Grundo shot her a wretched look. "Yes, I am," he

470

admitted. "I've done it ever since I was three years old. I – I put a glamour on you to make you – you love me and – and look after me above everyone else."

"But that was just because you were little and lonely then," Roddy protested quickly.

Grundo shook his head. "Not now. I do it all the time now, because – well, it's easier. You can read for me and help me with lessons and do magic for me that isn't back to front. And then I don't have to try."

"Laziness, in fact," Romanov said flatly.

Grundo nodded, looking so dismal that I swear even his nose drooped. "I'd better take it off now, hadn't I?" he grunted. Groaned, really.

"Yes," said Romanov. "If it's any comfort to you, I had back-to-front problems too as a boy. It only takes a month or so of real effort to learn to work with it. After that you find you can do things rather better than most other people, because they haven't had to try and you have."

Roddy, by this time, was so pale that she was sort of dough-coloured. "No!" she more or less screamed. "This isn't *true*! You're taking away the foundation of my *life*!"

Romanov shrugged. Grundo stuck his bottom lip out and said, "It *is* true. Sorry."

At this, Roddy shouted out a great yell of despair and went rushing out of the kitchen and out of the house. As the front door banged, Romanov gave me a curt nod and jerked his head at the door, meaning go after her. I stared at him for a second. It seemed to me that when someone's just discovered they've been living a lie, the last thing they want is me on top of it. But Romanov gave me an even fiercer jerk of the head and I went.

Roddy was standing with her back to me, halfway up the slope to the garden. Mini was beyond her, beside the garden wall, with her trunk drifting wistfully towards the fruit trees inside. She was doing her embarrassed leg-rubbing. "This girl seems awfully unhappy," she said to me.

"She is," I said.

Roddy spun round and saw me. "Go away!"

"In a bit," I said. "Tell me about it first."

"I can't!" Roddy stood with her face up. Her hands were clenched and her eyes were shut and oozing tears. Then she told me anyway. She obviously just had to tell someone. "Most of the time I've been alive," she said, "it's been a – an established *fact* that I cared for Grundo and looked after him – and defended him from his awful mother and sister as well. That made me better than Sybil and Alicia, you see. I've always thought of myself as a nice, loving, kind person. But now it turns out that Grundo was *making* me care for him, this means I'm not like that at all. I don't know *what* I'm like. I could be as vile and selfish as everyone else at Court for all I know! Don't you see? It's as if the world I thought I knew has suddenly turned out to be make-believe. *Nothing* seems to be valuable any more!"

"Yes, I see," I said. "And I'm almost impressed with that kid Grundo. He must be the only person in the multiverse who's more selfish than I am. But don't you think you might have liked him anyhow?"

She said, in a creaking, hysterical voice, "I don't *know!*"

"Well, look at it this way," I said. I was a bit flurried because she looked to me as if she about to go *really* off the deep end. "It can't have been necessarily a bad thing, you being made to care about Grundo. Like symbiosis – you know, cats and dogs and humans…"

"And elephants," Mini put in.

"And elephants," I said. "You and Grundo both sound to have been pretty lonely and miserable at Court, but if you were looking after him, OK, *he* was all right, but *you* had someone to be fond of too. And you strike me as being a pretty nice person. So maybe you'd have looked after him anyway. It's a shame he didn't trust you to try it on your own, that's all."

Roddy put her fists up to her face. "Oh, go away, Nick! I really do need to be alone. Anyway, you have to go back inside and explain to Romanov about the conspiracy. I can't trust Grundo to explain properly." There was a slightly horrible silence, then she said angrily, "I can't trust Grundo for *anything* now!" and burst into hard, hacking sobs, more like coughing than crying.

I put my arms round her. For just a mere, single instant, I had a real, heavy body in my arms and a moist face against my cheek, with a real, difficult personality to go with them. It was a fairly astonishing feeling. Then Roddy fiercely shook me off and went running away to the other side of the island.

I said to Mini, "You keep an eye on her," and went back into the house, hoping Romanov wouldn't think I'd given up too easily. But I was blowed if I was going to run after Roddy all over the island. That would *really* have irritated her.

Actually, when I went into the kitchen, Grundo was making a pretty good job of explaining the part he knew. As I came through the door, Romanov turned the razor-edge of his profile against my soul and asked, "What do *you* know about the Merlin's part in all this?"

"I don't," I said. "I never met him. Maxwell Hyde might know. All I know is that there's a lot of nasty types in Blest collecting salamanders for some sort of a power-push. And I saw Gwyn ap Nud carry Maxwell Hyde off. Roddy thinks he did that on the Merlin's orders. Or this woman Sybil's."

Romanov's razor profile raised an eyebrow at me and he said, "This woman who kidnaps a Magid, using the Merlin and the Lord of the Dead – there are going to be disturbances in a lot of worlds over this." He turned to Grundo. "*Who* did you say your mother is?"

"Her name's Sybil Temple," Grundo said.

A very strange look came over the slice of Romanov's face that I could see. It was if he didn't know whether to feel angry, surprised, contemptuous, anxious or sorry for someone – and probably more things I couldn't quite understand. "And I'm willing to bet she hasn't a notion what she's doing," he said at length. "She always was a greedy fool, my ex-wife Sybil."

"Oh," said Grundo.

"Yes," said Romanov. "Oh."

Things clunked about in my head, like slowly meshing gears. Then I said, "Oh," too. Romanov's face came round to mine so quickly that I went backwards a step. "It could be my fault she did this," I said. "She phoned while you were ill – er – ten years ago? And I got fed up with hearing her and tuned her out of your life. She was shouting threats about doing really big magic when I turned her off."

Romanov thought about this. His mouth pulled into a long, thin line in a way that quite scared me. "Water under the bridge," he said finally. "She was always making threats. I used to provoke her. No time to share out blame now— Has anyone done *anything* about the balance of magic?"

I said I didn't think so. Grundo said, "Nobody believed Roddy when she said there was a plot. One of the Little People told her to raise the land."

"Well? *Did* she?" Romanov snapped.

We stared at him, even the Izzies, impressed and alarmed at how urgent and dangerous he sounded. Grundo said, "We didn't know how to."

Romanov jumped up from his seat at the table. "Oh, of all the—! When one of the Little People gives advice like that, you take it! I'll tell her…" He looked at the door as if he expected to drag Roddy back through it, just by looking. "One of you go and find her. You – Toby. The rest of you give me the names of all the missing people that you know. I'd better find what's happened to them before I go to Blest."

# CHAPTER THIRTY-THREE

\*

No, I still feel awful when I think how I felt about Grundo – as if my whole mind was like one of those floating islands we crossed. Nothing to support it, dipping sickeningly about, and nothing but emptiness all round. I'm going to miss all that out. I know Nick will have plenty to say about Romanov.

# CHAPTER THIRTY-FOUR

*

*R*oddy looked like death when Toby came back with her.

By that time, Romanov had gone away to his workroom. Such a strong gush of magic came from there that Grundo and I broke out in a sweat and the Izzies went on about the way the hair on their arms was standing up. A right song and dance they made about it, too. They were *such* irritating kids.

Romanov shot back into the kitchen, saw Roddy and said, "Good. Come with me," and he led her away into the living room, saying, "I can only explain what you'd be trying to do and the way I'd set about it myself. You'll have to find your own means…"

That was all I heard before the door shut, but when Roddy came back, she looked as if she had slightly more interest in life. She said Romanov was in his workroom again. The Izzies wailed. But it wasn't long before the gush of magic stopped, thank goodness! Romanov came into the kitchen slowly, looking puzzled.

"I think I know where they all are," he said, "but it makes me wonder just what *is* going on. Have you all finished eating? Good. We'll go and collect the missing persons before I take you all back to Blest."

Romanov came to a decision and then did what he'd decided so quickly, that it made you feel left behind and breathless. He led us outside and there was Mini, waltzing towards the house, looking very pleased with herself. She had a long, double seat strapped to her back, with space for at least three people sitting back to back on either side. I'd ridden on a seat like that in a zoo once. This one was sky blue.

"You look smart!" I said.

"I do, don't I?" she said. "I do love going on expeditions. I've been on a lot now, but I never stop feeling excited."

"Are you sure you can carry all seven of us?" Romanov asked her.

She snorted through her trunk. "Easy. I'm a *big* elephant."

A sort of platform had appeared out of nowhere beside the house, with a ladder up to it, so that we could climb into the seat. Romanov warned us to arrange ourselves so that our weights balanced and, while Toby, Roddy and one Izzy were climbing up on to Mini's right side, he shot off to have a look at Helga. By the time Mini had turned herself round and Grundo and the other Izzy and I were getting into the left hand side of the seat, Romanov was back. He was grinning in a sharp slash across his face.

"Is Helga all right?" Toby called out anxiously.

"Fine – she's got two kids, a nanny and a billy," Romanov told him. Toby was glad, but he was upset too. He said we shouldn't have made Helga bring us here when she was so near to having kids. And the Izzies began squalling that they had to get down and *see* the new kids. Romanov stared at the nearest Izzy, enough to shut one of them up at least, and then looked up at me in a way that was almost like one normal person confiding in another. "One of each sex," he said. "That's a balance. Let's hope it's some kind of omen." Then he came up the steps and hopped across Mini's neck in front of the seat, where he sat sort of scrunched down like a mahout. "Right, Mini," he said. "Off you go. North quadrant."

Mini surged into a walk, round the end of the house, down the grassy bank and – with great sucking, sloshing noises – straight out into the marshy water there. The seat swayed about on her back. By the time we were a hundred yards out from the island, with a mild wind tossing our hair about and mosquitoes beginning to home in on us, I was trying not to feel seasick. Part of it was because

I was riding sideways. In order to see where we were going, I had to look across Grundo and an Izzy and over Romanov's head. But most of my unhappiness was due to the swaying and the steady sloshing of Mini's feet. I kept looking down nervously to make sure she was not out of her depth. But the water must have been very shallow all the way. She just churned up marshy stinks and set big, brown bubbles popping for ten feet all around.

I could really have done without those Izzies whining that it was not *fair*, they wanted to see the baby *goats*. Roddy snapped at them, but it made no difference. I just tuned them out in the end. By the time we were right out into the great sheet of water, and the island was out of sight behind us, I simply was not hearing them.

Soon after this, there was vague, misty shore ahead, rocky and pinkish. Mini heaved up on to it, sliding the Izzy into Grundo and Grundo into me, and marched on, stump, stump, stump, through what seemed to be rocky desert. There was nasty, steamy heat. Everything was sort of misty. The Izzies forgot the goats and whinged about the heat for a while, until Mini's mud-crusted feet began padding along a proper pavement, where we came under a high roof of some kind, and it was cooler.

I didn't realise where we were for a moment. I just knew it *smelt* familiar, in a way that made me faintly alarmed. Then I noticed that there were shops all along the side of the tunnel that I was facing. I craned round behind myself and saw a parapet, a cliff of shops and houses in the distance opposite, and bridges spanning in between. When we went swaying past a huge hoist, I was sure. We were in Loggia City.

But it looked quite a bit different. The pavement Mini's feet were on had hollow, worn places. There was litter blowing everywhere and the paint on the hoist was peeling. None of the shops at the back of the arcade appeared to be at all prosperous. Some were boarded up. The rest had desperate-looking notices in the windows, saying 90% OFF!! and EVERYTHING MUST GO!, and they didn't seem to have much for sale inside except for shoddy-looking rolls of plain cloth. Nobody was in there buying anything either.

"What's happened here?" I called over to Romanov.

"The workers on the top terrace left," he called back. "Someone told them they were producing works of art that people would pay a great deal for. They concentrated on tapestry after that. I helped them migrate to another world some years ago now. They're doing very well there."

I found I was crouching down in my end of the seat, trying to hide my hot face. Who would have thought it? I casually tell an old man that his tapestry was fabulous and, ten years later, the whole economy of a city is grinding to a halt. Who would have *thought* it?

Somebody shouted, "Hey, you! Halt!"

Mini's pacing feet faltered. "Keep going," Romanov said.

Her feet picked up their pace again. The person shouting got out of the way in a hasty scamper of yellow uniform, but he kept on shouting. "No animals on this level! What do you think you're *doing*?"

I looked down at his angry face as we slid swaying past him. And I knew him. He was the Important Policeman, evidently still on the job. But he had a seedy, down-on-his-luck look these days, as well as looking older and wrinkled and anxious. His yellow uniform was saggy around him, with darns in it, and he had lost weight. His moustache was still just as bushy though.

He looked up at me as I looked down. An expression came over his face of Where-have-I-seen-that-boy-before? Then he got it. His finger came up and pointed. "Hey, you! You're Nick Mallory! You skipped factory duty ten years ago. We want you!"

But Mini went imperturbably marching on. Important slid away behind. The great pillars of the stairway slid past, and a notice saying LIFTS OUT OF ORDER, and then we were out on a different and much more ruinous section of the arcade, where the sun came blinding down in long lines through gaps in the roof.

I looked back and Important was gone. Behind Mini, there were still houses in the walls of the great canyon, but they were ruins, with empty black spaces for windows, and half the bridges were down.

"What's happened?" Toby asked.

"This is the next world on," Romanov said. "The

people we're looking for are one world along from this one, but the sun is pretty harmful in all these canyon worlds, so I'm taking a route that keeps us in shade as much as possible."

Mini marched on, from arcade to empty arcade, always curving to the right out of the direct glare of the sun, until we went under the ruin of what looked like a factory and came out on the bare tops of the canyons. I think the canyons were not so deep in that world. At any rate, I could see them curving and branching in all directions around us, like the twigs and branches of a tree, as if the empty desert had cracked from the heat. At the end of the largest dark crack was something that glimmered.

"The people we want are in that xanadu there," Romanov said, pointing to the glimmer. "It's fairly well defended. I'm going to try to get us in underneath."

It was pretty extraordinary. He had taken us from world to world so smoothly that I never noticed us go. Or Mini had. Come to think of it, Mini must have had a gift for it. I envied her.

"Down you go, Mini," Romanov said to her. And we set off down a long slope where houses had dissolved away to rubble and formed a sort of ramp into the bottom of the chasm.

# CHAPTER THIRTY-FIVE

*

*I*t was peculiar but practical, I suppose, of Romanov
to load us all on his elephant. Romanov is one of the
most practical people I have met, and so full of energy he
made me feel tired. But the thought of him once being
married to Sybil still amazes me. It is odder even than
Grandad Hyde marrying Heppy. Still, it does explain
where Grundo and Alicia get their noses from.

Towards the end of our journey, I began to feel better,
though I was still feeling odd. Every time the elephant
seat lurched, I looked anxiously round at Grundo, and
then felt embarrassed at being anxious. It was habit, I
suppose. Grundo was all right anyway. He was watching
the walls of the gorge as we went down a sort of ramp

into it, and pointing out to Nick that the earliest of the ruined houses, on the ledges near the bottom, were carved straight out of the rock. Both of them were highly interested.

I was ashamed to see that Grundo nearly always *was* all right. Things that bothered me, like people being foul to him, just roll off Grundo's mind. He takes no notice because he is interested in *things* instead. Nick is the same. I felt very stupid not to have realised what Grundo was like before this.

The lurching was much less when we reached the bottom of the chasm. It was quite cold and dank there, because the sun never shone on it directly. There was a trickle of river running through the middle, but nothing grew there but green slime. The elephant picked her way along the edge of the river, between lumps of fallen house as big as she was, until the walls of the chasm seemed to meet together overhead and we were crunching along inside a huge, arched cave.

"Oh, my dear!" squealed one of the Izzies. "*Bats!*"

"Darkness," wailed the other one. "I'm *frightened!*"

I don't think they were frightened in the least. They were enjoying themselves. Their voices echoed and re-echoed in the cave, shriek upon shriek. And as soon as they heard the echoes, they made more noise than ever.

"Coo-eee!"

"Hall – oh – ho!"

Romanov turned round. "Be quiet," he said.

The Izzies stopped, just like that. I don't think Romanov used a spell on them. He just had the most forceful personality in many universes. Soon after that, he made a light. It was not the small, blue flame our teachers had shown us how to make, but a soft, spreading glow that seemed to come from the elephant's forehead. She seemed to appreciate it. She walked much faster. And the chain of caves we were going through sprang into life as we passed, quite astonishingly. Things like stone curtains hung from the arched roofs, folded and draped and banded with colours, reds, white, yellows – even greenish – and were reflected upside down in the black shiny waters of the river. Nick remarked that they looked like streaky bacon – well, he would! – which made Toby give a yelp of laughter.

Romanov said, "Quiet!" all sharp and tense, and after that none of us dared make a sound.

It was quite difficult not to exclaim, because we passed through archways with shell pink drapes where we all had to duck, and a hall where ivory fingers were pointing down from the vault, each one glittering with water, and along lacy terraces, and arcades of red pillars, where it was very hard not to call out at the strangeness. Once, the light swung across a high wall of jumbled red and black formations that shaped themselves into such a hideous glaring face that the Izzies were not the only ones who half-screamed.

Luckily, the river was noisy by then. Wherever we

came round a corner and met it again, it was tumbling in higher waterfalls. Probably it covered the noises we made at the hideous face, and again when a wall seemed to put out a huge clutching hand. By then, we were climbing steadily. The poor elephant was going slowly. I could hear her puffing amidst the noisy water and I could feel Romanov encouraging her.

At last, he said, "This will do, Mini. It's only twenty feet up from here."

The elephant turned head on to the nearest yellowish rock wall and we assumed she was going to stop. Instead, she went on walking. My hands clapped themselves over my mouth. Someone else squeaked. We were all sure we were going to crash into the rock. But the wall just didn't seem to be there, even though we could *see* it, and the elephant simply went on trudging upwards through it. There was rock right up against my face. I could see it and smell it, even *taste* it, but I couldn't feel a thing. And after an eternal twenty feet or so, we came up into daylight inside a giant dome.

It was daylight as you see it through sunglasses. I suppose the dome was tinted. But nearly all of us looked up nervously, expecting rain or thunder, even before we stared about and found ourselves in a thicket of fruit trees. They were all yellowy. Even allowing for that lurid light, I guessed those trees had not been tended for fifty years. I had a branch of misshapen figs almost in my lap and little undernourished oranges bobbed over my head. Grundo calmly picked figs. Nick reached up for an orange. Then they both threw them disgustedly away. I don't think any of the fruit was eatable.

Romanov pointed. "Go that way. No, don't worry about the vegetation. Go straight *there*."

The elephant turned and walked the way he pointed. She made an awful mess. She stepped on trees. Trees got shoved out of the way, causing fruit to shower off them. Branches snapped and tree trunks crashed, and our knees were scraped by twigs as she marched on through. Bark and leaves and fruit rained over us. I looked behind and saw a squashed, cloven path of ruined trees and trodden fruit where we had been. The elephant's funny little tail was quivering and jerking with excitement. I think she was enjoying this. When I looked to the front again, we were ploughing through apple trees, and the elephant's trunk was going out and back, out and back again, snatching apples and cramming them into her mouth – or it was until Romanov noticed.

"Cut that out, Mini!" he said and hit her quite hard on her head.

She flapped her ears crossly and forged on. Shortly, she crunched across a thicket of raspberry canes and came out into an overgrown field of melons. The melons were small and self-seeded, but all the same, you cannot *imagine* the effect an elephant has on a field of melons. There is the most incredible squelching and bursting. Seeds fly and the smell of ruined melon comes up in waves. I was leaning over, so fascinated by the carnage that I did not notice anything else until Toby said quietly, "I think we're here."

There was a space ahead that was fenced off with white plastic walls. Anyway, it was something half-transparent made into walls that came up to the elephant's shoulder. I thought I could see people beyond, though the light was queerer there, sort of filmy and foggy.

Romanov said, "Ten paces on, then stop and let us down."

The elephant obeyed him literally. This meant that she walked straight through the wall and it went *pop, pop,* CLAP as it tore in two, and then *clatter* as she trod on some of it. But none of the people just beyond seemed to notice. They were simply standing there, in a grassy space, covered in the stuff that was making the light so queer. It was coming down from the roof, this stuff, in cascades and swathes of what looked to be white cotton-wool cobwebs. Everyone I could see was draped in it. They were all alive though. That was what made it such a horrible thing to see. Every so often, one of them would shift from one foot to the other, or move their head as if they were trying to get rid of a crick in the neck – but slowly, slowly, like people moving in treacle. The only good thing about it was that most of them didn't seem quite conscious. The pink blurs of faces that I could see – though they were very hard to see through the white cobwebbing – seemed to be at least half asleep.

Mam and Dad are in there somewhere! I thought. I could hardly wait for the elephant to bend one of her front legs up so that Romanov could slither on to it and jump to the ground. And when he was down, he stood for a long, long moment, staring at the draped, white, slowly fidgeting crowd, until I nearly screamed at him to help us down to the grass too.

"This is a *very* strange spell," he said, turning to look up at us, all perched on our seat. "I'm going to need all the help you can give me to solve this one. Do any of you have any ideas?"

I was shaking my head, along with the others, "No," when I realised I was down on the ground. The elephant bulked above us, but almost at once she retreated to what was left of the fence and cowered there – if an elephant *can* cower. Nick went over and patted her trunk. "I know," he said. "None of the rest of us likes it either." Then he said, "Roddy!" and pointed.

It was the Izzies, naturally. They had gone right up to the edge of the silent, film-draped crowd. One of them was making mad balletic movements towards the nearest shrouded person, while the other one was dramatically on her knees with her hands clasped. "*Speak* to me!" she was saying. "I, the Isadora of Isadora, implore and command you! Speak!"

I got to her just as she tried to take hold of the swathe of veiling that anchored the person to the grass. From this close, it looked sticky, like slightly melted spun-sugar.

I dragged both of them clear of it. "Don't *touch* it, you little stupids!" I said. "It would probably get you too!"

"But I wanted to break the spell!" Isadora protested.

Ilsabil said tragically, "How *could* you do this to us! That's Heppy in there!"

It *was* Heppy, now that I looked closely. She was shorter and dumpier than any of the shrouded shapes around her. By peering, I could just pick out the muted glow of her orange hair through the whiteness. I could see her eyes most clearly of all. They seemed to track slowly across me as I leant towards her, but I had no idea if she knew me or not. For a moment, I felt absolute despair. Heppy was a witch after all. The people standing in there with her were all magic users. But if Heppy couldn't break this spell, if *none* of them could, what chance was there of anyone *ever* breaking it?

Something caught the light inside the white film. I looked and saw Heppy's hand moving, slowly, slowly, and the rings on her fingers glinting with the movement. I stared as Heppy's hand rose and moved back and forth, in what was clearly a slow-motion wave – or even a slow, slow blessing – a personal message to me to show me she knew me and was willing us well in our rescue attempt. My despair vanished and I could have shouted for joy. My grandmother was evidently a very powerful witch indeed and I had her blessing. Maybe after all this, we *did* like one another, just a little.

I smiled at her, though I am not sure she smiled back,

as I seized hold of the Izzies and towed them over to Grundo and Toby. "Take hold of an arm each," I told the boys, "and don't let either of them go, even for an instant." It did me good to give a few orders again. I felt brisk and confident.

The boys glowered at me. Toby shrugged and did what I said. Grundo reluctantly took hold of Ilsabil's arm and said, "It would be far easier to get them draped in this white spell too."

"You *dare!*" I said.

Romanov was walking slowly beside the draped crowd with Nick. Both of them kept bending and staring at the white stuff and looking mystified. Toby and Grundo went after them, each dragging their twin. I followed. I rather carefully didn't look at any more of the imprisoned people. More than half of them would be Court wizards whom I knew. Two of them must be my parents. I didn't want to see them like that, at least until there was some hope of freeing them.

*Goosegrass or cleavers* said the knowledge in my head, along with the image of the long skinny plant, covered in sticky whiskers and little green knobs. *Binding spells.* This seemed hopeful. I walked behind the others in a sort of dream, running through binding spells. There were hundreds, that was the problem. They were divided into *spoken* and *ritual,* and before I had run halfway through the *spoken* spells, I realised there were at least double the number I'd first thought, because you could reinforce any spoken spell by performing one or more *rituals* – and the other way round.

The very first *ritual* binding I came across was that old favourite *knots and crosses*. I discovered that you could make a net silently, or draw the pattern for tic-tac-toe, and bind most things to your will. If you made the net-pattern with goosegrass – nice sticky stuff – it was a truly strong binding for a short while; but if you said *words* as you made the pattern, the binding would last until the goosegrass rotted. And so on. You could make hundreds of other patterns – cobweb, cat's cradle, tatting, crochet, knitting – and use words, or you could perform other actions *and* say words. You could dance... Oh, it was hopeless!

Here we walked round a sort of bulge in the veiling and came across a painfully thin man sitting in a chair on his own. The chair was suffused in piles of the white stuff, but it only came up to the man's waist. His upper half was free and he was leaning wretchedly against a low wall of the same sort of plastic that the elephant had walked through. Beyond the wall, there seemed to be some kind of living-quarters. We could see armchairs and a table and, from somewhere beyond those, came a smell of cooking. The man seemed to have been put where he could smell the food but not get to it.

I was thinking, How cruel! when the man looked up and saw us. And he was the Merlin. I was utterly astonished. So was he.

"Who are *you*?" he said. I remembered his weak, throaty voice so well.

"Who are *you*?" Romanov replied.

"Me? I'm from Blest," the Merlin said, in a hesitating, apologetic way. "I was selected as the Merlin there, but I was carried off…"

Grundo said, "He has to be lying. Doesn't he?" and looked dubiously at me.

"I assure you I am not," said the Merlin. He leaned his head backwards against the wall, showing his chin all covered with scraggy new beard. The Adam's apple worked in his skinny neck and tears began to run from his eyes. I remembered Grandad being disgusted that this Merlin was a weeper, but I felt I could hardly blame the man now. "As far as I can tell," he said, "I was snatched away here about a month ago. Hauled out of my car, blindfolded and brought here. I was the only prisoner here then. He fetched the others in batches later. Three batches – some of them have only just arrived. I – I must confess that the first time I – I even advised him who to send for. I hoped the wizards might be able to break this terrible spell, you see." He put his hands over his face and sobbed.

"Have you any idea," Romanov asked in a level, unsympathetic voice, "of the nature of this spell at all?"

The Merlin shook his head behind his hands. "It's the queerest thing I ever met."

Toby asked, hushed and shocked, "Don't they give you anything to eat?"

"He tries," the Merlin said, "when he remembers. His mind's on the binding, you see. But it's hard for me to digest anything much. The binding slows everything down so." He took his hands from his tearful face and tried to smile at Toby.

"I don't *understand*!" Grundo declared. "You – the Merlin – you were in Blest not so long ago. It wasn't a month ago. I *saw* you. You were talking about the bespelled water in Sir James's Inner Garden."

"I swear to you…" The Merlin started to cry again. "I *swear* to you I was never in any Inner Garden! I never got that far. I was at the shrines in Derbyshire when they carried me off. And I've been here nearly a month. I marked the wall…"

"But I *saw* you!" Grundo insisted.

"Whoever you saw," the Merlin sobbed at him, "it was not me."

Grundo looked up at Romanov, who was staring down at the Merlin in a keen, pitiless, almost clinical way. "Weepers shed tears with the truth," he said to Grundo. "I think I'm inclined to believe him."

"But that means there's an impostor…" I started to say, when we saw another man coming towards us beyond the wall.

# CHAPTER THIRTY-SIX

*

*F*inding that Merlin-fellow was even worse than finding that crowd of veiled, living corpses. He was alive, see. He had been sick all down the wall and all over this feathery stuff he was sitting in. I think the stuff stopped him digesting properly. He'd used the sick to mark the days in.

Anyway, Roddy had just cried out that there was an impostor in Blest, when this heavy sort of man came marching over and leaned his hands on the wall to stare at us. I knew him at once. It's strange how some people hardly change at all as they grow up. When I first met Joel, as the older of the Prayermaster's two boys, he had had this thick pile of dark hair, cheekbones that stuck out, and eyebrows that seemed to express disgust with the whole world. Those eyebrows were just the same now. So were his rather fat lips and his blunt chin. I knew that chin perfectly, even though it was now covered with dark stubble. I remembered his sarcastic eyes, though they were bloodshot and tired. But then it had only been about three weeks since I last saw him, and it had been ten years for him and enough time to grow up in. And he stood there and didn't know *me* from Adam.

"What are you people doing here?" he said.

"You might say, looking for missing persons," Romanov answered. "Do you care to let any of them go?"

"No," he said. "Who are you?"

"They call me Romanov," Romanov answered. "You may have heard of me."

"Yes," Joel answered, in a dull, unfeeling way, as if his mind was on something else. "The abomination. You're not supposed to be alive. We sent..."

He looked at me then and made the connection. "We sent *you*," he said to me. "You were armed with a plague to kill Romanov and we offered Romanov money to kill you."

"And I love you too, Joel," I said.

He hardly seemed to hear me. He went on, as if he simply couldn't understand it. "I sent you off from London on Earth just before we brought the Merlin here. Why aren't you dead? Why are you here?"

So that's how it was, I thought. "No idea. This must

all be in the future for me," I said, fast as thought. I wasn't just meaning to confuse him. I was hoping to stop him putting his cotton-wool spell on me. He'd think he didn't need to if he thought Romanov was going to kill me sometime later. "Where's Japheth, then?"

"In Blest, of course, doing what he must," Joel said. "Go away, all of you. You'll get no joy here."

He turned away, but Romanov stopped him by saying sharply, "What must be done in Blest, Joel?"

Joel gave him a heavy, tired look over one shoulder. "Nothing you can stop, abomination. I can feel you picking at my workings, but I'm doing them the one true way and you can't touch them. Even if you did, it would be too late now. You're doomed, abomination, you and all your kind."

"But why *Blest*?" Romanov snapped out.

Joel gave him a bleary, sarcastic grin. "The balance," he said. "This is our great atonement, that we now tip the balance of all magics to our hands. By nightfall, Blest magic and the magics of many other worlds will be in the hands of righteousness. So now leave and tread your path to damnation, all of you."

He went walking wearily away, as if he simply could not be bothered with us, and sat himself down on a chair in the distance, bent over, staring at the grassy floor and frowning.

We all looked helplessly at Romanov. He was frowning too. It made a sort of pout above the zigzag of his nose and mouth. "Some sort of religious mania, evidently," he said. "Damn it! I can't even see what *form* of spell he's using!"

"It'll be some sort of Prayermaster thing," I said.

Romanov snapped round to face me, looking as if a great light had struck him. "*Right!*" he said. "And?"

But I didn't know any more than that. It was hopeless.

# PART TWELVE
# RODDY AND NICK

# CHAPTER THIRTY-SEVEN

*

While Nick stood there beside the gently heaving mass of white cobweb-stuff, looking helpless, I was thinking, thinking. I *knew* this had to be some kind of binding spell, but it didn't match any of the spells in the hurt woman's files. When Nick said the word "Prayermaster" though, I began going through *Goosegrass or cleavers* in a different way. My teachers had never said much about Prayermaster magic, but it stood to reason that it had to be mostly words – prayers. So I went back to *spoken bindings* and thought those through again. Most of them were quite simple and temporary – unless you were laying a strong *geas*, and it wasn't one of those. *Spoken bindings* mostly only became lasting if you combined them with actions, like making a net-pattern or a cat's cradle. Otherwise, you had to make the pattern with your words alone, and if you wanted it to last, you had to keep repeating it.

"Oh!" I said. "He's repeating it in his mind! No wonder he looks so tired!" I turned to Romanov. He was clicking his fingers in frustration and obviously searching through his mind in much the same way as I was. "It's a spoken binding," I said.

"A pretty complicated one," Romanov said irritably. "I can't get a handle on it at all."

"I don't think you will," I said, "unless you can break his concentration first. It won't even start to unravel unless you can force him to make a hole in his pattern."

"How do we do that?" Nick demanded, standing too close to me. I felt his warmth sort of pushing at me and moved away. He followed me, saying, "Joel came and had a conversation with us and didn't slip up for one moment as far as I can see. He must be doing it on autopilot."

Toby nudged Grundo and Grundo gave one of his smoothly wicked grins. "Why don't we," he suggested, "set the Izzies on him?"

The Izzies, who had been standing sighing and fidgeting and looking pious and wronged, at once became extremely indignant. "Do you take us for *dogs*?" Isadora demanded.

Ilsabil said, loudly and shrilly, "Take no notice, my dear. Per-thetic just wants us to get wrapped in white

504

cobwebs too. He *said* so."

"Please be quiet," Toby said, looking anxiously across at Joel, bowed over in his chair.

"And don't be silly," Grundo said. "You'd be quite safe if you put your glamour on him."

They heaved dramatic sighs. "Our glamour doesn't work any more," Ilsabil said tragically.

"Yes, it does," I said. "It just doesn't work on any of *us*."

"Look what you did to that fat teacher," Toby said.

"We're wise to you, you see," Grundo explained. "But *he* isn't. And he's got two-thirds of his mind on his binding anyway."

The Merlin was staring up at us with desperate hope. I looked at Romanov, who was watching the Izzies thoughtfully. "What do you think?" I asked him.

"It's worth a try," he said. "If they can make the slightest break in that spell, I can probably do the rest. I don't think we'll get anywhere without some kind of distraction. I'll give you strong protections," he said to the Izzies.

The Izzies looked at him the way courtiers do when a foreign ambassador offers a bribe, very haughty and honourable, with just a touch of well-judged doubt. "My dear, we couldn't possibly!"

Nick leant towards them across the Merlin's head. "I don't believe this!" he said. "You get offered the chance to behave as dreadfully as you can and you turn it down!

Where's your pride, both of you? Go and show us just how awful you can be."

They gave him wide-eyed looks. "You mean *flirt* with him?" Ilsabil asked.

"Be *rude*?" said Isadora. "But, my dear, I'm a polite person!"

"Then you can't do it," Nick said. "OK. You stopped that fat schoolmaster in the middle of a spell, but this one is about a hundred times more difficult. Sorry I asked. I can see it's too much for you."

The Izzies drew themselves tall. They looked at one another. "Shall we show him?" Ilsabil said.

"As a great favour," Isadora suggested. "Graciously."

"Right," Nick said and, without more ado, he lifted the nearest twin over the plastic wall. Romanov, grinning a bit, swung the other twin over beside her. "I still think you can't do it," Nick said.

Both Izzies stuck their chins up at him. But they had not done yet. They turned round, with their stomachs and their hands pressed against the wall, and looked sulky. "We need a bribe," said Isadora.

"We can't proceed without," said Ilsabil. Both pairs of their eyes flickered towards Romanov, calculatingly.

"Oh, for…!" Nick began, but Romanov interrupted him. "*What* bribe?"

"One of us is going to be turned out when we're fifteen," Ilsabil explained.

"So could you make it that Heppy dies, please?"

Isadora said. "So there will be only three Dimbers and we can *both* stay."

Quite honestly, they took my breath away. The Merlin's jaw dropped and we shook our heads at one another, speechless. The boys were not at all speechless. They all said in different hoarse whispers that the Izzies were unfeeling *brats* – and worse – and then looked nervously over at Joel's distant, brooding figure, in case he realised what was going on.

Romanov made no attempt to be furtive. He said, in that level, cutting voice of his, "You must have a very limited outlook. Do you really *want* to spend your lives in the same old place, doing the same old rituals, year after year? I couldn't. I was booked to do that and I couldn't face it. I got out."

The Izzies' two little pointy faces turned up to his, amazed and arrested. "Do you mean we don't *have* to?" said Ilsabil.

"But we're hereditary witches," Isadora said wistfully. "We can't both leave."

"I don't see why not," Romanov said. "Haven't you got any cousins?"

Ilsabil turned to Isadora. "The hereditary men are always having daughters," she said. Isadora nodded. They both looked expectantly up at Romanov.

"I'm sure I can arrange for one of those daughters to take over," the Merlin said. "But you have to get me free first."

They gave him startled looks, as if they had forgotten he was there. Their backs straightened. Their chins stuck out. "We'll do it," Ilsabil announced.

"As a *great* favour," Isadora added.

"Go on then," said Romanov.

They turned round. They raised their arms. Then they advanced upon Joel in his chair with little twinkling steps, wafting their arms like ballet dancers. "Where is this thick, sweaty man?" warbled one.

"I *love* men who pray all the time!" the other's voice rang out. "So godly!"

"Oh, you're *wonderfully* disgusting!" they both cried and threw their arms round Joel.

It was marvellous. I leant on the wall to watch. Joel was jerking around in his seat, looking panicked and bewildered.

"I don't think he's got a chance," Toby said, full of rare family pride.

"The glamour's on like a searchlight," Grundo agreed.

Beside me, Romanov was now crouching beside the Merlin's chair and sweating with effort and urgency. "Back me, friend," he said to the Merlin. "Help me find the pattern. The thing's like matted wool." Then he looked up at me, even more urgently. "You go to Blest and raise the land," he said to me. "Take the boys with you to help you. You should have done it *weeks* ago. I'll join you as soon as I've finished here. *That* way." He pointed along the wall. "Go that way. And *hurry*!"

The four of us set off along the wall at a run. Nick groaned, because, after a few yards, we were in a narrow, rocky passage with no light at all. "I seem to have spent *aeons* in these paths," he said, stumbling about. "Bloody ages!"

Grundo and Toby and I raised magelight the way we had been taught. This was the first time I had done it in earnest and, in spite of my dread that we were going to be too late getting to Blest, I was delighted when the blue light appeared, cupped in my hand. Or I was until our three blue lights blazed in the wide, green eyes of a huge, gaunt spotted cat that was trotting swiftly towards us. We all gasped and backed against the rock wall. But the creature simply trotted straight past us, intent on something else. It had such an intent look, in fact, that it brought me out in shivers. It was off to do something terrible.

"Romanov's called her," Nick said and sighed. Then he cursed again, because he couldn't seem to raise magelight.

"You had it on your forehead when I first saw you," I said.

"That was only because Maxwell Hyde gave it to me," he said. He was really mortified. He had to get Toby to lead him. "And I suppose we'll be blundering along here for hours," he grumbled.

I don't know if it was hours. It felt entirely timeless to me. And, as Grundo said, it was better than having to do goat-leaps across infinity. *Anything* was better, to my mind. I just kept hoping that we would arrive in time and that I could manage to raise the land in the way I had discussed with Romanov. And wondering what awful thing might happen if I did.

To take my mind off it, I said to Grundo, "You knew about the Izzies' glamour because you were doing the same thing to me, weren't you?"

He just gave me one of his smoothly guilty looks and changed the subject. "What did that man Joel mean about atonement?"

"He and another prayerboy murdered their Prayermaster ten years ago," Nick said. "He may think he's making up for that."

"What – by messing up Blest and a hundred other worlds?" Toby said. "That doesn't make sense!"

"Taking them over in the name of righteousness," Nick said. "It must make sense to him or he wouldn't have been working so hard."

They went on trying to understand it and it didn't help me at all. Nick had told me not to be so tense all the time, but I couldn't help it. It seemed to me I had every reason to be tense. I kept thinking of my parents, hidden in that cotton stuff so that I hadn't even been able to find them, draped in prayer-spell, hardly able to ease a crick in their necks, let alone their aching feet, standing, standing, while a religious madman wove the spell tighter and tighter yet. And I knew that if things had gone wrong, Romanov and the Izzies could be standing in that crowd by now, draped in prayer-spell too, and we might be the only ones left who could do anything to help Blest.

Just as I thought I couldn't bear any more, the dark path took us downhill into a bright misty morning, and we were back almost where we had started, in Grandad's garden in London.

Dora was standing by the stump of the goat's stake, looking woebegone. "The goat's gone," she said. "Did you know?"

She did not seem in the least surprised at our sudden arrival. When Toby went up to her and wrapped his arms around her, she patted his head in an absent-minded way and said, "Where were you all yesterday? You should have been here."

Toby looked up at her. "What day is it?"

"Sunday morning," Dora told him. "Not to worry. You're all here now."

Toby twisted round to look at Nick. "We should have rescued salamanders from the airport last night."

"There isn't a thing we can do about that now," Nick said. "Dora, you do drive Maxwell Hyde's car sometimes, don't you? Would you mind very much driving us all to…" He looked round at me. "Where, Roddy?"

Romanov had told me of five places where you could raise the land. "One place was not too far from London," I said. "It hasn't got a name. He just described it. If we take the main road west, I'll say when I think we're there."

Dora seemed perfectly willing to drive us. Nick said

we'd find some food and eat it in the car, and we were all hurrying towards the house, when Grundo growled in my ear, "Salamanders. They were all over the place when we were here before. Where are they?"

He was right to ask. When we had rushed out to find Helga, I hadn't exactly been looking for salamanders, but I had known they were there, either scooting out of our way or curled up in warm places watching us. Now they were not here. If I concentrated very hard, I could sense some of them. They were in hiding, very deep hiding, crouched up, nervous and afraid. The rest were just not there.

This was not the only thing wrong. Now I was attending, I knew everything was too quiet. I had been in London on a Sunday before, of course, and it was always much quieter than on a weekday. But before, there had always been the hum and mutter of distant people and remote traffic, or the occasional thunder of a bus. Now there was hardly any sound, not even from pigeons or sparrows. When I looked at Grandad's garden, it was standing perfectly still. No insects flew, not a leaf twitched. It was – well – not right.

# CHAPTER THIRTY-EIGHT

✳

Nick has just come down here to the dining room to tell me he thinks he can't write about some of this next part. I can't say I blame him. I'm going to do my best to put everything in, but there is at least one bit I don't know. I said he must write that. He says he'll try.

Anyway, my feeling of something being very wrong got worse as we drove out of London. Because it was such a hot, sultry day, Dora folded back the top of Grandad's car and we could look up at the sky. The sky was wrong. There were clouds in the blueness, very pale white, streaky clouds, and instead of being slanted across the sky as such clouds usually are, these were in a great stationary swirl, with long, vague arms of cloud stretching out of the swirl. Each long, vague arm went stretching away downwards to some point that was out of sight over the horizon. Nick said it was like the ghost of a tornado.

Everything was very misty too, and statue-still, with the normal summer colours looking unclear and rather dark, as if they were reflected in deep, thick water. None of it smelt quite right. And there were none of the transparent folks tumbling in the hedges in the wind from the car.

When the road brought us into sight of the green line of the Ridgeway Hills, running along the skyline to our left, those hills were nearly hidden by low, grey, moving clouds that formed big, puffy, blue-grey waves, which were all cascading and rushing westward faster than the car. By the time the road had brought us nearer to the hills, we were in those clouds. Hot white vapours almost hid the road. Dora was forced to slow right down, so that we could actually see the mist surging across us in waves, galloping into the west.

We were almost at the right place by then. I could feel the strange tug and pull of it. I was fairly sure it was the same place that Grundo and I had felt on our way to London. Grundo, Toby and I all cried out, "Here it is! We're nearly there!" and I said to Dora, "If you could take the next turning left…"

"Oh, no," she said.

This was where it got really frightening.

I said, "But this is truly the best place. Romanov said. I think it's a wood…"

"Oh, no," Dora said again. "It's much too near where Toby's father lives. I can't take you there."

"But you *have* to, Mum!" Toby cried out. "I went to them – I told them in the wood that I'd go back and call them out. They're *waiting* for me. I *promised* them!"

Dora said, "And I promised I would do at least this one thing for the group. They'll be very displeased if I don't." And she kept driving.

"Oh, *please!*" Toby said. I had never known him so upset. Tears were bursting out of his eyes and rolling down his shirt. I remembered, with a quiver of fright in my stomach, that Dora had always been at least half dotty, and Toby knew she was.

"Where *do* you think you're driving us then?" Nick said belligerently to Dora. He was in the front seat, and he more or less turned and shouted in Dora's face.

"Stonehenge," Dora said. "It'll be quite all right then. They promised me."

I almost relaxed at that. Stonehenge was one of the other four places Romanov had told me. But Nick said suspiciously, "*Who* told you to take us to Stonehenge? Toby's Dad?"

"And Mrs Blantyre," Dora said placidly. "And the sweet young man they get their orders from. I think he said he was the Merlin, but I'm not sure. He said that this was the least I could do. I was quite worried yesterday when I couldn't find any of you, because I didn't want to let them down, did I?"

"*Mum!*" Toby shouted. "*I* made a promise too! Stop the car!" He stood up and gave Dora's shoulder a shake, but the car swerved so violently that he sat down again quickly.

Nick tried cunning then. He said, "Dora, how about we stop the car and keep Toby's promise first? Then we can go on to Stonehenge and keep yours."

Dora shook her head. "No, dear. Please don't try any Oriental blandishments on me. I do know when someone's trying to get round me." And we bucketed on, with waves of mist rolling across us and away in front of us.

Nick and Toby both shot me desperate looks. Nick leaned over and tried to put on the handbrake – he says this is the only control that's the same as an Earth car – but he couldn't do it, even heaving with both hands. "What have you done to this?" he asked Dora.

"Nothing," she said, "but Mrs Blantyre did promise me she would make sure we got there. She's clever, isn't she? Now, do be good. It's so hard to see in all this fog."

Grundo leaned over the side to see if it was possible to jump out, but we were going far too fast. He sat down and looked at me. "It may be all right," I said. "Stonehenge was another of Romanov's places."

"Stonehenge is *the* place," Dora said happily. "The King is going to abdicate there today." As she said this, the roof of the car rolled back over us and we found that none of the doors would open. We roared onwards in a warm box surrounded in fog, and there seemed no way of stopping Dora that wouldn't crash the car. All my flower-files were useless, useless, because the hurt lady had never known about cars and I had never known much myself either.

I know the others tried things. Grundo tried an illusion of people in the road ahead, but he was upset, so they came out behind the car. Shadowy people chased us through the fog for miles. My idea was to give Dora cramp and a crick in her neck, but either this Mrs Blantyre of hers had thought of that or Dora just ignored what I did to her. Toby tried an illusion of the controls bursting into flame, but Dora knew it was him.

"Toby," she said reproachfully, "don't play tricks while I'm driving. It's not safe."

Toby sighed and the fire vanished. And Nick...

# CHAPTER THIRTY-NINE

*

Yes, well, I called that dragon.

I didn't do it just because I was scared spitless – although I was. The sight of the silly, dreamy smile on Dora's face while she refused to stop driving was one of the scariest things that had happened so far. But as soon as she mentioned the Merlin, I knew it was serious for a lot more reasons than just my own safety. I thought through the way Joel had talked, and how urgent Romanov had been, and what Roddy had told me, and I thought I'd better do what I could, and do it before we got out of range.

I shut my eyes and concentrated, the way Maxwell Hyde had tried to teach me. I'd never done it right before.

I suppose I'd lacked the incentive. It surprised the hell out of me when I found I was sort of floating beside the hillside, where the turf rolled back to show the dragon's vast white head. We were swamped in mist, both of us. His big, green eye was open and turning this way and that to watch the waves of cloud rushing across him, but the eye turned and looked at me when I got there, even though I was really sitting in a car speeding away from him.

"YOU AGAIN," he said. Just like Romanov. "HAVE YOU COME TO CALL ME OUT THIS TIME?"

"Yes," I said. "It's time. I summon you."

"YOU LEFT IT A BIT LATE," he said, "IN MY OPINION. VERY WELL. IT WILL TAKE ME A WHILE TO WORK LOOSE. AND REMEMBER WHAT I SAID. I DON'T LIKE BEING CALLED. PEOPLE ARE GOING TO GET HURT. YOU ARE GOING TO GET HURT. NOW GO AWAY."

I went away, fast. I flipped back into the car, shaking all over, and found we were on a stretch of road that was not in fog any longer. Dora was fair batting along it. She had her foot right down most of the rest of the way. It was frightening.

# CHAPTER FORTY

✳

*I*t was thoroughly frightening. It was also very hot too, as if the fine weather that my father had never been allowed to cancel was getting out of hand, somehow. With the heat, there was the sour, disinfectant-like smell you get when magic is being done. At first, I assumed it was coming from the spells that were holding the car doors shut, but then, slowly, I realised that it was coming from everywhere. It was outside, not simply in the car. And finally, I realised what it was. It was the smell of quantities of magic being moved. It was the way things smelt when all the magic in the countryside was being pulled, and sucked, and dragged, into one place.

"Oh, gods!" I said. Everyone except Dora looked

at me anxiously. "It's the magic," I said. "Someone's pulling in all the magic of Blest."

"So how do we stop it?" said Nick.

He said this as if he really thought it was possible – build a dam, suck in the opposite direction – I don't know what he thought, but it made Dora drive even faster, as if she was afraid Nick would really find some way to deal with the magic, huge as it was, unless we got to Stonehenge quickly. I could feel her adding in a speed-the-journey spell. It was a variant of the fifth one in my *Traveller's joy* file, and it had a foreign feel, as if someone else had provided it for her. It was strong. We were on Salisbury Plain five minutes after Nick asked his question.

Bare green distances rushed by. And suddenly, in that way it has of turning up, unexpectedly small and indescribably massive, there was Stonehenge.

We bumped across the grass right beside the enormous stones of it and Nick said, "There's a lot more of it standing than there is on Earth."

I hardly heard him. Too many other things grabbed my attention. I thought I caught a glimpse of Salisbury standing near one of the stones – just a sight of green rubber boots as we bumped past, and a flutter of ragged coat that might have been Old Sarum squatting beside the boots. But the main thing that held my attention was the great orderly jumble of cars, buses and lorries parked downhill from the henge. And despite all I knew, I found myself thinking, Oh, good! We've caught up with the Progress at last!

What a stupid way to think! I told myself, as Dora stopped the car. Every single person who might have been friendly to us was currently in a xanadu worlds away, shrouded in white spells of binding. As proof of this, the car was instantly surrounded by royal pages, who came running up while the car was still moving and pulled the doors open as soon as it stopped. They were Alicia's lot, all the people of Alicia's age whom I particularly did not like, and they stood in a close circle with official, polite looks on their faces – except that the polite looks were just slightly exaggerated, so that we knew it was a mass jeer really.

"If you will come this way, please," Alicia herself said, reaching in and hauling on my arm.

Her fingers dug, but I hardly noticed. We climbed out into such a storm of magic that it made me quite dazed. It set the hurt lady's knowledge racing randomly through my brain –*Purple vetch: vortex; Goosegrass or cleavers: bindings; Gorse: land and home magics; Woody nightshade: spells of evil intent, death spells and sacrifices; Foxglove: raising of power*, and so many more that I went dizzy and could only see things around me as sick-coloured shadows for a minute or so. Then my brain steadied on *Purple vetch* and I knew what was happening. We were at the centre of a vortex here, where all the magic in Blest, and for worlds around Blest, was coming roaring and soundlessly howling inwards to a spot right beside Stonehenge. I could feel it. I could see it too, in the swirls of white cloud that marked the lines of force in the blue sky, winding and dragging inwards to an icy spearpoint of power only yards away. I found I was bending sideways from it as Alicia hauled me politely towards it.

I hardly saw – but noticed all the same – a perfectly horrible woman leading Dora away, patting her and praising her as if she were a dog. "Good girl! *Well* done! *Doesn't* it feel better now you've done what you owed your friends to do?" Poor, silly Dora. She was beaming and nodding and looking shamed, all at once.

Another thing I hardly saw – but noticed all the same – was the way the pages expertly cleared a path for us through the crowds of people gathered in a ring around the point of the vortex. Some were people I knew from Court, but most of them were folk I'd never seen before, a lot of them like the horrid woman praising Dora, and crowds of men with beards and dishonest faces – many of these had too much hair and golden discs on their chests in the manner of priests – and large numbers of men and women who struck me as like Dora: not quite sure what they were doing here.

When we reached the space in the centre of the crowd, I hardly saw – but noticed all the same – that it was packed tight with the transparent folks. They had been pulled here by the magic and now they were being drawn on for their own magic. Their hard-to-see bodies bumped aside to let us through, and bumped and blundered high into the air, until they were crushed together into the white lines of the vortex clouds, where they were borne rushing downward again. The space was full of their soundless screams and their dreadful anxiety. They were terrified and horrified, but wildly excited as well, as if they couldn't help themselves.

There was more dreadful anxiety from the fringes of the crowd, but I couldn't find who it was coming from. All I knew was that a lot of someones were there, more worried than I cared to think about.

In the centre of the space was Sybil, dancing. Her big, square-toed feet were bare and her green skirts were hauled halfway up her massive legs. She must have been dancing for hours. When she saw us, she shouted, "*Hai*!" and flung her arms up, and I saw great dark patches of sweat spreading from her armpits almost to her waist.

Two chairs had been put facing one another on the grass, about ten yards apart. The King sat in one, looking royal and expressionless, with Prince Edmund standing beside him. The two Archbishops stood behind the chair, wearing robes and mitres. Each of them had a puzzled and slightly distant smile, as if they had no more idea than Dora what was going on, but felt they ought to look benevolent all the same.

The Merlin sat in the other chair. False Merlin, I should say. Now I had met the real one, I could see that this one's face was rattier and his hair fairer. But they were very alike. They both had the long neck and the big Adam's apple, and the same small, pointed face. Maybe this was what had put the idea of the conspiracy into this one's head. But I had the feeling that he wasn't pretending to be anyone except himself now. He was in plain brown robes that reeked of power and he sat in the same pose as a saint in a statue. Sir James was standing to one side of him, looking smug in a smart suit. There was a big box on the other side of the false Merlin. In front of him was a large silver bucket – or maybe it was a cauldron – that smoked cold, white smoke. This was where the point of the vortex of magic rested.

Grundo muttered beside me, "It would make more sense if they were inside Stonehenge. Why aren't they?"

"They can't. It won't let them," Nick answered, sort of absently. He was staring at the false Merlin as if he recognised him.

I glanced up at the grey huddle of stones beyond the crowds and saw that what Nick said was true. Stonehenge, in some strange way, was not really present. It seemed to have gone several layers of reality away from here. I think this is how it protects itself.

"He *has* to be Japheth," Nick said. "That ratty look."

Sybil rushed up to us and waved Alicia and the other pages aside. She finished the movement with her arms aloft again. "The ceremony can begin!" she shouted. "Our sacrifice is come among us!" In a big gust of sweat-smell, she seized Grundo's arm. "Now, you be good," she said to him, "and we won't hurt you more than we have to."

Toby and I stared at her. Under the sweat, her face was like red sandpaper and her eyes didn't quite see anything, like a drunk person's. She seemed to have no feeling for Grundo at all. Nick put his big hand over Sybil's chubby one and wrenched it off Grundo's arm. "*Leave* him!" he thundered out, glaring at Sybil. Sybil stared into air behind Nick and went on blindly grabbing at Grundo.

The false Merlin looked across at us.

He stared. Then he sprang up and came striding over to us, robes streaming, and pushed Alicia aside so that he could walk right up to Nick. He stood with his small, pale face more or less nose to nose with Nick's darker one. "*You*!" he said. "You're supposed to be *dead*! You *laughed* at me!"

I have never seen such hatred. Spittle came out of the false Merlin's lips with the strength of that hatred. He shook all over with it.

Nick tried to lean back, away from the flying spit. "What of it? You trod on an egg. It was funny."

"*What of it*!" the false Merlin more or less screamed. "I'll show you *what of it*! I've *dreamed* of you dead for ten years now! Today, you are going to *be* dead – as painfully as I can manage!" He turned and said to Sybil, in a normal, cold voice, "Leave that child. This boy will give us far more power." Then he went calmly back to his chair again.

Gods! I thought. He's mad, quite mad! And Nick had said he was a murderer too. I was terrified.

Sybil let go of Grundo. She seemed to be entirely under the false Merlin's influence. She beckoned to Nick. At once a skein of transparent folks swooped from the vortex, surrounded Nick, and pulled him into the open space. I tried to stop them. I am entirely in a muddle as to whether this was what I would have done for anyone or whether it was because it was Nick. I do know my heart hammered in my throat and that I put out my hands and tried to make the transparent folk stop. But your hands go through, or past, or slide off these people, and they were far too sunk in the storm of magic to heed me. I suppose to most of the onlookers it must have seemed as if Nick stumbled out into the open all by himself and then fell down on the grass.

"The sacrifice has presented himself!" Sybil proclaimed.

The false Merlin grinned. "So he has," he said. His long, skinny arm reached out to the box beside his chair, where he flipped up a small flap in the top, groped a bit and came up clutching a writhing bundle of salamanders. As the flap snapped down again, he reached forward and dipped the salamanders into the smoking silver bucket, quite slowly.

It was colder than the coldest ice in there. The

soundless scream from those poor salamanders as they met that cold went through us all like an electric shock. But it went through Nick in a much worse way. His body became covered at once in hurrying silver ripples. The ripples chased and overlapped one another and formed silver leaf-shapes, as if he was under shallow sea with the sun on the waves. He was in obvious agony from it. He rolled about, trying to scream – or not being able to scream - and every time the ripples formed into a leaf-shape this seemed to hurt him even more. He curled up, he uncurled, he flung his legs and arms about, much as the salamanders were doing in the false Merlin's fist.

"There is really nothing like a willing sacrifice," the false Merlin said. He looked to see if the salamanders were recovering a little and calmly dipped them in the smoking bucket again. Sir James – disgusting man! – leant eagerly over to watch.

"Oh, he mustn't!" Toby said despairingly. Possibly he was sorry for Nick but, being Toby, I suspect he was mostly feeling for those salamanders.

"No, he mustn't, must he?" Grundo agreed.

Here the King seemed to notice what was going on, or some of it. He looked from Nick to the false Merlin and said, "What's this? Eh?"

Toby was jigging about in his distress. Alicia jabbed him with her elbow and said, "Quiet. Don't interrupt."

"Your Majesty." The false Merlin smiled and stood up, flourishing his handful of agonised, dying salamanders.

"We are gathered here today to reinstate the old, true form of kingship. As has been explained to Your Majesty, yours are not the old, true forms. You make use of technology, and you have little or no dealings with the magic of Blest, and this has caused the old, true forms to warp and degenerate. You therefore intend to abdicate." He looked sternly at the King. "Don't you, Your Majesty?"

The King rubbed his hands across his face in a bewildered way. "Abdicate? Yes, I suppose we came here for something like that," he agreed, but not as if he was at all sure. "What happens then?"

"Why then we install a true king!" the false Merlin announced, as ringingly as such a reedy voice as his was able. "We ratify the Prince Edmund in your place, in the presence of both Archbishops and the priests of all other religions, and we seal it in proper form with the blood of a sacrifice."

"Oh," said the King. For a moment he looked startled and a little disgusted. Then he said placidly, "Very well then. If Edmund…"

He stopped, distracted, because the false Merlin stooped and once more plunged the wretched salamanders into the white smokes of the bucket. This time they died. The shock was like the crack of a whip. The ripples were so thick over Nick that you could hardly see him, just a rolling, thrashing *something* under a moving silver web.

"Look here," said Prince Edmund. He came out from

behind the King to stand and stare at what could be seen of Nick. "I don't think this is— I mean, is this a *human* sacrifice you're talking about? I'm not sure— What happens then?"

Well fancy this! I thought. Prince Edmund is a decent human being after all! But that was before Sybil came tramping up to him and laid her fat hand against his arm. "Your Highness," she said, in the kind of low, tactful voice that everyone can hear, "if you are unwilling, please say so at once. Your Highness has four younger brothers, any of whom might wish to guide these islands along the one true way in your place."

You could see this not appealing to the Prince at all. He never did like his brothers. He said, "Oh, in that case..."

"Then hearken to the Merlin as he prophesies," Sybil suggested and stood back.

The Prince and the King both looked enquiringly at the false Merlin, who gave them a merry smile, tossed the dead salamanders on the grass, and put his hands in the rope-pulling position, by which we were supposed to understand that he was making a prophecy. But I could see he was just pretending. He said, "This sacrifice both anoints our new King and brings the power of all Blest to the crown. By this sacrifice, we shall raise the land and bring peace and prosperity..."

I think he went on for some time, but I stopped listening. As soon as he said "raise the land", I realised that this was exactly what he *was* doing. And he couldn't be allowed to, not like this! Doing it by a blood sacrifice would bring Blest and all the worlds surrounding it into the realm of purest black magic. The balance would be tipped entirely the wrong way.

I fought my way out from the hurricane of magic and horror and tried to think through the hurt woman's files again. They rushed into my head, file after file – *Purple vetch, Goosegrass, Foxglove, Teazle, Gorse, Mullein, Dog rose, Thistle, Nightshade, Poison, Invisible peoples, Sex magics, Journeys, The Dead, Bird magic, Shape-shifting, Summoning, Unbinding* – on and on, in a wild waterfall of spells. At first they seemed to be no use at all. But that phrase *raise the land* had given me such a jolt that before long it seemed to steady the rush down. I saw that they did not come into my head in any old order: they started with *Purple vetch* for *vortex*, and followed that with spells of binding and unbinding. Seeing that stopped the rush of files almost entirely. And I knew that I *had* known how to raise the land, long before Romanov tried to explain it to me.

Each file, down at the very end, had what the hurt woman called its Great Spell, one that encompassed all the others. What Romanov had told me amounted simply to unbinding these. You started with *vortex*. Then you went on to *unbinding* in its Great form and, as you unbound the *vortex*, you fed into it each of the other Great Spells, good and bad alike, and you made them all unravel. The gods alone knew what would happen then! I almost turned to Grundo then. I wanted to ask him if he thought we would all be entirely without magic ever after.

Grundo's face had gone white and secretive and he wouldn't look at me. All my earlier hurt came back. Grundo never needed me, he just *used* me, he never cared— Then I realised that Grundo was trying to work magic too. It was something directional, by his look, which was always difficult for him, because he had to turn everything round the other way, against the grain of his mind. He was scowling, pouting the skin above his long nose as he concentrated.

By this time, as the false Merlin blathered on, the ripples were dying away from Nick. He was lying with his face in his arms, exhausted by the convulsions they had put him through. The false Merlin noticed. A mean look came over his face and, still prophesying, he went over to the box and reached for another handful of salamanders.

Grundo burst the box open as he did so.

Toby cheered. It was wonderful for a moment. The sides fell out and the lid flew up and hit the false Merlin in the face. The salamanders inside, hundreds and hundreds of them, had been packed and crammed in there, thoroughly miserable anyway, and then panic-stricken when the first handful died. They came out like a small volcano. They showered into the air and then ran everywhere, incandescent with fear, setting the grass alight, raising smoke and flames and howls from the people in the ring of spectators. The false Merlin howled as loud as anyone. Sir James got a salamander on his smart hat and tried to beat the fire out on the chair, while Sybil ran and pranced and jumped to avoid red-hot salamanders running across her bare feet.

But it only lasted a minute or so. Those salamanders were so truly terrified that they all ran away as fast as they could, flashing among the feet of the crowd and diving under cars and buses, cooling off as they ran. By far the most of them seemed to race uphill, in among the great trilithons of Stonehenge. I think they were safe there. They seemed to be able to go away into the same distant layer of reality as Stonehenge itself, and stay there.

Alicia had realised that it was Grundo who let them out. Well, she would. She took him by one ear and shook him, silently and fiercely, with her nails digging in. "Little beast!" she whispered. "Little *pig!*"

Two days ago that would have got all my attention at once. Now I realised that Grundo was distracting Alicia from me, just when I needed it. It was quite hard, but I'm afraid I let Grundo suffer. I began trying to raise the land.

*Vortex* was there already. I only had to touch the spell in *Purple vetch* to make it my magic and not Sybil's or the false Merlin's. The whirling in my head intensified, but I tried to ignore it and went on to *Goosegrass or cleavers* and the Great Unbinding at the end of it. Ideally, you had to make a model of what you needed to unbind – it was like a hideously complicated cat's cradle – and then say the words as you undid it. Because I couldn't do that, I was forced to do it all in my head, imagining each strand of the cradle and the movements I might have used to untwist them, and saying the words in my head too. Try as I might, I couldn't help making small twisting movements with my fingers. It was too difficult otherwise. And I couldn't manage a translation of the words. I had to think them through in the hurt woman's language, and I believe I was murmuring them as I worked.

My greatest fear was that nothing would happen. But I knew I was doing *something* when a great cluster of transparent people sped out of the lines of cloud and hung in the air above me, attracted by the magic. I was afraid that Alicia or one of the other pages might notice them, but they didn't. Toby distracted them all by sinking his teeth into Alicia's hand as it gripped Grundo's ear. All the pages crowded in to separate Toby from Alicia and Alicia from Grundo – but quietly, because you didn't make a noise in front of the King. I was able to move to one side and continue unbinding.

The King was still sitting there. I don't think he noticed the salamanders. He didn't seem to see that the false Merlin's nose was bleeding. The false Merlin wiped the blood carefully on a handkerchief and handed it to Sybil. "Blood for a summoning," he said to her. "We've no salamanders. We want that Old Power here instead, quickly." He went and stood with one foot on Nick's back, in case Nick recovered and tried to get up, while

Sybil waved the red-blotched hanky about and began chanting.

"I can't think why they think they need any *more* magic here," Grundo grunted, appearing by my shoulder with one ear bleeding. I always forget how good Grundo is at slithering out of scraps. But at that stage I was only two-thirds of the way through the Great Unbinding. I made frantic noddings and face-twistings at him not to distract me. His mouth made an "Oh" of quiet understanding. Then he ducked out of my sight and several of the pages yelped almost at once.

Gratefully, I went on to the last third of the unbinding. Slowly and carefully, I undid nine twists and three knots. Then I was done, right on to the very last, which was to pull an imaginary straight unknotted string through my fingers, to show that it was now free of all tangles. I wished that had been all. But I had to go on to feed all my flower-files to the vortex, while my head spun with it, and pages heaved and gasped to one side of me, and Sybil, out in the open, got on with her summoning too.

I don't know how long I took to feed everything into the vortex. On one level, it took no time at all, just a crazy unreeling of file after file, plant after dry, thorny plant rushing through my mind and speeding into the twisted clouds, while I said to each, "I hereby call you to raise the land." On another level, I could see myself reaching out and slowly pulling to myself layer after layer of different magics. Sometimes I paused to marvel at them. *Songs* and *thoughts* looked truly beautiful, all intricate, curled-up colours, but when I turned them round to look at the other side, they were quite drab, and some had oozing nastinesses. *Time* and *eternity* took my breath away, though I tried not to look too hard at the demons that rode with them.

And I remember being slightly astonished at all the beings waiting in the wood where Toby had promised to go. I recognised the kingly man in the red cloak. He was on horseback, surrounded by his knights and standard bearers. I knew he was the Count of Blest. But there were ladies with him that I didn't know, and large numbers of tall people who didn't look quite as solid as the Count and his court. They all looked relieved when they saw me standing between two trees and called out to know if it was time. "Yes," I said. "My cousin is not able to come, but it *is* time." They started to move at once, while the trees around them tossed and surged.

I called good things and bad things, and things that were neither, birds, animals, growing things, and things that never changed. I called the sun. I called stars, moon and planets. Last of all, I called the world and Blest rolled towards me.

Everything seemed to come loose.

The wonder of it was that this only seemed to take seconds. When I finished, Sybil was still chanting, the false Merlin still had his foot on Nick's back, and Grundo and Toby were still silently wrestling with Alicia and the other pages. Nobody seemed to notice what was happening.

What was happening was terrifying. Blest was rolling loose among the universes, shedding strips of magic like bandages unwinding from a mummy. I saw the islands we had crossed behind Helga dipping and spinning. One actually pitched sideways and sank. Another seemed to be melting, and nearly all of them had lost their clear, luminous colours. They were patchy, with brown clouds.

I saw London walk among his towers and carefully put his huge foot down on a house, crushing it to brick dust.

I saw a huge wave rise out of a sea on another world and rush across a land full of brown people in houses. There were no houses after that. In another world, a vast being standing guard on the top of a green hill turned and looked doubtfully over his shoulder. He seemed to have lost his purpose. After a while, he came down from his hill and walked across the plains to meet three other beings like him, who looked equally lost. I was sorry about that, because this was the world where we had accidentally arrived in that library, and they depended for their magics on these Guardians of the Four Quarters. When I looked at another world, I saw that all its magic had entered its railway lines, causing incredible confusion. And I turned to a world of giant canyons, just in time to see a glistening xanadu collapse into the caves beneath it, followed by half the rocky landscape in great plumes of dust. That horrified me, because I had no idea if my parents were in there or not.

Here, in the Islands of Blest, lines of power were winking out and, from every river, there was rising a slimy, shell-covered head. "Free!" they growled. "Loose at last!" and their waters began to rise. Manchester, in a red dress, was hurriedly building city walls. Things that had been buried under the Pennines for centuries were crawling out from under confining blocks of magic. Not all these things were evil, but all over the country, moors and forests were becoming strange and powerful as the layers of magic shredded away. And the sea was rising.

What have I done? I thought. What *have* I done?

The magic was still shredding. In my head the file *Gorse: home and country* continued to unreel into the vortex long after the others had gone. It made sense. The magic of the Islands of Blest had more layers than anywhere else. I watched the strips unwind, layer after layer, until I thought for a moment that I was looking at the bedrock of our country. It was a brown-green lumpy shape, right at the bottom of things. Then it stirred, stretched, and sat up. It shook loose hair back and smiled at me, and I recognised the lady who had taken away the virtue from the Inner Garden.

"I never knew you were alive before," I said.

"Of course I am," she said. "So is every land. Thank you. Now I can put things back as I want them." She lay back, like someone settling into a really comfortable sofa, and began pulling bands and scarves of magic across herself, slowly and carefully, looking at each strip before she laid it on herself. Some she shook her head at and threw away, some she put aside to lay on later, and some she smiled at and gave special treatment to, like wrapping them round her shoulders or her head.

Perhaps I haven't destroyed everything then, I thought.

A tremendous roar came out of the east. It was like an answer.

I had never heard anything that remotely resembled that noise, but Nick tells me that he thought it was a jet plane, flying very low. He was half-delirious at that stage, shaken with shudders of pain, and he says he thought he was back on Earth suddenly. But the roar came a second time, and he realised what it was. And where he was, which he says was not so good. Everyone turned to look to the east, even Sybil, but no one could see anything for the huge bank of mist rolling up from there.

The dragon came flying above the mist, against the blue sky. He was white as chalk and touched gold from the sinking sun. He was enormous. The King stood up, which was fitting, although everyone else half-crouched, except for the false Merlin, who stared up at the dragon, dumbfounded. The Archbishops fell to their knees and prayed, as did quite a few of the priests in the crowd.

The dragon came flying on and he was even more enormous. When he was about half a mile away, his huge cry came again. There were words in it, but they were too loud to understand. Nick raised his head and shouted back, "*This* one! The one standing on me!"

"AH!" said the dragon. Everyone clearly saw the flame flicker in its huge mouth.

Then it was there. It cut through the vortex as if that did not exist, and hundreds of transparent folk sped away outwards, frantic to get out of its way. For a moment, it was like being under a great ivory-coloured tent. The dragon's wings were so huge that they covered Stonehenge in one direction and all the cars and buses of the Court in the other.

A shining white claw came down from the ivory hugeness – it shone like marble, but you could see it was hard as granite – and hooked itself around the false Merlin. He screamed, a high, childlike scream as he was snatched away upwards. The gigantic wings beat with a dull boom, like thunder, or strong wind in a tent, pulling the mist in across us. It started to snow then, in lines that twisted with the vortex, filling everyone's hair with furry whiteness, but I honestly think nobody really noticed. We were all staring up at the dragon as he rose, huge and white and perfect, dangling the tiny dark figure of the false Merlin in one clawed front foot.

He circled with his prey, round against the sun, until he was far out over the plain, to the west. Then he dropped the false Merlin. Most of us watched the little dark shape hurtle downwards. Most of us strained to hear the noise of that shape hitting the ground, but there was no sound. It was too far away.

But Sir James strode through the whirling snow and came up to Sybil beside the two Archbishops. He didn't bother with them, nor with the King and Prince Edmund, who were both standing by Sybil. He said to Sybil, "*Much* better. Now there's only two of us to share everything. Let's get this sacrifice over, shall we? Shall I kill him, or do you still insist on your ritual?"

Now the false Merlin was gone, Sybil seemed much more herself. She drew herself up. "My ritual..." she began. She stopped, looking irritable, and moved aside.

My Grandfather Gwyn was there, looming above her on his white mare. His cloak clapped about in the snow and strips of bloody horsehide swirled from his standard. All his people were behind him, dimly visible in the mist and the snow.

"About time too!" Sybil shouted up at him. "You should *obey* when I call! Kill this boy at once. We want your stake through his heart according to the ritual."

Nick sat up at this and scrambled round on his knees.

My Grandfather Gwyn did not look at him. He said to Sybil, "No. I warned you, but you never listened, did you now? You have called me three times already. Now you have called me yet again and I have the right to call you. And I now call you."

Here, for a while, so many things happened at once that I have had to ask the others what *they* saw and did. I was mostly watching Sybil. I think she truly saw

Grandfather Gwyn for the first time then. She stared up at him and her face was like uncooked prettybread, blotched with red over yellow-white. Her mouth came open and she flopped to her knees with her hands clasped. "Spare me," she said.

"No," my grandfather said. "From now on, you follow me."

He started to ride forward. Sybil was scrambling round on her knees to obey him – she never argued or even tried to protest – when more riders loomed through the fog and the snow, coming from the opposite direction. The one in front was wearing a dark-red cloak which billowed and whirled around his armour. He saw Grandfather Gwyn and his people and stopped. I had just a glimpse of the elegant, practised way his gloved left hand drew up his reins, and of the way his horse tossed its head and champed, not at all willing to stop, while the rider raised his right hand courteously to my grandfather. Then I had to look at the upheaval going on beside me.

Grundo says that a piece of the wet, snowy grass unfolded beside him to let a crowd of Little People come swarming out on their bent-back legs. I think they were the ones I had felt watching so anxiously. They wanted Grundo and Toby for some reason. Grundo says he had no idea why, but he knew at once that they wanted him. He grabbed Toby and got clear. I didn't see any of that. All I saw was a seething struggle between Little People and snow-sodden royal pages, human youngsters being seized around the legs and bitten by long sharp teeth, and the humans kicking and punching in return. I had a flying glimpse of Grundo with his hair filled with snow, forging through the other side of the struggle, and I nearly went to help him. Then I thought that this was what he had bespelled me to do and I stopped. And *then* I thought that you helped people if they needed it, and I started forward again. But it was over by then. The Little People dragged Alicia away through the open fold and the fold slid shut.

Do you know, I *envied* Alicia! I still do. What an interesting thing to happen to her, I thought. It's not fair!

When I looked out into the driving, spiralling snow, Grandfather Gwyn had almost finished riding round the open space, selecting people from the crowd to follow him. He had Sybil and most of the other Court wizards walking obediently behind his line of horses by then. I think one of the other people may have been Toby's father.

# Chapter Forty-One

*

*I* suppose I'd better tell this bit. Roddy says she was busy trying to convince the royal pages that Alicia had gone for good. And they wanted to know where, but she had no more idea than they did.

I was so dazed and scared, and sore and frozen, that it all seemed more like a tumultuous dream than anything. I sat on the sopping grass, with snow catching on my eyelashes, and watched Gwyn ap Nud greet the Count of Britain – at least, they call him the Count of Blest here, but *I* call him the Count of Britain. I think he was King Arthur once, but I'm not sure.

They were very courtly and stately with one another and you could see they were equals. The Count of Blest in his red cloak said, "Well met in this time of change, Prince. Are you taking all here?"

Gwyn ap Nud bowed. He has the most terrible grim smile. "Well met indeed, Majesty. I am taking in my harvest, but there is one that must be yours." He pointed with his flapping grisly horsehead to the man Roddy says was Sir James. Then he rode away and I didn't see him any more.

The Count of Blest beckoned with his free hand to someone behind him. "Take him and tie him to the tail of the last horse," he said. And that person – he was a big, muscular knight – leaned down and dragged Sir James away to somewhere behind. Sir James was going on about this being an outrage, but nobody took any notice and after a while he stopped and I didn't see *him* any more either. But the Count of Blest began slowly riding on again, while I sat and noticed in a dazzled way that the swirls of snow from the blizzard were following exactly the lines of the vortex and sort of centring over that smoking bucket that Japheth had left standing there.

I looked up because the King – the present day King of Blest, that is – was trying to catch hold of the Count of Blest's bridle. The poor man looked almost as miserable as I felt. His face was the bright red that you go in snow and his beard was fluffy with white flakes. "Forgive me," he said, looking up at the Count of Blest. "I haven't exactly done well, have I?"

"Others have done almost as badly," the Count of

Blest said, quite kindly, riding on. He kept going, so that the King had more or less to trot beside him. "It is no easy matter to hold a kingdom in trust."

"I know, I *know*!" the King cried out. "I'll do better from now on, I swear! How long have I got?"

I think this was what the King *really* wanted to know, but the Count of Blest answered, "That is not a question I should answer or one you should ask. But choose your advisors more carefully in future. Now, forgive me. I have to ride the realm."

He rode away, and lots of tall horse legs went past me, some with armed men, some with incredible-looking ladies and some with weirder people. The King hurried after them for a while, looking snubbed and despairing, and then gave up. Endless riders went mistily past us both.

At the same time – Grundo says it had been going on all this while – hosts of the transparent folks came hurtling down from the spirals of snow, and a lot of others came with them, who looked to be the dark, riotous, bloodthirsty invisibles that usually only came out at night. And the whole lot came sweeping crosswise through the circle of people who had been watching. They kept pouring through, hundreds of them, thousands. They ought to have got in the way of the Count of Blest's riders, but in some queer way, they seemed to be on a different band of space. I sat watching them screaming by me and all the people who hadn't run for cover in those buses, including the two Archbishops, running away from them madly. And, at the same time, I watched princely knights and great ladies riding through the same spot. It was really odd.

The dragon came back in the midst of it all. Everything got darker underneath him. When I looked up through the driving, winding snow, I could faintly see the vast grey shape of him hovering above the weather. His huge voice boomed down to me.

"GIVE ME THE END OF IT."

I knew what he meant. I got up and tottered through the streams of transparent people, and among horses' legs that went past without touching me, to Japheth's smoking bucket. Grundo and Toby were there, trying to shelter behind it – not that they could, because the snow was blinding in from all directions. I was really glad to see them. I was shaky all over and I kept jerking with the salamander magic. I knew I couldn't manage on my own.

"Help me," I said. "We've got to get the end of this vortex up to the dragon."

They looked pretty scared, but they put out their arms and helped me try to lift it. It was surprisingly easy. Toby said, "It's quite loose!" It was, and it wasn't heavy, either, just awkward. I had to lift it by myself the last foot or so, because I was so much taller than they were, and it hummed and slithered and wobbled in my arms, but I managed to hang on to it until a great shiny claw reached down through the storm and hooked it off me.

"NOW FOR CHANGES," the dragon said.

I am not sure what he did. I heard his wings thunder. Then things went different. About ninety degrees different, and then stuck there. *Magic* was different, all over everywhere.

# CHAPTER FORTY-TWO

*

*I* had cast magic loose: the dragon fixed it again. He turned the vortex through a quarter circle and sealed it that way. I felt the change, but I was watching my Grandfather Gwyn ride away out into the distance, dark against the snow, with a long line of people trudging after the horses, getting smaller and smaller. He had never looked at me once. Knowing what I know about him, I suppose that was a good thing, but I had wanted him to *see* me. I wanted him to give me at least a look of approval. But he just rode away.

I blinked. The tears in my eyes seemed to have got into the landscape. All the melting snow was winking rainbow colours in the low sun, and flaring off the white slabs of snow along the trilithons of Stonehenge. Stonehenge was back in the same world with us now. I looked where I had seen – or thought I saw – Salisbury and Old Sarum, and there was no sign of them. That was when I realised how much the magic had changed. It was going to be much harder to see things or do things now. As far as I could tell, that went for all the other worlds too.

The dragon was gone. I was almost the only person standing in that flaring, melting landscape.

Everyone seemed to have run away or driven off. In the distance, the King's two limousines and one of the buses were bumping over the grass to the road, but there were a lot of empty cars and buses left behind. One was the car we had come here in. Dora had gone. Some witches had given her a lift back to London.

The three boys were sitting beside a rusty old bucket not far away, all very bedraggled. Nick kept shaking and jerking. As soon as I saw him, *Rosemary* came into my head, *healing*. I was so relieved I nearly cried again. I had carefully not looked for the hurt woman's knowledge, in case I had lost it in the vortex. I dragged myself over to Nick, running through the *Rosemary* file to see what would help him.

Before I got there, people shouted from up the hill, and the elephant came treading cautiously down from the direction of Stonehenge. Romanov was riding on the elephant's neck and, in the seat swaying on her back, leaning out anxiously on either side, were Mam and Dad.

Grandad – my sane, mortal Grandad Hyde – was riding with them and so was Mrs Candace.

"Magic has changed here too," Romanov remarked. The elephant stopped and he slid down on to her bent-up leg. "We got held up in the changes," he said as he reached the slushy ground. "Sorry about that."

He helped the others down. While my parents were hugging me, Grandad had one arm around Toby and the other hand on Nick's shoulder. "What's up with you, lad?" At this, Romanov looked at Nick and moved in too. They had him feeling better in moments, without my having to try using the changed magic. At least, they got Nick's body right, but Grandad says it will take much longer to heal his mind. "Don't look so chagrined, Roddy," Grandad said to me. "Romanov and I are used to working in changing conditions." Then he got out of the way, because the elephant trampled in and twined her trunk delightedly round Nick.

"I thought you were inside that dome when it collapsed!" I kept saying to my parents. "I'm so *glad*!"

Then I found Mrs Candace beside me. She leaned on Dad's arm, looking terribly tired but still amazingly elegant. "Your mother has been telling me how much she wishes you didn't have to live with the Progress," she said, staring into my eyes with her own peculiarly luminous green-blue ones. She nodded. "Yes," she said. "I wondered when I first saw you and now I'm sure. You are my next Lady of Governance, child. You must come and live with me and learn the ways of it."

Mam let out a wail at that. "That wasn't what I meant! Oh, I *knew* something like this would happen if I let my horrible old father get his hands on her!"

"It's all right, Mam," I said. "He only showed me how to find out about things."

Mrs Candace said, "It will take me some weeks to recover from that ghastly cavern, or whatever it was, and to get used to this shift in the magics. She can come to me in a month's time."

"Fine," said Dad, before Mam could raise more outcries. He was looking around, sniffing the air and frowning. "I'd better join the Court at once. Unless I get to my weather table soon, there's going to be a serious shift in the climate."

"I think your weather table's still here," I said. "I can see the lorry where they usually pack it."

"Excellent!" said my father and he dashed over to the lorry at once, sliding and sending up showers of slush in his hurry.

Grandad Hyde had seen his own car standing where Dora had left it. He rubbed his hands together with pleasure. "If she's left the keys in, fine," he said. "If not, it'll have to be Magid methods. Nick, Toby, come along. Let's get to London before nightfall if we can."

Nick untwined the elephant's trunk from his neck regretfully. "I wish I could come with you," he said to Romanov. "I want to be a free operator like you."

Romanov looked thoroughly taken aback. Then he shrugged. "If you want. I'm going to be taking my son with me anyway."

He nodded at Grundo. Grundo, in that way that he has, had somehow caused everyone to forget him. He had collected a heap of things that people had dropped – combs, hairpins, paper, pens, coins, some glowing rowan berries, and even a fiery little brooch that must have been dropped by the Count of Blest's people – and he was busy building them into a long, wavery tower. Actually, he had made it rather beautiful, like a mad sculpture. "I can work with this new magic," he said, when he saw us looking at him. "It's much easier."

Grandad Hyde frowned down at Grundo's artwork. "I don't think you *can* take him, you know," he said to Romanov. "I suspect he's likely to be the next Merlin. This one won't last long. Not up to strength really, you know."

Romanov frowned too. "Only if he *wants* the post," he said. "They wanted me for the Merlin once and I know how *that* feels." He and Grandad directed their frowns at one another. It was quite a clash. "I'm not leaving him with Sybil, whatever you want," Romanov said. "Where *is* Sybil, by the way?"

"Gone," Nick said. "Ap Nud took her."

Romanov tried to look sober and sorry, but his face bent into wholly new zigzags of relief and delight, however he tried. "Well, well," he settled for saying.

"Then I'll have to take him, but we can visit you – once a month, if you want."

Grandad was not pleased, but he had no chance to say so because the square brown car came slewing and sliding across the grass then to take Mrs Candace home. Old Sarum was at its wheel. He scowled and scrunched his face up at me. That made me laugh. I don't know if Old Sarum meant to do this, but he made me feel a lot better about being separated from everyone I knew. I went and helped Mrs Candace politely into the car.

"I'll be along to collect you next month, child," she said before she was driven away.

Grandad was just rounding on Romanov again to restart their argument, when Stonehenge suddenly became full of people. The first one to slip between the stones and start towards us was the real Merlin, grinning shyly at Romanov. But Heppy was close behind him. We heard her parrot voice even before we saw her.

"But this is the *Henge*! How does he suppose we're going to get home from here, Jude, that's what I want to know! It's miles away!"

The Izzies were only too evidently with her. "Oh, I love that Merlin!" their voices trilled. "His chin is so *weak*!"

My grandfather was galvanised. "Quick!" he said. "Into my car, Nick, Toby, Grundo, Roddy – all of you. I'll have Roddy for the month, Annie. Can you stay and sort things out here?" he asked Romanov over one shoulder as he rushed to the car. "Come and fetch whichever boys you want in a month's time."

That was typical Grandad, getting his own way in spite of everything. Romanov actually laughed as we drove away.

It was typical too that Grandad didn't scold Dora – though I think he should have done – when she crept into his house late that night. And it was equally typical that, as soon as he saw how upset Nick was, he immediately started us on what he calls The Grand Project, which is for me and Nick to write down exactly what happened to both of us. He says he needs it for Magid reasons. So for this last month we have done just that, me in the dining room and Nick up in the room he shares with Grundo. I think it might have made Nick feel a little better. And there isn't much else to do, because Dad has changed the weather to rain and rain, and yet more rain. Toby and Grundo have been quite bored, now that they have got all the salamanders put where they can be dry. And it has taken me the entire month to write everything down, but I think I've finished now – which is just as well, because I can hear Mrs Candace's voice in the hall. I feel *so* nervous.

# CHAPTER FORTY-THREE

*

*I*'ve done what Maxwell Hyde wanted – he says his Upper Room needs to see this – but I still feel – well – maimed. It was not so much what Japheth did, although that hurt like crazy, it was being sort of *invaded* by someone else's hatred. And I can't get over the way such small things led to such incredibly large, violent events. It's like the way I told that old man in Loggia City that his tapestry was beautiful – and that destroyed the city. I answered the phone to Sybil, and that seems to have set her on to grab power and make her conspiracy. And I laughed at Japheth. That was all I did.

Maxwell Hyde said, when I told him this, that large things often do hinge on very small incidents. "And I don't believe for a moment your laughing at him set that Japheth on to murder his Prayermaster," he said. "I'd very much like to know what other criminal activities those two got up to between rushing off in that flier and turning up just recently."

I got up the courage to ask him what had happened to Joel then. "Well," he said, "I was fighting my way out of a skein of cotton wool at the time, but I got the impression that a spotted cat of some kind tore him to bits. The creature was covered with blood when I saw it. But don't tell Roddy. It's not the kind of thing she can take."

He may be right, although Roddy is actually quite tough. I got to know her quite well, in a subdued sort of way, this last month. The trouble with Roddy is that she is too eaten up inside with magic. It's going to take me years to get through to her. But I'm going to keep trying. The problem is, I don't know quite how I shall manage it, what with her being on Blest and me being on Earth. I shall have to go back to see Dad. He needs looking after. I see that now. I shouldn't have blurted out to Romanov that I wanted to go with him.

But I do want to see Romanov and get him to teach me, even though Romanov is bound to be ten times more demanding than Maxwell Hyde. I do want to be a free operator like Romanov. Much as I like Maxwell Hyde, I keep running up against his limits. In the last resort, he always has to do what his bosses in the Upper Room want, and I don't think I could stand that. I'd go mad after six months.

There was a noise in the street. I went to look and saw Mrs Candace getting out of that brown car. I shall have to go down and say goodbye to Roddy. But the noise was from the ring of kids standing round Mini. Romanov has come to fetch Grundo too. I have to go and explain to him that I'm not going with Grundo, not yet, and make an arrangement to get to his island later. I'll go when I've made sure that my dad will be all right for the rest of his life.

# MAGICAL BOOKS FROM

# Diana Wynne Jones

...Magic rules the world!

Spells are the hardest things to get right...

No magic allowed here!

Follow your dreams...

'Always perfectly magical' Neil Gaiman

'The best writer of magic there is' Neil Gaiman

Four tales of Chrestomanci

MAGICAL BOOKS FROM

# Diana Wynne Jones

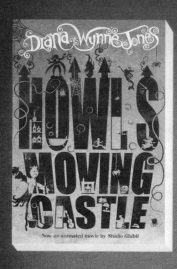

Now an animated movie by *Studio Ghibli*

An exotically magical sequel to *Howl's Moving Castle*

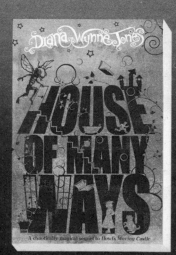

A chaotically magical sequel to *Howl's Moving Castle*